The WEREWOLF of FEVER SWAMP

Goosebumps®

The WEREWOLF of FEVER SWAMP

R.L. STINE

■SCHOLASTIC

Scholastic Children's Books
An imprint of Scholastic Ltd
Euston House, 24 Eversholt Street
London, NW1 1DB, UK
Registered office: Westfield Road, Southam, Warwickshire, CV47 0RA
SCHOLASTIC and associated logos are trademarks and/or
registered trademarks of Scholastic Inc.

First published in the US by Scholastic Inc, 1993
First published in the UK by Scholastic Ltd, 1995
This edition published by Scholastic Ltd, 2015

Copyright © Scholastic Inc, 1993

ISBN 978 1407 15752 8

Goosebumps book series created by Parachute Press, Inc.

SCHOLASTIC, GOOSEBUMPS, GOOSEBUMPS HORRORLAND,
and associated logos are trademarks and/or registered trademarks of Scholastic Inc.

"Behind the Screams" bonus material by Gabrielle S. Balkan

A CIP catalogue record for this book is available from the British Library.

Printed and bound by CPI Group (UK) Ltd, Croydon, CR0 4YY
Papers used by Scholastic Children's Books are made from wood grown in
sustainable forests.

11

www.scholastic.co.uk

We moved to Florida during Christmas vacation. A week later, I heard the frightening howls in the swamp for the first time.

Night after night, the howls made me sit up in bed. I would hold my breath and wrap my arms around myself to keep from shivering.

I would stare out my bedroom window at the chalk-colored full moon. And I would listen.

What kind of creature makes such a cry? I would ask myself.

And how close is it? Why does it sound as if it's right outside my window?

The wails rose and fell like police car sirens. They weren't sad or mournful. They were menacing.

Angry.

They sounded to me like a warning. *Stay out of the swamp. You do not belong here.*

When my family first moved to Florida, to our

1

new house at the edge of the swamp, I couldn't wait to explore. I stood in the backyard with the binoculars my dad had given me for my twelfth birthday and gazed toward the swamp.

Trees with slender white trunks tilted over each other. Their flat, broad leaves appeared to form a roof, covering the swamp floor in blue shadow.

Behind me, the deer paced uneasily in their wire-mesh pen. I could hear them pawing the soft, sandy ground, rubbing their antlers against the walls of their pen.

Lowering my binoculars, I turned to look at them. The deer were the reason we had moved to Florida.

You see, my dad, Michael F. Tucker, is a scientist. He works for the University of Vermont in Burlington, which, believe me, is a *long* way from the Florida swamps!

Dad got these six deer from some country in South America. They're called swamp deer. They're not like regular deer. I mean, they don't look like Bambi. For one thing, their fur is very red, not brown. And their hooves are really big and kind of webbed. For walking on wet, swampy ground, I guess.

Dad wants to see if these South American swamp deer can survive in Florida. He plans to put little radio transmitters on them and set them free in the swamp. Then he'll study how they get along.

When he told us back in Burlington that we were moving to Florida because of the deer, we all totally freaked. We didn't want to move.

My sister, Emily, cried for days. She's sixteen, and she didn't want to miss her senior year in high school. I didn't want to leave my friends, either.

But Dad quickly got Mom on his side. Mom is a scientist, too. She and Dad work together on a lot of projects. So, of course, she agreed with him.

And the two of them tried to persuade Emily and me that this was the chance of a lifetime, that it was going to be really exciting. An adventure we'd never forget.

So here we were, living in a little white house in a neighborhood of four or five other little white houses. We had six weird-looking red deer penned up behind the house. The hot Florida sun was beaming down. And an endless swamp stretched beyond our flat, grassy backyard.

I turned away from the deer and raised the binoculars to my face. "Oh," I cried out as two dark eyes seemed to be staring back at me.

I pulled the binoculars away and squinted toward the swamp. In the near distance I saw a large white bird on two long, spindly legs.

"It's a crane," Emily said. I hadn't realized Emily had stepped up beside me. She was wearing a sleeveless white T-shirt and red denim shorts. My sister is tall and thin and very blond. She looks a lot like a crane.

The bird turned and began high-stepping toward the swamp.

"Let's follow it," I said.

Emily made her pouting face, an expression we'd all seen a lot of since moving down here. "No way. It's too hot."

"Aw, come on." I tugged her skinny arm. "Let's do some exploring, check out the swamp."

She shook her head, her white-blond ponytail swinging behind her. "I really don't want to, Grady." She adjusted her sunglasses on her nose. "I'm kind of waiting for the mail."

Since we're so far from the nearest post office, we only get mail two times a week. Emily had been spending most of her time waiting for the mail.

"Waiting for a love letter from Martin?" I asked with a grin. She hated when I teased her about Martin, her boyfriend back in Burlington. So I teased her as often as I could.

"Maybe," she said. She reached out with both hands and messed up my hair. She knows I hate to have my hair messed up.

"Please?" I pleaded. "Come on, Emily. Just a short walk. Very short."

"Emily, take a short walk with Grady," Dad's voice broke in. We turned to see him inside the deer pen. He had a clipboard in one hand and was going from deer to deer, taking notes. "Go

4

ahead," he urged my sister. "You're not doing anything else."

"But, Dad — " Emily could whine with the best of them when she wanted.

"Go ahead, Em," Dad insisted. "It will be interesting. More interesting than standing around in the heat arguing with him."

Emily pushed the sunglasses up again. They kept slipping down her nose. "Well . . ."

"Great!" I cried. I was really excited. I'd never been in a real swamp before. "Let's go!" I grabbed my sister's hand and pulled.

Emily reluctantly followed, a fretful expression on her face. "I have a bad feeling about this," she muttered.

My shadow slanting behind me, I hurried toward the low, tilting trees. "Emily, what could go wrong?" I asked.

It was hot and wet under the trees. The air felt sticky against my face. The broad palm leaves were so low, I could almost reach up and touch them. They nearly blocked out the sun, but shafts of yellow light broke through, beaming down on the swamp floor like spotlights.

Scratchy weeds and fern leaves brushed against my bare legs. I wished I'd worn jeans instead of shorts. I kept close to my sister as we made our way along a narrow, winding trail. The binoculars, strapped around my neck, began to feel heavy against my chest. I should've left them at home, I realized.

"It's so noisy here," Emily complained, stepping over a decaying log.

She was right. The most surprising thing about the swamp was all the sounds.

A bird trilled from somewhere above. Another bird replied with a shrill whistle. Insects chittered loudly all around us. I heard a steady *tap-tap-tap*, like someone hammering on wood. A woodpecker? Palm leaves crackled as they swayed. Slender tree trunks creaked. My sandals made *thup thup* sounds, sinking into the marshy ground as I walked.

"Hey, look," Emily said, pointing. She pulled off her dark glasses to see better.

We had come to a small, oval-shaped pond. The water was dark green, half hidden in shade. Floating on top were white water lilies, bending gracefully over flat green lily pads.

"Pretty," Emily said, brushing a bug off her shoulder. "I'm going to come back here with my camera and take pictures of this pond. Look at the great light."

I followed her gaze. The near end of the pond was darkened by long shadows. But light slanted down through the trees at the other end, forming what looked like a bright curtain that spilled into the still pond water.

"It is kind of cool," I admitted. I wasn't really into ponds. I was more interested in wildlife.

I let Emily admire the pond and the water lilies a little longer. Then I headed around the pond and deeper into the swamp.

My sandals slapped over the wet ground. Up ahead, a swarm of tiny gnats, thousands of them, danced silently in a shaft of sunlight.

7

"Yuck," Emily muttered. "I hate gnats. It makes me itchy just to look at them." She scratched her arms.

We turned away — and both saw something scamper behind a fallen moss-covered log.

"Hey — what was *that*?" Emily cried, grabbing my elbow.

"An alligator!" I shouted. "A hungry alligator!"

She uttered a short, frightened cry.

I laughed. "What's your problem, Em? It was just some kind of lizard."

She squeezed my arm hard, trying to make me flinch. "You're a creep, Grady," she muttered. She scratched her arms some more." "It's too itchy in this swamp," she complained. "Let's head back."

"Just a little bit farther," I pleaded.

"No. Come on. I really want to get back." She tried to pull me, but I backed out of her grasp. "Grady —"

I turned and started walking away from her, deeper into the swamp. I heard the *tap-tap-tap* again, directly overhead. The low palm leaves scraped against each other, shifting in a soft, wet breeze. The shrill chittering of the insects grew louder.

"I'm going home and leaving you here," Emily threatened.

I ignored her and kept walking. I knew she was bluffing.

8

My sandals crackled over dried, brown palm leaves. Without turning around, I could hear Emily a few steps behind me.

Another little lizard scampered across the path, just in front of my sandals. It looked like a dark arrow, shooting into the underbrush.

The ground suddenly sloped upward. We found ourselves climbing a low hill into bright sunlight. A clearing of some sort.

Beads of sweat ran down my cheeks. The air was so wet, I felt as if I were swimming.

At the top of the hill, we stopped to look around. "Hey — another pond!" I cried, running over fat yellow swamp grass, hurrying up to the water's edge.

But this pond looked different.

The dark green water wasn't flat and smooth. Leaning over it, I could see that it was murky and thick, like split-pea soup. It made disgusting gurgling and plopping sounds as it churned.

I leaned down closer to get a better look.

"It's quicksand!" I heard Emily cry in horror.

And then two hands shoved me hard from behind.

As I started to fall into the bubbling green stew, the same hands grabbed my waist and pulled me back.

Emily giggled. "Gotcha!" she cried, holding on to me, keeping me from turning around and slugging her.

"Hey — let go!" I cried angrily. "You almost pushed me into *quicksand*! That's not funny!"

She laughed some more, then let me go. "It isn't quicksand, dork," she muttered. "It's a bog."

"Huh?" I turned to stare into the gloppy green water.

"It's a bog. A peat bog," she repeated impatiently. "Don't you know anything?"

"What's a peat bog?" I asked, ignoring her insults. Emily the Know-It-All. She's always bragging about how she knows everything and I'm a stupid clod. But she gets B's in school, and I get A's. So who's the smart one?

"We learned about this last year when we studied the wetlands and rain forests," she replied smugly. "The pond is thick because it has peat moss growing in it. The moss grows and grows. It absorbs twenty-five times its own weight in water."

"It's gross-looking," I said.

"Why don't you drink some and see how it tastes," she urged.

She tried to push me again, but I ducked and skirted away. "I'm not thirsty," I muttered. I realize it wasn't too clever, but it was the best reply I could think of.

"Let's get going," she said, wiping sweat off her forehead with her hand. "I'm really hot."

"Yeah. Okay," I reluctantly agreed. "This was a pretty neat walk."

We turned away from the peat bog and started back down the hill. "Hey, look!" I cried, pointing to two black shadows floating high above us under a white cloud.

"Falcons," Emily said, shielding her eyes with one hand as she gazed up. "I *think* they're falcons. It's hard to see. They sure are big."

We watched them soar out of sight. Then we continued down the hill, making our way carefully on the damp sandy ground.

At the bottom of the hill, back under the deep shade of the trees, we stopped to catch our breath.

11

I was really sweating now. The back of my neck felt hot and itchy. I rubbed it with one hand, but it didn't seem to help.

The breeze had stopped. The air felt heavy. Nothing moved.

Loud cawing sounds made me glance up. Two enormous blackbirds peered down at us from a low branch of a cypress tree. They cawed again, as if telling us to go away.

"This way," Emily said with a sigh.

I followed her, feeling prickly and itchy all over. "I wish we had a swimming pool at our new house," I said. "I'd jump right in with my clothes on!"

We walked for several minutes. The trees grew thicker. The light grew dimmer. The path ended. We had to push our way through tall, leafy ferns.

"I — I don't think we've been here before," I stammered. "I don't think this is the right way."

We stared at each other, watching each other's face fill with fright.

We both realized we were lost. Completely lost.

"I don't *believe* this!" Emily shrieked.

Her loud shout made the two blackbirds flutter off their tree limb. They soared away, cawing angrily.

"What am I *doing* here?" she cried. Emily is not good in emergencies. When she got a flat tire during one of her first driving lessons back home in Burlington, she jumped out of the car and ran away!

So I didn't exactly expect her to be calm and cool now. Since we were totally lost in the middle of a dark, hot swamp, I expected her to panic. And she did.

I'm the calm one in the family. I take after Dad. Cool and scientific. "Let's just figure out the direction of the sun," I said, ignoring the fluttering in my chest.

"What sun?" Emily cried, throwing her hands up.

13

It was really dark. The palm trees with their wide leaves formed a pretty solid roof above us.

"Well, we could check out some moss," I suggested. The fluttering in my chest was growing stronger. "Isn't moss supposed to grow on the north side of the trees?"

"East side, I think," Emily muttered. "Or is it the west?"

"I'm pretty sure it's the north," I insisted, gazing around.

"Pretty sure? What good is pretty sure?" Emily cried shrilly.

"Forget the moss," I said, rolling my eyes. "I'm not even sure what moss looks like."

We stared at each other for a long time.

"Didn't you used to carry a compass with you wherever you went?" Emily asked, sounding a little shaky.

"Yeah. When I was four," I replied.

"I can't believe we were so stupid," Emily wailed. "We should have worn one of the radio transmitters. You know. For the deer. Then Dad could track us down."

"I should have worn jeans," I muttered, noticing some tiny red bumps along my calf. Poison ivy? Some kind of rash?

"What should we do?" Emily asked impatiently, wiping sweat off her forehead with her hand.

"Go back up the hill, I guess," I told her. "There were no trees there. It was sunny. Once we see where the sun is, we can figure out the direction to get back."

"But which way is the hill?" Emily demanded.

I spun around. Was it behind us? To our right? A cold chill ran down my back as I realized I wasn't sure.

I shrugged. "We're really lost," I murmured with a sigh.

"Let's go this way," Emily said, starting to walk away. "I just have a feeling this is the way. If we come to that bog, we'll know we're going right."

"And if we don't?" I demanded.

"We'll come to something else, maybe," she replied.

Brilliant.

But I didn't see any good in arguing with her. So I followed.

We walked in silence, the shrill ringing of the insects on all sides, the calls of birds startling us from above. After a short while, we pushed our way through a clump of tall, stiff reeds.

"Have we been here before?" Emily asked.

I couldn't remember. I pushed a reed away to step through and realized it had left something sticky on my hand. "Yuck!"

"Hey, look!" Emily's excited cry made me glance up from the sticky green gunk that clung to my hand.

The bog! It was right in front of us. The same bog we had stopped at before.

"Yay!" Emily cried. "I *knew* I was right. I just had a feeling."

The sight of the gurgling green pond cheered us both up. Once past it, we began to run. We knew we were on the right path, nearly home.

"Way to go!" I cried happily, running past my sister. "Way to go!"

I was feeling really good again.

Then something reached up, grabbed my ankle, and pulled me down to the swampy ground.

I hit the ground hard, landing on my elbows and knees.

My heart leaped into my mouth.

I tasted blood.

"Get up! Get up!" Emily was screaming.

"It — it's *got* me!" I cried in a tight, trembling voice.

The fluttering in my chest had become a pounding. Again, I tasted blood.

I raised my eyes to see Emily laughing.

Laughing?

"It's just a tree root," she said, pointing.

I followed the direction of her finger — and instantly realized I hadn't been pulled down. I had tripped over one of the many upraised tree roots that arched over the ground.

I stared at the bonelike root. It was bent in the middle and looked like a skinny white leg.

But what was the blood I tasted?

17

I felt my aching lip. I had bitten it when I fell.

With a loud groan, I pulled myself to my feet. My knees ached. My lip throbbed. Blood trickled down my chin.

"That was pretty clumsy," Emily said softly. And then she added, "Are you okay?" She brushed some dried leaves off the back of my T-shirt.

"Yeah, I guess," I replied, still feeling a little shaky. "I really thought something had grabbed me." I forced a laugh.

She rested a hand on my shoulder, and we started walking again, slower than before, side by side.

Slender beams of light poked down through the thick tree leaves, dotting the ground in front of us. It all looked unreal, like something in a dream.

Some creature scampered noisily behind the tangle of low shrubs at our right. Emily and I didn't even turn to try to see it. We just wanted to get home.

It didn't take us long to realize we were headed in the wrong direction.

We stopped at the edge of a small, round clearing. Birds chattered noisily above us. A light breeze made the palm leaves scrape and creak.

"What are those huge gray things?" I asked, lingering behind my sister.

"Mushrooms, I think," she replied quietly.

"Mushrooms as big as footballs," I murmured.

We both saw the small shack at the same time.

It was hidden in the shadow of two low cypress trees beyond the field of giant mushrooms at the other side of the clearing.

We both gaped at it in surprise, studying it in shocked silence. We took a few steps toward it. Then a few more.

The shack was tiny, built low to the ground, not much taller than me. It had some kind of thatched roof, made of long reeds or dried grass. The walls were made of layers of dried palm leaves.

The door, built of slender tree limbs bound together, was shut tight. There were no windows.

A pile of gray ashes formed a circle a few yards from the door. Signs of a campfire.

I saw a pair of battered old workboots lying at the side of the shack. Beside them were several empty tin cans on their sides and a plastic water bottle, also empty, partly crumpled.

I turned to Emily and whispered, "Do you think someone lives here? In the middle of the swamp?"

She shrugged, her features tight with fear.

"If someone lives here, maybe he can tell us which way to go to get home," I suggested.

"Maybe," Emily murmured. Her eyes were straight ahead on the tiny shack covered in blue shadow.

We took another couple of steps closer.

Why would someone want to live in a tiny shack like this in the middle of a swamp? I wondered.

An answer flashed into my mind: *Because whoever it is wants to hide from the world.*

"It's a hideout," I muttered, not realizing I was speaking out loud. "A criminal. A bank robber. Or a *killer*. He's hiding here."

"*Sshhh.*" Emily put a finger on my mouth to silence me, hitting the cut on my lip. I pulled away.

"Anyone home?" she called. Her voice came out low and shaky, so low, I could barely hear her. "Anyone home?" she repeated, a little more forcefully.

I decided to join in. We shouted together: "Anyone home? Anyone in there?"

We listened.

No reply.

We stepped up to the low door.

"Anyone in there?" I called one more time.

Then I reached for the doorknob.

Just as I was about to pull open the crude wooden door, it swung out, nearly hitting us both. We leaped back as a man burst out from the dark doorway of the hut.

He glared at us with wild black eyes. He had long gray-white hair, down past his shoulders, tied behind him in a loose ponytail.

His face was bright red, sunburned, maybe. Or maybe red from anger. He stared at us with a menacing scowl, standing bent over, stooped from being inside the low hut.

He wore a loose-fitting white T-shirt, dirt-stained and wrinkled, over heavy black trousers that bagged over his sandals.

As he glared at us with those amazing black eyes, his mouth opened, revealing rows of jagged yellow teeth.

Huddling close to my sister, I took a step back.

I wanted to ask him who he was, why he lived

in the swamp. I wanted to ask if he could help us find our way back home.

A dozen questions flashed through my mind.

But all I could utter was, "Uh . . . sorry."

Then I realized that Emily was already running away. Her ponytail flew behind her as she dived through the tall weeds.

And a second later, I was running after her. My heart pounded. My sandals squished over the soft ground.

"Hey, Emily — wait up! Wait up!"

I ran over the rough carpet of dead leaves and twigs.

As I struggled to catch up to her, I glanced behind me — and cried out in terror. "Emily — he's *chasing* us!"

Bent low to the ground, the man from the hut moved steadily after us, taking long strides. His hands bobbed at his sides. He was breathing hard, and his mouth was open, revealing the jagged teeth.

"Run!" Emily cried. "Run, Grady!"

We were following a narrow path between tall weeds. The trees thinned out. We ran through shadow and sunlight and back into shadow.

"Emily — wait up!" I called breathlessly. But she didn't slow down.

A long, narrow pond appeared to our left. Strange trees lifted up from the middle of the water. The slender trunks were surrounded by a thicket of dark roots. Mangrove trees.

I wanted to stop and look at the eerie-looking trees. But this wasn't the time for sightseeing.

We ran along the edge of the pond, our sandals sinking into the marshy ground. Then, my chest heaving, my throat choked and dry, I followed Emily as the path curved into the trees.

A sharp pain in my side made me cry out. I stopped running. I gasped for breath.

"Hey — he's gone," Emily said, swallowing hard. She stopped a few yards ahead of me and leaned against a tree trunk. "We lost him."

I bent over, trying to force away the pain in my side. After a short while, my breathing slowed to normal. "Weird," I said. I couldn't think of anything else.

"Yeah. Weird," Emily agreed. She walked back to me and pulled me up straight. "You okay?"

"I guess." At least the pain had faded away. I always get a pain in my right side when I run a long time. This one was worse than usual. I usually don't have to run for my life!

"Come on," Emily said. She let go of me and started walking quickly, following the path.

"Hey, this looks familiar," I said. I began to feel a little better. I started to jog. We passed clusters of trees and ferns that looked familiar. I could see our footprints in the sandy ground, going the other way.

A short while later, our backyard came into view. "Home sweet home!" I cried.

Emily and I stepped out from the low trees and began running across the grass toward the back of the house.

Mom and Dad were in the backyard setting up

outdoor furniture. Dad was lowering an umbrella into the white umbrella table. Mom was washing off the white lawn chairs with the garden hose.

"Hey — welcome back," Dad said, smiling.

"We thought you got lost," Mom said.

"We did!" I cried breathlessly.

Mom turned off the nozzle, stopping the spray of water. "You *what*?"

"A man chased us!" Emily exclaimed. "A strange man with long white hair."

"He lives in a hut. In the middle of the swamp," I added, dropping down into one of the lawn chairs. It was wet, but I didn't care.

"Huh? He chased you?" Dad's eyes narrowed in alarm. Then he said, "I heard in town there's a swamp hermit out there."

"Yes, he chased us!" Emily repeated. Her normally pale face was bright red. Her hair had come loose and fell wildly around her face. "It — it was scary."

"A guy in the hardware store told me about him," Dad said. "Said he was strange but perfectly harmless. No one knows his name."

"Harmless?" Emily cried. "Then why did he chase us?"

Dad shrugged. "I'm only repeating what I heard. Evidently he's lived in the swamp most of his life. By himself. He never comes to town."

Mom dropped the hose and walked over to Emily. She placed a hand on Emily's shoulder. In the bright sunlight, they looked like sisters. They're both tall and thin, with long, straight blond hair. I look more like my dad. Wavy brown hair. Dark eyes. A little chunky.

"Maybe they shouldn't go back in the swamp by themselves," Mom said, biting her lower lip fretfully. She started to gather Emily's hair back up into a ponytail.

"The hermit is supposed to be completely harmless," Dad repeated. He was still struggling to lower the umbrella into the concrete base. Every time he lowered it, he missed the opening.

"Here, Dad. I'll help you." I scooted under the table and guided the umbrella stem into the base.

"Don't worry," Emily said. "You won't catch *me* back in that swamp." She scratched both shoulders. "I'm going to be itchy for the rest of my life!" she groaned.

"We saw a lot of neat things," I said, starting to feel normal again. "A peat bog and mangrove trees . . ."

"I told you this was going to be an experience," Dad said, arranging the white chairs around the table.

"Some experience," Emily grumbled, rolling her eyes. "I'm going in to take a shower. Maybe if I stay in it for an hour or so, I'll stop itching."

Mom shook her head, watching Emily stomp

toward the back door. "This is going to be a hard year for Em," she muttered.

Dad wiped his dirty hands on the sides of his jeans. "Come with me, Grady," he said, motioning for me to follow him. "Time to feed the deer."

We talked more about the swamp at dinner. Dad told us stories about how they hunted and trapped the swamp deer that he was using for his experiment.

Dad and his helpers searched the South American jungles for weeks. They used tranquilizer guns to capture the deer. Then they had to bring in helicopters to pull the deer out, and the deer were not too happy about flying.

"The swamp you two were exploring this afternoon," he said, twirling his spaghetti. "Know what it's called? Fever Swamp. That's what the local people call it, anyway."

"Why?" Emily asked. "Because it's so hot in there?"

Dad chewed and swallowed a mouthful of spaghetti. He had orange splotches of tomato sauce on both sides of his mouth. "I don't know why it's called Fever Swamp. But I'm sure we'll find out eventually."

"It was probably discovered by a guy named Mr. Fever," Mom joked.

"I want to go home to Vermont!" Emily wailed.

*   *   *

After dinner, I found myself feeling a little homesick, too. I took a tennis ball out to the back of the house. I thought maybe I could bounce it off the wall and catch it the way I had done back home.

But the deer pen was in the way.

I thought about my two best friends in Burlington, Ben and Adam. We had lived on the same block and used to hang out after dinner. We'd throw a ball around or walk down to the playground and just mess around.

Staring at the deer, who milled silently at one end of the pen, I realized I really missed my friends. I wondered what they were doing right now. Probably hanging out in Ben's backyard.

Feeling glum, I was about to go back inside and see what was on TV — when a hand grabbed me from behind.

The swamp hermit!

He found me!

The swamp hermit found me! And now he's got me!

Those are the thoughts that burst into my mind.

I spun around — and uttered a startled cry when I saw that it wasn't the swamp hermit. It was a boy.

"Hi," he said. "I thought you saw me. I didn't mean to scare you." He had a funny voice, gravelly and hoarse.

"Oh. Uh . . . that's okay," I stammered.

"I saw you in your yard," he said. "I live over there." He pointed to the house two doors down. "You just moved in?"

I nodded. "Yeah. I'm Grady Tucker." I slapped the tennis ball into my hand. "What's your name?"

"Will. Will Blake," he said in his hoarse voice. He was about my height, but he was heavier, bigger somehow. His shoulders were broader. His neck was thicker. He reminded me of a football lineman.

He had dark brown hair cut very short. It stood straight up on top, like a flattop, and was swept back on the sides. He wore a blue-and-white-striped T-shirt and denim cutoffs.

"How old are you?" he asked.

"Twelve," I answered.

"Me, too," he told me, glancing over my shoulder at the deer. "I thought maybe you were eleven. I mean, you look kind of young."

I was insulted by that remark, but I decided to ignore it. "How long have you lived here?" I asked, tossing the tennis ball from hand to hand.

"A few months," Will said.

"Are there any other kids our age?" I asked, glancing down the row of six houses.

"Yeah. One," Will replied. "But she's a girl. And she's kind of weird."

In the distance, the sun was lowering itself behind the swamp trees. The sky was a dark scarlet. The air suddenly became cooler. Gazing high in the sky, I could see a pale moon, nearly full.

Will headed over to the deer pen, and I followed him. He walked heavily, his big shoulders bobbing with each step. He poked his hand through the wire mesh and let a deer lick his palm.

30

"Your father works for the Forest Service, too?" he asked, his eyes studying the deer.

"No," I told him. "My mom and dad are both scientists. They're doing studies with these deer."

"Weird-looking deer," Will said. He pulled his wet hand from the pen and held it up. "Yuck. Deer slime."

I laughed. "They're called swamp deer," I told him. I tossed him the tennis ball. We backed away from the deer pen and started to throw the ball back and forth.

"Have you been in the swamp?" he asked.

I missed the ball and had to chase it across the grass. "Yeah. This afternoon," I told him. "My sister and I, we got lost."

He snickered.

"Do you know why it's called Fever Swamp?" I asked, tossing him a high one.

It was getting pretty dark, harder to see. But he caught the ball one-handed. "Yeah. My dad told me the story," Will said. "I think it was a hundred years ago. Maybe longer. Everyone in town came down with a strange fever."

"Everyone?" I asked.

He nodded. "Everyone who had been in the swamp." He held on to the ball and moved closer. "My dad said the fever lasted for weeks, sometimes even months. And lots of people died from it."

"That's horrible," I murmured, glancing across the backyard to the darkening trees at the swamp edge.

"And those who didn't die from the fever began acting very strange," Will continued. He had small, round eyes. And as he told his story, his eyes gleamed. "They started talking crazy, not making any sense, just saying nonsense words. And they couldn't walk very well. They'd fall down a lot or walk around in circles."

"Weird," I said, my eyes still trained on the swamp. The sky darkened from scarlet to a deep purple. The nearly full moon seemed to glow brighter.

"Ever since that time, they called it Fever Swamp," Will said, finishing his story. He flipped the tennis ball to me. "I'd better get home."

"Did you ever see the swamp hermit?" I asked.

He shook his head. "No. I heard about him, but I've never seen him."

"I did," I told him. "My sister and I saw him this afternoon. We found his hut."

"That's cool!" Will exclaimed. "Did you talk to him or anything?"

"No way," I replied. "He chased us."

"He did?" Will's expression turned thoughtful. "Why?"

"I don't know. We were pretty scared," I admitted.

"I've got to go," Will said. He started jogging toward his house. "Hey, maybe you and I can go exploring in the swamp together," he called back.

"Yeah. Great!" I replied.

I felt a little cheered up. I'd made a new friend. *Maybe it won't be so bad living here*, I thought.

I watched Will head around the side of his house two doors down. His house looked almost identical to ours, except there was no deer pen in back, of course.

I saw a swing set with a small slide and seesaw in his backyard. I wondered if he had a little brother or sister.

I thought about Emily as I headed to the house. I knew she'd be jealous that I'd made a friend. Poor Emily was really sad without that goon Martin hanging around her.

I never liked Martin. He always called me "Kiddo."

I watched one of the deer lower itself to the ground, folding its legs gracefully. Another deer did the same. They were settling in for the night.

I made my way inside and joined my family in the living room. They were watching a show about sharks on the Discovery Channel. My parents *love* the Discovery Channel. Big surprise, huh?

I watched for a short while. Then I began to realize I wasn't feeling very well. I had a headache, a sharp throbbing at my temples. And I had chills.

I told Mom. She got up and walked over to my chair. "You look a little flushed," she said, studying me with concern. She placed a cool hand on my forehead and left it there for a few seconds.

"Grady, I think you have a little fever," she said.

A few nights later, I heard the strange, frightening howls for the first time.

My fever had gone up to 101 degrees and stayed there for a day. Then it went away. Then it came back.

"It's the swamp fever!" I told my parents earlier that night. "Pretty soon I'm going to start acting crazy."

"You *already* act crazy," Mom teased. She handed me a glass of orange juice. "Drink. Keep drinking."

"Drinking won't help swamp fever," I insisted glumly, taking the glass anyway. "There's no cure for it."

Mom tsk-tsked. Dad continued to read his science magazine.

I had strange dreams that night, disturbing dreams. I was back in Vermont, running through the snow. Something was chasing me. I thought maybe it was the swamp hermit. I kept running

35

and running. I was very cold. I was shivering in the dream.

I turned back to see who was chasing me. There wasn't anyone there. And suddenly, I was in the swamp. I was sinking in a peat bog. It gurgled all around me, green and thick, making these sick sucking sounds.

It was sucking me down. Down . . .

The howls woke me up.

I sat straight up in my bed and stared out the window at the nearly full moon. It floated right beyond the window, silvery and bright against the blue-black sky.

Another long howl rose on the night air.

I realized I was shaking all over. I was sweating. My pajama shirt stuck to my back.

Gripping the covers with both hands, I listened hard.

Another howl. The cry of an animal.

From the swamp?

The cries sounded so close. Right outside the window. Long, angry howls.

I shoved down the covers and lowered my feet to the floor. I was still trembling, and my head throbbed as I stood up. I guessed I still had a fever.

Another long howl.

I made my way to the hall on shaky legs. I had to find out if my parents had heard the howls, too.

Walking through the darkness, I bumped into a low table in the hall. I still wasn't used to this new house.

My feet were cold as ice, but my head felt burning hot, as if it were on fire. Rubbing the knee I had banged, I waited for my eyes to adjust to the darkness. Then I continued down the hall.

My parents' room was just past the kitchen in the back of the house. I was halfway across the kitchen when I stopped short.

What was that sound?

A scratching sound.

My breath caught in my throat. I froze, my arms stiff at my sides.

I listened.

There it was again.

Over the pounding of my heart I heard it.

Scratch scratch scratch.

Someone — or something — scratching at the kitchen door.

Then — another howl. So close. So terrifyingly close.

Scratch scratch scratch.

What could it be? Some kind of animal? Just outside the house?

Some kind of swamp animal howling and scratching at the door?

I realized I'd been holding my breath a long while. I let it out in a *whoosh*, then sucked in another breath.

37

I listened hard, straining to hear over the pounding of my heart.

The refrigerator clicked on. The loud click nearly made me jump out of my skin. I grabbed the countertop. My hands were as cold as my feet, cold and clammy.

I listened.

Scratch scratch scratch.

I took a step toward the kitchen door.

One step, then I stopped.

A shudder of fear ran down my back.

I realized I wasn't alone.

Someone was there, breathing beside me in the dark kitchen.

I gasped. I was gripping the countertop so hard, my hand ached.

"Wh-who's there?" I whispered.

The kitchen light flashed on.

"Emily!" I practically shouted her name, in surprise and relief. "Emily —"

"Did you hear the howls?" she asked, speaking just above a whisper. Her blue eyes burned into mine.

"Yes. They woke me up," I said. "They sound so angry."

"Like a cry of attack," Emily whispered. "Why do you look so weird, Grady?"

"Huh?" Her question caught me off guard.

"Your face is all red," she said. "And look at you — you're all shaky."

"I think my fever is back," I told her.

"Swamp fever," she murmured, examining me with her eyes. "Maybe it's the swamp fever you were telling me about."

I turned to the kitchen door. "Did you hear the scratching sounds?" I asked. "Something was scratching at the back door."

"Yes," she whispered. She stared at the door.

We both listened.

Silence.

"Do you think one of the deer escaped?" she asked, taking a few steps toward the door, her arms crossed in front of her pink-and-white robe.

"Do you think a deer would scratch at the door?" I asked.

It was such a silly question, we both burst out laughing.

"Maybe it wanted a glass of water!" Emily exclaimed, and we both laughed some more. Giddy laughter. Nervous laughter.

We both cut our laughter short at the same time and listened.

Another howl rose up outside like a police siren.

I saw Emily's eyes narrow in fear. "It's a wolf!" she cried in a hushed whisper. She raised a hand to her mouth. "Only a wolf makes a sound like that, Grady."

"Emily, come on —" I started to protest.

"No. I'm right," she insisted. "It's a wolf howl."

"Em, stop," I said, sinking onto a kitchen stool. "There are no wolves in the Florida swamps. You can look in the guidebooks. Or better yet, ask Mom and Dad. Wolves don't live in swamps."

She started to argue, but a scratching at the door made her stop.

Scratch scratch scratch.

We both heard it. We both reacted with sharp gasps.

"What *is* that?" I whispered. And then, reading her expression, I quickly added, "Don't say it's a wolf."

"I — I don't know," she replied, both hands raised to her face. I recognized her look of panic. "Let's get Mom and Dad."

I grabbed the door handle. "Let's just take a look," I said.

I don't know where my sudden courage came from. Maybe it was the fever. But suddenly I just wanted to solve the mystery.

Who or what was scratching at the door?

There was one good way to find out — open the door and look outside.

"No, Grady — wait!" Emily pleaded.

But I waved away her protests.

Then I turned the knob and pulled open the kitchen door.

A gust of hot, wet air rushed in through the open door. The chirp of cicadas greeted my ears.

Holding on to the door, I peered into the darkness of the backyard.

Nothing.

The nearly full moon, yellow as a lemon, floated high in the sky. Then wisps of black clouds drifted over it.

The cicadas stopped suddenly, and all was quiet.

Too quiet.

I squinted into the distance, toward the blackness of the swamp.

Nothing moved. Nothing made a sound.

I waited for my eyes to adjust to the darkness. The moonlight sent a pale glow over the grass. In the far distance, I could see the black outline of slanting trees where the swamp began.

Who or what had scratched at the door? Were they hiding in the darkness now?

Watching me?

Waiting for me to close the door so they could begin their frightening howls again?

"Grady — close the door."

I could hear my sister's voice behind me. She sounded so frightened.

"Grady — do you see something? Do you?"

"No," I told her. "Just the moon."

I ventured out onto the back stoop. The air was hot and steamy, like the air in the bathroom after you've taken a hot shower.

"Grady — come back. Close the door." Emily's voice was shrill and trembly.

I gazed toward the deer pen. I could see their shadowy forms, still and silent. The hot wind rustled the grass. The cicadas began chirping again.

"Is anybody out here?" I called. I immediately felt foolish.

There was no one out here.

"Grady — shut the door. Now."

I felt Emily's hand on my pajama sleeve. She tugged me back into the kitchen. I closed the door and locked it.

My face felt wet from the damp night air. I had chills. My knees were shaking.

"You look kind of sick," Emily said. She glanced over my shoulder to the door. "Did you see anything?"

"No," I told her. "Nothing. It's so dark in back, even with a full moon."

43

"What's going on in here?" A stern voice interrupted us. Dad lumbered into the kitchen, adjusting the collar of the long nightshirt he always wore. "It's past midnight." He glanced from Emily to me, then back to Emily, looking for a clue.

"We heard noises," Emily said. "Howls outside."

"And then something was scratching at the door," I added, trying to keep my knees from shaking.

"Fever dreams," Dad said to me. "Look at you. You're as red as a tomato. And you're shaking. Let's take your temperature. You must be burning up." He started toward the bathroom to get the thermometer.

"It wasn't a dream," Emily called after him. "I heard the noises, too."

Dad stopped in the doorway. "Did you check the deer?"

"Yeah. They're okay," I said.

"Then maybe it was just the wind. Or some creatures in the swamp. It's hard to sleep in a new house. The sounds are all so new, so unfamiliar. But you'll both get used to them after a while."

I'll never *get used to those horrible howls*, I thought stubbornly. But I headed back to my room.

44

Dad took my temperature. It was just slightly above normal. "You should be fine by tomorrow," he said, smoothing my blanket over me. "No more wandering around tonight, okay?"

I murmured a reply and almost instantly drifted into a restless sleep.

Again I had strange, troubling dreams. I dreamed I was walking in the swamp. I heard the howls. I could see the full moon between the slender tree trunks of the swamp.

I started to run. And then suddenly I was up to my waist in a thick green bog. And the howls continued, one after the other, echoing through the trees as I sank into the murky bog.

When I awoke the next morning, the dream lingered in my mind. I wondered if the howls were real or just part of the dream.

Climbing out of bed, I realized I felt fine. Yellow morning sunlight poured in through the window. I could see a clear blue sky. The beautiful morning made me forget my nightmares.

I wondered if Will was around this morning. Maybe he and I could go exploring in the swamp.

I got dressed quickly, pulling on pale blue jeans and a black-and-silver Raiders T-shirt. (I'm not a Raiders fan. I just like their colors.)

I gulped down a bowl of Frosted Flakes, allowed

my mom to feel my head to make sure my fever was gone, and hurried to the back door.

"Whoa. Hold on," Mom called, setting down her coffee cup. "Where are you going so early?"

"I want to see if Will is home," I said. "Maybe we'll hang out or something."

"Okay. Just don't overdo it," she warned. "Promise?"

"Yeah. Promise," I replied.

I pulled open the kitchen door, stepped out into blinding sunlight — and screamed as an enormous, dark monster leaped onto my chest and heaved me to the ground.

"It — it's *got* me!" I screamed as it pushed me to the ground and jumped on my chest.

"Help! It — it's *licking my face!*"

I was so startled, it took me a long time to realize my attacker was a dog.

By the time Mom and Dad came to my rescue and started to pull the big creature off my chest, I was laughing. "Hey — that tickles! Stop!"

I wiped the dog spit off my face with my hands and scrambled to my feet.

"Where'd *you* come from?" Mom asked the dog. She and Dad were holding on to the enormous beast.

They both let go, and it stood wagging its tail excitedly, panting, its big red tongue hanging down practically to the ground.

"He's enormous!" Dad exclaimed. "He must be part shepherd."

I was still wiping the sticky saliva off my cheeks. "He scared me to death," I confessed. "Didn't you, fella?" I reached down and stroked the dark gray fur on the top of his head. His long tail started wagging faster.

"He likes you," Mom said.

"He practically *killed* me!" I exclaimed. "Look at him. He must weigh more than a hundred pounds!"

"Were *you* the one scratching at our door last night?" Emily appeared in the doorway, still in the long T-shirt she used as a nightshirt. "I think this clears up the mystery," she said to me, yawning sleepily and pulling her blond hair behind her shoulders with both hands.

"I guess," I muttered. I got down on my knees beside the big dog and stroked his back. He turned his head and licked my cheek again. "Yuck! Quit that!" I told him.

"I wonder who he belongs to?" Mom said, staring at the dog thoughtfully. "Grady, check his collar. There's probably an ID tag."

I reached up to the dog's broad neck and felt around in his fur for a collar. "Nothing there," I reported.

"Maybe he's a stray," Emily said from inside the kitchen. "Maybe that's why he was scratching at the door last night."

"Yeah," I said quickly. "He needs a place to live."

"Whoa," Mom said, shaking her head. "I don't

think we need a dog right now, Grady. We just moved in, and —"

"But I *need* a pet!" I insisted. "It's so lonely here. A dog would be great, Mom. He could keep me company."

"You have the deer for pets," Dad said, frowning. He turned to the deer pen. The six deer were all standing quietly at attention, staring warily at the dog.

"You can't walk a deer!" I protested. "Besides, you're going to set the deer free, right?"

"The dog probably belongs to someone," Mom said. "You can't just claim any dog that wanders by. Besides, he's so big, Grady. He's too big to —"

"Aw, let him keep it," Emily called from the house.

I stared at her in shock. I couldn't remember the last time Emily and I had been on the same side of a family argument.

The discussion continued for several minutes more. Everyone agreed that he seemed like a sweet-tempered, gentle dog despite his huge size. And he certainly was affectionate. I couldn't make him stop licking me.

Glancing up, I saw Will come out of his house and head across the back lawns toward us. He was wearing a sleeveless blue T-shirt and blue Lycra bicycle shorts. "Hi! Look what we found!" I called.

I introduced Will to my mom and dad. Emily had disappeared back to her room to get dressed.

"Have you seen this dog before?" Dad asked Will. "Does he belong to someone in the neighborhood?"

Will shook his head. 'Nope. Never seen him." He cautiously petted the dog's head.

"Where'd you come from, fella?" I asked, staring into the creature's eyes. They were blue. Sky blue.

"He looks more like a wolf than a dog," Will said.

"Yeah. He really does," I agreed. "Was that you howling like a wolf all last night?" I asked the dog. He tried to lick my nose, but I pulled my face back in time.

I glanced up at Will. "Did you hear those howls last night? They were really weird."

"No. I didn't hear anything," Will replied. "I'm a very sound sleeper. My dad comes into my room and shouts through a megaphone to wake me up in the morning. Really!"

We all laughed.

"He really *does* look like a wolf," Mom commented, staring at the dog's blue eyes.

"Wolves are skinnier," Dad remarked. "Their snouts are narrower. He could be *part* wolf, I suppose. But it's not very likely in this geographical area."

50

"Let's call him Wolf," I suggested enthusiastically. "It's the perfect name for him." I climbed to my feet. "Hi, Wolf," I called to the dog. "Wolf! Hi, Wolf!"

His ears perked straight up.

"See? He likes the name!" I exclaimed. "Wolf! Wolf!"

He barked at me, a single yip.

"Can I keep him?" I asked.

Mom and Dad exchanged long glances. "We'll see," Mom said.

That afternoon, Will and I headed to the swamp to do some exploring. My nightmares about the swamp lingered in my mind. But I did my best to force them away.

It was a blazing hot day. The sun burned down in a clear, cloudless sky. As we crossed my backyard, I hoped it would be cooler in the leafy shade of the swamp.

I glanced back at Wolf. He was napping in the hot sunlight, lying on his side, his four legs stretched straight out in front of him.

We had fed him before lunch, some leftover roast beef scraps from our dinner the night before. He gobbled it up hungrily. Then, after slurping up an entire bowl of water, he dropped down in the grass in front of the back stoop to take his nap.

Will and I followed the dirt path into the slanting trees. Black-and-orange monarch butterflies, four or five of them, fluttered over a bank of tall wildflowers.

"Hey!" I cried out as my foot sank into a marshy spot in the dirt. When I pulled my sneaker out, it was covered with wet sand.

"Have you seen the bog?" Will asked. "It's kind of neat."

"Yeah. Let's go there," I said enthusiastically. "We can throw sticks in and stuff, and watch them sink."

"Do you think any people ever got sunk in the bog?" Will asked thoughtfully. He brushed a mosquito off his broad forehead, then scratched his short dark brown hair.

"Maybe," I replied, following him as he turned off the path and headed through a wide patch of tall reeds. "Do you think it would really suck you down into it, like quicksand?"

"My dad says there's no such thing as quicksand," Will said.

"I bet there is," I told him. "I bet people have fallen into the bog accidentally and gotten sucked down. If we brought a fishing rod, we could cast a line in and pull up their bones."

"Gross," he said.

We were walking over a carpet of dead brown leaves. Our sneakers crunched noisily as we made our way under tangled palm trees toward the bog.

Suddenly, Will stopped. *"Ssshhh."* He raised a finger to his lips.

I heard it, too.

Crunching behind us.

Footsteps.

We both froze in place, listening hard. The footsteps drew closer.

Will's dark eyes narrowed in fear. "Someone's following us," he murmured. "It's the swamp hermit!"

13

"Quick — hide!" I cried.

Will dived behind a thick clump of tall weeds. I tried to follow him, but there wasn't room for both of us.

Crawling on my hands and knees, I searched frantically for something to hide behind.

The crackling of dead leaves became louder. The footsteps hurried closer.

I scrambled toward a nest of brambles. No. They wouldn't hide me.

A clump of ferns across from me was too low.

The footsteps crackled closer.

Closer.

"Hide! Hide!" Will urged.

But I was trapped out in the open. Caught.

I struggled to my feet just as our pursuer came into view.

"Wolf!" I cried.

The big dog's tail began wagging furiously as

54

soon as he saw me. He uttered a joyful bark — and jumped.

"No!" I managed to cry.

His front paws landed hard on my chest. I stumbled backwards into the tall weeds and fell onto Will.

"Hey!" He cried out and scrambled to his feet.

Wolf barked happily and practically smothered me, trying to lick my face.

"Wolf — down! Down!" I shouted. I stood up and started brushing dead leaves off my T-shirt. "Wolf, you've got to stop doing that, boy," I told him. "You're not a little puppy, you know?"

"How did he find us?" Will asked, pulling a burr off the seat of his blue Lycra shorts.

"Good nose, I guess," I replied, staring down at the happily panting dog. "Maybe he's part hunting dog or something."

"Let's get to the bog," Will said impatiently. He began leading the way, but Wolf pushed past him, nearly bumping him over, and continued trotting toward the bog, his powerful legs taking long, steady strides.

"Wolf acts as if he knows where we're going," I said, a little surprised.

"Maybe he's been here before," Will replied. "Maybe he's a swamp dog.

"Maybe," I replied thoughtfully, staring down at Wolf. *Where* do *you come from, dog?* I wondered. He certainly did seem at home in the swamp.

In a short while, we came to the edge of the peat bog. I wiped the sweat off my forehead with the back of my hand and stared across the oval-shaped pond.

Shafts of sunlight made the green surface sparkle. Thousands of tiny white insects fluttered just above it, catching the light, glistening like little diamonds.

Will picked up a small tree branch. He cracked it in half between his hands. Then he heaved one of the halves high into the air.

It hit the surface of the bog with more of a *thunk* than a *splash*. And then it just lay there. It didn't sink.

"Weird," I said. "Let's try something heavier."

I started to search for something, but a low growl caught my attention. I turned toward the sound. To my surprise, it was coming from Wolf.

The dog had lowered its big head. Its entire body stood tensed, as if in attack position. Its dark lips were pulled back, revealing two sharp rows of teeth. It uttered a low growl, then another.

"I think he senses danger," Will said softly.

Wolf uttered another menacing growl, baring his jagged teeth. The fur on his back stood up stiffly. His legs tensed as if preparing to attack.

The sound of crackling twigs made me raise my eyes. I saw a gray figure darting behind tall weeds on the other side of the bog.

"Who — who's that?" Will whispered.

I stared straight ahead, unable to speak.

"Is that —" Will started.

"Yes," I managed to choke out. "It's him. The swamp hermit." I dropped quickly to my knees, hoping to keep out of view.

But had he already seen us?

Had he been there at the other side of the bog all along?

Will must have been sharing my thoughts. "Has that weirdo been *spying* on us?" he demanded, huddling beside me.

Wolf uttered a quiet growl, still frozen in place, ready to attack.

Keeping low, I scooted closer to the dog. For protection, I guess.

I watched the strange man as he made his way through the weeds. His long gray-white hair was wild, standing straight out around his face. He kept glancing behind him as he walked, as if making sure he wasn't being followed.

He carried a brown sack over one shoulder.

He turned his gaze in our direction. I dropped down lower, trying to hide behind Wolf, my heart pounding.

Wolf hadn't moved, but he was silent now. His ears were still pulled back, his lips still open in a soundless snarl.

What were those dark stains on the front of the swamp hermit's grimy shirt?

Bloodstains?

A shiver of fear ran down my back.

Wolf stared straight ahead without blinking, without moving a muscle.

The swamp hermit disappeared behind the tall weeds. We couldn't see him, but we could still hear his footsteps crunching over dead leaves and fallen twigs.

I glanced over at Wolf. The big dog shook himself, as if shaking the swamp hermit from his mind. His tail wagged slowly. His body relaxed. He uttered soft whimpers, as if telling me how scared he had been.

"It's okay, boy," I said quietly and rubbed the soft fur on top of the dog's head. He stopped whimpering and licked at my wrist.

"That guy is creepy!" Will exclaimed, climbing slowly to his feet.

"He even scared the dog," I said, petting Wolf some more. "What do you think he had in the sack?"

"Probably someone's head!" Will said, his dark eyes wide with horror.

I laughed. But I stopped when I saw that Will wasn't joking. "Everyone says he's harmless," I said.

"He had blood all over the front of his shirt," Will said with a shudder. He scratched his short dark hair nervously.

The sunlight faded quickly as clouds rolled over the sun. Long shadows crept over the bog. The stick Will had thrown had disappeared, sucked into the thick, murky water.

"Let's get home," I suggested.

"Yeah. Okay," Will agreed quickly.

I called to Wolf, who was exploring in the tall weeds. Then we turned and started to make our way back along the twisting dirt path.

A soft breeze fluttered the trees, making the palm leaves scrape and clatter. Tall ferns shivered in the wind. The shadows grew deeper and darker.

I could hear Wolf behind us. I could hear his body brushing through low shrubs and weeds.

We were nearly to where the trees ended and the flat grass leading to our backyards began. We were nearly out of the swamp when Will stopped suddenly.

I saw his mouth drop open in horror.

I turned to follow his gaze.

Then I uttered a shocked cry and covered my eyes to shut out the gruesome sight.

When I opened my eyes, the hideous pile of feathers and blood-covered flesh was still at my feet.

"Wh-what *is* it?" Will stammered.

It took me a long while to realize we were staring at a bird. A large heron.

It was hard to recognize because it had been torn apart.

Long white feathers were scattered over the soft ground. The poor bird's chest had been torn wide open.

"The swamp hermit!" Will cried.

"Huh?" I cried. I turned away from the hideous sight and tried to force the image from my mind.

"That's why he had blood all over his shirt!" Will declared.

"But why would he rip a bird apart?" I asked weakly.

"Because . . . because he's a *monster*!" Will exclaimed.

"He's just a weird old guy who lives alone in the swamp," I said. "He didn't do this, Will. Some kind of animal did it. Look!" I pointed to the ground.

There were paw prints in the soft ground. All around the dead bird.

"They look like a dog's paws," I said, thinking out loud.

"Dogs don't rip apart birds," Will replied quietly.

At that moment, Wolf came bounding up to us through the weeds. He came to a stop in front of the dead bird and started to sniff it.

"Get away from there, Wolf," I ordered. "Come on. Get away." I tugged him back, pulling him with both hands around his thick neck.

"Let's get home," Will said. "Let's get away from this thing. I'm going to have bad dreams. I really will."

I pulled Wolf with both hands. We stepped carefully around the dead heron and then hurried toward the swamp edge. Neither of us said a word. I guess we were both still picturing what we had seen.

As we reached the flat grass behind our houses, I said good-bye to Will. I watched him hurry to his house. Wolf scampered after him for part of the way. Then he turned and hurried back to me.

The late afternoon sun burned its way through

the clouds. I shielded my eyes from the sudden brightness and saw my dad working in the deer pen behind the house.

"Hey, Dad —" I ran toward him over the grass.

He glanced up when I called to him. He was wearing denim cutoffs and a sleeveless yellow T-shirt. He had an Orlando Magic cap pulled down over his forehead. "What's up, Grady?"

"Will and I — we saw a dead heron," I told him breathlessly.

"Where? In the swamp?" he asked casually. He pulled off the cap, wiped his forehead with the back of his hand, and replaced the cap.

"Dad, it — it was torn apart!" I cried.

He didn't react. "That's part of life in the wild," he said, pulling up one of the deer's hooves to examine the bottom. "You know that, Grady. It can get pretty violent out there. We've talked about survival of the fittest and stuff like that."

"No, Dad. This is different," I insisted. "The heron — it was ripped in two. I mean, like someone took it and —"

"Another bird, maybe," Dad said, concentrating on the deer hoof. "A larger bird of prey. It could have been —"

"We saw the swamp hermit," I interrupted. "He had blood all over his shirt. Then we saw paw prints in the ground. All around the dead bird."

"Grady, calm down," Dad said, setting down the deer's leg. "If you go exploring in the swamp, you're going to see a lot of frightening-looking things. But don't let your imagination run away with you."

"Will said it was done by a monster!" I exclaimed.

Dad frowned and scratched his head through the cap. "I see your new friend has a good imagination, too," he said quietly.

That night, I was glad my parents agreed to let Wolf sleep in my room. I felt a lot safer with the big dog curled up on the rug beside my bed.

I hadn't been able to shake the ugly picture of the dead heron from my mind. I watched some TV until dinnertime. Then after dinner, I played a long chess game with Emily.

But no matter what I did, I kept seeing the white feathers scattered over the ground, the torn-apart bird lying crumpled on the path.

So now I felt a little comforted with Wolf sleeping in the room. "You'll protect me, won't you, boy?" I whispered from my bed.

He uttered a low snort. Light from the full moon spilled over him through the window. I saw that he was sleeping with his head resting on his two front paws.

Then I drifted into a dreamless sleep.

I don't know how long I slept.

I was awakened some time later by a horrifying crash.

I sat straight up with a startled gasp.

The crash had come from the living room, I realized.

Someone was breaking in!

Was it a burglar?

I climbed out of bed, my heart pounding, and crept to the door.

Another crash. A loud *thump*.

Footsteps.

"Who — who is it?" I cried. My voice came out in a choked whisper.

Keeping against the wall, I made my way slowly toward the living room. "Who's there?" I shouted.

Mom and Dad and Emily met me in the dark hallway. Even in the darkness I could see the fear and confusion on their faces.

I was the first to the living room. Pale yellow light from the full moon washed across the room. "Hey!" I called out.

Wolf leaped against the big front window. His shoulders made a loud *thud* against the glass.

"Wolf — stop!" I cried.

66

In the pale light, I saw what had caused the loud crash. Wolf had knocked over the table and a lamp that had stood in front of the window.

"He — he's trying to get outside," I stammered.

I felt Dad's hand on the shoulder of my pajama shirt. "What a mess he's made," he murmured.

"Wolf — stop!" I called again.

The big dog turned, breathing hard. His eyes glowed red in the moonlight through the window.

"Why is he so desperate to get out?" Emily demanded.

"We can't have him in the house if he does this every night," Mom said, her voice hoarse from sleep.

The big dog lowered his head and let out an excited growl. His tail stood straight up behind him.

"Open the front door. Let him out," Mom said. "Before he wrecks the whole house."

Dad hurried across the room and pulled open the door. Wolf didn't hesitate for a second. He bounded to the door and burst out.

I ran to the window to watch him. But the big dog disappeared around the side of the house, running toward the backyard.

"He's heading to the swamp," I guessed.

"He tried to break right through the window," Mom said.

Emily clicked on a lamp. "He's so strong, he probably could have broken the window," she said quietly.

Dad closed the front door. He yawned. Then he turned his gaze on me. "You know what this means, don't you, Grady?"

I was still staring out at the full moon. "No. What?"

"Wolf will have to stay outdoors from now on," Dad said. He stooped and began picking up pieces of the broken lamp.

"But, Dad —" I started to protest.

"He's too big and too restless to stay in the house," Dad continued. He handed the lamp pieces to Emily. Then he pulled the table rightside up and returned it to its place in front of the window.

"Wolf didn't mean to break the lamp," I argued weakly.

"He'll break everything we have," Mom said quietly.

"He's just too big," Dad added. "He'll have to stay outside, Grady."

"Why did he want out so desperately?" Emily demanded.

"He's probably used to being outside," Dad told her. "He'll be happier out there," he said, turning to me.

"Yeah. Maybe," I replied glumly. I liked having Wolf sleep beside me in my bedroom. But I knew there was no way I could convince my parents to give the dog a second chance. Their minds were made up.

And at least they were letting me keep Wolf.

I pulled the vacuum cleaner out of the closet and plugged it in. Dad took the nozzle and began vacuuming up the tiny pieces of glass from the carpet.

That crazy dog, I thought, shaking my head unhappily. *What is his* problem, *anyway?*

When Dad finished, I carried the vacuum cleaner back to the closet.

"Now maybe we can all sleep in peace," Mom said, yawning.

She was wrong.

17

I heard the frightening howls again a short while later.

At first I thought I was dreaming them.

But when I opened my eyes and gazed around my dark bedroom, the howls continued. Still half asleep, I gripped the covers with both hands and pulled them up to my chin.

The howls sounded so close, as if they were right outside my window. They didn't seem like the cries of an animal. They were too angry, too deliberate.

Too human.

Stop trying to frighten yourself, I thought. *It's a wolf. It has to be some kind of swamp wolf.*

In the back of my mind, I knew it might be Wolf making those frightening sounds. But I kept pushing the thought away.

Why would the dog howl like that?

Dogs bark. They don't howl unless they're very sad or upset.

I shut my eyes, wishing the frightening wails away.

Suddenly, they stopped. Silence.

Then I heard rapid thumps on the ground. Footsteps.

Some kind of a struggle.

I heard a short, terrifying cry. It cut off almost as soon as it began.

It's right in back of the house, I realized.

Wide-awake now, I jumped out of bed, dragging the covers with me. I stumbled to the bedroom window and grabbed the windowsill.

The full moon had risen high in the night sky. The backyard stretched out silvery in the moonlight, the dewy grass shimmering in the bright light.

Pressing my forehead against the windowpane, I peered out toward the dark swamp. I uttered a near-silent gasp when I saw the shadowy creature running toward the trees.

A large creature, running on all fours.

It was only a black outline fading into the darkness. But I could see how big it was, and I could see how fast it was running.

And I heard its howls. *Triumphant howls,* I thought.

Is it Wolf? I wondered. I peered out the window without moving, even though the darkness had swallowed the creature up. I could see only the outline of distant trees.

But I could still hear the howls rising and falling on the heavy night air.

Is it Wolf?

It can't be Wolf — can it?

I lowered my gaze. My breath caught in my throat. I saw something. In the middle of the backyard. A few feet from the deer pen.

At first I thought it was a pile of rags.

My hands trembled as I pulled open my window.

I had to get a better look. I had to see what that was in the backyard.

I pulled up my pajama bottoms. Then, gripping the windowsill, I lowered myself out the window onto the grass.

The wet grass felt cold under my bare feet. I turned to the deer pen. The six swamp deer were standing tensely, huddled together against the house. Their dark eyes followed me as I began to creep across the grass.

What is *that thing?* I wondered, staring into the silvery light.

Is it just a pile of old rags?

No.

What is *it?*

My bare feet felt cold and wet as I made my way slowly across the dew-covered grass. The night air was heavy and still, still as death.

When I came close enough to see what was lying in a heap on the grass, I uttered a faint cry and started to gag.

I pressed a hand against my mouth and swallowed hard.

I realized I was staring down at a rabbit. Its small black eyes were frozen open in terror. One of its ears had been pulled off.

The rabbit had been ripped open, nearly torn in half.

I forced myself to look away.

My stomach still heaving, I hurried back over the wet grass to my open window and scrambled back in.

As I struggled to pull the window shut, the howls rang out again, rising triumphantly from the nearby swamp.

*   *   *

After breakfast the next morning, I led Dad out to the backyard to show him the murdered rabbit. It was a bright, hot day, and a red sun climbed a pale, clear sky.

As soon as we stepped off the back stoop, Wolf appeared from around the side of the house. His tail began wagging furiously. He came running excitedly to greet me, as if he hadn't seen me in years, leaping onto my chest, nearly knocking me over.

"Down, Wolf! Down!" I cried, laughing as the dog stretched to lick my face.

"Your dog is a killer," a voice said behind me. I turned to see that Emily had followed us. She was wearing a red T-shirt over white tennis shorts. She had her arms crossed in front of her, and she was glaring disapprovingly at Wolf. "Look what he did to that poor bunny rabbit," she said, shaking her head.

"Whoa. Hold on," I replied, petting Wolf's gray fur. "Who said Wolf did this?"

"Who else would have done it?" Emily demanded. "He's a killer."

"Oh, yeah? Look how gentle he is," I insisted. I put my wrist in Wolf's mouth. He clamped down gently on it, being careful not to hurt me.

"Wolf *may* be a bit of a hunter," Dad said thoughtfully. He had been staring down at the rabbit, but now he turned his glance to the deer pen.

Huddled together at one end of the pen, the deer were all staring warily at Wolf. They had their heads lowered cautiously as they followed the dog's every move.

"I'm glad they're safe inside that pen," Dad said softly.

"Dad, you have to get rid of this dog," Emily said shrilly.

"No way!" I cried. I turned angrily to my sister. "You have no proof that Wolf did anything wrong!" I shouted. "No proof at all!"

"You have no proof that he *didn't* do it!" Emily replied nastily.

"Of *course* he didn't!" I cried, feeling myself lose control. "Didn't you hear the howls last night? Didn't you hear those frightening howls? It wasn't a *dog* howling like that. Dogs don't howl like that!"

"Then what was it?" Emily demanded.

"I heard them, too," Dad said, stepping between us. "They sounded more like wolf howls. Or maybe a coyote."

"See?" I told Emily.

"But I'd be very surprised to find a wolf or coyote in *this* area," Dad continued, gazing out toward the swamp.

Emily still had her arms crossed tightly over

her chest. She gazed down at Wolf and shuddered. "He's dangerous, Dad. You really have to get rid of him."

Dad walked over and patted Wolf's head. He scratched Wolf under the chin. Wolf licked Dad's hand.

"Let's just be careful around him," Dad said. "He seems very gentle. But we don't really know anything about him — do we? So let's be very careful, okay?"

"I'm going to be careful," Emily replied, narrowing her eyes at Wolf. "I'm going to stay as far away from that *monster* as I can." She turned and stormed back to the house.

Dad made his way to the shed to get a shovel and box for carrying away the dead rabbit.

I dropped to my knees and hugged Wolf's broad neck. "You aren't a monster, are you, boy?" I asked. "Emily is crazy, isn't she? You're not a monster. That wasn't you I saw running toward the swamp last night, was it?"

Wolf raised his deep blue eyes to mine. He stared hard at me.

He seemed to be trying to tell me something.

But I had no idea what it could be.

That night I didn't hear the howls.

I woke up in the middle of the night and stared out the window. Wolf was gone, probably exploring the swamp. In the morning, I knew he'd come running back to greet me as if I were a long-lost friend.

The next morning Will showed up just as I was giving Wolf his breakfast, a big bowl of crunchy dry dog food. "Hey, what's up?" Will asked, his usual greeting.

"Nothing much," I said. I rolled up the top of the big bag of dog food and dragged it back into the kitchen. Wolf stood over his bowl, his head lowered, chewing noisily away.

I pushed open the screen door and returned to Will. He was wearing a dark blue muscle shirt and black Lycra bike shorts. He had a green-and-yellow Forest Service cap pulled down over his dark hair.

"Want to go exploring?" he asked in his hoarse voice, watching Wolf hungrily gobble down his breakfast. "You know. In the swamp?"

"Yeah. Sure," I said. I called inside to tell my parents where I was going. Then I followed Will across the back lawn toward the swamp.

Wolf came scampering after us. He'd run past us, then let us catch up. Then he'd run in crazy zigzags in front of us, behind us, romping happily under the hot morning sun.

"Did you hear about Mr. Warner?" Will asked. He stopped to pick up a long blade of grass and put it between his teeth.

"Who?"

"Ed Warner," Will replied. "I guess you haven't met the Warners yet. They live in the very last house." He turned and pointed behind us to the last white house at the end of the row of white houses.

"What about him?" I asked, nearly tripping over Wolf, who had come rumbling past my feet.

"He's missing," Will replied, chewing on the grass blade. "He didn't come home last night."

"Huh? From where?" I asked, turning to stare at the Warners' house. Heat waves shimmered up from the grass, making the house appear to bend and quiver.

"From the swamp," Will replied darkly. "Mrs. Warner called my mom this morning. She said Mr. Warner went hunting yesterday afternoon.

He likes to hunt wild turkeys. He took me with him a couple times. He's real good at chasing them down. When he kills one, he hangs its feet up on his den wall."

"He does?" I cried. It sounded pretty gross to me.

"Yeah. You know. Like a trophy," Will continued. "Anyway, he went hunting wild turkeys in the swamp yesterday afternoon, and he hasn't come home."

"Weird," I said, watching Wolf stop at the edge of the trees. "Maybe he got lost."

"No way," Will insisted, shaking his head. "Not Mr. Warner. He's lived here a long time. He was the first one to move here. Mr. Warner wouldn't get lost."

"Then maybe the werewolf got him!" called a strange voice behind us.

Startled, we both spun around to see a girl about our age. She had rust-colored hair tied in a ponytail on one side. She had catlike green eyes, a short stub of a nose, and freckles all over her face. She was wearing faded red denim jeans and a T-shirt with a grinning green alligator on the front.

"Cassie, what are *you* doing here?" Will demanded.

"Following you," she replied, making a face at him. She turned to me. "You're the new kid, Grady, right? Will told me about you."

"Hi," I said awkwardly. "He told me a girl lived in the neighborhood. But he didn't tell me much about you."

"What's to tell?" Will teased.

"I'm Cassie O'Rourke," she said. She shot up her hand and pulled the blade of grass from Will's mouth.

"Hey!" He playfully tried to slug her, but missed.

"What did you say about a werewolf?" I asked.

"Don't start with that stuff again," Will grumbled to Cassie. "It's so stupid."

"You're just afraid," Cassie accused.

"No, I'm not. It's too stupid," Will insisted.

We stepped into the shade of the trees at the swamp edge. A funnel cloud of white gnats whirred crazily in a shaft of light between the trees.

"There's a werewolf in the swamp," Cassie said, lowering her voice as we ducked past the gnats and moved deeper into the shade.

"And I'm going to flap my wings and fly to Mars," Will said sarcastically.

"Shut up, Will," Cassie snapped. "Grady doesn't think it's stupid — do you?"

I shrugged. "I don't know," I said. "I don't think I believe in werewolves."

Will laughed. "Cassie believes in the Easter Bunny, too," he said.

Cassie socked him hard in the chest.

"Hey!" Will cried out angrily as he staggered back. "What's your problem?"

"Mosquito," she said, pointing. "A big one. I got him."

Scowling, Will glanced down. "I don't see any mosquito. Give me a break, Cassie."

We made our way along the winding path. It had rained the day before. The ground was marshier than usual. We kept slipping in the soft mud.

"Do you hear the howling sounds at night?" I asked Cassie.

"That's the werewolf," she replied softly. Her green cat-eyes burned into mine. "I'm not kidding around, Grady. I'm serious. Those howls aren't human. Those howls come from a werewolf who has just killed."

Will snickered. "You've got a good imagination, Cassie. I guess you watch a lot of scary movies on TV, huh?"

"Real life is scarier than the movies," she said, lowering her voice to a whisper.

"Ooh, stop. You're making me shake all over!" Will exclaimed sarcastically.

She didn't reply. She was still staring at me as we walked. "You believe me, don't you?"

"I don't know," I said.

The bog came into view. The air became heavier, wetter. The tall weeds on the other side stood straight up. The bog gurgled quietly. Two big flies danced over the dark green surface.

"There's no such thing as werewolves, Cassie," Will muttered, searching for something to throw into the bog. He grinned at her. "Unless maybe *you're* one!"

She rolled her eyes. "Very funny." She made biting motions with her teeth as if she were going to bite him.

I heard a rustling sound across the oval-shaped bog. The tall weeds suddenly parted, and Wolf appeared at the edge of the water.

"What does the werewolf look like?" Will asked sarcastically "Does it have red hair and freckles?"

Cassie didn't reply.

I turned to see a look of terror freeze on her face. Her green eyes grew wide, and her freckles seemed to fade. "Th-there's the *werewolf*!" she stammered in a choked whisper. She pointed.

Feeling a chill of fear, I turned to see where she was pointing.

To my horror, she was pointing right at Wolf!

"No!" I started to protest.

But then I saw that I had misunderstood. Cassie wasn't pointing at Wolf. She was pointing to the figure moving through the tall weeds behind the dog.

The swamp hermit!

I saw him walking quickly behind the weeds, his shoulders bent, his mangy head bobbing with each step.

As he moved into a small break in the weeds, I could see why he was leaning forward. He carried something over one shoulder. A bag of some sort.

Wolf started to growl.

The hermit stopped walking.

It wasn't a bag slung over his shoulder, I saw. It was a turkey. A wild turkey.

A chilling thought burst into my mind: Had he taken it from Mr. Warner?

Was Cassie right about the swamp hermit? Was he a werewolf? Had he done something horrible to Mr. Warner and claimed the wild turkey as his prize?

I tried to dismiss these horrible thoughts. They were crazy. Impossible.

But Cassie looked so frightened, staring across the gurgling green bog at the wild-eyed hermit. And the howls at night, the howls had been so frightening, so human.

And the dead animals I'd seen, torn so brutally apart, as if . . . as if by a werewolf!

Wolf uttered another warning growl. He stared at the hermit, his tail standing stiffly behind him, his fur rising up on his back.

The hermit moved quickly. I saw his dark eyes flash just before he disappeared behind the weeds.

"It's him!" Cassie cried, still pointing. "It's the werewolf!"

"Cassie — *shut up!*" Will warned. "He'll *hear* you!"

I swallowed hard, frozen in place by my fear. I saw the weeds tremble across the bog. I heard rustling sounds growing closer.

"Run!" Will cried, his hoarse voice shrill and frightened. "Come on — run!"

Too late.

The swamp hermit burst out of the weeds right

85

behind us. "I'm the werewolf!" he shrieked. His eyes were wild, excited. His face, surrounded by his long, tangled hair, was bright red. "I'm the werewolf!"

He *had* heard Cassie!

Laughing at the top of his lungs, he tossed up both hands, then began to swing the turkey in a wide circle over his head. "I'm the werewolf!" he cried.

Cassie, Will, and I all cried out at the same time.

Then we started to run.

Out of the corner of my eye, I could see Wolf. He hadn't moved from his spot across the bog. But now, as I started to run, he came bounding toward us, barking excitedly.

"I'm the werewolf!" the hermit shrieked. He howled with laughter, still swinging the turkey as he chased after us.

"Leave us alone!" Cassie cried, running beside Will a few steps ahead of me. "Do you *hear* me? Leave us alone!"

Her pleas made the hermit howl again.

My shoes slipped in the muddy ground.

I turned back. He was gaining on me. Right behind me.

Gasping for breath, I struggled to run faster. Sharp vines and heavy leaves slapped at my face and arms as I plunged forward.

It was all a blur now. A blur of light and shade, trees and vines, tall weeds and sharp brambles.

"I'm the werewolf! I'm the werewolf!"

The crazed hermit's high-pitched wails of laughter echoed through the swamp.

Keep going, Grady, I urged myself. *Keep going.*

Then, with a terrified cry, I felt my feet slide out from under me.

I fell face forward into the mud, landing hard on my hands and knees.

He's got me, I realized.

The werewolf has got me.

22

I tried frantically to scramble up from the mud. But I slipped again and tumbled forward with a *splat*.

He's got me now, I thought.

The werewolf has got me now. I cannot escape.

My muscles all froze in panic. I struggled to crawl away.

I turned back, expecting the hermit to grab me.

But he had stopped several yards away. The turkey dangled to the ground as he stared down at me, a strange grin on his weathered face.

Where is Wolf? I wondered.

Wolf had been growling furiously at the swamp hermit. Why hadn't Wolf attacked?

"Help! Will! Cassie!" I called desperately.

Silence.

They were gone. They were both probably out of the swamp by now, running for home.

88

I was alone. Alone to face the hermit.

I stumbled to my feet, my eyes locked on his. Why was he grinning at me like that?

"Go on. Go," he murmured, gesturing with his free hand. "Just teasing you."

"What?" My voice came out tiny and frightened.

"Go. I'm not going to bite you," he said. His grin faded. The light seemed to dim in his shiny black eyes.

Wolf appeared behind him. The dog gazed up at the hermit, then lowered his eyes to the dead turkey. He barked once, a shrill *yip*. But I could see that Wolf had relaxed. He had no intention of attacking the hermit.

"This dog yours?" the hermit asked, eyeing Wolf warily.

"Yeah," I replied, still breathing hard. "I . . . found him."

"Watch out for him," the hermit said sharply. Then he turned and, hoisting the large bird on his shoulder, headed back into the weeds.

"W-watch out for him?" I stammered. "What do you mean?"

But the hermit didn't reply. I could hear him brushing the tall weeds away as he disappeared back into the swamp.

"What do you mean?" I called after him.

But he was gone. The swamp was silent now except for the chirping and clicking of insects and

89

the dry sound of palm leaves brushing against each other.

I stared straight ahead at the tall weeds. I guess I expected the swamp hermit to return, to burst back into view, to attack again.

Two white moths fluttered together over the weeds. Nothing else moved.

He was teasing us, he had said.

That's all it was, just teasing.

I swallowed hard. Then I forced myself to breathe normally again.

After a while, I lowered my gaze to Wolf. The dog was busily sniffing the ground where the hermit had stood.

"Wolf — why didn't you protect me?" I scolded.

The dog glanced up, then returned to his sniffing.

"Hey, dog — are you a big coward?" I asked, brushing at the wet dirt on the knees of my jeans. "Is that your problem? You sound real tough, but you're actually a big chicken?"

Wolf ignored me.

I turned and headed home, thinking about the hermit's warning. As I made my way along the narrow path, I could hear Wolf running through the weeds and tall grass, following close behind.

"Watch out for him," the hermit had said.

Was he teasing about that, too? Was he just trying to scare me?

The strange man saw that Will, Cassie, and I were afraid of him. So he decided to have some fun with us.

That's all it was, I decided.

He heard Cassie call him a werewolf. So he decided to give us a real scare.

As I walked along the marshy ground under the shade of the tilted palm trees, my mind spun with thoughts about Cassie and Will and Wolf and werewolves.

I didn't see the snake until I stepped on it.

I glanced down in time to see its bright green head shoot forward.

I felt a sharp stab of pain as its fangs dug into my ankle.

The pain jolted up my leg.

I uttered a choked gasp before I crumpled to the ground.

23

I hit the ground and curled into a tight ball as the pain throbbed through my body.

Red dots formed in my eyes. The dots grew larger and larger until I saw only red. The color shimmered in rhythm to the throbbing pain.

Through the curtain of red, I saw the snake slither into the bushes.

I grabbed my ankle, trying to force the pain down.

Slowly, the red faded, then vanished, leaving only the pain.

My hand suddenly felt wet.

Blood?

I glanced down to see Wolf licking my hand. Fierce licking, as if trying to cure me, trying to make everything okay again.

Despite the pain, I laughed. "It's okay, boy," I said. "I'm okay."

He kept licking my hand until I climbed to my feet. I felt a little dizzy. My legs were shaky.

I tried putting weight on the foot that had been bitten.

It felt a little better.

I took a step, limping. Then another.

"Let's go, Wolf," I said. He gazed up at me sympathetically.

I knew I had to get home quickly. If the snake was poisonous, I was in big trouble. I had no way of knowing how much time I had before the venom would paralyze me completely — or worse.

Wolf stayed by my side as I limped over the soft ground toward home. I was gasping for breath. My chest felt tight. The ground swayed beneath me.

Was it because of the snake venom? Or was it just because I was so frightened?

Pain shot up my side with every step I took.

But I kept pulling myself along, talking to Wolf all the while, ignoring the throbbing ache of my ankle.

"We're almost there, Wolf," I said, panting loudly. "Almost there, boy."

The dog sensed that something was seriously wrong. He stayed by my side instead of running his usual zigzag patterns in front of me and behind me.

The end of the trees came into view. I could see bright sunlight just beyond the swamp.

"Hey —" a voice called to me. I saw Will and Cassie waiting for me on the flat grass.

They began running toward me. "Are you okay?" Cassie called.

"No. I . . . I got *bit*!" I managed to choke out. "Please — go get my dad!"

They both took off, running full speed to my house. I dropped down on the grass, spreading my legs straight out, and waited.

I tried to stay calm, but it was impossible.

Was the snake poisonous? Was the venom heading straight to my heart? Was I about to die any second?

I reached down with both hands and carefully, carefully, pulled off my mud-covered sneaker. Then, moving it a tiny bit at a time, I lowered my white sock down over the ankle and off my foot.

The ankle was a little swollen. The skin was red except for a white puckered spot around the bite. Inside that spot, I saw two small puncture marks, bright red droplets of blood oozing from each hole.

When I raised my eyes from the wound, I saw my dad, dressed in brown shorts and a white T-shirt, hurrying along the flat grass toward me, followed closely by Will and Cassie.

"What happened?" I heard my dad ask them. "What happened to Grady?"

"He was bitten by a werewolf!" I heard Cassie reply.

94

*　　*　　*

"Keep the ice pack on it," Dad instructed. "The swelling will go down."

I groaned and held the ice pack against my ankle.

Mom tsk-tsked from the kitchen table. She had a newspaper spread out in front of her. I couldn't tell if she was tsk-tsking over me or over the day's news.

Outside the screen door I could see Wolf, on his side on the grass just past the back stoop, sound asleep. Emily was in the front room, watching some soap on TV.

"How does it feel?" Mom asked.

"A lot better," I told her. "I think I was mainly scared."

"Green snakes aren't poisonous," Dad reminded me for the tenth time. "But I took every precaution, just in case. We'll wrap it up really good when you're through putting ice on it."

"What was all that talk about werewolves?" Mom asked.

"Cassie has werewolves on the brain," I said. "She thinks the swamp hermit is a werewolf."

"She seems like a sweet girl," Mom said quietly. "I had a nice talk with her while your father was taking care of your bite. You're lucky, Grady, to find two kids your age out here on the edge of a swamp."

"Yeah, I guess," I replied, shifting the ice pack on the ankle. "But she was driving Will and me nuts with all her werewolf talk."

Dad was washing his hands in the kitchen sink. He dried them on a dish towel, then turned to me. "That old swamp hermit is supposed to be harmless," he said. "At least, that's what everyone says."

"Well, he gave us a real scare," I told him. "He chased us through the swamp, shouting, 'I'm the werewolf!'"

"Weird," Dad replied thoughtfully. He tossed the dish towel onto the counter.

"You should stay away from him," Mom said, looking up from the newspaper.

"Do you believe in werewolves?" I asked.

Dad snickered. "Your mom and I are scientists, Grady. We're not supposed to believe in supernatural things like werewolves."

"Your father is a werewolf," Mom joked. "I have to shave his back every morning so he'll look human."

"Ha-ha," I said sarcastically. "I'm serious. I mean, haven't you heard the weird howls at night?"

"Lot's of creatures howl," Mom replied. "I'll bet *you* howled when that snake bit your ankle!"

"Can't you be serious?" I cried shrilly. "You know, the howls didn't start until it was a full moon."

"I remember. The howls didn't start until that dog showed up!" Emily called from the front room.

"Emily, give me a break!" I shouted.

"Your dog is a werewolf!" Emily called.

"Enough werewolf talk," Mom muttered. "Look. I've got hair growing on my palms!" She held up her hands.

"That's just ink off the newspaper," Dad said. He turned to me. "See? There's a scientific explanation for everything."

"I really would like to be taken seriously," I said through clenched teeth.

"Well . . ." Dad glanced outside. Wolf had rolled onto his back and was sleeping with all four legs up in the air. "The moon will look full for only two more nights," Dad told me. "Tonight and tomorrow night. If the howl stops after tomorrow night, we'll know it was a werewolf, howling at the full moon."

Dad chuckled. He thought it was all a big joke.

We had no idea that something was about to happen that night that might change his opinion about werewolves — forever.

24

Will and Cassie came over after dinner. Mom and Dad were still loading dishes into the dishwasher and cleaning up. Emily had hurried into town to go to the only movie playing.

I was walking around pretty well. The ankle barely hurt at all. Dad's a pretty good doctor, I guess.

The three of us settled in the front room, and we instantly got into an argument about werewolves.

Cassie insisted that the swamp hermit wasn't kidding, that he really was a werewolf.

Will told her she was a complete jerk. "He only chased us because he heard you call him a werewolf," he told Cassie angrily.

"Why do you think he lives by himself way deep in the swamp?" Cassie demanded of Will. "Because he knows what happens to him when the moon is full, and he doesn't want anyone else to know it!"

"Then why did he scream to us that he was a werewolf this afternoon?" Will asked impatiently. "Because he was just joking, that's why."

"Come on, guys. Let's change the subject," I said. "My parents are both scientists, and they say there's no proof that werewolves exist."

"That's what scientists always say," Cassie insisted.

"They're right," Will said. "There are no werewolves except in movies. You're a real jerk, Cassie."

"*You're* a jerk!" Cassie shouted back.

I could see they'd had fights like this before. "Let's play a game or something," I suggested. "Want to play some Nintendo? It's in my room."

"Mr. Warner still hasn't shown up," Cassie told Will, ignoring me. She tugged at her red ponytail, then tossed it behind her head. "You know why? Because he was murdered by the werewolf!"

"Don't be stupid," Will said. "How do *you* know?"

"Maybe *you're* the werewolf!" I told Cassie.

Will laughed. "Yeah. That's why you're such an expert, Cassie."

"Oh, shut up," Cassie grumbled. "You look more like a werewolf than me, Will!"

"You look like a *vampire*!" he told her.

"Well, you look like King Kong!" she cried.

"What are you kids talking about?" Mom interrupted, poking her head into the room.

"Just talking about movies and things," I replied quickly.

I couldn't get to sleep that night. I kept rolling on to one side, then the other. I couldn't get comfortable.

I kept listening for the howls.

A strong wind had come up from the Gulf. I could hear it rushing past our small house. It rattled the wire mesh of the deer pen out back. It made a constant *ssshhhhh* sound, and I strained to hear the familiar howls.

I had just about drifted off to sleep when the howls began.

Instantly alert, I jumped to my feet. My left ankle ached as I stepped down on it.

Another howl. Far off. Barely carrying over the steady rush of the wind.

I limped to my bedroom window. The ankle had stiffened up a bit while I was lying in bed. I pressed my face against the glass and peered out.

The full moon, gray as a skull, hovered low in the charcoal sky. The dewy grass gleamed under its blanket of pale light.

A burst of wind rattled my window.

Startled, I pulled back. And listened.

Another howl. Closer.

This one sent a cold shudder down my back.

It sounded really close. Or was the wind carrying it from the swamp?

I squinted out the window. Swirls of wind made the grass sway from side to side. The ground appeared to be spinning, glowing in the pale moonlight as it twirled.

Another howl. Even closer.

I couldn't see anything. I *had* to know who or what was making that terrifying sound.

I pulled my jeans on over my pajama bottoms. Struggling in the dark, I managed to slide my feet into a pair of flip-flops.

I started out of my room but stopped short when I heard banging. Then a loud crash. And a harsh *thud*.

Right outside.

Right outside my house.

My heart pounding, I ran through the dark hallway. My ankle ached, but I ignored it.

I hurried through the kitchen, unlocked the back door, and pulled it open. A strong gust of wind pushed me back as I opened the screen door.

The wind was hot and wet. Another strong gust pushed me back.

The wind is trying to keep me inside, I thought. *Trying to keep me from solving the mystery of the terrifying howls.*

I lowered my head against the driving gusts and leaped down off the stoop.

"Ow!" I cried out as pain shot up my leg.

Waiting for my eyes to adjust to the dim light, I listened hard.

No howls now. Just the shrill, steady rush of wind, pushing, pushing me back against the house.

The backyard glowed in the moonlight. Everything was silver and gray.

And silent.

I searched the backyard, my eyes sweeping slowly across the shifting grass. Empty.

But what had caused all the commotion I'd heard in my room. The banging? The loud *thuds*? The rattling sounds?

Why had the howls stopped when I came outside?

What a mystery, I thought. *What a strange mystery.*

The wind swirled around me. My face was dripping wet from the heavy dampness of the air.

Feeling defeated, I turned back toward the house.

And uttered a shocked cry when I saw that the werewolf had murdered again.

I took a step through the swirling wind toward the deer pen.

"Dad!" I called. But my voice came out a hushed whisper. "Dad!" I tried to shout, but my throat was too dry and choked with fear.

Staring straight ahead, I took another step. I could see it all clearly now. A scene of death. Pale light and shadows. The only sounds were the pounding of my heart, the swell of the wind, and the rattling of the wire mesh of the pen.

I took another step closer. "Dad? Dad?" I cried out without thinking, without hearing myself, knowing he couldn't hear.

But I wanted him to be there. I wanted *someone* to be there with me. I didn't want to be all alone out there in the backyard.

I didn't want to be staring at the hole that had been ripped from the side of the pen. I didn't want to see the murdered deer lying so pitifully on its side.

The five remaining deer huddled together at the other end of the pen. Their eyes were on me. Frightened eyes.

The wind swept around me, hot and wet. But I felt cold all over. A cold shudder of terror ran down my body. I swallowed hard. Once. Twice. Trying to choke down the heavy lump in my throat.

Then, before I even realized what I was doing, I began running to the house, screaming, "Dad! Mom! Dad! Mom!" at the top of my lungs.

My cries rose on the gusting wind like the terrifying howls I'd heard just a few moments before.

His pajama shirt flapping over the jeans he had pulled on, Dad dragged the dead deer to the back of the yard. Then, as I watched from the kitchen window, he patched the deer pen with a large sheet of box cardboard.

As he tried to return to the house, the strong winds nearly blew the screen door off its hinges. Dad jerked the door shut, then locked it.

His face was dripping with perspiration. He had mud down the side of one pajama sleeve.

Mom poured him a glass of water from the sink, and he drank it down without taking a breath. Then he wiped the sweat from his forehead with a dish towel.

"I'm afraid your dog is a killer," he said softly

to me. He tossed the towel back onto the counter.

"It wasn't Wolf!" I cried. "It wasn't!"

Dad didn't reply. He took a deep breath, then let it out slowly. Mom and Emily watched silently from in front of the sink.

"What makes you think it was Wolf?" I demanded.

"I saw the prints on the ground," he replied, frowning. "Paw prints."

"It wasn't Wolf," I insisted.

"I'm going to have to take him to the pound in the morning," Dad said. "The one over in the next county."

"But they'll kill him!" I cried.

"The dog is a killer," Dad insisted softly. "I know how you feel, Grady. I know. But the dog is a killer."

"It wasn't Wolf," I cried. "Dad, I know it wasn't Wolf. I heard the howls, Dad. It was a wolf."

"Grady, please —" he started wearily.

Then the words just burst out of me. I lost all control of them. They just poured out in a flood. "It was a werewolf, Dad. There's a werewolf in the swamp. Cassie is right. It wasn't a dog, and it wasn't a wolf. It's a werewolf who's been killing animals, who killed your deer."

"Grady, stop —" Dad pleaded impatiently.

But I couldn't stop. "I know I'm right, Dad," I cried in a shrill voice that didn't sound like me.

"It's been a full moon this week, right? And that's when the howls began. It's a werewolf, Dad. The swamp hermit. That crazy guy who lives in the shack in the swamp. He's a werewolf. He told us he is. He chased us and told us he's a werewolf. *He* did it, Dad. Not Wolf. *He* killed the deer tonight. I hear him howling outside, and then — then —"

My voice caught in my throat. I started to choke.

Dad filled the glass with water and handed it to me. I gulped it down thirstily.

He put a hand on my shoulder. "Grady, let's talk about it in the morning, okay? We're both too tired to think straight now. What do you say?"

"It wasn't Wolf!" I cried stubbornly. "I know it wasn't."

"In the morning," Dad repeated, his hand still on my shoulder. He held it there to comfort me, to steady me.

I felt shaky. I was panting. My heart pounded.

"Yeah. Okay," I agreed finally. "In the morning."

I made my way slowly to my room, but I knew I wouldn't sleep.

The next morning, Dad was gone when I got up. "He went to the lumberyard," Mom told me, "to get wire mesh to repair the pen."

I yawned and stretched. I had fallen into a restless sleep at about two-thirty. But I still felt tired and nervous.

"Is Wolf out there?" I asked anxiously. I ran to the kitchen window before she could reply.

I could see Wolf at the head of the driveway. He had a blue rubber ball between his front paws, and he was chewing at it furiously.

"But he's hungry for breakfast," I muttered.

I heard the crunch of the gravel, and Dad's car pulled up the drive. The trunk was opened partway, a roll of wire mesh bulging inside.

"Morning," Dad said as he came into the kitchen. His expression was grim.

"Are you going to take Wolf?" I demanded immediately. My eyes were on the dog, chewing on the rubber ball outside. He looked so cute.

"People in town are upset," Dad replied, pouring himself a cup of coffee from the coffeemaker. "A lot of animals have been killed this week. And a guy who lives down the way, Ed Warner, has disappeared in the swamp. People are very worried. They've heard the howls, too."

"Are you taking Wolf away?" I repeated shrilly, my voice trembling.

Dad nodded. His expression remained grim. He took a long sip of coffee. "Go look at the paw prints outside the pen, Grady," he said, locking his eyes on mine. "Go ahead. Take a look."

"I don't care about prints," I moaned. "I just know —"

"I can't take any more chances," Dad said.

"I don't care! He's my dog!" I screamed.

"Grady —" Dad set down the cup and started toward me.

But I burst past him and ran to the door. Pushing open the screen door, I leaped off the back stoop.

Wolf stood up as soon as he saw me. His tail started to wag. Leaving the blue rubber ball behind, he began loping toward me eagerly.

Dad was right behind me. "I'm going to take the dog away now, Grady," he said. "Do you want to come along?"

"No!" I cried.

"I have no choice," Dad said, his voice just above a whisper. He stepped forward and reached for Wolf.

"No!" I shouted. "No! Run, Wolf! Run!"

I gave the dog a shove. Wolf turned to me uncertainly.

"Run!" I screamed. "Run! Run!"

I gave Wolf another hard shove. "Run! Run, boy! Go!"

Dad had his hands around Wolf's shoulders, but he didn't have a good grip.

Wolf broke free and started to run toward the swamp.

"Hey!" Dad called angrily. He chased Wolf to the end of the backyard. But the big dog was too fast for him.

I stood behind the house, breathing hard, and watched Wolf until he disappeared into the low trees at the edge of the swamp.

Dad turned back toward me, an angry expression on his face. "That was dumb, Grady," he muttered.

I didn't say anything.

"Wolf will come back later," Dad said. "When he does, I'll have to take him away."

"But, Dad —" I started.

"No more discussion," he said sternly. "As soon as the dog returns, I'm taking him to the pound."

"You *can't!*" I screamed.

"The dog is a killer, Grady. I have no choice." Dad headed toward the car. "Come help me unload this wire mesh. I'll need your help getting the pen patched up."

I gazed toward the swamp as I followed Dad to the car. *Don't come back, Wolf,* I pleaded silently.

Please, don't come back.

All day long, I watched the swamp. I felt nervous, shaky. I had no appetite at all. After I helped Dad repair the deer pen, I stayed in my room. I tried to read a book, but the words were just a blur.

By evening, Wolf hadn't returned.

You're safe, Wolf, I thought. *At least for today.*

My whole family was tense. At dinner, we hardly spoke. Emily talked about the movie she had seen the night before, but no one joined in with any comments.

I went to bed early. I was really tired. From tension, I guess. And from being up most of the night before.

My room was darker than usual. It was the last night of the full moon, but heavy blankets of clouds covered the moonlight.

I settled my head onto my pillow and tried to get to sleep. But I kept thinking about Wolf.

The howls started a short while later.

I crept out of bed and hurried to the window. I squinted out into the darkness. Heavy black clouds still covered the moon. The air was still. Nothing moved.

I heard a low growl, and Wolf came into focus.

He was standing stiffly in the middle of the backyard, his head tilted up to the sky, uttering low growls. As I stared out the window at him, the big dog began to pace, back and forth from one side of the yard to the other.

He's pacing like a caged animal, I thought. *Pacing and growling, as if something is really troubling him.*

Or scaring *him.*

As he paced, he kept raising his head toward the full moon behind the clouds and growling.

What is going on? I wondered. I had to find out.

I got dressed quickly in the darkness, pulling on the jeans and T-shirt I had worn all day.

I fumbled into my sneakers. At first I had the left one on the right foot. It was so dark in my room without the moonlight pouring in!

As soon as my sneakers were tied, I hurried back to the window. Wolf was leaving the backyard, I saw. He was lumbering slowly in the direction of the swamp.

I'm going to follow Wolf, I decided. *I'm going to prove once and for all that he isn't a killer — or a werewolf.*

I was afraid my parents might hear me if I went to the kitchen door. So I crawled out my window.

The grass was wet from a heavy dew. The air was wet, too, and nearly as hot as during the day. My sneakers squeaked and slid on the damp grass as I hurried to follow Wolf.

I stopped at the end of the backyard. I'd lost him.

I could still hear him somewhere up ahead. I could hear the soft *thud* of his paws on the marshy ground.

But it was too dark to see him.

I followed the sound of his footsteps, gazing up at the shifting, shadowy clouds.

I was nearly to the swamp when I heard footsteps behind me.

With a gasp of fright, I stopped and listened hard.

Yes. Footsteps.

Moving rapidly toward me.

"Hey!"

I let out a choked cry and spun around.

At first, all I could see was blackness. "Hey — who's there?" My voice came out in a hushed whisper.

Will stepped out from the darkness. "Grady — it's you!" he cried. He came closer. He was wearing a dark sweatshirt over black jeans.

"Will — what are you *doing* out here?" I asked breathlessly.

"I heard the howls," he replied. "I decided to investigate."

"Me, too. I'm so glad to see you!" I exclaimed. "We can explore together."

"I'm glad to see you, too," he said. "It was so dark, I — I didn't know it was you. I thought —"

"I'm following Wolf," I told him. I led the way into the swamp. It grew even darker as we made our way under the low trees.

As we walked, I told Will about the night before, about the murdered deer, the paw prints around the deer pen. I told him about how people in town were talking. And about how my dad planned to take Wolf away to the pound.

"I know Wolf isn't the killer," I told him. "I just know it. But Cassie got me so scared with all her werewolf stories, and —"

"Cassie is a jerk," Will muttered. He pointed into the weeds. "Look — there's Wolf!"

I could see his black outline moving steadily through the heavy darkness. "I was so stupid. I should have brought a flashlight," I murmured.

Wolf disappeared behind the weeds. Will and I followed the sound of his footsteps. We walked for several minutes. Suddenly, I realized I could no longer hear the dog.

"Where's Wolf?" I whispered, my eyes searching the dark bushes and low trees. "I don't want to lose him."

"He went this way," Will called back to me. "Follow me."

Our sneakers slid over the damp, marshy ground. I slapped at a mosquito on the back of my neck. Too late. I could feel warm blood.

Deeper into the swamp. Past the bog, eerily silent now.

"Hey, Will?"

I stopped — and searched. "Oh." A soft cry escaped my lips as I realized I had lost him.

Somehow we had gotten separated.

I heard rustling up ahead. The crack of twigs. The whispering brush of weeds being stepped on and pushed out of the way.

"Will, is that you?"

Or was it Wolf?

"Will? . . . Where *are* you?"

Pale light suddenly washed over me, washed slowly over the ground. Glancing up, I saw the heavy clouds pull away. The yellow full moon hovered high in the sky.

As the light slowly swept over the swamp, a low structure came into view straight ahead of me.

At first, I couldn't figure out what it was. Some kind of gigantic plant?

No.

As the moonlight shone down, I realized I was staring at the swamp hermit's shack.

I stopped, frozen in sudden fear.

And then the howls began.

The frightening sound tore through the heavy silence. A horrifying wail, so loud, so nearby, rose on the still air, rose and then fell.

The sound was so terrifying, I raised my hands to cover my ears.

The swamp hermit! I thought. *He* is *a werewolf!*

I knew *he was the werewolf!*

I've got to get away from here, I realized. *I've got to get home.*

I turned away from the small shack.

My legs were trembling so hard, I didn't know if I could walk.

Got to go! Got to go! Got to go! The words repeated in my mind.

But before I could move, the werewolf burst out from behind a tree — and, howling its hideous howl, leaped onto my shoulders and shoved me to the ground.

As the yellow light of the full moon shone down, I gazed into the face of the werewolf as it pinned me to the ground.

Its dark eyes glared out at me from an almost human face covered in wolf fur. It howled its rage, its animal snout opening wide to reveal two gleaming rows of wolf fangs.

It's a human wolf! I realized to my terror. *A werewolf!*

"Get off!" I shrieked. "Will — get off me!"

It was Will. The werewolf was Will.

Even through the thick, matted wolf fur, I could recognize his dark features, his small, black eyes, his thick, stubby neck.

"Will!" I screamed.

I struggled to push him away, to squirm out from under.

But he was too powerful. I couldn't move.

"Will — *get off*!"

He raised his fur-covered face to the moon and uttered an animal howl. Then, snarling out his rage, he lowered his beastly head and dug his fangs into my shoulder.

I let out a shriek of pain.

Blinding flashes of red filled my eyes.

I thrust out my hands, kicked my legs — struggled blindly to free myself.

But he had animal strength. He was much too strong for me . . . too strong. . . .

The flashing red faded, turned to black. Everything was fading to black. I could feel myself sinking, sinking down a black tunnel, sinking forever into deep, deep, endlessly deep darkness.

A loud growl brought me back.

Bewildered, I gazed up to see Wolf leap onto Will.

Will uttered a shrill howl of anger and turned to wrestle with the snarling dog.

I watched in stunned disbelief as they scrabbled over the ground, biting and clawing, raging at each other, growling and grunting.

"Will . . . Will, it was you . . . it was you all along. . . ." I murmured, struggling to my feet.

I gripped a tree trunk. The ground appeared to be sliding beneath me.

The two creatures continued to battle, grunting and growling as they clawed at each other, wrestling over the wet ground.

"I knew it wasn't Wolf," I muttered aloud. "I knew . . ."

And then a deafening high-pitched shriek startled me, and I tumbled to my knees.

I looked up in time to see Will running away, fleeing on all fours through the tall weeds. Wolf followed close behind, snapping at Will's ankles, jumping on him, biting and clawing him as they ran.

Then I heard Will utter another cry of pain, a wail of defeat.

As the anguished sound faded, I sank down, down, down into the blue-black darkness.

"You have a slight fever," Mom said. "But you'll be okay."

"Swamp fever," I murmured weakly. I gazed up at her, trying to focus. Her face was blurred, hovering over me in the soft light.

It took me a long while to realize I was in my own bedroom. "How — how did I get here?" I stammered.

"The swamp hermit — he found you in the swamp and carried you home," Mom said.

"He did?" I tried to sit up, but my shoulder ached. To my surprise, it was tightly bandaged. "The — werewolf — Will — he bit me," I said, swallowing hard.

Dad's face hovered beside Mom's. "What are you saying, Grady? Why do you keep muttering about a werewolf?"

I pulled myself up a little and told them the whole story. They listened in silence, glancing at each other from time to time as I talked.

"Will is a werewolf," I concluded. "He changed. Under the full moon. He changed into a wolf, and —"

"I'm going to check this out right now," Dad said, staring intently down at me. "Your story is crazy, Grady. Just crazy. Maybe it's the fever. I don't know. But I'm going right over to your friend's house and see what's what."

"Dad — be careful," I called after him. "Be careful."

Dad returned a short while later, a bewildered look on his face. I was sitting in the living room, feeling a lot better, a big bowl of popcorn in my lap.

"There's no one there," Dad said, scratching his head.

"Huh? What do you mean?" Mom asked.

"The house is empty," Dad told us. "Deserted. It doesn't look like anyone has lived there in months!"

"Wow, Grady. You certainly have strange friends!" Emily exclaimed, rolling her eyes.

"I don't get it," Dad said, shaking his head.

I didn't, either. But I didn't care. Will was gone. The werewolf was gone for good.

"So can I keep Wolf?" I asked Dad, climbing up from the chair and crossing the room to him. "Wolf saved my life. Can I keep him?"

Dad stared back at me thoughtfully but didn't reply.

"The swamp hermit told us he saw the dog chase some kind of animal away from Grady," Mom said.

"Probably a squirrel," Emily joked.

"Emily, give me a break," I groaned. "Wolf really saved my life," I told them.

"I guess you can keep him," Dad said reluctantly.

"YAY!" I thanked him and eagerly made my way to the backyard to give Wolf a happy hug.

That all happened nearly a month ago.

Since then, Wolf and I have had a wonderful time exploring the swamp. I've gotten to know just about every inch of Fever Swamp. It's like my second home.

Sometimes Wolf and I let Cassie come along exploring with us. She's kind of fun, even though she's always on the lookout for werewolves. I really wish she'd just drop the subject.

I'm standing at my bedroom window now, watching the full moon rising over the distant trees. This first full moon in a month makes me think of Will.

Will may be gone, but he changed my life. I know I'll never forget him.

I can feel the fur sprouting on my face. My snout

is expanding, and my fangs are sliding out between my dark lips.

Yes, when he bit me, Will passed the curse on to me.

But I don't mind. I'm not upset.

I mean, with Will out of the way, the swamp is now mine! All mine!

I'm climbing out of my window now. There's Wolf waiting for me, eager to do some night exploring.

I drop easily to the ground on all fours. I raise my fur-covered face to the moon and utter a long, joyful howl.

Let's go, Wolf. Let's hurry to Fever Swamp.

I'm ready to hunt.

BEHIND THE SCREAMS

The WEREWOLF of FEVER SWAMP

CONTENTS

Bonus material written and compiled
by Matthew D. Payne

About the Author

R.L. Stine's books are read all over the world.
So far, his books have sold more than 300 million
copies, making him one of the most popular children's authors in history. Besides Goosebumps,
R.L. Stine has written the teen series Fear Street.
R.L. Stine lives in New York with his wife, Jane,
and Minnie, his King Charles spaniel. You can
learn more about him at www.RLStine.com.

Q & A with R.L. Stine

The werewolf is one of the world's most famous monsters, seen over and over again in books and film. Why is the werewolf so cool?

R.L. Stine (RLS): *I love the whole idea of the werewolf. You're a normal guy, walking around. The full moon comes up. You grow fur, snap your fangs, let out a long howl—and go wild. It's everyone's dream—isn't it?*

Has your dog ever done anything to make you think SHE might be a werewolf?

RLS: *Well, she's certainly got the fur for it. And she's a ferocious hunter. But you know what she loves to hunt?* Butterflies. *Here's the sad part: She only chases their shadows and is always so surprised when she pounces on a shadow and it disappears.*

You live smack-dab in the middle of one of the busiest cities in the world: New York City. Do you ever wish to be alone like the swamp hermit?

RLS: *Some people say I am a swamp hermit. I spend most of the day in my apartment just staring at the cold, silvery light of my computer monitor.*

What sort of music do you like to listen to? Chopin's "Funeral March," perhaps? Or the Addams Family theme?

RLS: *I never listen to music when I write. But when I'm not writing I like all kinds of music. I have satellite radio so I have something like 200 stations to listen to. And I like to play my music LOUD!*

Do you spend a lot of time on the Internet?

RLS: *I love the Internet. A friend of mine says the Internet is like a magic hat—you can pull anything out of it. I spend a lot of time on rlstine.com. In addition to looking at the creepy stuff, I love reading messages from my readers.*

Fright Gallery: The Werewolf

ORIGINAL 1993 COVER

THE WEREWOLF OF FEVER SWAMP

FIRST APPEARANCE
The Werewolf of Fever Swamp

OTHER APPEARANCES
Werewolf Skin

ORIGINS No one is sure where the first werewolf came from. But, in a twisted game of tag ("tag, you're BIT"), the evil werewolf curse is passed from werewolves to regular humans, who—once they become werewolfs—pass it on again.

SPECIAL POWERS Werewolves are extremely powerful, can run superfast for long periods of time, have an amazing sense of smell, and are fantastic hunters. Combine these powers with a strong bite, and a werewolf is not something you'd want to run into during a full moon!

WEAKNESSES Silver bullets. Big dogs.

LIVING OR DEAD? Alive

FAVORITE PHRASE "AROOOOOOH!"

HOBBIES AND INTERESTS Moon gazing. Singing (OK . . . more like "howling").

SPLAT STATS

STRENGTH	•	•	•	•	•	•	•	•	
INTELLIGENCE	•	•	•	•	•	•	•		
SPEED	•	•	•	•	•	•	•	•	•
ATTACK SKILLS	•	•	•	•	•	•	•		
HUMOR	•	•							
EVIL	•	•	•	•					

FULL-MOON MADNESS!

Maniac, cuckoo, madman. What do these words have in common? They are all synonyms for the word "lunatic," which comes from *luna*, Latin for "moon." Does the full moon make people crazy? Not as crazy as a fictional werewolf, perhaps, but one recent study claims that 80% of doctors believe that a full moon can affect a person's sanity . . . or INSANITY! Legend certainly supports the fact that a full moon can drive people nutty and make them dangerous (thanks, Mr. Werewolf), but where are the facts?

Take a look at what's been said to happen during the full moon.

- Some doctors and nurses swear there is a larger number of **EMERGENCY ROOM PATIENTS**.
- Reports of **ERRATIC DRIVERS** increase.
- Studies have shown that **VIOLENT CRIME** rises during a full moon.
- Brighton, England, puts **MORE POLICE ON PATROL**.
- A study in Leeds, England, found incidences of **PRISONERS BEHAVING BADLY**.

And it's not just crazy people—crazy things are thought to happen during a full moon as well. Some people claim a full moon can:

- increase the number of **AVALANCHES**
- trigger an **EARTHQUAKE**

- cause **BLACK CATS** to mysteriously **DISAPPEAR**
- encourage **PLANTS** to **GROW BETTER**—perhaps Jack from "Jack and the Beanstalk" planted his magic seeds during a full moon. . . .

Still, even with some evidence, science can't prove that a full moon actually makes people crazy. Studies on dog bites during a full moon have shown two different results: one shows MORE dog bites during a full moon. Others have shown FEWER. Studies on insane asylums actually show there are FEWER new patients during the full moon. So if more people are going crazy, where is the proof?

Science just can't say. One theory revolves around the moon's effect on water. Your science teacher might have taught you that the changing position of the moon affects the ocean's tide. Some think the moon has the same pull on humans, who are made mostly of water. But scientists say the moon's gravity is so small it can't affect us.

What scientists DO think is that people see full-moon madness all around them because they BELIEVE in it and go out of their way to find evidence of it.

In any case, it's still a good idea to keep a cautious eye out during a full moon. You never know when you might run into a crazy person, dog, or werewolf put under the spell of Luna.

QUIZ! Can You Survive the Swamp?

Before you head INTO your creepy neighborhood swamp, take this simple quiz to find out if you'll make it OUT. Keep track of your answers, and use the key at the end of the next page to tally up your points and see your chances for survival.

1. You find yourself knee-deep in quicksand! You . . .
   a. struggle as much as possible
   b. slowly reach out and grab a vine that's fallen from a tree
   c. wait patiently while screaming your head off

2. You see an alligator ahead! You . . .
   a. grab a stick and poke the gator in the eye
   b. play dead
   c. run away from the alligator in a straight line as fast as you can

3. You've found a hut in the middle of a dry field in the swamp. You . . .
   a. move on and hope whoever owns the hut is not around
   b. head inside without knocking and make yourself at home
   c. knock and wait to introduce yourself

4. You're STARVING and need to find some food fast. You . . .

    a. trap a poisonous water snake, kill it, skin it, and eat it

    b. chow down a handful of peat from a peat bog

    c. scarf a handful of every bright berry you come across

5. P-U! You smell swamp gas. You . . .

    a. find another way around the stinky area

    b. light a match to get rid of that terrible smell

    c. cover your face with your T-shirt and keep moving

Use the key below to add up the points for each answer. Your total will let you know if you're ready to brave the swamp.

15–11 Points: You'll definitely make it out of this swamp alive—jump in and have a great time!

10–6 Points: Hmmm . . . you might want to brush up on your swamp skills before you start a swamp adventure.

5–1 Points: Don't even think about heading into the swamp—you don't stand a chance!!!

(1) A = 1 Point, B = 3 Points, C = 2 Points
(2) A = 1 Point, B = 2 Points, C = 3 Points
(3) A = 3 Points, B = 1 Point, C = 2 Points
(4) A = 3 Points, B = 2 Points, C = 1 Point
(5) A = 3 Points, B = 1 Point, C = 2 Points

You Might Be a Werewolf if You . . .

. . . shave ten times a day.

. . . buy a whole bunch of flea collars—
for YOURSELF!

. . . howl at a full moon. Half howl at a half moon.
Crescent howl at a—oh, you get the picture!

. . . leave so much hair on seats people
won't let you ride in their cars.

. . . can scratch behind your ears—
with your FOOT!

. . . pack doggie biscuits with your lunch.

. . . get hissed at by cats for no reason.

. . . like your steak really, REALLY rare.

. . . eat a foot-long sandwich in ONE bite.

Turn the page for a peek at the next
all-terrifying thrill ride from R.L. Stine.

1

"Hey, Jodie — wait up!"

I turned and squinted into the bright sunlight. My brother, Mark, was still on the concrete train platform. The train had clattered off. I could see it snaking its way through the low green meadows in the distance.

I turned to Stanley. Stanley is the hired man on my grandparents' farm. He stood beside me, carrying both suitcases. "Look in the dictionary for the word *slowpoke*," I said, "and you'll see Mark's picture."

Stanley smiled at me. "I like the dictionary, Jodie," he said. "Sometimes I read it for hours."

"Hey, Mark — get a move on!" I cried. But he was taking his good time, walking slowly, in a daze as usual.

I tossed my blond hair behind my shoulders and turned back to Stanley. Mark and I hadn't visited the farm for a year. But Stanley still looked the same.

He's so skinny. "Like a noodle," my grandma always says. His denim overalls always look five sizes too big on him.

Stanley is about forty or forty-five, I think. He wears his dark hair in a crew cut, shaved close to his head. His ears are huge. They stick way out and are always bright red. And he has big round brown eyes that remind me of puppy eyes.

Stanley isn't very smart. Grandpa Kurt always says that Stanley isn't working with a full one hundred watts.

But Mark and I really like him. He has a quiet sense of humor. And he is kind and gentle and friendly, and always has lots of amazing things to show us whenever we visit the farm.

"You look nice, Jodie," Stanley said, his cheeks turning as red as his ears. "How old are you now?"

"Twelve," I told him. "And Mark is eleven."

He thought about it. "That makes twenty-three," he joked.

We both laughed. You never know *what* Stanley is going to say!

"I think I stepped in something gross," Mark complained, catching up to us.

I *always* know what Mark is going to say. My brother only knows three words — *cool*, *weird*, and *gross*. Really. That's his whole vocabulary.

As a joke, I gave him a dictionary for his last birthday. "You're *weird*," Mark said when I handed it to him. "What a *gross* gift."

He scraped his white high-tops on the ground as we followed Stanley to the beat-up red pickup truck. "Carry my backpack for me," Mark said, trying to shove the bulging backpack at me.

"No way," I told him. "Carry it yourself."

The backpack contained his iPod, comic books, his Game Boy, and at least fifty game cartridges. I knew he planned to spend the whole month lying in the hammock on the screened-in back porch of the farmhouse, listening to music and playing video games.

Well . . . no way!

Mom and Dad said it was *my* job to make sure Mark got outside and enjoyed the farm. We were so cooped up in the city all year. That's why they sent us to visit Grandpa Kurt and Grandma Miriam for a month each summer — to enjoy the great outdoors.

We stopped beside the truck while Stanley searched his overall pockets for the key. "It's going to get pretty hot today," Stanley said, "unless it cools down."

A typical Stanley weather report.

I gazed out at the wide, grassy field beyond the small train station parking lot. Thousands of tiny white puffballs floated up against the clear blue sky.

It was so beautiful!

Naturally, I sneezed.

I love visiting my grandparents' farm. My only problem is, I'm allergic to just about everything on it.

So Mom packs several bottles of my allergy medicine for me — and lots of tissues.

"Gesundheit," Stanley said. He tossed our two suitcases in the back of the pickup. Mark slid his backpack in, too. "Can I ride in back?" he asked.

He loves to lie flat in the back, staring up at the sky and bumping up and down really hard.

Stanley is a terrible driver. He can't seem to concentrate on steering and driving at the right speed at the same time. So there are always lots of quick turns and heavy bumps.

Mark lifted himself into the back of the pickup and stretched out next to the suitcases. I climbed in front beside Stanley.

A short while later, we were bouncing along the narrow, twisting road that led to the farm. I stared out the dusty window at the passing meadows and farmhouses. Everything looked so green and alive.

Stanley drove with both hands wrapped tightly around the top of the steering wheel. He sat forward stiffly, leaning over the wheel, staring straight ahead through the windshield without blinking.

"Mr. Mortimer doesn't farm his place anymore," he said, lifting one hand from the wheel to point to a big white farmhouse on top of a sloping green hill.

"Why not?" I asked.

"Because he died," Stanley replied solemnly.

See what I mean? You never know what Stanley is going to say.

We bounced over a deep rut in the road. I was sure Mark was having a great time in back.

The road leads through the small town, so small that it doesn't even have a name. The farmers have always called it Town.

It has a feed store, a combination gas station and grocery store, a white-steepled church, a hardware store, and a mailbox.

There were two trucks parked in front of the feed store. I didn't see anyone as we barreled past.

My grandparents' farm is about two miles from town. I recognized the cornfields as we approached.

"The corn is so high already!" I exclaimed, staring through the bouncing window. "Have you eaten any yet?"

"Just at dinner," Stanley replied.

Suddenly, he slowed the truck and turned his eyes to me. "The scarecrow walks at midnight," he uttered in a low voice.

"Huh?" I wasn't sure I'd heard correctly.

"The scarecrow walks at midnight," he repeated, training his big puppy eyes on me. "I read it in the book."

I didn't know what to say, so I laughed. I thought maybe he was making a joke.

Days later, I realized it was no joke.

Watching the farm spread out in front of us filled me with happiness. It's not a big farm or a fancy farm, but I like everything about it.

I like the barn with its sweet smells. I like the low mooing sounds of the cows way off in the far pasture. I like to watch the tall stalks of corn, all swaying together in the wind.

Corny, huh?

I also like the scary ghost stories Grandpa Kurt tells us at night in front of the fireplace.

And I have to include Grandma Miriam's chocolate chip pancakes. They're so good, I sometimes dream about them back home in the city.

I also like the happy expressions on my grandparents' faces when we come rushing up to greet them.

Of course, I was the first one out of the truck. Mark was as slow as usual. I went running up to the screened-in back porch of their big old farmhouse. I couldn't *wait* to see my grandparents.

Grandma Miriam came waddling out, her arms outstretched. The screen door slammed behind her. But then I saw Grandpa Kurt push it open and he hurried out, too.

His limp was worse, I noticed right away. He leaned heavily on a white cane. He'd never needed one before.

I didn't have time to think about it as Mark and I were smothered in hugs. "So good to see you! It's been so long, so long!" Grandma Miriam cried happily.

There were the usual comments about how much taller we were and how grown-up we looked.

"Jodie, where'd you get that blond hair? There aren't any blonds in *my* family," Grandpa Kurt would say, shaking his mane of white hair. "You must get that from your father's side.

"No, I know. I bet you got it from a store," he said, grinning. It was his little joke. He greeted me with it every summer. And his blue eyes would sparkle excitedly.

"You're right. It's a wig," I told him, laughing.

He gave my long blond hair a playful tug.

"Did you get cable yet?" Mark asked, dragging his backpack along the ground.

"Cable TV?" Grandpa Kurt stared hard at Mark. "Not yet. But we still get three channels. How many more do we need?"

Mark rolled his eyes. "No MTV," he groaned.

Stanley made his way past us, carrying our suitcases into the house.

"Let's go in. I'll bet you're starving," Grandma Miriam said. "I made soup and sandwiches. We'll have chicken and corn tonight. The corn is very sweet this year. I know how you two love it."

I watched my grandparents as they led the way to the house. They both looked older to me. They moved more slowly than I remembered. Grandpa Kurt's limp was definitely worse. They both seemed tired.

Grandma Miriam is short and chubby. She has a round face surrounded by curly red hair. Bright red. There's no way to describe the color. I don't know what she uses to dye it that color. I've never seen it on anyone else!

She wears square-shaped eyeglasses that give her a really old-fashioned look. She likes big, roomy housedresses. I don't think I've ever seen her in jeans or pants.

Grandpa Kurt is tall and broad-shouldered. Mom says he was really handsome when he was young. "Like a move star," she always tells me.

Now he has wavy white hair, still very thick, that he wets and slicks down flat on his head. He has sparkling blue eyes that always make me smile. And white stubble on his slender face. Grandpa Kurt doesn't like to shave.

Today he was wearing a long-sleeved, red-and-green-plaid shirt, buttoned to the collar despite the hot day, and baggy jeans, stained on one knee, held up by white suspenders.

Lunch was fun. We sat around the long kitchen table. Sunlight poured in through the big window. I could see the barn in back and the cornfields stretching behind it.

Mark and I told all our news — about school, about my basketball team going to the championships, about our new car, about Dad growing a mustache.

For some reason, Stanley thought that was very funny. He was laughing so hard, he choked on his split pea soup. And Grandpa Kurt had to reach over and slap him on the back.

It's hard to know what will crack Stanley up. As Mark would say, Stanley is definitely *weird*.

All through lunch, I kept staring at my grandparents. I couldn't get over how much they had changed in one year. They seemed so much quieter, so much slower.

That's what it means to get older, I told myself.

"Stanley will have to show you his scarecrows," Grandma Miriam said, passing the bowl of potato chips. "Won't you, Stanley?"

Grandpa Kurt cleared his throat loudly. I had the feeling he was telling Grandma Miriam to change the subject or something.

"I made them," Stanley said, grinning proudly. He turned his big eyes on me. "The book — it told me how."

"Are you still taking guitar lessons?" Grandpa Kurt asked Mark.

I could see that, for some reason, Grandpa Kurt didn't want to talk about Stanley's scarecrows.

"Yeah," Mark answered with a mouthful of potato chips. "But I sold my acoustic. I switched to electric."

"You mean you have to plug it in?" Stanley asked. He started to giggle, as if he had just cracked a funny joke.

"What a shame you didn't bring your guitar," Grandma Miriam said to Mark.

"No, it isn't," I teased. "The cows would start giving sour milk!"

"Shut up, Jodie!" Mark snapped. He has no sense of humor.

"They already *do* give sour milk," Grandpa Kurt muttered, lowering his eyes.

"Bad luck. When cows give sour milk, it means bad luck," Stanley declared, his eyes widening, his expression suddenly fearful.

"It's okay, Stanley," Grandma Miriam assured him quickly, placing a hand gently on his shoulder. "Grandpa Kurt was only teasing."

"If you kids are finished, why not go with Stanley," Grandpa Kurt said. "He'll give you a tour of the farm. You always enjoy that." He sighed. "I'd go along, but my leg — it's been acting up again."

Grandma Miriam started to clear the dishes. Mark and I followed Stanley out the back door. The grass in the backyard had recently been mowed. The air was heavy with its sweet smell.

I saw a hummingbird fluttering over the flower garden beside the house. I pointed it out to Mark, but by the time he turned, it had hummed away.

At the back of the long green yard stood the old barn. Its white walls were badly stained and peeling. It really needed a paint job. The doors were open, and I could see square bales of straw inside.

Far to the right of the barn, almost to the cornfields, stood the small guesthouse, where Stanley lived with his teenage son, Sticks.

"Stanley — where's Sticks?" I asked. "Why wasn't he at lunch?"

"Went to town," Stanley answered quietly. "Went to town, riding on a pony."

Mark and I exchanged glances. We never can figure Stanley out.

Poking up from the cornfields stood some dark figures, the scarecrows Grandma Miriam had started to talk about. I stared out at them, shielding my eyes from the sun with one hand.

"So many scarecrows!" I exclaimed. "Stanley, last summer there was only one. Why are there so many now?"

He didn't reply. He didn't seem to hear me. He had a black baseball cap pulled down low over his forehead. He was taking long strides, leaning forward with that storklike walk of his, his hands shoved into the pockets of his baggy denim overalls.

"We've seen the farm a hundred times," Mark complained, whispering to me. "Why do we have to take the grand tour again?"

"Mark — cool your jets," I told him. "We *always* take a tour of the farm. It's a tradition."

Mark grumbled to himself. He really is lazy. He never wants to do anything.

Stanley led the way past the barn into the cornfields. The stalks were way over my head. Their golden tassels gleamed in the bright sunlight.

Stanley reached up and pulled an ear off the stalk. "Let's see if it's ready," he said, grinning at Mark and me.

He held the ear in his left hand and started to shuck it with his right.

After a few seconds, he pulled the husk away, revealing the ear of corn inside.

I stared at it — and let out a horrified cry.

The Original Bone-Chilling Series

HOW TO BOIL
AN EGG

... and 184 other
recipes f

KT-432-919

HOW TO
BOIL
AN EGG

...and 184 other simple
recipes for one

Jan Arkless

RIGHT WAY

Typeset in 10/12pt Times by County Typesetters, Margate, Kent.

Printed and bound in Great Britain by Cox & Wyman Ltd., Reading,
Berkshire.

The *Right Way series* is published by Elliot Right Way Books,
Brighton Road, Lower Kingswood, Tadworth, Surrey, KT20 6TD,
U.K. For information about our company and the other books we
publish, visit our web site at www.right-way.co.uk

CONTENTS

For Jon Jon,
whose architectural aspirations
inspired this book.

1

INTRODUCTION

I originally wrote this book to help my son with his cooking when he first went to university. I have since realised that the recipes contained here are not only useful for students but for anyone, of any age, who find themselves alone, and for the first time have to cook for themselves, whether in their own home or in new accommodation.

Other cookery books assume some basic knowledge of cooking techniques but in this book I have assumed none as I wrote it specifically for the person who knows *absolutely nothing* or *very little* about cooking, or meal planning.

The book explains the simple things that one is supposed to know by instinct, such as how to boil an egg or fry sausages, how to prepare and cook vegetables *and* have them ready to eat at the same time as the main course! It includes recipes and suggestions for a variety of snacks and main meals (not all cooked in the frying pan or made from mince), using fish, chicken, beef, lamb and pork. The majority of the meals are quick, easy and economical to make, but there is a 'Sunday Lunch' chapter near the end of the book.

There are just a few recipes for desserts and cakes as you can easily buy biscuits and ready-made or frozen cakes. Remember that yoghurt makes a good, cheap sweet, and that fresh fruit is the best pud you can eat. Also, fresh fruit juice or milk is far better for you than fizzy drinks or alcohol.

Most recipes in other cookery books are geared towards feeding four or six people, but the recipes contained here are designed for the single person living on his or her own. However, this book does include a few recipes which cater for two people. This is because it is easier to cook larger portions of stews and casseroles as very small helpings tend to dry up during cooking.

AMOUNTS TO USE WHEN COOKING FOR ONE

Pasta, Noodles, Shapes, etc.
1 very generous cup (3 oz/75g) of uncooked pasta.

Potatoes
3–4 (8 oz/225g) according to size.

Rice
½ cup (2–3 oz/50–75g) dry uncooked rice.

Vegetables
See the individual vegetables in Chapter 5.

Oily Fish
1 whole fish (trout, mackerel, herring).

White Fish
6–8 oz (175–225g) fillet of cod, haddock, etc.

Roast Beef
Approximately 6 oz (175g) per person. A joint weighing 2½–3 lb (1–1.5kg) should serve 6–8 helpings; remember you can use cold meat for dinner the next day.

Minced Beef
4–6 oz (100–175g).

Beef Steak
6–8 oz (175–225g) is a fair-sized steak.

Stewing Steak
4–6 oz (100–175g).

Chicken
Allow a 6–8 oz (175–225g) chicken joint (leg or breast) per person. A 2½–3 lb (1–1.5kg) chicken serves 3–4 people.

Lamb or Pork Chops
1 per person.

Lamb Cutlets
1–3 according to size and appetite.

Roast Lamb
Because you are buying meat with a bone in, you need to buy a larger joint to account for the bone. A joint weighing about 2½ lb (1kg) will serve 4 people well.

Roast Pork
Approximately 8 oz (225g) per serving. A boneless joint weighing 2½–3 lb (1–1.5kg) will give 5–6 generous helpings.

Pork or Gammon Steaks
1 per person or 6 oz (175g).

USING THE OVEN
Temperatures are given for both gas and electric ovens.

Remember always to heat the oven for a few minutes before cooking food in it, so that the whole of the oven reaches the appropriate temperature.

REHEATING FOOD

One note of warning: be very careful about reheating cooked dishes. If you must do this, always be sure that the food is re-cooked right through, not merely warmed. *Food just reheated can make you extremely ill if not cooked thoroughly, especially pork and chicken – you have been warned!*

FOLLOWING THE RECIPES

I have given 'preparation and cooking' times for the recipes in this book so that, before you start cooking, you will know approximately how much time to set aside for preparing and cooking the meal. Read the recipe right the way through so that you know what it involves.

The ingredients used in each recipe are all readily available and listed in the order they are used in the method. Collect all the specified ingredients *before* you start cooking, otherwise you may find yourself lacking a vital ingredient when you have already prepared half the meal. When the meal is ready, there should be no ingredients left – if there are, you have missed something out!

Measurements

The ingredients are given in both imperial and metric measurements. Follow one type of measurement or the other, but do not combine the two, as the quantities are not exact conversions.

I have used size 2 or 3 eggs in the recipes so you can use whichever you happen to have in stock. Meat, fish and vegetables can be weighed in the shop when you buy them, or will have the weight on the packet. Don't buy more than you need for the recipe; extra bits tend to get left at the back of the cupboard or fridge and wasted. But it is worthwhile buying some goods in the larger size packets – rice, pasta, tomato ketchup, etc. – as they will keep fresh for ages and be on hand when you need them.

In case you don't own kitchen scales many of the measurements are also given in spoonfuls or tea cups (normal drinking size, which approximates to ¼ pint/5 fl oz/ 150ml; it isn't the American measure of a cup). The following measurements may also be helpful:

Butter, margarine or lard, etc.
1 inch cube (2.5cm cube) = 1 oz (25g); it is easy to divide up a new packet and mark it out in squares.

Cheese
1 inch cube (2.5cm cube) = 1 oz (25g) approximately.

Flour, cornflour
1 very heaped tbsp = 1 oz (25g) approximately.

Pasta (shells, bows, etc.)
1 very full cup = 3 oz (75g) approximately.

Rice
½ cup dry uncooked rice = 2 oz (50g) approximately.

Sugar
1 heaped tbsp = 1 oz (25g) approximately.

Sausages
Chipolatas: 8 sausages in an 8 oz (225g) packet.
Thick sausages: 4 sausages in an 8 oz (225g) packet.

Abbreviations
tsp = teaspoon
dsp = dessertspoon
tbsp = tablespoon (serving spoon)
1 spoonful = 1 slightly rounded spoonful
1 level spoonful = 1 flat spoonful

1 cupful	= 1 tea cup (drinking size cup) approximately ¼ pint/5 fl oz/150ml (*not* the American measure)
pt	= pint

USEFUL STORES & KITCHEN EQUIPMENT

This section may be particularly useful if you're a student living away from home and cooking for yourself for the first time in your life. Beg or borrow these items from home or try to collect them at the beginning of term, then just replace them during the year as necessary.

Beef, chicken and vegetable stock cubes
Coffee (instant)
Coffee (real)
Cooking oil
Cornflour
Curry powder
Dried mixed herbs
Drinking chocolate
Flour
Garlic powder (or paste)
Gravy granules
Horseradish sauce
Mustard
Milk powder (for coffee)
Orange/lemon squash
Pasta
Pepper
Pickle
Rice (long grain)
Salt
Soy sauce
Sugar
Tabasco sauce
Tea bags
Tomato purée (in a jar or tube)
Tomato sauce
Vinegar
Worcester sauce

Also
Dish cloth, washing-up liquid, tea towels, pan scrubber, oven cleaning powder, oven cloth.

Store sugar, rice, flour, pasta, biscuits and cakes in airtight containers rather than leaving them in open packets on the shelf. This keeps them fresh and clean for much longer and protects them from ants and other insects. Try to collect some storage jars and plastic containers for this purpose. (Large, empty coffee jars with screw lids, and plastic ice-cream cartons are ideal.)

Perishable Foods
These don't keep so long but are useful to have as a start.

Bacon
Biscuits
Bread
Butter
Cereals (such as cornflakes)
Cheese
Chocolate spread
Eggs
Fruit juice

Frozen vegetables
Honey
Jam
Margarine
Marmalade
Milk
Peanut butter
Potatoes

Handy Cans for a Quick Meal
Baked beans
Beans with sausages
Chicken in white sauce
Corned beef
Evaporated milk
Frankfurter sausages
Italian tomatoes
Luncheon meat
Minced beef
Rice pudding
Sardines
Soups (also packet soups)
Spaghetti

Spaghetti hoops
Stewed steak
Sweetcorn
Tinned fruit
Tuna fish
Vegetables (peas, carrots, etc.)

Also
Blancmange powders
Instant whip
Jellies
Pot noodles

Useful Kitchen Equipment
Basin (small)
Bottle opener

Casserole pan (thick heavy ones are the best)
Chopping/bread board
Cling film
Cooking foil
Cooking tongs
Dessertspoons
Fish slice
Frying pan
Grater
Kettle
Kitchen paper
Kitchen scissors
Knives: bread knife with serrated edge;
            sharp chopping knife for meat;
            vegetable knife
Measuring jug
Oven-proof dish (pyrex-type): 1 pint/0.5 litre size is big
    enough for one
Plastic storage containers (large ice-cream tubs are useful, to
    store biscuits, cakes, pasta, etc.)
Saucepans: 1 small; 1 or 2 large ones
Storage jars (large empty coffee jars are ideal)
Tablespoons
·Teaspoons
Tin opener
Wooden spoon

Handy but not Essential Kitchen Equipment
Baking tin (for meat)
Baking tins (various)
Basin (large) or bowl
Bread bin
Colander
Egg whisk or egg beater
Electric frying pan/multi cooker (very useful if your cooker is
    very small, old or unreliable)
Electric kettle

Foil dishes (these are cheap and last for several bakings; useful if you need a tin of a particular shape or size)
Kitchen scales
Liquidiser
Measuring jug (can also be used as a basin)
Mixer or food processor
Potato masher
Saucepans (extra) and/or casserole dishes
Sieve
Toaster

GLOSSARY

Various cooking terms used in the book (some of which may be unfamiliar to you) are explained in this glossary.

Al dente
Refers to pasta that is cooked and feels firm when bitten.

Basting
Spooning fat or butter or meat juices over food that is being roasted (particularly meat and poultry) to keep it moist.

Beating
Mixing food with a wooden spoon or whisk so that the lumps disappear and it becomes smooth.

Binding
Adding eggs, cream or butter to a dry mixture to hold it together.

Blending
Mixing dry ingredients (such as flour) with a little liquid to make a smooth, runny lumpfree mixture.

Boiling
Cooking food in boiling water (i.e. at a temperature of 212°F/100°C) with the water bubbling gently.

Boning
Removing the bones from meat, poultry or fish.

Braising
Frying food in a hot fat so that it is browned, and then cooking it slowly in a covered dish with a little liquid and some vegetables.

Casserole
An oven-proof dish with lid; also a slow-cooked stew.

Chilling
Cooling food in a fridge without freezing.

Colander
A perforated metal or plastic basket used for straining food.

Deep-frying
Immersing food in hot fat or oil and frying it.

Dicing
Cutting food into small cubes.

Dot with butter
Cover food with small pieces of butter.

Flaking
Separating fish into flaky pieces.

Frying
Cooking food in oil or fat in a pan (usually a flat frying pan).

Grilling
Cooking food by direct heat under a grill.

Mixing
Combining ingredients by stirring.

Nest (making a)
Arranging food (such as rice or potatoes) around the outside of a plate to make a circular border and putting other food into the middle of this 'nest'.

Poaching
Cooking food in water which is just below boiling point.

Purée
Food that has been passed through a sieve and reduced to pulp (or pulped in a liquidiser or electric mixer).

Roasting
Cooking food in a hot oven.

Sautéing
Frying food quickly in hot, shallow fat, and turning it frequently in the pan so that it browns evenly.

Seasoning
Adding salt, pepper, herbs and/or spices to food.

Simmering
Cooking food in water which is just below boiling point so that only an occasional bubble appears.

Straining
Separating solid food from liquid by draining it through a sieve or colander, e.g. potatoes, peas, etc., that have been cooked in boiling water.

2

EGGS

Eggs are super value, quick to cook and can make a nourishing snack or main meal in minutes.

In view of the publicity over salmonella in eggs, take care about the eggs you buy and store them sensibly and hygienically – eggs have porous shells and should never be stored where they are in contact with uncooked meat or fish, dust or dirt of any kind. They also absorb smells through the shells, so beware if you are buying fresh fruit, washing powder, household cleaners, firelighters, etc., and keep them in separate shopping bags. Heed the advice on fresh eggs given out by the health authorities: only buy eggs from a reputable supplier and *do not serve raw or lightly cooked egg dishes to babies, pregnant women or the elderly unless you're sure that the eggs are free from bacteria.* There are egg substitutes available in the shops (although you may have to search for them) which you may prefer for safety reasons instead of fresh eggs. Don't panic, but do take reasonable care with egg cookery.

BOILED EGG

Use an egg already at room temperature if possible, not one straight from the fridge as otherwise it may crack. If you prick the top of the shell once with a special gadget or a clean pin, the egg will not crack while cooking (my daughter-in-law Barbara taught me this, and it really does work). Slip the egg carefully into a small saucepan, cover with warm (not boiling) water and add ½ tsp salt (to seal up any cracks). Bring to the boil, note the time and turn down the heat before the egg starts rattling about in the pan. Simmer gently, timing from when the water begins to boil, using the table below:

Size	Time	Description
Large (sizes 1 or 2)	3 mins.	soft-boiled
Standard (sizes 3 or 4)	2½ mins.	soft-boiled
Large	4 mins.	soft yolk, hard white
Standard	3½ mins.	soft yolk, hard white
Large	10 mins.	hard-boiled
Standard	9 mins.	hard-boiled

SOFT-BOILED

Remove carefully from the pan with a spoon, put into an egg cup and tap the top to crack the shell and stop the egg continuing to cook inside.

HARD-BOILED

Remove the pan from the heat and place under cold, running water to prevent a black ring forming round the yolk. Peel off shell and rinse in cold water to remove any shell still clinging to the egg.

POACHED EGG

Put about 1 in (2.5cm) water into a clean frying pan and bring to the boil. Reduce the heat so that the water is just simmering. Crack the egg carefully into a cup, and slide it into the simmering water. Cook very gently, just simmering in the hot water, for about 3 minutes, until the egg is set to your liking. Lift it out with a slotted spoon or fish slice, being careful not to break the yolk underneath.

FRIED EGG

Heat a small amount of cooking oil, butter or dripping in a frying pan over a moderate heat (not too hot, or the egg white will frazzle). Carefully break the egg into a cup to check that it is not bad, then pour it into the frying pan and fry gently for 2 to 3 minutes. To cook the top of the egg, either baste the egg occasionally by spooning a little of the hot fat over it, or put the lid on the pan and let the heat cook it. You may prefer the egg carefully flipped over when half done to cook on both sides, but be prepared for a broken yolk. Remove the egg from the pan with a fish slice or wide-bladed knife.

SCRAMBLED EGGS

Usually you will want to scramble 2 or more eggs at a time.

Chopped chives are tasty with scrambled eggs. Simply wash them, cut off their roots and chop them.

Beat the egg well with a fork in a basin or large cup. Add salt, pepper and chopped chives. Melt a large knob of butter in a small, preferably thick, saucepan. Turn heat to low, and pour in the beaten egg, stirring all the time, until the egg looks thick and creamy. Do not overcook, as the egg will continue to cook even when removed from the heat. Stir in (if required) 1 to 2 tsp cream or top of the milk, or a small knob of butter (this helps to stop the egg cooking any more).

CHEESY SCRAMBLED EGGS
Add 1 oz (25g) grated or chopped cheese to the beaten eggs, before cooking.

PAN SCRAMBLE
If you are cooking sausages or bacon as well as scrambled eggs, fry the meat first and then cook the eggs in the same hot fat.

PIPERADE
Serves 1

Scrambled eggs plus a bit extra.

Preparation and cooking time: 30 minutes.

1 small onion
Small green pepper
2 tomatoes (fresh or tinned)
1 tbsp oil, or knob of butter (for frying)
Pinch of garlic powder
Salt and pepper
2–3 eggs

Peel and slice the onion. Wash, core and chop the green pepper. Wash and chop the fresh tomatoes or drain the tinned tomatoes and chop roughly. Heat the butter or oil in a saucepan and cook the onion and pepper over a medium heat, stirring well, until soft (about 5 minutes).

Add the chopped tomatoes, garlic, salt, pepper and stir. Put a lid on the pan and continue to cook gently over a low heat, stirring occasionally, for about 15 to 20 minutes, to make a thick saucy mixture.

Break the eggs into a small basin or large cup. Lightly beat them with a fork, then pour them into the vegetable mixture, stirring hard with a wooden spoon, until the eggs are just setting. Pour onto a warm plate, and eat with hot buttered toast or crusty fresh bread rolls.

SAVOURY EGGS
Serves 1

A cheap and tasty variation on the bacon 'n egg theme; makes a good, quick supper.

For a change, cooked sliced sausages or slices of salami can be used instead of bacon.

Preparation and cooking time: 25 minutes.

1 small onion
1 small eating apple
1 rasher of bacon
2 tsp cooking oil or large knob of butter (for frying)
Salt and pepper
¼ tsp sugar
2 eggs

Peel and slice the onion. Wash, core and slice the apple. De-rind the bacon and cut into ½ in (1.25cm) pieces. Heat the oil or butter in a frying pan over a moderate heat. Add the bacon, onion and apple, and fry, stirring occasionally, until soft (about 5 minutes). Stir in the salt, pepper and sugar.

Remove from the heat. Break the eggs into a cup, one at a time, and pour on top of the onion mixture. Cover the pan with a lid, and cook for a further 3 to 5 minutes over a very low heat, until the eggs are as firm as you like them.

CHEESY BAKED EGG
Serves 1

Quite delicious, and so easy to make.

Preparation and cooking time: 20 minutes.

3–4 oz (75–100g) cheese
2 eggs
Salt and pepper
Large knob of butter

Heat the oven (350°F/180°C/Gas Mark 4). Grease an oven-proof dish well with some butter.

Grate the cheese and cover the base of the dish with half of the cheese. Break the eggs, one at a time, into a cup, then slide them carefully on top of the cheese. Season well with the salt and pepper, and cover the eggs completely with the rest of the cheese.

Dot with the butter and bake in the hot oven for about 15 minutes, until the cheese is bubbling and the eggs are just set. Serve at once, with crusty French bread, rolls or crisp toast, or a salad.

EGG NESTS   *Serves 1*

These can be served plain, or with the addition of grated cheese, to make a very cheap lunch or supper.

Preparation and cooking time: 30 minutes.

2–4 potatoes
Large knob of butter
2 oz (50g) cheese (optional)
Salt and pepper
2 eggs

Peel the potatoes, cut into thick slices and cook in boiling, salted water in a saucepan for 10 to 15 minutes, until soft. Drain and mash with a fork, then beat in the large knob of butter, using a wooden spoon. Grate the cheese, if used, and beat half of it into the potato. Season with the salt and pepper.

1.   Egg nest

Grease an oven-proof dish. Spread the potato into this, and make a nest for the eggs. Keep it warm. Boil 1 in (2.5cm) water in a clean frying pan and poach the eggs. If making cheesy eggs, heat the grill. Carefully lift the eggs out of the water when cooked and put them into the potato nest. If making plain eggs serve at once, otherwise cover the eggs with the remainder of the grated cheese and brown for a few moments under the hot grill. Can be served with a fresh tomato or a salad.

SICILIAN EGGS
Serves 1

Saucy tomatoes with eggs and bacon. Serve with hot toast.

Preparation and cooking time: 25 minutes.

2 eggs
1 small onion
Knob of butter
1 small tin (8 oz/230g) tomatoes
Salt and pepper
Pinch of sugar
Pinch of dried herbs
2 rashers of bacon (de-rinded)

Hard boil the eggs for 10 minutes. Cool them in cold, running water. Shell them, rinse clean, slice thickly and arrange in a greased, heat-proof dish.

Peel and slice the onion, and fry it in the butter in a small saucepan over a moderate heat, until soft (about 5 minutes). Add the tomatoes, salt, pepper, sugar and herbs, and cook gently for a further 5 minutes. Heat the grill.

Pour the tomato mixture over the eggs, top with the de-rinded bacon rashers and place under the hot grill until the bacon is cooked.

If you do not have a grill, fry the bacon in the pan with the onions, remove it and keep it hot while the tomatoes are cooking, then top the tomato mixture with the hot, cooked bacon.

EGG, CHEESE AND ONION SAVOURY   *Serves 1*
Cheap and cheerful, eaten with chunks of hot, crusty bread.

Preparation and cooking time: 30 minutes.

2 eggs
1 onion
Knob of butter (for frying)
1 oz (25g) cheese

For the cheese sauce (you can omit this and just use grated cheese or alternatively use packet sauce mix):
1 oz (25g) cheese
2 tsp flour (or cornflour)
1 cup (¼ pt/150ml) milk
½ oz (12g) butter
Salt and pepper
Pinch of mustard

Hard boil the eggs for 10 minutes. Peel and slice the onion and fry gently in the knob of butter in a small saucepan over a moderate heat, for 4 to 5 minutes, until soft and cooked. Grate the cheese.

For the cheese sauce: EITHER mix the flour or cornflour into a smooth paste with a little of the milk in a small basin. Boil the rest of the milk and pour onto the flour mixture, stirring all the time. Then pour the whole mixture back into the saucepan and stir over the heat until the mixture thickens. Stir in the butter and beat well. Add the 1 oz (25g) grated cheese, salt, pepper and mustard. OR make up the packet sauce mix.

Put the onion into a greased oven-proof dish. Slice the cold, peeled hard-boiled eggs, and arrange on top of the onion. Cover with the cheese sauce and sprinkle with the rest of the grated cheese. Brown under a hot grill for a few minutes, until the cheese is melted, crisp and bubbly.

MURPHY'S EGGS *Serves 1*

A cheap and filling supper dish if you have time to wait for it to cook in the oven.

Preparation and cooking time: 1 hour 15 minutes.

½ lb (225g) potatoes (about 3 or 4 according to appetite)
1 onion
1 rasher of bacon
Salt and pepper
½–1 cup (¼ pt/150ml approx.) hot milk
Knob of butter
2 eggs

Peel the potatoes, cut into small ½ in (1.25cm) dice. Peel and slice the onion. De-rind and chop the bacon. Grease an oven-proof dish. Mix the potatoes, onion and bacon in a bowl, and put into the dish, seasoning well with the salt and pepper. Add the hot milk (enough to come halfway up the dish) and dot with the butter.

Bake in a hot oven (400°F/200°C/Gas Mark 6), covered with a lid or foil, for 45 minutes to 1 hour, until the potatoes are cooked and all the milk is absorbed.

Break each egg into a cup. Remove the dish of potatoes from the oven, make two hollows in the top of the potatoes with a spoon, and slip the raw eggs into the hollows. Return the dish to the oven for 6 to 8 minutes until the eggs are set. Serve at once.

EGGY BREAD OR FRENCH TOAST   *Serves 1*

A boarding school favourite.

Serve with golden syrup, honey or jam, or sprinkled with white or brown sugar.

Or to make it savoury, sprinkle with salt, pepper, and a blob of tomato sauce. Savoury eggy bread goes well with bacon, sausages and baked beans.

Preparation and cooking time: 15 minutes.

1 egg
1–2 tsp sugar (according to taste)
½ cup milk
3–4 thick slices of white bread
2 oz (50g) butter (for frying)

Break the egg into a basin or a large cup, add the sugar and beat well with a whisk, mixer or fork, gradually adding the milk. Pour this egg mixture into a shallow dish or soup plate, and soak each slice of bread in the egg, until it is all soaked up.

Heat a frying pan over a moderate heat. Melt the butter in the pan and fry the soaked bread slices in the hot butter, turning to cook both sides, until golden brown and crispy. Serve at once as above.

FRENCH OMELETTE

Serves 1

The best-known type of omelette: light golden egg, folded over into an envelope shape. Served plain or with a wide variety of sweet or savoury fillings, folded inside. There is no need for a special omelette pan (unless you happen to own one, of course). Use any clean, ordinary frying pan.

Preparation and cooking time: 10 minutes.

2–3 eggs
1 tsp cold water per egg
Pinch of salt and pepper (omit for sweet omelettes)
Knob of butter
Filling as required (see opposite)

Prepare the filling (see list opposite). Warm a plate. Break the eggs into a basin or large cup, add the water, salt and pepper and beat with a fork.

Put the butter in a frying pan and heat over a moderate heat until it is just sizzling (but not brown). Place the egg mixture in the pan at once. Carefully, with a wide-bladed knife or wooden spoon, draw the mixture from the middle to the sides of the pan, so that the uncooked egg in the middle can run onto the hot pan and set. Continue until all the egg is very lightly cooked underneath and the top is still running and soft (about one minute). The top will cook in its own heat, when it is folded over.

With the wide-bladed knife or a fish slice loosen the omelette so that you can remove it easily from the pan. Put the filling across the middle of the omelette and fold both sides over it to make an envelope. If using a cold filling, cook for a further minute. Remove from the pan and place on the warm plate. Serve at once, with French bread, bread rolls, sauté or new potatoes, a side salad or just a fresh tomato. Delicious!

OMELETTE AND PANCAKE FILLINGS
For pancakes, see page 183.

Savoury

Asparagus
Use ½ small can (10 oz/298g size) asparagus tips. Heat them through in a small saucepan. Drain and keep hot.

Bacon
Fry 1–2 rashers of bacon in a little oil or fat. Keep hot.

Cheese
1–2 oz (25–50g) grated or finely cubed.

Chicken
2–3 tbsp chopped, cooked chicken. (You can use the pickings from a roast chicken.)

Fresh or Dried Herbs
Add 1 tsp chopped herbs to the beaten eggs, water and seasoning.

Cooked Meat
Chop 1–2 slices cooked ham, salami or garlic sausage, etc.

Mushrooms
Wash and chop 2 oz (50g or 4–5 mushrooms). Cook gently in a small pan, with a knob of butter, for 2–3 minutes, stirring occasionally. Keep hot.

Tomato
Wash 1–2 tomatoes, slice and fry them in a little oil or fat and keep hot.

Sweet
Choose one of the following fillings, then sprinkle the omelettes with 1 tsp icing or granulated sugar, just before serving.

Fruit
Add 2–3 tbsp sliced, tinned fruit (peaches, pineapple or apricot) or 2–3 tbsp sliced fresh fruit (bananas, peaches, strawberries or raspberries).

Honey
Add 2–3 tbsp honey.

Honey and Walnut
Use 2–3 tbsp honey, 1 tbsp chopped walnuts.

Jam
Add 1–2 tbsp jam or bramble jelly. Warm the jam by standing it in a saucepan with 2 in (5cm) hot water, and warming gently over a low heat.

Marmalade
Add 2–3 tbsp orange or ginger marmalade.

SPANISH OMELETTE   *Serves 1*

A delicious, filling, savoury omelette. Served flat like a thick pancake, mixed with onion, potato, cooked meat and other vegetables – a good way of using up cold, cooked, leftovers. (A large omelette, made with 4 eggs and some extra vegetables, can be cut in half, serving 2 people.)

Preparation and cooking time: 15 minutes.

EXTRAS (optional):
Bacon: 1–2 rashers of bacon, chopped and fried with the onion
Cooked meat: 1–2 slices of chopped, cooked ham, salami, or garlic sausage, etc.
Green peppers: 1–2 tbsp green peppers, chopped and mixed with the onion
Sausages: 1–2 cold, cooked sausages, sliced

Vegetables: 1–2 tbsp cold cooked vegetables (peas, sweetcorn, green beans, mixed vegetables)

1 small onion
2–3 boiled potatoes
2–3 eggs
1 tsp cold water per egg
Salt and pepper
Pinch of dried herbs (optional)
1 tbsp oil (for frying)

Prepare the 'extras' if used. Peel and chop the onion. Dice the cooked potatoes. Beat the eggs, water, seasoning and herbs lightly with a fork in a small basin.

Heat the oil in an omelette or frying pan over a medium heat, and fry the onion for 3 to 5 minutes, until soft. Add the diced potato and continue frying until the potato is thoroughly heated. Add the extra meat or vegetables (if used) and heat through again. Heat the grill and warm a plate. Pour the beaten egg mixture into the pan, over the vegetables, and cook without stirring until the bottom is firm, but with the top remaining creamy and moist (about 1 to 2 minutes). Shake the pan occasionally to prevent sticking.

Place under the hot grill for ½ minute, until the top is set – beware in case the pan handle gets hot. Slide the omelette flat onto the warm plate and serve at once.

QUICK EGG AND VEGETABLE CURRY   *Serves 1*
A fast and easy curry recipe.

Preparation and cooking time: 35 minutes.

1 onion
Knob of butter
1 tsp cooking oil
1 tsp curry powder (or more or less according to taste)
1 tsp flour or cornflour
Small can (10 oz/295g) mulligatawny soup
2 eggs
½ cup (2–3 oz/50-75g) long grain rice
1 cup or 2 oz (50g) frozen mixed vegetables

Peel and chop the onion, and fry in the oil and butter in a saucepan over a medium heat, until soft (about 3 to 4 minutes). Stir in the curry powder and flour, and cook very gently for a further 2 minutes, stirring all the time. Gradually stir in the soup, bring to the boil, reduce the heat to a simmer, put on the lid, and cook gently for about 20 minutes, stirring occasionally, to make a thick sauce.

Hard boil the eggs for 10 minutes. Rinse them under cold, running water, peel them, wash off the shell and cut in half, lengthways. Cook the rice for 10 to 12 minutes in a large pan of boiling salted water (see page 81). Drain and keep hot, fluffing with a fork to stop it going lumpy. Add the mixed vegetables to the curry sauce, bring back to the boil and simmer for a few minutes to cook the vegetables.

Put the rice onto a warm plate, spreading round with a spoon to form a ring. Arrange the eggs in the centre and cover with the vegetable curry sauce. Serve with any side dishes you like (see page 128).

DRINKING EGG OR EGG NOG   *Serves 1*

A nourishing breakfast for those in a hurry, or an easily-digested meal for those feeling fragile!

Preparation time: 5 minutes.

1 egg
2 tsp sugar
2 cups (½ pt/300ml) milk (cold or warm)
2 tsp brandy, rum or whisky (optional, but not for breakfast!)
** or 1 tbsp sherry (optional, but not for breakfast!)**
Pinch of nutmeg or cinnamon

Break the egg into a basin, beat it lightly with a mixer, egg whisk or fork, adding the sugar and gradually beating in the milk. Add the spirits (if used). Pour into a tall glass, sprinkle nutmeg or cinnamon on top and serve at once.

HOW TO SEPARATE AN EGG

METHOD 1

Have 2 cups or basins ready. Crack the egg carefully, and pull the 2 halves apart, letting the white drain into one basin, and keeping the yolk in the shell, until all the white has drained out. Tip the yolk into the other basin. If the yolk breaks, tip the whole lot into another basin and start again with another egg.

METHOD 2

Carefully break the egg and tip it onto a saucer, making sure the yolk is not broken. Place a glass over the yolk, and gently tip the white into a basin, keeping the yolk on the saucer with the glass.

ENGLISH
CHEDDAR

FARMHOUSE
CHEDDAR

EDAM

GRATED
PARMESAN
CHEESE

BRIE

PREPACKED INDIVIDUAL
CHEESE SLICES

3

CHEESE

Here are some delicious snacks using cheese – they're simple and quick to make.

EASY WELSH RAREBIT (CHEESE ON TOAST)

Serves 1

This is the quickest method of making cheese on toast. It can be served plain, or topped with pickle, sliced tomato or crispy, cooked bacon.

Preparation and cooking time: 5–10 minutes.

1–3 rashers of bacon (optional)
1–2 tomatoes (optional)
2–3 oz (50–75g/2–3 slices) cheese *(continued overleaf)*

(Easy Welsh Rarebit continued)
2–3 slices of bread (white or brown)
Butter (for spreading)
1 tbsp pickle (optional)

Heat the grill. Lightly grill the bacon, if used. Slice the tomatoes, if used. Slice the cheese, making enough slices to cover the pieces of bread. Toast the bread lightly on both sides and spread one side with the butter. Arrange the slices of cheese on the buttered side of the toast and put under the grill for 1 to 2 minutes, until the cheese begins to bubble. Top with the tomato slices, bacon or pickle and return to the grill for another minute, to heat the topping and brown the cheese. Eat at once.

TRADITIONAL WELSH RAREBIT   *Serves 1*
More soft and creamy than cheese on toast, and only takes a few more minutes to prepare.

Preparation and cooking time: 10 minutes.

1–3 rashers of bacon (optional)
1–2 tomatoes (optional)
2–3 oz (50–75g) cheese
1 tsp milk
Pinch of mustard
Shake of pepper
1 tbsp pickle (optional)
2–3 slices of bread, and butter

Heat the grill. Lightly grill the bacon, if used. Slice the tomatoes, if used. Grate the cheese and mix into a stiff paste with the milk in a bowl, stirring in the mustard and pepper. Lightly toast the bread, and spread one side with butter, then generously cover it with the cheese mixture. Put under the hot grill for 1 to 2 minutes, until the cheese starts to bubble. Top with the bacon, tomato slices or pickle, and return to the grill for another minute, to heat the topping and brown the cheese. Serve at once.

BUCK RAREBIT   *Serves 1*

Welsh Rarebit with poached eggs. When the toast is covered
with the cheese, and ready to pop back under the grill to
brown, prepare 1 or 2 poached eggs, by cooking them gently
in simmering water for 2 to 3 minutes. While the eggs are
cooking, put the toast and cheese slices under the grill to
brown. When they are golden and bubbling, and the eggs are
cooked, carefully remove the eggs from the water, and slide
them onto the hot cheesy toast. Serve immediately.

BOOZY WELSH RAREBIT   *Serves 1*

Open a can of beer, use a little in the cooking, and drink the
rest with your meal.

Preparation and cooking time: 10–15 minutes.

2–3 oz (50–75g) cheese
Knob of butter
1–2 tbsp beer
Shake of pepper
Pinch of mustard
1–2 slices of bread (white or brown)

Grate the cheese and heat the grill. Melt the butter in a small
saucepan over a moderate heat. Add the cheese, beer,
pepper and mustard, and stir well over the heat, until the
cheese begins to melt, and the mixture begins to boil.
Remove the saucepan from the heat. Toast the bread lightly
on both sides. Carefully pour the cheese mixture onto the
toast, and put back under the grill for a few moments, until
the cheese is hot, bubbling and golden brown. Serve at once,
delicious!

CHEESY FRANKFURTER TOASTS   *Serves 1*

A quick snack, made with food from the store cupboard.

Preparation and cooking time: 15 minutes.

2–3 slices of bread
½ oz (12g) butter
**2–3 slices of cooked ham, garlic sausage or luncheon meat
 (optional)**
**Small can (8 oz/227g; actual weight of sausages 4 oz/163g)
 Frankfurter sausages**
2–3 slices of cheese (pre-packed slices are ideal)

Heat the grill. Lightly toast the bread on one side. Butter the untoasted side of the bread. Lay the ham or garlic sausage on the untoasted side and top with the Frankfurters. Cover with the cheese slices, and cook under the hot grill until the cheese has melted. Eat at once.

If you don't have a grill the bread can be heated in a hot oven (400°F/200°C/Gas Mark 6) for a few minutes, and then buttered. Place the 'toast' with the topping back into the oven, on an oven-proof dish, and cook for 5 to 10 minutes, until the cheese has melted.

CAULIFLOWER CHEESE *Serves 1*

Filling enough for a supper dish with crusty French bread and butter, or serve as a vegetable dish with meat or fish.

Preparation and cooking time: 30 minutes.

1 portion (3–4 florets) cauliflower
1 slice of bread (crumbled or grated into crumbs)
Knob of butter
1 sliced tomato (optional)

For the cheese sauce (alternatively use packet sauce mix or 2 oz/50g grated cheese):
2 oz (50g) cheese
2 tsp cornflour or flour
1 cup (¼ pt/150ml) milk
½ oz (12g) butter or margarine
Salt and pepper
Pinch of mustard

Trim the cauliflower's stalk, divide it into florets and wash thoroughly. Cook it in boiling, salted water for 5 minutes, until just tender. Drain well.

Make the cheese sauce (see page 174).

Put the cauliflower into a greased oven-proof dish. Cover with the cheese sauce, sprinkle the breadcrumbs on top and add a knob of butter and the tomato slices. Place under a hot grill for a few minutes, until golden-brown and crispy. (If you do not have time to make the cheese sauce, cover the cauliflower with 2 oz (50g) grated cheese and grill as above.)

4

SNACKS, SAVOURIES
AND SALADS

Just a few ideas and suggestions for quick snacks and
packed lunches. Other recipes can be found in Chapters 2
and 3.

SANDWICHES FOR PACKED LUNCHES

Try and ring the changes with different kinds of bread –
white, brown, granary, sliced, crusty rolls, soft baps, French
bread and Arab bread are a few suggestions. Crisp breads
make a change too.

Butter the bread lightly, this stops it going soggy if the

filling is moist, and holds the filling in place (have you ever tried eating unbuttered egg sandwiches?). Wrap the sandwiches in cling film to keep them fresh – it's worth buying a roll if you take sandwiches often – or put them into a polythene bag. A plastic container will stop them getting squashed.

Lettuce, tomato, cucumber, celery and green peppers are a good addition, either sliced in the sandwiches or eaten separately, with them. Treat yourself to some fresh fruit as well, according to what is in season.

Cheese
Slice or grate the cheese.

Cheese and Pickle
As above, and mix with a little pickle or chutney.

Cheese Slices
Quick and easy. Use straight from the packet. Spread pickle on top of the cheese if liked.

Cheese and Tomato
Slice a tomato layer on top of the cheese.

Cheese and Onion
Peel and thinly slice an onion, lay it thinly on top of the sliced cheese.

Cold Meat
Sliced, cooked meat, from the supermarket or delicatessen: ham, tongue, turkey roll, chicken roll, salami, garlic sausage, etc. Buy according to your taste and pocket. Buy fresh as you need it; do not store too long in the fridge.

Cold Meat from the Joint
Beef and mustard or horseradish sauce
Slice the beef thinly, and spread with the mustard or horseradish.

Cold Lamb and Mint Sauce
Slice the meat, cut off any excess fat. Add the mint sauce.

Cold Pork and Apple Sauce and Stuffing
Slice the pork, spread with any leftover apple sauce and stuffing.

Cold Chicken
Use up the fiddly bits from a roast chicken or buy chicken roll slices. Spread with cranberry jelly and stuffing. Do not store for too long in the fridge; buy just a little at a time.

Egg
Cook for 10 minutes in boiling water. Shell, wash and mash with a fork. Mix it either with a little mayonnaise or tomato chutney. One egg will fill two rounds of cut bread sandwiches.

Marmite
Very good for you, especially with a chunk of cheese, or topped with sliced cheese.

Peanut Butter
No need to butter the bread first. Top with seedless jam (jelly) if liked.

Salad
Washed lettuce, sliced tomato, sliced cucumber, layered together.

Salmon
Open a can, drain off any excess juice, and tip the salmon into a bowl. Discard the bones and skin, and mash with a little vinegar and pepper. Spread on the buttered bread, top with cucumber slices or lettuce if liked.

Tuna Fish
Open a can, drain off the oil. Tip the tuna fish into a bowl

and mash with vinegar and pepper, or mayonnaise. Spread on the buttered bread, top with lettuce or cucumber slices.

Liver Pâté
Choose from the numerous smooth or rough pâtés in the supermarket. Brown or granary bread is particularly good with pâté.

Eat with your Packed Lunch:
Cottage Cheese (plain or flavoured)
Eat from the carton with a fresh buttered roll, or an apple if you're slimming. Don't forget to take a spoon.

Yoghurt
Eat from the carton – remember to take a spoon.

Hard-boiled Egg
Hard boil an egg. Shell and wash it. Pop it into a polythene bag and eat with a fresh buttered roll.

Scotch Egg
Buy fresh from the supermarket.

FRIED BREAD *Serves 1*

Best cooked in the frying pan in the fat left from frying bacon or sausages.

Preparation and cooking time: 4–5 minutes.

1–2 slices of bread
Fat left in the pan from cooking sausages or bacon (or 2 tsp cooking oil and large knob of butter)

Remove the sausage or bacon from the pan and keep hot. Cut the bread slices in half, and fry in the hot fat over a moderate heat for 1 to 2 minutes on each side, until golden brown and crispy, adding a little extra butter to the pan if necessary.

FRIED CHEESE SANDWICHES   *Serves 1*
A very quick and tasty snack.

Preparation and cooking time: 10 minutes.

2–4 slices of bread
½ oz (12g) butter
**2–4 thin cheese slices (you can use pre-packed cheese slices if
   you wish)**
1 tbsp cooking oil and a large knob of butter (for frying)

Extra fillings (optional):
1 thinly-sliced tomato
1 tsp pickle
**1–2 rashers of crisply fried bacon – fry this ready before you
   start the sandwiches**

Lightly butter the slices of bread. Make them into sandwiches with 1 to 2 slices of cheese in each sandwich, adding
any of the optional extras you like.

Heat the oil and knob of butter in a frying pan, over a
moderate heat. Put the sandwiches into the hot fat, and fry
for a few minutes on each side, until the bread is golden and
crispy, and the cheese is beginning to melt.

Remove from the pan, drain on a piece of kitchen paper if
they seem a bit greasy. Eat at once while hot.

GARLIC BREAD   *Serves 1*
A sophisticated alternative to hot bread rolls.

Preparation and cooking time: 18–20 minutes.

1 clove of garlic (or ½ tsp garlic powder or paste)
2 oz (50g) butter
½ French loaf or 1–2 bread rolls (according to appetite)
Large piece of cooking foil (for wrapping)

Peel, chop and crush the garlic clove, if used, until smooth.
(You can crush it with a pestle and mortar or garlic press, if
you have one, or use the flat side of a knife but this is more
fiddly.) Cream together the butter and crushed garlic (or
garlic powder or paste), until soft and well-mixed.
   Cut the loaf nearly through into 1 in (2.5cm) slices (be
careful not to cut the slices completely or the loaf will drop
into bits) or cut the rolls in half. Butter the slices of the loaf,
or the rolls, generously on both sides with the garlic butter
and press the loaf or rolls together again. Wrap the loaf or
rolls loosely in the foil. Heat the bread in a hot oven (400°F/
200°C/Gas Mark 6–7) until hot and crisp (approximately 5
minutes). Serve at once, with the foil unfolded.

HERB BREAD   *Serves 1*
If you don't like garlic, omit garlic from the above recipe and
make a herb loaf, adding a really generous handful of freshly
chopped or snipped mixed herbs and a tsp lemon juice to the
butter.

BEANS (OR SPAGHETTI) ON TOAST   *Serves 1*

If you've never cooked these before, here is the method.

Preparation and cooking time: 5 minutes.

1 oz (25g) cheese (optional)
1 small (8 oz/225g) tin beans, spaghetti, spaghetti hoops, etc.
2–3 slices of bread
Butter

Grate the cheese, or chop it finely (if used).

Put the beans or spaghetti into a small saucepan, and heat slowly over a moderate heat, stirring occasionally. Toast the bread and spread one side of it with butter. When the beans are beginning to bubble, stir gently until they are thoroughly heated.

Put the toast onto a warm plate, and pour the beans on top of the buttered side (some people prefer the toast left at the side of the plate). Sprinkle the cheese on top. Eat at once.

GARLIC MUSHROOMS   *Serves 1*

Delicious, but don't breathe over other people after eating these! Serve with fried bacon to make it more substantial.

Preparation and cooking time: 10 minutes.

3–4 oz (75–100g) mushrooms
1 clove of fresh garlic (or garlic powder or garlic paste)
1–2 rashers of bacon (optional)
1 oz (25g) butter with 1 tsp cooking oil
2 thick slices of bread

Wash the mushrooms. Peel, chop and crush the fresh garlic, if used. Fry the bacon and keep hot. Melt the butter and oil in a saucepan over a moderate heat. Add the garlic (fresh, powder or paste) and mushrooms.

Stir well, and fry gently for 3 to 5 minutes, stirring and spooning the garlic-flavoured butter over the mushrooms. While the mushrooms are cooking, toast the bread lightly, cut in half and put onto a hot plate. Spoon the mushrooms onto the toast and pour the remaining garlic butter over the top. Top with bacon, if used. Eat at once.

PIZZA

There are so many makes, shapes and sizes of pizza available now, both fresh and frozen, that it hardly seems worth the effort of making your own. However, these commercial ones are usually improved by adding your own extras during the cooking, either when under the grill or in the oven according to the instructions on the packet.

Add these extras for the last 5 to 10 minutes of cooking time by spreading them on top of the pizza:

Cheese
Use grated or thinly sliced.

Ham
Chop and sprinkle over the pizza.

Salami, Garlic Sausage
Chop or fold slices and arrange on top of the pizza.

Mushrooms
Wash and slice thinly, spread over the pizza.

Tomatoes
Slice thinly, spread over the pizza.

Olives
A few spread on top add colour and flavour.

Anchovies or Sardines
Arrange criss-cross over the pizza.

BASIC GREEN SALAD
Serves 1

Preparation time: 5 minutes.

3–4 washed lettuce leaves
½ small onion
1 tbsp vinaigrette

Leave the lettuce leaves whole if small, or shred as finely as you like. Peel and slice the onion. Put the lettuce and onion into a salad bowl, add the vinaigrette and lightly turn the lettuce over in the dressing, until well mixed.

Other salad vegetables can be added:

Beetroot (cooked, if necessary, and sliced)
Celery (washed, scraped, if necessary, cut into 1 in (2.5cm) lengths)
Cucumber (washed, cut into rings or chunks)
Pepper (washed, cored, cut into rings)
Radishes (with tops cut off, roots removed and washed)
Spring onion (washed, cut off roots and yellow leaves, cut into rings or leave whole)
Tomatoes (washed, sliced or cut into quarters)
Watercress, mustard and cress (washed, sprinkled on top of the other vegetables).

WINTER SALAD
Serves 1

Trim, shred and wash a quarter of a white or green cabbage. Drain well and dry in a salad shaker (if you have one) or put into a clean tea-towel and shake or pat dry. Put the cabbage in a dish, with any other salad vegetables, such as raw, grated carrot, tomato quarters, cucumber, celery, peppers, peeled sliced onion.

It can either be served on its own, or with a dressing made from the following ingredients mixed together thoroughly: 4 tsp salad oil, 2 tsp vinegar, pinch of salt, pepper and sugar.

COLESLAW
Serves 1

A quick and tasty way of using up extra raw cabbage. Serve with cold meat, or with hot dishes.

Preparation time: 15 minutes.

¼ crisp white cabbage
1 small carrot
1 eating apple (red-skinned if possible)
Lemon juice (if possible)
1 small onion
1–2 tbsp mayonnaise
Salt and pepper

Trim off the outer leaves and stalk of the cabbage. Shred it finely, wash it well in cold water. Scrape the carrot. Chop it finely or grate it. Peel and core the apple. Chop it finely or grate it. Sprinkle with a little lemon juice. Peel the onion. Chop or grate it finely. Drain the cabbage well.

Mix all the vegetables together in a bowl. Toss lightly in the mayonnaise until all the ingredients are well-coated. Season to taste.

Many different fruit or vegetables can be used in this recipe. A few chopped salted nuts, a tbsp of washed, dried sultanas, a little chopped green pepper are some ideas you might like to try.

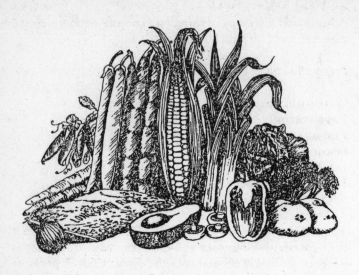

5

VEGETABLES, VEGETABLE DISHES AND RICE

This chapter gives basic instructions on preparing and cooking fresh vegetables (listed in alphabetical order) to be eaten as part of a meal, together with recipes using vegetables which are substantial enough to be used as a lunch or supper dish by themselves.

When cooking vegetables in water, remember that a lot of the goodness and flavour soaks from the vegetables into the cooking water. So do not use too much water or overcook them. When possible, use the vegetable water for making gravy. Frozen vegetables are convenient but are generally dearer than fresh vegetables. Vegetable prices vary tremendously according to the season, so look out for the best buys at the vegetable counter.

GLOBE ARTICHOKES

2. Globe Artichokes

These are the green, leafy type of artichoke. They look large, but as you only eat the bottom tip of each leaf, you do need *a whole artichoke for each person*. As they are expensive, cook them mainly for special occasions.

Cut off the stem of the artichoke to make the base level, snip off the points of the leaves, and wash the artichoke well in cold water. Put in a large saucepan, cover with boiling salted water, and boil for 30 to 40 minutes, until a leaf will pull off easily.

Drain the water from the pan and then turn the artichoke upside down in the pan for a few moments to drain any remaining water. Serve with plenty of butter.

JERUSALEM ARTICHOKES

3. Jerusalem Artichokes

These artichokes look like knobbly potatoes. Cook them immediately they are peeled, as they go brown very quickly even in cold water. A little lemon juice in the cooking water helps to keep them white.

8 oz (225g) serves 1–2 portions.

BOILED

Peel the artichokes and cut them into evenly-sized lumps about the size of small potatoes. Boil them in a pan of salted water for 20 to 30 minutes, until tender. Drain and serve with a dab of butter.

BOILED WITH CHICKEN SAUCE

Cook in salted water (as above) until tender. Drain, and put back in the saucepan with ½ can (10 oz/300g size) of condensed chicken soup. Bring back to the boil, stirring occasionally. Tip the artichokes onto a warm plate, pouring the chicken sauce over them.

FRIED

Peel the artichokes and cut them into thick slices or chunks. Put 1 tsp cooking oil and ½ oz (12g) butter into a frying pan, add the artichoke pieces and cook gently, turning frequently, for 15 to 20 minutes, until soft. Tip the artichokes onto a warm plate, pouring the buttery sauce over them.

ASPARAGUS

A very expensive treat! *Usually sold in bundles, enough for 2–4 servings.*

Cut off the woody ends of the stems and then scrape off the white tough parts of the stems. Rinse. Tie the stems into a bundle, with clean string or white cotton, and stand them tips uppermost in a pan with 1 in (2.5cm) boiling water. Cover the pan with a lid or a dome of foil, and boil for 8 to 10 minutes, until tender. Remove them carefully from the pan. Asparagus is traditionally eaten with the fingers. To eat, just dip the tips in butter and leave any woody parts that still remain on the stems.

AUBERGINES

The English name for the aubergine is the 'egg plant'. These lovely, shiny purple-skinned vegetables are best left unpeeled.

Fry 1 medium-sized aubergine per person.

To get rid of any bitter taste before cooking, slice the aubergine into ½ in (1.25cm) pieces. Put into a colander or strainer (if you do not have one, lay the slices on a piece of kitchen paper), sprinkle with salt, press a heavy plate down on top and leave for 30 minutes so that the bitter juices are pressed out. Wash and dry the slices. Heat a little oil in a frying pan, and fry gently until soft (about 5 minutes).

AVOCADO PEARS

Buy avocados when the price is down – the price varies considerably during the year, as they are imported from several countries. They make a nourishing change.

Choose pears that yield slightly when pressed gently. Unripe pears feel very hard.

Slice the avocado in half lengthways, cutting through to the stone. Then separate the two halves by twisting gently. Remove the stone with the tip of the knife, trying not to damage the flesh, which should be soft and buttery in texture.

Cut avocados discolour very quickly, so prepare them just before serving, or rub the cut halves with lemon juice to stop them going brown. Serve avocados plain with a squeeze of lemon juice, with a vinaigrette dressing or with any one of the numerous fillings spooned into the cavity from where the stone was removed. Brown bread and butter is the traditional accompaniment, with a garnish of lettuce, tomato and cucumber.

Some Filling Ideas

Vinaigrette: Mix well 2 tsp oil, 1 tsp vinegar, salt, pepper and a pinch of sugar.

Mayonnaise: 1 tbsp mayonnaise.

Cottage Cheese: Mix well together 2 tbsp cottage cheese (plain or with chives, pineapple, etc.) and 1 tsp mayonnaise.

Prawn or Shrimp: Mix gently together 1–2 tbsp shelled prawns or shrimps (fresh, frozen or canned), 1 tbsp mayonnaise and/or cottage cheese. A sauce can also be made with a mixture of 1 tbsp salad cream and a dash of tomato ketchup.

Egg: Shell and chop 1 hard-boiled egg. Mix gently with 1 tbsp mayonnaise and/or cottage cheese.

Yoghurt: 2 tbsp yoghurt on its own, or mixed with a chopped tomato and a few slices chopped cucumber.

CREAMY AVOCADO TOAST   *Serves 1*

Use a soft avocado pear for this. They are often sold off cheaply when they become very ripe and the shop wants to sell them quickly.

Preparation time: 5 minutes.

1 ripe avocado
Salt and pepper
2 thick slices of bread (brown or granary)
Knob of butter

Cut the avocado in half, lengthways and remove the stone. Scoop out the soft flesh with a teaspoon, put it into a small basin, and mash to a soft cream. Season with the salt and pepper.

Toast the bread on both sides, spread one side with butter, then spread the avocado cream thickly on the top. Eat while the toast is hot.

SAVOURY AVOCADO SNACK   *Serves 1*

If you're a vegetarian and don't want to eat bacon, you may prefer to sprinkle ½ tbsp chopped walnuts on top of the cheese instead.

Preparation and cooking time: 15 minutes.

1–2 rashers of bacon
Oil (for frying)
1 small avocado pear
1 oz (25g) cheese
Chunk of French bread
Knob of butter

De-rind the bacon. Fry it in a little oil in a frying pan over a moderate heat until crisp.

Peel the avocado pear and slice it, removing the stone. Grate or slice the cheese.

Cut the French bread in half lengthways, and spread with the butter. Arrange layers of the avocado and bacon on the bread. Top with the cheese slices or grated cheese.

Grill under a hot grill for a few minutes, until the cheese is golden, bubbling and melted. Eat at once.

BROAD BEANS

Buy 4–8 oz (100–225g) unshelled beans per person, according to the size of the beans. The smaller, younger beans go further, as you can cook them whole, like French beans, whereas older, larger beans need to be shelled.

TINY NEW BROAD BEANS

Top and tail the beans with a vegetable knife or a pair of scissors. Either leave them whole or cut them into shorter lengths (4 in/10cm) depending on their size. Boil them in water for 5 to 10 minutes, according to size, until tender. Drain and serve with a knob of butter.

LARGER BROAD BEANS

Remove the beans from the pods. Cook in boiling water for 5 to 10 minutes, until tender. Drain and serve with a knob of butter, or parsley sauce, if you feel very ambitious.

FROZEN BROAD BEANS

Allow approximately 4 oz (100g) per serving. Cook as instructed on the packet, and serve as above.

FRENCH BEANS

Can be rather expensive, but as there is very little waste you need only buy a small amount. *Allow approximately 4 oz (100g) per serving.*

Top and tail the beans with a vegetable knife or a pair of scissors. Wash the beans and cut the longer beans in half (about 4 in/10cm). Put them into a pan of boiling, salted water and cook for 2 to 5 minutes, until just tender. Drain well and serve them with a knob of butter.

FROZEN WHOLE FRENCH BEANS

Allow approximately 3–4 oz (75–100g) per serving. Cook in boiling, salted water as directed on the packet and serve as above with a knob of butter. Very tasty, but be careful not to overcook them.

RUNNER BEANS

These are sold frozen and ready to cook all year round, but lovely fresh beans are available in August and September. Choose crisp, green beans; limp, pallid ones are not as fresh as they should be. *Allow 4 oz (100g) beans per person.*

Top and tail the beans. Cut down the sides of the large beans to remove any tough stringy bits, and slice the beans evenly into whatever size you prefer, up to 1 in (2.5cm) long. Wash them in cold water. Cook in boiling, salted water for 5 to 10 minutes, according to size, until just tender. Drain well and serve hot.

FROZEN BEANS
Allow 3–4 oz (75–100g) per serving. Cook according to the instructions on the packet, in boiling, salted water.

BEAN SPROUTS

These can be cooked on their own, but are better when cooked with a mixture of stir-fried vegetables. *Allow 4 oz (100g) per portion.* Soak for 10 minutes in cold water, then drain the bean sprouts well. Heat 1 tbsp oil in a frying pan or a wok, add the bean sprouts and fry for 1 to 2 minutes, stirring all the time. Serve at once.

BROCCOLI

Green broccoli and purple sprouting broccoli are both cooked in the same way. *Allow 2–3 pieces or 8 oz (225g) per serving.*

Remove any coarse outer leaves and cut off the ends of the stalks. Wash well in cold water. Boil for 5 to 10 minutes in salted water, until tender. Drain well; press out the water gently with a fork if necessary. Serve with a knob of butter.

FROZEN BROCCOLI
Allow 4–6 oz (100–150g) per serving, according to appetite. Cook as directed on the packet, in boiling, salted water.

BRUSSELS SPROUTS

Try to buy firm, green sprouts of approximately the same size. Yellow outside leaves are a sign of old age.

Allow 4–6 oz (100-150g) per serving.

Cut off the stalk ends, and trim off the outer leaves if necessary. Wash well. Cook in boiling, salted water for 5 to 10 minutes, until tender. Drain well.

FROZEN SPROUTS
Allow 3–4 oz (75–100g) per serving. Cook in boiling, salted water as directed on the packet.

WHITE OR GREEN CABBAGE

A much maligned vegetable, evoking memories of school days. If cooked properly, cabbage is really delicious and much cheaper than a lot of other vegetables. Cabbage goes a very long way, so either buy a *small cabbage* and use it for several meals (cooked, or raw in a winter salad) or *just buy half or a quarter of a cabbage*.

Trim off the outer leaves and the stalk. Cut into quarters and shred, not too finely, removing the central core and cutting that into small pieces. Wash the cabbage. Boil it in salted water for 2 to 5 minutes. Do not overcook. Drain well, serve with a knob of butter, or with a cheese sauce.

To make cabbage cheese, instead of cauliflower cheese, substitute the cabbage for the cauliflower on page 39.

CRISPY CABBAGE CASSEROLE

Serves 1

This is filling enough to serve as a cheap supper dish, with hot bread rolls, butter and a chunk of cheese. It is delicious as a vegetable accompaniment with meat.

Preparation and cooking time: 35 minutes.

1 portion of cabbage (¼ of a cabbage)
1 small onion
1–2 sticks of celery
1 tsp oil and ½ oz (12g) butter (for frying)
1 slice of bread

For the white sauce (or use 1 packet of sauce mix):
2 tsp cornflour (or flour)
1 cup (¼ pt/150ml) milk
½ oz (12g) butter (or margarine)
Salt and pepper

Grease an oven-proof dish or casserole. Trim the outer leaves and stalk from the cabbage. Shred it, not too finely, wash it well and drain. Peel and chop the onion. Scrape and wash the celery and cut into 1 in (2.5cm) lengths. Heat the oil and butter in a frying pan, and fry the onion gently for 2 to 3 minutes until soft. Add the celery and drained cabbage, fry gently for a further 5 minutes, stirring occasionally.

Heat the oven at (400°F/200°C/Gas Mark 6–7). Make the white sauce (see page 174). Put the vegetable mixture into the greased dish. Pour the white sauce over the top. Crumble or grate the bread into crumbs, and sprinkle these on top of the sauce. Dot with a knob of butter. Bake for 15 minutes in the hot oven until the top is crunchy and golden brown.

RED CABBAGE　　　　　　　　　　*Serves 1*

Usually cooked in a casserole, to make a lovely warming winter vegetable dish. Why not put some jacket potatoes in the oven to eat with it?

Preparation and cooking time: 1 hour (cooked on top of the stove); 1 hour 15 minutes (cooked in the oven).

1 rasher of bacon (optional)
1 small onion
½ small red cabbage
1 eating apple
1 tsp oil
½ oz (12g) butter
Salt and pepper
1 tsp sugar (brown if possible, but white will do)
1 tsp vinegar
½ cup boiling water

Chop the bacon with a sharp knife or a pair of scissors. Peel and chop the onion. Cut off the stalk from the cabbage. Remove any battered outside leaves. Shred the cabbage finely, wash and drain. Peel, core and slice the apple. Melt the oil and butter in a frying pan and fry the bacon until crisp. Remove the bacon, put it on a plate. Add the onion to the pan and fry gently for 2 to 3 minutes, until soft.

PAN METHOD
In a saucepan, put layers of the cabbage, apple, onion and bacon, seasoning each layer with salt, pepper, sugar and vinegar. Pour ½ cup of boiling water over it and lightly sprinkle with sugar. Put on the saucepan lid and simmer gently for 45 minutes, stirring occasionally.

OVEN METHOD
Use a casserole dish (with a lid) that can be put in the oven. Put the vegetables in layers as in the pan method, adding ½ cup of boiling water and the sugar and cook in the oven

(350°F/180°C/Gas Mark 4), stirring occasionally, for about an hour. Jacket potatoes can be cooked with the casserole. Serve hot. Red cabbage cooked in this way is tasty with pork and lamb.

CARROTS

New carrots can simply be scrubbed and cooked whole, like new potatoes. Older, larger carrots should be scraped or peeled, then cut in halves, quarters, slices, rings or dice, as preferred. The smaller the pieces the quicker the carrots will cook.

Allow 4 oz (100g) per serving.

Scrub, peel and slice the carrots as necessary. Boil them in salted water for 5 to 20 minutes, according to their size, until just tender. Serve with a knob of butter.

BUTTERED CARROTS

Prepare the carrots as above: leaving tender, young carrots whole, or slicing old carrots into rings. Put the carrots in a saucepan, with ½ a cup of water, ½ oz (12g) butter, 1 tsp sugar and a pinch of salt. Bring to the boil, then reduce the heat and simmer for 20 minutes, until the carrots are tender. Take the lid off the saucepan, turn up the heat for a few minutes, and let the liquid bubble away until only a little sauce is left. Put the carrots onto a plate, and pour the sauce over them.

FROZEN CARROTS OR MIXED VEGETABLES

Allow 3–4 oz (75–100g) per serving. Cook in boiling, salted water as directed on the packet, and serve as above.

CAULIFLOWER

Most cauliflowers are too large for one person, but they can be cut in half and the remainder kept in the fridge for use in the next few days. Try not to bruise the florets when cutting them, as they will discolour easily. Very small caulis and packets of cauliflower florets are sold in some supermarkets.

Allow 3–4 florets per serving.

Trim off tough stem and outer leaves. The cauli can either be left whole or divided into florets. Wash thoroughly. Cook in boiling, salted water for 5 to 15 minutes, according to size, until just tender. Drain well. Serve hot, with a knob of butter, a spoonful of soured cream, or white sauce (see page 174). For cauliflower cheese, see page 39.

FROZEN CAULIFLOWER
Allow 4–6 oz (100–150g) per serving. Cook as directed on the packet and serve as above.

CELERIAC

4. Celeriac

The root of a variety of celery, celeriac is one of the more unusual vegetables now available in good greengrocers and larger supermarkets.

Allow 4–8 oz (100–225g) per person.

Peel fairly thickly, and cut into evenly-sized chunks. Put into a saucepan with boiling water, and cook for 30 to 40 minutes. Drain well. Serve with butter, or mash with a potato masher, fork or whisk, with a little butter and top of the milk. Season with salt and pepper.

CELERY

Most popular eaten raw, with cheese, or chopped up in a salad. It can be cooked and served as a hot vegetable; the tougher outer stems can be used for cooking, leaving the tender inner stems to be eaten raw.

Allow 3–4 stalks of celery per serving.

Trim the celery stalk. Divide it into separate stems. Wash each stem well and scrape off any stringy bits with a knife. The celery is now ready to eat raw. To cook, chop the celery into 1 in (2.5cm) lengths. Put it into a saucepan, with boiling, salted water, and cook for 10 minutes, until just tender. Drain well, serve with a knob of butter, or put into a greased, oven-proof dish, top with 1–2 oz (25–50g) grated cheese, and brown under a hot grill.

CHICORY

This can be used raw in salads, or cooked carefully in water and butter, and served hot.

Allow 6–8 oz (175–225g/one head) per serving.

5. Chicory

Remove any damaged outer leaves and trim the stalk. With a pointed vegetable knife, cut a cone-shaped core out of the base, to ensure even cooking and reduce bitterness. Wash in cold water. Put the chicory into a saucepan with a knob of butter, 2–3 tbsp water and a pinch of salt. Cook gently for about 20 minutes, until just tender, making sure that all the liquid does not disappear. Serve with melted butter.

CHINESE LEAVES

These can be used raw in salads. Keep the Chinese leaves in a polythene bag in the fridge to keep them crisp until you want to use them.

Allow ¼–½ small cabbage per serving.

Trim off any spoiled leaves and stalks. Shred finely. Wash and drain well (in a salad shaker or a clean tea-towel). Use in salad with any other salad vegetables (cucumber, tomato, cress, spring onions, raddish etc.) and a vinaigrette dressing (2 tbsp oil, 1 tsp vinegar, pinch of salt, pepper and sugar, all mixed well together).

COURGETTES

These are baby marrows. They are very quick and easy to prepare, and are quite economical as there is almost no waste with them. *Allow 1 or 2 courgettes (4–6 oz/100–175g) per serving, according to size.*

Top and tail very tiny courgettes, and leave them whole. Slice larger ones into rings (½–1 in/1.25–2.5cm) or large dice. Wash well.

BOILED

Prepare the courgettes as above. Boil them gently in salted water for 2 to 5 minutes, until just tender. Drain them very well, as they tend to be a bit watery. (You can get them really dry by shaking them in the pan over a very low heat for a moment.) Serve topped with a knob of butter, or tip them into a greased, oven-proof dish and top with 1 oz (25g) grated cheese, and brown under a hot grill. Courgettes can also be served with white, cheese or parsley sauce.

FRIED

Prepare the courgettes as above. Wash and drain them well and dry on kitchen paper. Melt a little cooking oil and butter in a frying pan, add the courgettes and fry gently for a few minutes, until tender. Drain on kitchen paper. Serve hot.

CUCUMBER

Most widely used as a salad vegetable and eaten raw, although it can be cut in chunks and added to casseroles, or cooked in the same way as courgettes or celery. Cucumbers are usually bought *whole, or cut in half*. They keep best in the fridge, wrapped in a polythene bag.

Wash the cucumber. Peel thinly (if you wish) or leave unpeeled. Cut into thin slices and use with salad, or munch a chunk like an apple, with a ploughman's lunch.

LEEKS

These must be thoroughly washed or they will taste gritty.

Allow 1 or 2 leeks per serving, according to size and appetite.

Cut off the roots and the tough green part, just leaving any green that looks appetising. Slit down one side and rinse well in cold, running water to get rid of all the soil and grit – this is a bit fiddly and it will take a few minutes to get them thoroughly clean. Leave them whole, or cut them into shorter lengths if they are very large, or into rings.

Cook in a very little boiling, salted water for 5 to 10 minutes, according to size, or sauté in a little oil or butter for a few minutes. Drain well. Serve at once, or put into a greased oven-proof dish, cover with 1 oz (25g) grated cheese and brown under a hot grill or serve with white sauce which can be prepared while the leeks are cooking.

LETTUCE

Cheapest and best in spring and summer, when various kinds are available. Choose a lettuce that looks crisp and firm, with a solid heart; if it looks limp and flabby it is old and stale. Lettuce will keep for a few days in a polythene bag or a box in the fridge, but goes slimy if left too long, so buy *a small lettuce* unless you're going to eat a lot of salad.

Cut off the stalk and discard any brown or battered leaves. Pull the leaves off the stem and wash separately in cold, running water. Dry thoroughly in a salad shaker or clean tea-towel. Put into a polythene bag or box in the fridge if not using immediately, to keep it crisp. Serve as a basic green salad or as a garnish with bread rolls, cheese or cold meat, or as a side salad with hot dishes (alone or with a French dressing).

MARROW

Very cheap when in season, during the autumn. *A small marrow* will serve three or four people as a vegetable with meat or fish, or can be stuffed with meat or rice to make a dinner or supper dish.

Wash the marrow in cold water. Peel thinly. Cut into 1 in (2.5cm) rings or cubes, according to size. Boil gently in salted water for 3 to 6 minutes, until just tender. Drain very well, as marrow can be a bit watery. (You can get the pieces really dry by shaking them in the pan over a very low heat for a few moments.) Serve topped with a knob of butter, or tip the pieces into a greased oven-proof dish and top with 1 oz (25g) grated cheese, and brown under a hot grill. Marrow can also be served with white, cheese or parsley sauce.

MUSHROOMS

Buy in small amounts, *2 oz (50g)*, so that they can be eaten fresh. Fresh mushrooms are pale-coloured and look plump and firm; older ones look dried-up and brownish. Keep mushrooms in the fridge. Mushrooms can be fried or grilled with bacon, sausages, chops or steaks. Add them to casseroles or stews or make a tasty snack by cooking them in butter and garlic and serving on toast (see page 46).

Allow 2–3 mushrooms each, according to size, or 1–2 oz (25–50g).

FRIED
Wash the mushrooms in cold water. Leave them whole or slice large ones if you wish. Fry them gently in a little butter

and oil for a few minutes, until soft. They can be put in the frying pan with bacon or sausages, or cooked alone in a smaller saucepan.

GRILLED
Put a small knob of butter in each mushroom and grill them for a few minutes in the base of the grill pan. If you are grilling them with bacon, sausages or chops put them under the grill rack; the juice from the meat and mushrooms makes a tasty sauce.

OKRA

6. Okra

Known as Ladies' Fingers, okra consists of curved seed pods. It can be served as a vegetable with meat or curry, or fried with tomatoes, onions and spices with rice as a supper dish.
  Allow 2 oz (50g) per serving.
  Top and tail the okra. Wash it in cold water. Put 1–2 tbsp cooking oil in a pan, add the okra and cook gently, stirring occasionally for 15 to 20 minutes, until the okra feels tender when tested with a pointed knife. It should have a slightly glutinous texture.

ONIONS

The best way to peel onions without crying is to cut off their tops and tails and then peel off their skins with a vegetable knife under cold running water.

To chop onions evenly, peel them under cold water, then slice them downwards vertically into evenly-sized rings. If you want finely-chopped onion pieces, slice the rings through again horizontally.

ROAST ONION

Allow 1 medium or large onion per person. Spanish onions are good for roasting. Top, tail and peel the onion. Heat a little oil or fat in a roasting tin (400°F/200°C/Gas Mark 6). When hot (3 to 5 minutes) place the onion carefully in the hot fat – it will spit, beware! Roast for 45 minutes to 1 hour. Onions are delicious roasted with a joint of meat and roast potatoes.

BAKED ONION

Allow 1 large onion per person. Spanish onions are the best. Rinse the onion, top and tail it, but do not peel it. Put it in a tin or baking dish, and bake for 45 minutes to 1 hour (400°F/200°C/Gas Mark 6). Slit and serve with butter.

BOILED ONION

Allow 1 medium onion per person. Top, tail and peel the onion. Put it in a pan of boiling water and simmer for 20 to 30 minutes, according to its size, until tender.

FRIED ONION

Allow 1 onion per person. Top, tail and peel the onion and slice into rings. Fry them gently in a saucepan with a little oil and butter, for 5 to 10 minutes, until soft and golden, stirring occasionally. Delicious with liver and bacon.

PARSNIPS

These are very tasty and can be roasted on their own, or with roast potatoes.

Allow 1 parsnip per person if small, or a large parsnip will cut into 5 or 6 pieces.

Parsnips are cooked in the same way as roast potatoes (see page 72), but do not cut them into too small pieces or they get too crispy. If you peel them before you are ready to cook them, keep them covered in a pan of cold water, as they go brown very quickly. (If this should happen, the parsnips will still be all right to cook, they will just look a bit speckled.)

PEAS

Most commonly available tinned or frozen nowadays. But fresh peas are a lovely treat in the summer, so try some.

Allow 8 oz (225g) peas in the pod per serving.

Shell the peas and remove any maggotty ones. Boil them gently in salted water, with a sprig of mint if possible, for 5 to 10 minutes. Drain them well, remove the mint and serve with a sprinkle of sugar and a knob of butter.

FROZEN PEAS

Allow 3–4 oz (75–100g) per serving. Cook as directed on the packet.

MANGETOUT PEAS OR SUGAR SNAP PEAS

Becoming widely available in supermarkets. Quite expensive but can be bought in small amounts and you eat the lot, including the pods!

Allow approximately 4 oz (100g) per serving.

Top and tail the peas with a vegetable knife or a pair of scissors. Wash them and leave them whole. Put them into a pan of boiling, salted water and boil for 2 to 3 minutes. They are slightly crumbly when cooked. Serve hot with a knob of butter.

GREEN, RED OR YELLOW PEPPERS

Use raw in a green salad, or cook, filled with rice or meat stuffing, for a lunch or supper dish (see below), or stewed in oil with tomatoes and garlic as a filling vegetable dish. *Peppers can be bought singly.* Choose crisp, firm-looking ones and store them in the fridge to keep them fresh.

Rinse them in cold water, cut off the top, scoop out the core and seeds. Cut into rings or chunks and use in salad or as a garnish.

STUFFED PEPPERS   *Serves 1*

Green peppers are available in the shops all year round, but their price varies considerably, so shop around for a 'good buy'. As with avocados, peppers come from different countries and the price will vary during the year. Serve with a side salad and brown crusty bread.

Preparation and cooking time: 45 minutes.

1 small onion
1 tbsp oil (for frying)
4 oz (100g) minced beef
1 small tomato
1 tsp tomato purée (or ketchup)
½ stock cube
½ cup boiling water
Salt and pepper
Pinch of herbs
1 tbsp raw rice or 2 tbsp cooked rice if you have any left-over
   (optional)
1–2 green peppers

Peel and chop the onion. Heat the oil in a saucepan. Add the onion and fry gently for a few minutes, until soft. Add the minced beef to the onion, and continue to fry for 2 to 3 minutes, stirring frequently. Wash and chop the tomato. Add it to the meat in the pan, with the tomato purée (or ketchup).

Dissolve the stock cube in the boiling water. Add it to the meat, with the salt, pepper and herbs. Continue simmering over a moderate heat. Stir in the washed raw rice and leave to simmer for 15 to 20 minutes, stirring occasionally. The stock should be almost completely absorbed. Cut the tops off the peppers. Remove the seeds and wash the peppers.

Grease an oven-proof dish. Remove the meat mixture from the heat. Strain off any excess liquid (the mixture wants to be damp but not swimming in gravy). If you are using left-over cooked rice, mix it in with the meat mixture. Fill the peppers with the meat mixture and put them into the greased oven-proof dish. Bake in a hot oven (350°F/180°C/Gas Mark 4–5) for 30 minutes.

BOILED POTATOES

Try to select potatoes of the same size to cook together, or cut large potatoes into evenly-sized pieces, so that all the potatoes will be cooked at the same time. (Very big potatoes will go soggy on the outside before the inside is cooked if left whole.) Do not let the water boil too fast, or the potatoes will tend to break up.

Allow 2–4 potato pieces per person.

Peel the potatoes as thinly as you can. Dig out any eyes or any black bits with as little waste as possible. Put them in a saucepan. Cover with hot water and add a pinch of salt. Bring to the boil, then lower the heat and simmer for 15 to 20 minutes, until they feel just soft when tested with a knife. Drain and serve hot.

MASHED POTATOES

The best way of serving boiled potatoes that have broken up during cooking. Prepare the boiled potatoes as described above. (If you are in a hurry, cut the potatoes into thick slices and cook for less time, about 10 minutes.) When they are cooked, drain the potatoes well. Mash them with a fork or masher until fluffy, then heap onto a serving dish.

CREAMED POTATOES

Prepare mashed potatoes as above. When they are really fluffy beat in a knob of butter and a little top of the milk. Fork into a heap on a serving dish and top with a dab of butter.

POTATO CASTLES

Prepare creamed potatoes as above. Grease a flat baking tin or an oven-proof plate, and pile the potatoes onto it, in 2 or 3 evenly-sized heaps. Fork them into castles, top with a bit of butter and either brown under the grill for a minute or two, or put them into a hot oven (400°F/200°C/Gas Mark 6) for 5 to 10 minutes, until crisp and golden brown.

CHEESY POTATOES

Prepare creamed potatoes as above, beating 1–2 oz (25–50g) grated cheese into the potatoes with the butter. Pile the potatoes into a greased oven-proof dish, fork down evenly and top with a little grated cheese. Brown under a hot grill for a minute or two, or put into a hot oven (400°F/200°C/Gas Mark 6) for 5 to 10 minutes, until golden.

ROAST POTATOES

These can be cooked around the joint if you are cooking a roast dinner, or in a baking tin, with a little hot fat, to cook on their own. *Allow 2–4 potato pieces per person.*

Peel the potatoes and cut them into evenly-sized pieces. Put them in a saucepan of hot water, bring to the boil and simmer for 2 to 3 minutes. Put a little fat in a roasting tin. (Use lard, margarine, dripping or oil. Do not use butter on its own as it burns and goes brown.) Heat the tin in the oven (400–425°F/200–220°C/Gas Mark 6–7). Drain the potatoes and shake them in the pan over the heat for a moment to dry them. Put the potatoes into the hot roasting tin, but be careful that the hot fat does not spit and burn you. Roast for 45 to 60 minutes, according to size, until crisp and golden brown.

NEW POTATOES

Lovely and easy – no peeling! *Allow 3–6 new potatoes, according to size and appetite.*

Wash the potatoes well under running water and scrub them with a pan scrubber or a brush. If you prefer, scrape them with a vegetable knife also. Put them in a pan, cover with boiling water, add salt and a sprig of mint. Bring to the boil and simmer for 15 to 20 minutes, until tender. Drain well, tip onto a plate and top with a little butter.

SAUTÉ POTATOES

A way of using up left-over boiled or roast potatoes. Alternatively potatoes can be boiled specially, and then sautéed when they have gone cold. *Allow approximately 3–4 cold cooked potato pieces, according to appetite.*

Slice the potatoes thinly. Heat a little oil and butter in a frying pan. Add the potato slices and fry them gently for 5 minutes, until crisp and golden, turning frequently with a fish slice or spatula.

ONION SAUTÉ POTATOES

Peel and thinly slice a small onion. Fry the onion in a frying pan with a little oil and butter until it is just soft, then add the cold, sliced potatoes and fry as above until crisp and delicious. Serve at once.

JACKET SPUDS

These can be served as an accompaniment to meat or fish or made into a meal on their own, with any one of a number of fillings heaped on top of them. *Allow 1 medium – large potato per person.*

Choose potatoes that do not have any mouldy-looking patches on the skin. Remember that very large potatoes will take longer to cook, so if you're hungry it's better to cook 2 medium-sized spuds. Wash and scrub the potato. Prick it several times with a fork. For quicker cooking, spear potatoes onto a metal skewer or potato baker.

TRADITIONAL WAY
Put the potato into the oven (400°F/200°C/Gas Mark 6) for 1 to 1½ hours according to size. The skin should be crisp and the inside soft and fluffy when ready. If you prefer softer skin, or don't want to risk the potato bursting all over the oven, wrap the spud loosely in a piece of cooking foil before putting it into the oven.

QUICKER WAY
Put the potato into a saucepan, cover with hot water, bring to the boil and cook for 5 to 10 minutes according to size. Drain it carefully, lift the potato out with a cloth, and put into a hot oven (400°F/200°C/Gas Mark 6) for 30 to 60 minutes, according to size, until it feels soft.

If you are cooking a casserole in the oven at a lower temperature, put the potato in the oven with it, and allow extra cooking time.

BAKED STUFFED POTATO
Useful to serve with cold meat or with steak, as it can be prepared in advance and heated up at the last minute.

Scrub and bake a largish jacket potato as described above. When the potato is soft, remove from the oven, and cut it carefully in half lengthways. Scoop the soft potato into a bowl, and mash with a fork, adding ½ oz (12g) butter and ½ oz (12g) grated cheese. Pile the filling back into the skin again and fork down evenly. Place on a baking tin or oven-proof plate, sprinkle a little grated cheese on top, and either brown under the hot grill for a few minutes, or put into a hot oven (400°F/200°C/Gas Mark 6) for 5 to 10 minutes, until browned.

A FEW FILLINGS

Prepare and cook the jacket spuds. When soft, put them onto a plate, split open and top with your chosen filling and a knob of butter.

Cheese
1–2 oz (25–50g) grated cheese.

Cheese and Onion
1 small finely-sliced onion and 1–2 oz (25–50g) grated cheese.

Cheese and Pickle
1–2 oz (25–50g) grated cheese and 1 tsp pickle or chutney.

Cottage Cheese
2–3 tbsp cottage cheese (plain or with chives, pineapple, etc.).

Baked Beans
Heat a small tin of baked beans and pour over the potato.

Bolognese
Top with Bolognese sauce (see page 158). This is a good way of using up any extra sauce left over from Spaghetti Bolognese.

Bacon
Chop 1–2 rashers of bacon into pieces. Fry them for a few minutes, until crisp, then pour over the potato.

Egg
Top with 1–2 fried eggs, a scrambled egg or an omelette.

Curry
Top with any left-over curry sauce, heated gently in a saucepan until piping hot.

SCALLOPED POTATOES

Tasty and impressive-looking potatoes. Quick to prepare but they take an hour to cook, so they can be put in the oven and left while you are preparing the rest of the meal, or they can cook on a shelf above a casserole in the oven. (The potatoes need a higher temperature so put them on the top shelf and the casserole lower down.)

Allow 1–2 potatoes per person according to size and appetite.

Grease an oven-proof dish well. Peel the potatoes and slice them as thinly as possible. Put them in layers in the greased dish, sprinkling each layer with a little flour, salt and pepper. Almost cover them with ½–1 cup of milk (or milk and water). Dot with a large knob of butter. Put the dish, uncovered, in a hot oven (400°F/200°C/Gas Mark 6) for about an hour, until the potatoes are soft and most of the liquid has been absorbed. The top should be crispy.

Packets of scalloped potatoes are available in supermarkets. They are more expensive than making your own, but are easy to prepare following the packet instructions.

CHIPS

If you must make your own chips do take great care. There are many good 'ready-made' frozen chips which you can buy at the supermarket, which can be cooked in the oven or shallow-fried in a little fat in an ordinary frying pan. You would be well-advised to use these when you want chips, unless you are an experienced cook and have the correct equipment for deep-fat frying. Please, please don't attempt to make chips, or indeed do any deep-fat frying, unless you have the use of a 'proper' chip pan (the electric thermostatically-controlled type preferably) and have had some previous experience of deep-fat frying under supervision. *Allow 2–3 large potatoes per person.*

Only pour enough oil into the chip pan to cover as far as the marks on the pan, which will be no more than a quarter of the way up the pan, as the hot fat rises alarmingly when the chips or other foods are lowered into it. If the pan should catch alight, turn off the cooker and put the lid on the pan immediately. Do not move the pan or throw water over it. Follow the manufacturer's instructions carefully about using the pan, and heat the oil to the correct setting (probably about 380°F/190°C), so that it is hot and just hazing, not smoking, when you are ready to cook the chips.

Peel the potatoes, and cut them into slices ¼ in (0.5cm) thick, and cut these slices into chips. Dry the chips on a clean cloth or kitchen paper, and sprinkle with a little salt, if desired. When the fat is the correct temperature, put the chips into the chip basket and lower this carefully into the fat. Cook for 3 to 4 minutes, shaking the basket occasionally to ensure the chips are cooking evenly – don't let the fat splash onto you or the surroundings.

Remove the basket and rest it on the rim of the pan, letting the oil on the chips drip into the oil in the pan. Allow the oil in the pan to heat up again. Plunge the basket back into the oil for another minute to crisp the chips. Remove from the fat and drain as before for just a moment, then tip the hot chips onto the kitchen paper to drain. SWITCH OFF THE CHIP PAN. Serve the chips immediately. When the fat is cold, it should be strained through a fine sieve to get rid of any burnt bits or crumbs, and stored for future use, either in the chip pan or in a clean jar.

INSTANT MASH

Although more expensive then fresh potato, this makes a quick standby which saves you the trouble of peeling potatoes. The flavour and price of the different makes vary (the most expensive may not necessarily be the best), so try them out until you find one you prefer. Afterwards, it is usually more economical to buy the large size, as it keeps fresh in a container for ages. To make up the potato, follow the packet instructions. The amounts given are for rather small servings, and you may need to make extra if you're hungry. A big knob of butter (added just before serving) improves both the flavour and the appearance.

PUMPKIN

Generally associated with Hallowe'en, Cinderella and American Thanksgiving Day! It is available fresh in England around the end of October when it may be quite cheap. It is prepared and cooked in the same way as marrow. See page 66.

SALSIFY

A less well-known root vegetable, with soft, white flesh.

Allow 1–2 salsify roots per person.

Scrape the roots in a bowl of cold water. The roots must be kept under the cold water when being scraped, to stop discolouration. Cut them into evenly-sized rings. Cook, as soon as possible, in boiling water for 5 to 15 minutes, until tender. Drain, and serve with a knob of butter.

SPINACH

Allow 8 oz (225g) per person.

Spinach must be washed thoroughly in cold water, to get rid of all dust and grit. This will take several rinses. Remove any tough-looking leaves and stalks and cut into convenient-sized lengths (4 in/10cm). Put the spinach in a large saucepan, with no extra water, and cook over a medium heat for 7 to 10 minutes, until soft. As the spinach boils down, chop it about with a metal spoon or knife, and turn it over so that it cooks evenly, in its own juices. Drain very well, pressing the water out to get the spinach as dry as possible. Put a knob of butter in the pan with the drained spinach, and reheat for a few moments. Serve with the melted butter, seasoned well with salt and pepper.

FROZEN SPINACH

Allow 4 oz (100g) per person. Packets of frozen spinach are available all the year round in supermarkets. Cook as instructed on the packet and serve with butter as above.

SWEDE ('NEEPS' IN SCOTLAND)

Known as 'poisonous' by one member of our family, but really it is a delicious winter vegetable.

Buy a very small swede for one person, or a slightly larger one for 2 servings.

Peel thickly, so that no brown or green skin remains. Cut into ½ in (1.25cm) chunks. Cook in boiling, salted water for 15 to 20 minutes, until tender. Drain well (if you are making gravy at the same time, save the water for the gravy liquid), and mash with a fork or potato masher, adding a knob of butter and plenty of pepper.

If you wish, peel 1 or 2 carrots, cut them into rings and cook them with the swede, mashing the two vegetables together with butter as above, or just mix the two together without mashing.

SWEETCORN

Frozen corn-on-the-cob is available all the year round. Cook as directed on the packet. Fresh cobs are in the shops from August to October, although imported sweetcorn is sometimes available at other times.

Cut off the stalk, remove the leaves and silky threads – this may be a bit fiddly, but try and pull all the threads off. Put the sweetcorn into a large pan of boiling, unsalted water, and simmer for 8 to 10 minutes, until the kernels are tender. Drain and serve with plenty of butter by melting a little in the hot saucepan and pouring it over the cobs. Tooth picks, cocktail sticks or 2 forks will serve as corn-on-the-cob holders.

SWEET POTATOES

Not directly related to ordinary potatoes. Becoming more widely available in many supermarkets. Peel, boil and purée them like creamed potatoes or cook them like roast potatoes.

TOMATOES

'Love apples' add colour and flavour to many dishes. They are used raw in salads or as a garnish, can be grilled or fried, chopped up and added to casseroles or stews, or stuffed as a supper dish. Choose firm tomatoes and keep them in the fridge for freshness. Cheaper soft tomatoes are a good buy for cooking, provided that you are going to use them straightaway.

Wash and dry the tomatoes, cut them into slices or quarters to use in a salad or as a garnish. Tomatoes are easy to cut or slice thinly if you use a bread knife or a vegetable knife with a serrated edge. The skin will then cut more easily without the inside squidging out.

GRILLED

Cut them in half, dot with butter and grill for 3 to 5 minutes. Alternatively, put them in the grill pan under the grid when grilling sausages, bacon, chops or steak, as the tomatoes will then cook with the meat.

FRIED

Cut the tomatoes in half and fry them in a little oil or fat, on both sides, over a medium heat, for a few minutes until soft. Serve with bacon and sausages, or place on a slice of toast or fried bread.

BAKED

Cut a cross in the top of any small or medium-sized tomatoes and halve any large ones. Put them into a greased, oven-proof dish or tin, with a knob of butter on top. Bake for 10 to 15 minutes (350°F/180°C/Gas Mark 4), until soft.

TURNIPS

Small white root vegetables, not to be confused with swedes.

Allow ½–2 turnips per serving, according to size and appetite.

Peel the turnips thickly. Leave small ones whole but cut large turnips in half or quarters. Cook them in boiling, salted water for 10 minutes, until soft. Drain them well. Return the turnips to the pan and shake over a low heat for a few moments to dry them out. Serve with a knob of butter.

Turnips can also be served with 1 or 2 diced carrots. Just peel them and cut them into large dice, mix them with the carrots and boil them together for 5 to 10 minutes. Drain and dry as above.

PURÉE

Peel the turnips and cut them into chunks. Cook them in boiling water for 5 to 10 minutes, until soft. Drain well, and dry as above. Mash with a fork or potato masher, with a knob of butter and some pepper.

BOILED RICE

A good quick standby, which saves peeling potatoes. Long grain, or Patna type, rice is used for savoury rice; the smaller, round grain type is used for puddings. Brown rice is also used for savoury dishes, but takes longer to cook. Rice is cheaper to buy in a large packet, and keeps for ages if decanted into a jar or plastic container. You can buy prepared and 'easy cook' rice of several types in the supermarkets, which must be cooked exactly as described on the packet. This type of rice is very good and easy to cook, but is usually more expensive than plain, long grain rice.

METHOD ONE

I prefer to use this method, as I tend to let the pan boil dry with the alternative method! However, you do need a largish pan and it's a bit steamy as the rice must be cooked without the lid on, otherwise it boils over.

Preparation and cooking time: 13 minutes.

½ cup (3 oz/75g) long grain rice – white or brown
½ tsp salt

Wash the rice well to get rid of the starch (put it into a saucepan and slosh it around in several rinses of cold water). Put the rice into a largish pan. Fill the pan two-thirds full of boiling water. Add the salt. Bring back to the boil and boil gently for 10 to 12 minutes for white rice, 20 to 25 minutes for brown rice, until the rice is cooked but still firm. Do not overcook or it will go sticky and puddingy. Drain well. Fluff with a fork and serve.

METHOD TWO
Be careful that the rice doesn't boil dry.

Preparation and cooking time: 13–16 minutes.

½ cup (3 oz/75g) long grain white rice
1 tsp oil or small knob of butter
1 cup boiling water
Pinch of salt

Wash the rice as in method one. Put the oil or butter in a smallish saucepan and heat gently. Then add the rice, stirring all the time, to coat each grain. Add the boiling water and a pinch of salt, bring up to simmering point and stir. Put on the lid and leave the rice to simmer over a very gentle heat for 12 to 15 minutes. Test to see if the rice is cooked: all the liquid should be absorbed and the rice should be cooked but not soggy. Lightly fluff with a fork and serve.

FRIED RICE   *Serves 1*

A good way of using up left-over boiled rice.

Preparation and cooking time: 15 minutes (plus 15 minutes if you have to boil the rice first).

1 cup cooked boiled rice (use ½ cup raw rice)
½ onion or 1 spring onion
½ slice cooked, chopped ham (optional)
1 tbsp cooking oil
1 tbsp frozen peas and/or sweetcorn (optional)

Cook the rice if necessary (see page 81). Peel and chop the onion, or wash and chop the spring onion. Chop the ham. Heat the oil in a frying pan over a medium heat. Add the chopped onion and fry, turning frequently, until soft. Add the cooked rice, and fry for 4 to 5 minutes, stirring all the time. Add the frozen peas (still frozen; they will defrost in the pan), sweetcorn and ham, and cook for a further 2 to 3 minutes, stirring all the time, until it is all heated through.

You can make this more substantial by adding more vegetables and chopped cooked meat (ham, salami, garlic sausage, etc.) if you wish.

BUBBLE AND SQUEAK   *Serves 1*

A lovely warm way of using up cold, left-over vegetables; you can, of course, cook some fresh vegetables specially if you wish.

Preparation and cooking time: 15 minutes.

3–4 cold cooked potatoes
1 cup cold cooked cabbage (or Brussels sprouts)
Little oil and a knob of butter

Slice the potatoes and chop up the cabbage or slice the sprouts. Heat the oil and butter in a frying pan over a medium heat. Put the potatoes and cabbage (or sprouts) into the frying pan and fry gently for 5 to 10 minutes, turning frequently, until the cabbage is cooked and the potatoes are golden and crispy. Serve hot with cold meat, bacon or fried eggs.

RISOTTO   *Serves 1*

A cheap meal if you have any 'pickings' of chicken left over.
Or use a thick slice of cooked ham, chicken or turkey. It can
be served with a green salad. (You don't need all the
vegetables listed here; choose those you like.)

Preparation and cooking time: 35 minutes.

1 egg
1 cup rice
1 small onion
1 tbsp oil (or large knob of butter or fat)
1 stock cube and 2 cups (½ pt/300ml) boiling water
1 slice (1–2 oz/25–50g) of cooked ham, chicken or turkey
2–3 mushrooms (sliced)
1 tomato
1 tbsp frozen or canned peas
1 tbsp frozen or canned sweetcorn
Salt, pepper, Worcester sauce
1 oz (25g) grated cheese and Parmesan cheese (optional)

Hard boil the egg for 10 minutes. Wash the rice in several
rinses of cold water to get rid of the starch. Peel and chop the
onion finely. Heat the oil or fat in a medium saucepan or
frying pan with a lid. Fry the onion for 3 to 4 minutes, until
soft. Add the rice and fry, stirring well, for a further 3
minutes. Dissolve the stock cube in the boiling water. Add
this to the rice, stir and leave to simmer with the lid on,
stirring occasionally, for 10 to 15 minutes, until the rice is
tender, and the liquid almost absorbed.

   Chop the meat. Peel and chop the hard-boiled egg. Wash
the sliced mushrooms. Wash and chop the tomato. Add the
peas, sweetcorn, mushrooms and tomato to the rice. Cook
for 2 to 3 minutes, stirring gently. Then add the chopped
meat and egg, and continue stirring gently until heated right
through. Season with salt, pepper and Worcester sauce.
Serve with lots of grated cheese and/or Parmesan and a dash
of Worcester sauce.

VEGETABLE HOT POT   *Serves 1*

This can be made with or without cheese, to provide a tasty dish for lunch or supper, or it can be served as a vegetable accompaniment to meat, to make a substantial meal if you're really hungry. You can either buy fresh, raw vegetables, or use up left-over vegetables. This recipe is particularly suitable for vegetarians.

Preparation and cooking time: 50 minutes.

1 small onion
1–2 oz (25–50g) cheese (optional)
2–3 potatoes
Oil and knob of butter
1–2 cups (4–8 oz/100–225g) mixed vegetables – carrots, cauliflower, leeks, celery, swede, turnip etc. Keep raw and cooked vegetables separate at this stage.
1 cup (½ small can/¼ pt/150ml) vegetable soup
Salt and pepper

Peel and slice the onion. Grate the cheese. Peel the potatoes and cut them into thick slices (¼ in/0.5cm). Heat the oil and butter in a saucepan over a moderate heat, and fry the onion for 2 to 3 minutes, until soft. Add the raw vegetables (not the potatoes) and continue to fry gently for a few minutes. Stir in the soup. Bring to the boil, and then lower the heat and simmer gently for 5 to 10 minutes, until the vegetables are tender, adding any cooked vegetables for the last 2 to 3 minutes to heat them through.

Meanwhile partly cook the sliced potatoes separately in boiling, salted water for 4 to 5 minutes. Drain them. Arrange the mixed vegetables in a casserole or oven-proof dish. Stir in half the cheese and cover with the hot soup. Season with salt and pepper. Top with a thick layer of potato slices. Dot with some butter. Sprinkle with the rest of the cheese. Bake in a hot oven (400°F/200°C/Gas Mark 6–7) for 15 to 20 minutes, until the top is golden brown. Serve hot.

VEGETABLE CURRY   *Serves 1*
You can use either fresh raw vegetables, left-over cooked vegetables, frozen vegetables (sold for stews or casseroles), or a mixture of them all. Serve with boiled rice.

Preparation and cooking time: 50 minutes.

1 small onion
2 cups (8 oz/225g) mixed vegetables: carrots, cauliflower, potatoes, celery, swede, turnip, etc. Keep the raw and cooked vegetables separate at this stage if you are using both.
Little oil for frying
1–2 tsp curry powder (or to taste)
½ tsp paprika pepper
1 tsp tomato purée (or ketchup)
1 tsp apricot jam (or redcurrant jelly)
½ tsp lemon juice
1 cup (¼ pt/150ml) milk (or milk and water)
1 tbsp sultanas (or raisins)
1 egg (optional)

Peel and chop the onion. Wash and prepare the fresh vegetables and cut them into largish pieces. Heat the oil in a saucepan over a moderate heat and fry the onion for a few minutes, stirring occasionally, until soft. Add the curry powder and paprika, and cook, stirring as before, for 2 to 3 minutes. Stir in the tomato purée, apricot jam (or redcurrant jelly), lemon juice, milk and/or water and the sultanas (or raisins). Bring to the boil, then reduce the heat and leave to simmer with the lid on for 10 minutes.

Cook the raw or frozen vegetables, in boiling water, for 5 to 10 minutes. Drain them. Hard boil the egg in boiling water for 10 minutes. Then peel it and slice it thickly. Gently stir the vegetables into the curry sauce and simmer for a further 5 to 10 minutes, until the vegetables are completely cooked and the curry is hot. While the curry is simmering, cook the boiled rice. Garnish the curry with the hard-boiled egg.

6

BACON, SAUSAGES AND HAM

Lots of quick, but substantial snacks in this chapter. Bacon and sausages don't take long to cook and are useful when you come home hungry and want a meal in a hurry.

BACON

Streaky bacon is the cheapest, then shoulder rashers, while back and gammon are the most expensive. *Serve 1 to 2 rashers of bacon per person.* How well cooked you like your bacon is a very personal thing; I know someone who likes hers cremated! As a rough guide: cook for between 1 and 5 minutes. Tomatoes and/or mushrooms can be cooked in the grill pan under the rashers of bacon; the fat from the bacon will give them a good flavour.

Cut off the bacon rinds if you wish or just snip the rinds at intervals.

GRILLED
Heat the grill. Put the bacon on the grid in the grill pan and cook, turning occasionally, until it is cooked to your taste.

FRIED
Heat a smear of oil or fat in a frying pan. Add the bacon, and fry over a medium-hot heat, turning occasionally, until the bacon is as you like it.

SAUSAGES

These come in all shapes, sizes and pieces; the thicker the sausage the longer it takes to cook. Have you tried eating sausages with marmalade? I'm told it is delicious, and a boarding school speciality.

Cook as many sausages as you can eat. Always prick the sausages (except for skinless ones) with a fork before cooking to stop the sausages bursting open.

GRILLED
Heat the grill. Put the sausages on the grid in the grill pan, and cook, turning occasionally, until brown and delicious (about 10 to 20 minutes). Thicker sausages may brown on the outside before the middle is cooked, so turn the heat down to medium for the last 5 to 10 minutes of cooking time.

FRIED
Heat a smear of oil or fat in a frying pan, over a medium heat (too hot a pan will make the sausages burst their skins), add the sausages and fry gently, turning occasionally, until they are brown and crispy (10 to 20 minutes). Cook thick sausages

for the longer time, using a lower heat if the outsides start getting too brown.

ROAST

Roast chipolata (thin) sausages are traditionally served as accompaniments to roast turkey and chicken. Roasting is an easy way of cooking sausages if you're not in a hurry. Place the sausages in a lightly-greased tin and bake in a hot oven (400°F/200°C/Gas Mark 6), turning occasionally to cook all over, until crisp and brown (20 to 30 minutes). Thicker sausages take the longer time.

A PROPER BREAKFAST *Serves 1*
Tastes just as good for lunch or supper.

Preparation and cooking time: 20 minutes.

Use any combination of ingredients according to taste and appetite:
1–4 sausages
1–2 rashers of bacon – streaky, back or collar
1 tomato
3–4 mushrooms
1–2 left-over cold boiled potatoes
1 tbsp oil (for frying)
1–2 eggs
1 slice of bread (for fried bread)
Knob of butter
Several slices of bread (for toast)

The breakfast, apart from the eggs, potatoes and fried bread which are better fried, can be grilled if you prefer. Get everything ready before you actually start cooking: prick the sausages, de-rind the bacon, wash and halve the tomato, wash the mushrooms and slice the potatoes. Warm a plate, put the kettle on ready for tea or coffee, get the bread ready to make the toast, and you're all set to start. In both methods, start cooking the sausages first, as they take the longest to cook, gradually adding the rest of the ingredients to the pan.

FRYING

Heat the oil in a frying pan over a moderate heat and fry the sausages gently, turning occasionally, allowing 10 to 20 minutes for them to cook according to size. When the sausages are half-cooked, put the bacon in the pan with them and fry for 1 to 5 minutes with the sausages, until they are cooked to your taste. Push the sausages and bacon to one side or remove and keep warm. Put the potato slices into the pan and fry until crispy. Fry the tomato and mushrooms at the same time, turning them occasionally until cooked (about 4 to 5 minutes).

Remove the food from the pan and keep hot. Break the eggs into a cup, and slide into the hot fat in the pan over a low heat. Fry them gently until cooked (see page 20). Remove them from the pan and put them with the bacon, sausages, etc. Cut the slice of bread in half, and fry in the fat in the pan, adding a little extra oil or butter if necessary, until golden and crispy, turning to cook both sides (1 to 2 minutes). Remove from the pan and put onto the plate with the rest of the breakfast. Make the toast, coffee or tea, and eat at once.

GRILLING

Heat the grill. Put the tomato halves and mushrooms in the base of the grill pan, arrange the sausages above on the grid, and grill until half cooked (5 to 10 minutes) turning to cook on all sides. Arrange the bacon on the grid with the sausages, and continue cooking for a further 3 to 5 minutes, turning to cook both sides. Remove everything from the pan and keep it warm. Pour the fat from the grill pan into a frying pan, add extra oil or butter if necessary, then fry the potato slices, eggs and fried bread as described above, and enjoy it all with lots of toast, marmalade, and lovely strong coffee or tea.

BANGERS AND MASH
Serves 1

Fast, filling, cheap and tasty!

Preparation and cooking time: 30 minutes.

2–3 potatoes – according to size and appetite (or instant mashed potato – use amount specified in the instructions on the packet)
2–4 sausages – according to size and appetite
Knob of butter

Gravy:
1 tsp flour or cornflour and 1 tsp gravy flavouring powder or 2 tsp gravy granules
1 cup (¼ pt/150ml) water (use the water the potatoes cooked in)
Little fat from the sausages

Peel the potatoes, cut into small, evenly-sized pieces, and cook in boiling, salted water for 10 to 20 minutes, according to size, until soft. Prick the sausages, cook under a hot grill for 10 to 15 minutes, turning frequently, or fry over a medium heat, with a smear of oil to stop them sticking, turning often, for 10 to 15 minutes, until brown. (Make the instant mash, if used, according to the instructions on the packet. Keep it warm.) Test the potatoes for softness, and drain them as soon as they are cooked. Mash them with a fork or potato masher, and beat in the knob of butter. Keep them warm.

Make the gravy, by mixing the flour or cornflour and gravy flavouring powder, or gravy granules, into a smooth paste with a little cold water, or wine, sherry, beer, etc. Add one cup of the vegetable water and any juices from the sausages. Pour the mixture into a small saucepan, and bring to the boil, stirring all the time. Cook until the mixture thickens. Add more liquid if it's too thick. Arrange the mashed potato on a hot plate, stick the sausages round it and pour the gravy over the top.

BRAISED SAUSAGES   *Serves 1*

These take longer to cook, but make a change from the usual fried or grilled sausages. Serve with mashed potatoes.

Preparation and cooking time: 50–60 minutes.

2–3 thick sausages (the spicy, herb sort are the best)
1–2 rashers of streaky bacon
1 small onion (or 2–3 shallots)
2–3 mushrooms
2 tsp oil
1 tsp flour
1 small cup (¼ pt/150ml approx.) wine, beer, or cider or ½
  stock cube dissolved in 1 cup boiling water
Pinch of dried herbs
Pinch of garlic powder
Salt and pepper

Prick the sausages. De-rind and chop the bacon. Peel and thickly slice the onion or peel the shallots and leave whole. Wash the mushrooms and slice if large.

Heat the oil in a casserole or thick saucepan, over a moderate heat, and lightly brown the sausages. Remove them from the pan.

Add the bacon and onion, and fry for 2 to 3 minutes. Stir in the flour, and gradually add the wine, beer, cider or stock, stirring as the sauce thickens.

Return the sausages to the pan. Add the mushrooms, herbs, garlic, salt and pepper. Reheat, then put on the lid, lower the heat and leave to simmer gently for 35 to 45 minutes, removing the lid for the last 15 minutes of cooking time. Add a little more liquid if it gets too dry.

SAVOURY SAUSAGE-MEAT PIE   *Serves 1*
The apple gives the sausage-meat a tangy taste.

Preparation.and cooking time: 50 minutes.

**3–4 potato pieces (or a large serving of instant mashed potato,
    use amount specified in the instructions on the packet)**
1 cooking apple
1 onion
2 tomatoes (tinned or fresh)
1 tsp sugar
4 oz (100g) sausage-meat (or 2–4 sausages)
Knob of butter

Prepare the mashed potato (see page 71) or make up the
instant potato as instructed on the packet. Peel, core and
slice the apple. Peel and chop the onion. Slice the fresh
tomatoes, or drain and slice the tinned tomatoes.

Place the apple slices in the base of a greased, oven-proof
dish. Sprinkle with the sugar. If using sausages, slit the
sausage skins to remove the sausage-meat and dispose of the
skins. Mix the chopped onion with the sausage-meat or the
skinned sausages and spread the sausage mixture over the
apples.

Spoon the mashed potato round the dish to make a border
or 'nest' for the sausage. Cover the sausage with the
tomatoes. Dot the potato with the butter, and bake in an
oven (400°F/200°C/Gas Mark 6) for 30 minutes, until the
sausage is cooked and the potato is crisp and golden-brown
on top.

TOAD IN THE HOLE   *Serves 1*

You can use either large sausages (toads) or chipolatas (frogs) for this meal, whichever you prefer! Some people believe that a better Yorkshire Pudding is made if the ingredients are mixed together first and the batter is then left to stand in the fridge while you prepare the rest of the meal. Alternatively, make the batter while the sausages are cooking.

Preparation and cooking time: 45–55 minutes.

3–6 sausages (according to appetite and size)
1 tbsp cooking oil

Yorkshire Pudding batter:
2 heaped tbsp plain flour
Pinch of salt
1 egg
1 cup (¼ pt/150ml) milk

Heat the oven (425°F/220°C/Gas Mark 7–8). Prick the sausages. Put them into a baking tin with the oil. (Any baking tin can be used, but not one with a loose base. You do not get as good a result with a pyrex-type dish.) Cook the chipolatas for 5 minutes or the larger ones for 10 minutes.

Make the batter while the sausages are cooking. Put the flour and salt in a basin, add the egg, and beat it into the flour, gradually adding the milk, to make a smooth batter. (This is easier with a hand or electric mixer, but with a bit of old-fashioned effort you can get just as good a result using a whisk, wooden spoon or even a fork.) Pour the batter into the baking tin on top of the hot sausages. Bake for a further 20 to 25 minutes, until the Yorkshire pud is golden. Try not to open the oven door for the first 10 to 15 minutes, so that the pudding will rise well. Serve at once.

HAWAIIAN SAUSAGES
Serves 1

An unusual variation on the sausage and bean theme.

Preparation and cooking time: 30 minutes.

3–6 sausages, according to size and appetite
½ small can (7¾ oz/220g size) pineapple rings
1 small onion (or 2 spring onions)
Knob of butter
1 small can (7.9 oz/225g) baked beans
1 tsp vinegar
Salt and pepper

Prick the sausages. Fry or grill them until cooked and brown (see page 88). Add 1 or 2 pineapple rings and heat through with the sausages for a minute or two. Save 2 sausages, and keep hot with the pineapple rings (for decoration). Slice the rest of the sausages.

Peel and slice the onion, or wash and chop the spring onions. Chop another 1 or 2 pineapple rings.

Heat the butter in a saucepan over a moderate heat, and fry the onion and pineapple pieces until soft (2 to 3 minutes). Add the beans, sliced sausages, vinegar, salt and pepper, and simmer for 3 to 4 minutes.

Pour into a warm serving dish. Decorate with the whole sausages and pineapple rings you are keeping hot. Serve with crispy bread rolls or hot toast.

SAUSAGE AND BACON HUBBLE BUBBLE *Serves 1*
A tasty way of using up odds and ends from the fridge.

Preparation and cooking time: 30 minutes.

2–3 cooked boiled potatoes
1 small onion
1 rasher of bacon
2–4 sausages
2 tsp oil (for frying)
1 egg
½ cup milk
Salt and pepper

Heat the oven (375°F/190°C/Gas Mark 5–6). Grease an oven-proof dish.

Slice the cooked potatoes. Peel and chop the onion. De-rind the bacon. Prick the sausages.

Heat the oil in a frying pan, and fry the sausages, bacon and onion gently for 5 minutes, turning frequently.

Place the potato slices in the dish. Arrange the onions, sausages and bacon on top. Beat the egg with the milk, salt and pepper in a small basin, using a whisk or fork. Pour the egg mixture over the top, and bake in a hot oven for about 15 minutes, until the egg mixture is set.

CHEESY SAUSAGES   *Serves 1*
A quick and tasty lunch or supper.

Preparation and cooking time: 25 minutes.

2 or 3 thick sausages
2 or 3 rashers of back bacon
1–2 oz (25–50g) Cheddar cheese
1 tbsp pickle (or sweet chutney)
Few wooden cocktail sticks or toothpicks
1–2 slices of bread
Little butter

Prick the sausages with a fork. Grill them under a moderate heat for about 15 minutes. Make a slit in each sausage, lengthways, and wedge a slice of cheese in each slit. Cut the rind from the bacon, and spread with the chutney.

7. Cheesy sausages

Wrap the bacon round the sausages and pin securely with cocktail sticks or toothpicks (not plastic ones!). Return to the hot grill, and cook for about 5 minutes, until the bacon is crisp and the cheese is melting. Toast the bread, spread with the butter and serve with the sausages.

GAMMON STEAK WITH PINEAPPLE OR
FRIED EGG

Serves 1

Buy a thick slice (½ in/1.25cm at least) of gammon, if possible, as thin slices just go crispy, like bacon. Serve with boiled new potatoes and salad in summer and sauté or jacket potatoes and peas in winter.

Preparation and cooking time: 6–10 minutes according to taste.

1 steak or slice (about 6 oz/175g) gammon
Little oil
1–2 tinned pineapple rings
** or 1 egg**

GRILLED

Heat the grill. Snip the gammon rind at intervals. Brush or wipe both sides of the gammon with a smear of oil. Place the gammon on the grid of the grill pan and cook each side under the hot grill for 3 to 5 minutes, until brown. Put the pineapple slices on top of the gammon and heat for a few moments or fry the egg in a frying pan, in a little hot fat. Serve the gammon with the pineapple slices or with the egg on top.

FRIED

Snip the gammon rind at intervals. Heat a smear of oil or fat in a frying pan. Add the gammon and cook each side for 3 to 5 minutes, until brown. Add the pineapple rings to the pan and heat for a few moments or fry the egg in the hot fat. Serve the gammon with the pineapple rings or with the egg on top.

ST DAVID'S DAY SUPPER   *Serves 2*

Leeks, of course, are the main ingredients.

Preparation and cooking time: 40 minutes.

5–6 potatoes
2 medium-sized leeks
Salt and pepper
4 oz (100g) cooked ham
1 small can (10.4 oz/295g) cream of chicken soup
1 tomato

Wash and peel the potatoes. Cut them into thick slices. Cut off the roots and leaves of the leeks and wash thoroughly (see page 65) and slice.

Put the potato and leek slices in a saucepan, cover with boiling, salted water, and cook for 8 to 10 minutes, until half cooked. Drain well.

Grease an oven-proof dish, put the vegetable mixture into the dish, and sprinkle with the salt and pepper. Chop the ham. Put the ham on top of the vegetables. Pour the chicken soup over the top, and heat through in the oven (400°F/ 200°C/Gas Mark 6) for about 20 minutes.

Wash and slice the tomato and place on top of the vegetables for the last 5 minutes of cooking time. Serve with hot bread rolls and butter.

LUNCHEON MEAT PATTIES *Serves 1*

Cheap and tasty, and filling enough for lunch or supper if served with fried eggs.

Preparation and cooking time: 20 minutes.

3–4 potatoes
1 small onion
4 oz (100g) luncheon meat (canned or sliced)
A little beaten egg
Salt and pepper
Pinch of dried herbs
Oil (for frying)
Knob of butter (for frying)

Peel and thickly slice the potatoes. Cook them in boiling, salted water for 10 minutes, until soft. Drain them and mash well.

Peel and finely chop or grate the onion. Chop the luncheon meat.

Mix together the potato, onion, luncheon meat, and bind with the well-beaten egg, adding sufficient egg to hold it all together. Season with the salt, pepper and herbs. Form the mixture into 3 or 4 equal portions. Shape each into a ball and then flatten to form 'beefburger' shapes about ¾ in (2cm) thick.

Heat the oil and butter in a frying pan, and fry over a moderate heat for 3 to 5 minutes, turning to cook both sides, until crisp and golden brown. Serve with fresh or fried tomatoes and/or a couple of fried eggs, if you're really hungry.

BACON-STUFFED COURGETTES   *Serves 1*

In the autumn, when marrows are cheap, you can make a very economical and tasty meal using marrow instead.

Preparation and cooking time: 1 hour.

1 onion
4 oz (100g/2–3 rashers) bacon – odd slices of bacon, sometimes sold cheaply as they are left-over end pieces, are suitable for this dish too
1 tomato
2 tsp cooking oil
½ tsp dried mixed herbs
Salt and pepper
2 medium courgettes

Peel and chop the onion. Cut the rind from the bacon; cut or chop it into small pieces. Chop the tomato. Heat the oil in a frying pan, add the onion and fry gently for 3 to 4 minutes, until soft. Add the bacon, and cook for a further 8 to 10 minutes, stirring well. Add the tomato and seasoning.

Wash the courgettes in cold water and cut a wedge-shaped 'lid' along the length of each courgette, to leave a hollow. Pile the filling into the hollow. Put the courgettes carefully into a greased, oven-proof dish and top with the 'lids'. Cover with a piece of foil and bake in a moderate oven (350°F/ 180°C/Gas Mark 4–5) for about 45 minutes. Serve with hot, brown bread rolls and butter, and a green salad.

VEGETABLE MARROW

These are often fairly large, so increase the quantity of stuffing, and make enough for several people. Remove a thick slice from the top of the marrow (to be used later). Scoop out the seeds. Fill the marrow with the prepared stuffing. Top with the 'lid' you sliced off. Brush lightly with a little cooking oil or softened butter, and carefully put the marrow on a greased baking dish. Bake in a moderate oven (350°F/180°C/Gas Mark 4–5) for about 1 hour.

FARMHOUSE SUPPER   *Serves 1*

A tasty way of using up cooked potato and food from the fridge to make a meal.

Preparation and cooking time: 20 minutes.

3–4 cooked, boiled potatoes (see page 71 if you don't have any cooked)
1 small onion
1–2 rashers of bacon
½ small green pepper
1 oz (25g) cheese
Little oil for frying
Knob of butter
1–2 eggs

Slice and dice the potatoes. Peel and chop the onion. De-rind and dice the bacon. Core and chop the pepper. Grate the cheese.

Heat the oil in a frying pan, add the bacon, and fry gently for 3 to 4 minutes. Remove the bacon from the pan and save on a saucer.

Put the potatoes, onion and green pepper into the hot fat in the pan, and continue to fry gently for 5 to 10 minutes, until lightly browned.

Mix the bacon with the vegetables and place in an oven-proof dish. Melt the butter in the pan and fry the eggs. Carefully put the eggs on top of the vegetables and bacon. Cover with the grated cheese, and brown for a few minutes under a hot grill, until the cheese is bubbly. Serve at once.

7

OFFAL AND COOKED MEATS

This means kidney, liver, tripe and sweetbreads etc. They are extraordinarily cheap, and besides being such good value for money, are very nourishing. Lamb's liver and kidney are more expensive than pig's liver and kidney which have a stronger taste, are very cheap, and make a tasty meal as well.

FRIED LIVER AND BACON WITH FRIED ONIONS
Serves 1

Lamb's liver is delicious fried, but if you are really counting the pennies, buy pig's liver and soak it for an hour in a little milk to give it a more delicate flavour.

Preparation and cooking time: 15 minutes (plus 30–60 minutes soaking time for the pig's liver).

4–6 oz (100–175g) lamb's or pig's liver (sliced)
Milk (for soaking)
1 rasher of bacon
1 onion
Little oil (for frying)
Knob of butter (for frying)

Gravy:
2 tsp gravy granules
  or 1 tsp flour (or cornflour) and 1 tsp gravy flavouring powder
1 tsp cold water, sherry or wine (optional)
½ cup water (or water used in cooking the vegetables)

Put the pig's liver slices in a shallow dish, cover with a little milk, and leave to soak for 30 to 60 minutes. Lamb's liver does not need soaking. De-rind the bacon. Peel and slice the onion into rings. Dry the liver on kitchen paper. Heat the oil and butter in a frying pan over a moderate heat. Add the onion slices and fry for 3 to 4 minutes, stirring frequently, until soft. Push the onion to one side of the pan and stir occasionally while frying the bacon and liver.

Put the bacon and liver in the hot fat in the pan, and fry gently for 3 to 5 minutes, turning frequently, until cooked to taste – liver should be soft on the outside, not crispy. Remove the liver, bacon and onion from the pan and serve on a hot plate.

Either pour the meat juices from the pan over the liver and serve with crusty new bread; or make gravy with the juices and serve with boiled potatoes and a green vegetable. For the gravy: mix the gravy granules (or flour and gravy flavouring powder) into a smooth paste with the sherry, wine or cold water. Add the half cup of vegetable water or cold water and mix well. Pour onto the meat juices in the pan, stirring well. Bring to the boil, stirring all the time until the gravy thickens. Pour over the liver and vegetables.

SAVOURY CORNED BEEF HASH   *Serves 1*
Every cowboy's favourite standby!

Preparation and cooking time: 30 minutes.

3–4 potatoes
½ small onion
2–4 oz (50–100g) corned beef
Salt and pepper
1 tbsp oil (for frying)
1 egg
1 tsp tomato purée (or ketchup)
1 tbsp hot water
A dash of Worcester sauce
A dash of tabasco sauce

Peel the potatoes, cut into large dice, and cook for 5 to 6 minutes, in boiling, salted water, until half cooked. Drain well.

Peel and finely chop the onion. Dice the corned beef. Mix together the potato cubes, onion and corned beef. Season with salt and pepper. Grease well a frying pan with oil and put the meat and potato mixture into the pan.

Beat the egg. Dissolve the tomato purée or ketchup in 1 tbsp of hot water, beat this into the egg, add the Worcester and tabasco sauces then pour onto the meat mixture. Fry gently for about 15 minutes, stirring occasionally. Serve hot.

I have known people to make this gourmet dish using cooked rice instead of cooked potatoes, but it has not been particularly successful.

SAUCY LIVER SAVOURY   *Serves 1*

This is a real money saver, as it can be made with the cheaper pig's liver (but remember to allow the soaking time to give the liver a more delicate flavour – see method below). Serve with creamy, mashed potatoes or plain boiled rice or crusty bread rolls and butter, and a green salad.

Preparation and cooking time: 25 minutes (plus 30–60 minutes soaking time).

4–6 oz (100–175g) pig's or lamb's liver
½ cup cold milk
1 onion
Clove of garlic (or pinch of garlic powder or garlic paste)
Knob of butter (for frying)
Little oil (for frying)
1 tsp flour
1 tbsp tomato purée (or tomato ketchup)
Pinch of dried mixed herbs
Salt and pepper
½ stock cube and ½ cup hot water

Cut the liver into 1 in (2.5cm) strips, and soak the pig's liver in cold milk for 30 to 60 minutes, if possible. Lamb's liver need not be soaked. Peel and slice the onion. Peel and chop the fresh garlic. Remove the liver from the milk, but reserve the milk to use in the sauce.

Heat the butter and oil in a frying pan over a moderate heat, and fry the onion for 2 to 3 minutes, stirring occasionally, until just soft. Add the liver pieces, fry gently, turning frequently to brown on all sides (3 to 5 minutes). Stir in the flour, garlic, tomato purée, herbs, salt and pepper. Remove from the heat. Dissolve the stock cube in the hot water. Gradually mix in the stock and milk, return to the heat and stir continuously until the sauce thickens. Lower the heat, cover the pan and leave to simmer for 10 minutes until the liver is tender.

LIVER HOT POT

Serves 1

Make this with the really cheap pig's liver if you're counting the pennies, but remember to soak the slices to give it a more delicate flavour. Serve hot with a green vegetable.

Preparation and cooking time: 1 hour (plus 30–60 minutes soaking time).

4–6 oz (100–175g) lamb's or pig's liver (sliced)
Milk (for soaking)
3–4 potatoes
1 onion
1 tomato
2–3 mushrooms
Oil (for frying)
Salt and pepper
Pinch of dried herbs
½ stock cube
½ cup hot water
Knob of butter

Soak the pig's liver slices in milk for 30 to 60 minutes, if possible. Lamb's liver need not be soaked. Peel the potatoes, thickly slice them (¼ in/0.5cm) and cook for 5 minutes in boiling, salted water, until partly cooked. Drain them. Peel and slice the onion into rings. Wash and slice the tomato and mushrooms. Heat the oil in a frying pan, and fry the onion rings gently for 2 to 3 minutes, until just soft. Push them to one side of the pan. Add the liver slices and fry these, turning to cook both sides, for 1 to 2 minutes.

Grease an oven-proof dish or casserole, and arrange the slices of onion, liver, mushrooms and tomato in layers. Sprinkle with the salt, pepper and herbs. Dissolve the stock cube in the ½ cup of hot water and pour the stock into the casserole. Cover the casserole with a thick layer of the sliced potatoes. Dot the potatoes with the butter, and bake in an oven (375°F/190°C/Gas Mark 5–6) for about 35 to 45 minutes, until the potatoes are brown and crispy on the top.

KIDNEY STROGANOFF   *Serves 1*

A special kidney dish, but much cheaper than beef stroga-
noff, so treat yourself to lamb's kidneys and enjoy them.
Serve with plain, boiled rice.

Preparation and cooking time: 35 minutes.

1 small onion
2–3 mushrooms
3–4 lamb's kidneys
Knob of butter (for frying)
1 tsp oil (for frying)
1 tsp flour (or cornflour)
Salt and pepper
⅔ cup milk (just under ¼ pint/150ml)
½ cup (3 oz/75g) raw, long grain rice
2 tbsp plain yoghurt

Peel and chop the onion. Wash and slice the mushrooms. Cut
the kidneys in half lengthways. Remove the white fatty core
and cut the kidneys into quarters

Melt the butter and oil in a saucepan over a moderate
heat, and fry the onion gently for 2 to 3 minutes to soften.
Add the mushrooms and stir. Add the kidneys, flour, salt
and pepper, and continue to cook for another 3 to 5 minutes
until the kidneys are browned on all sides.

Remove the pan from the heat and gradually stir in the
milk. Return to the heat and slowly bring the sauce to the
boil, stirring gently all the time as the sauce thickens. Lower
the heat, cover the pan and simmer very gently for 10 to 15
minutes, until the kidneys are cooked. Cook the rice (while
the kidneys are simmering) in boiling, salted water. Stir the
yoghurt into the kidney sauce. Drain the rice and serve hot
with the kidneys.

QUICK KIDNEY SPECIAL   *Serves 1*

This is delicious made with lamb's kidney, and makes a complete supper with sauté potatoes, served with a green salad.

Preparation and cooking time: 35 minutes.

3–4 small potatoes
1 small onion
2–3 lamb's kidneys
Oil (for frying)
Knob of butter (for frying)
Salt and pepper
Pinch of garlic powder (or clove of garlic)
1 tbsp sherry (or wine)
1 tbsp cream (or sour cream or plain yoghurt)

Peel the potatoes. Slice them thickly (¼ in/0.5cm) and cook gently in boiling, salted water for 5 to 10 minutes, until just soft. Drain them.

Peel the onion, slice it into thin rings. Cut the kidneys in halves, and remove the fatty white core. Then cut the kidneys into quarters.

Heat the oil and butter in a frying pan, and fry the potatoes, turning occasionally, for a few minutes, until golden and crispy. Remove from the pan, drain on kitchen paper and keep warm on a hot plate.

Add a little more butter to the frying pan if necessary, and fry the onion rings and kidneys over a gentle heat, stirring gently, for 5 to 10 minutes, until the kidneys are cooked. Season with the salt and pepper and garlic. Stir in the sherry and cream, stirring to heat thoroughly, but do not allow to boil. Make the potatoes into a 'nest'. Pour the kidneys and sauce into the middle of the potatoes and serve at once.

KIDNEY DINNER   *Serves 1*

This can be made with lamb's kidneys or the cheaper pig's
kidney, according to how rich you are feeling – both are tasty
and delicious. Serve with boiled rice or boiled new potatoes;
these can be prepared in advance and kept warm while the
kidneys are cooking.

Preparation and cooking time: 20 minutes.

8 oz (225g/3–4) lamb's kidneys or (1–1½) pig's kidneys
1 tsp oil (for frying)
Knob of butter (for frying)
½ small tin (10.4 oz/295g size) of kidney (or oxtail) soup
1 tsp flour (or cornflour) and ½ tsp gravy flavouring powder
   or 2 tsp gravy granules
1 tbsp water or sherry or wine (your choice)
1 tbsp cream (optional)

Cut the kidneys in half, lengthways, and remove the white,
fatty core. Cut the kidneys into pieces.

Heat the oil and butter gently in a saucepan. Add the
kidneys and fry over a moderate heat, stirring until the
kidneys are browned on all sides. Gradually stir in about 1
cup of soup and leave to simmer for 10 minutes, over a very
low heat, until the kidneys are tender.

Mix the flour and gravy flavouring powder (or gravy
granules) into a smooth paste with the sherry, wine or water,
and add to the kidney sauce, stirring as the sauce thickens.
Stir in the cream, if using, and heat through, but do not let
the cream boil.

KEBABS
Serves 1

This is an economical recipe, using kidney, sausages and bacon, instead of the much more expensive steak, cubed pork or lamb. The supermarkets sell packets of ready-prepared assorted kebab meats, which are good value, as it is rather expensive buying small quantities of different meats. Serve with boiled rice or bread rolls, and a green salad and barbecue sauce.

Preparation and cooking time: 20–25 minutes.

Use any mixture of the following:

1–2 rashers of bacon
1–2 chipolata sausages
1–2 lamb's kidneys
2–4 button mushrooms
1–2 tomatoes
Few pieces of green pepper
1 onion
1–2 pickled onions
Few pineapple cubes
Allow 1–2 long skewers per person
Oil for cooking

Heat the oven (400°F/200°C/Gas Mark 6–7) or the grill. Start cooking the rice, if used, in boiling salted water (see page 81). Prepare the salad and put aside.

Assemble and prepare your chosen ingredients as follows. De-rind the bacon. Cut the rashers in half to make them shorter in length, and roll them into little bacon rolls. Twist and halve the chipolata sausages. Halve the kidneys length-ways and remove the white, fatty core. Wash the mushrooms. Wash the tomatoes, cut into halves or quarters, according to size. Slice the green pepper into chunks. Peel the onion and cut into quarters. Drain the pickled onions and the pineapple cubes.

8. Kebabs

Thread the skewers with the chosen food, arranging it as you wish. Brush or wipe with oil. Either grill under a moderate grill on the grill rack, or balance the skewers across a baking tin in the hot oven, and cook for about 15 minutes, turning frequently. Drain the rice. Serve the kebabs on the skewers – be careful: they will be hot, so have a paper napkin handy.

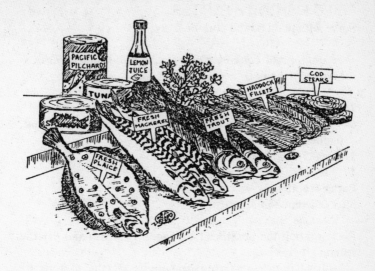

8

FISH

Fresh or frozen fish can be used in these recipes according to availability. Fishmongers and market stalls sell wet fish, but most fish sold in the supermarkets is frozen and ready to use. The inevitable fish finger is well-known and widely available, along with other packets of frozen fish ready for frying. These need not be deep-fried, but are good cooked in a frying pan in a little butter and oil, or grilled. Eaten with bread, butter and tomato sauce these make a really quick supper. There are also many commercially-frozen fish dishes sold in the supermarkets, which are quite cheap, and quick and easy to cook, often by simply heating the packets in a saucepan of boiling water. Follow the instructions given on the packet carefully (short cuts aren't usually very successful) and serve with boiled or mashed potatoes, fresh or frozen vegetables, bread rolls or a side salad.

FRIED FISH WITH BUTTER   *Serves 1*
Serve with plain boiled potatoes.

Preparation and cooking time: 15–20 minutes (according to the type of fish used).

2–4 potato pieces
6–8 oz (175–225g) fillet of white fish (fresh or frozen) – cod, haddock, or plaice are the cheapest
1–2 oz (25–50g) butter
1 tsp cooking oil
Parsley (optional)
Slice of lemon (optional)

Peel and boil the potatoes (see page 71). Wash and dry the fish on kitchen paper.

Melt the butter in a frying pan with the oil (the oil stops the butter going too brown), add the fish and fry until tender (about 5 to 10 minutes), spooning the melted butter over it as it cooks. (The thicker the fish the longer it will take to cook.)

Lift the fish carefully onto a warm plate, add a little chopped parsley (if used) to the butter in the pan and heat thoroughly. Pour the buttery juice over the fish and garnish with the lemon slice. Drain the potatoes and serve.

FRIED OR GRILLED TROUT (OR MACKEREL)

Serves 1

These can be bought quite cheaply fresh from trout farms, but frozen trout are also good value, as they provide a filling meal with just bread and butter. Mackerel are cheap, delicious and are cooked in the same way.

Preparation and cooking time: 15–20 minutes.

1 trout or mackerel
1 tsp oil (for frying)
½ oz (12g) butter
Slice of lemon (optional)
Vinegar (optional)

Clean the fish by removing its head, entrails, fins and gills. (The fishmonger will usually do this for you. Frozen fish is already cleaned.)

FRIED
Heat the oil and butter in a frying pan, and fry the fish over a moderate heat, for about 5 minutes on each side.

GRILLED
Dot with the butter and grill on both sides until done (about 5 minutes each side for a medium-sized fish).

Serve with a slice of lemon, or vinegar, and brown or French bread and butter.

CHEESY COD STEAKS　　　　　　　　*Serves 1*

Thick pieces of cod or haddock, or frozen fish steaks can be used. The frozen steaks are easy to cook and keep a good shape as they are individually wrapped and so can be separated easily while still frozen.

Preparation and cooking time: 20 minutes.

6–8 oz (175–225g) piece of cod (or 1–2 frozen fish steaks)
Salt and pepper
½ slice of bread
½ oz (12g) Cheddar cheese
½ oz (12g) butter

Wipe the fish and season with salt and pepper. Grate or crumble the bread, grate or finely chop the cheese, and mix together.

Put the fish in the base of a greased grill pan, dot with half the butter and grill for 5 minutes. Turn the fish over, cover with the cheese mixture, dot with the remaining butter and grill for another 5 minutes.

Serve on a warm plate.

TOMATO FISH BAKE   *Serves 1*

Brill is very tasty in this recipe, but cod or haddock are good too (and probably cheaper).

Preparation and cooking time: 35 minutes.

1 portion (6 oz/150g) fillet of brill, cod or haddock
2 tsp cooking oil
½ small onion
½ small can (8 oz/230g size) tomatoes (or use 1 or 2 fresh tomatoes)
Salt and pepper
¼ green pepper (optional)
1 stick of celery (optional)

Put the fish in a greased oven-proof dish.

Heat the oil in a small saucepan, chop the onion and fry it gently in the oil, until soft (2 to 3 minutes).

Add the tinned tomatoes or chopped fresh tomatoes and seasoning. Bring to the boil and cook gently until the liquid is reduced to a thin purée (3 to 5 minutes).

Chop the celery and/or pepper if used, stir into the tomato mixture, and spoon the sauce over the fish. Cover with a lid or cooking foil, and bake for about 20 minutes in an oven (375°F/190°C/Gas Mark 5). Serve hot.

TUNA BAKE   *Serves 1*

Serve with crispy bread rolls or toast.

Preparation and cooking time: 20 minutes.

½–1 can (200g size) tuna fish (use the rest for sandwiches or in Tuna Fiesta or Tuna Continental)
½ can (10 oz/298g size) condensed mushroom soup
1 slice of bread (crumbled into breadcrumbs)
1 oz (25g) butter
Few mushrooms (optional)

Drain the tuna fish and flake it into large flakes. Heat the soup in a saucepan, add the fish and cook for 2 to 3 minutes.

Pour the mixture into a heat-proof dish. Sprinkle with the breadcrumbs and dot with half the butter. Grill for 5 minutes or until golden brown.

Meanwhile wash the mushrooms, if used, melt the remaining butter in the pan, add the mushrooms and cook gently for 4 to 5 minutes. Place on top of the hot tuna bake and serve at once.

Do not leave the remainder of the tuna fish or the soup in the cans. Put them into covered containers or cups in the fridge and use within 24 hours.

TUNA FIESTA   *Serves 1*
Serve with boiled rice or mashed potatoes.

Preparation and cooking time: 25 minutes.

½ cup (3 oz/75g) long grained rice, or 2–4 potato pieces
1 small onion
½ oz (12g) margarine (or butter or 1 tsp cooking oil)
2 oz (50g) mushrooms
½ green pepper
2 oz (50g) peas
2 tbsp tinned tomato soup
Salt and pepper
Garlic powder
½ can (200g size) tuna fish (use the rest for sandwiches or
   in Tuna Bake or Tuna Continental)

Peel the potatoes (or wash the rice) and boil (see pages 71 and 81).

Peel and slice the onion and fry it gently in the butter or oil in a saucepan, until soft (2 to 3 minutes).

Wash and slice the mushrooms and pepper. Add them to the onion and fry gently, until soft (2 minutes). Add the peas, tomato soup, salt, pepper and garlic. Gently stir in the drained tuna and cook for a few minutes, until hot.

Strain the potatoes and mash (or drain and fork the rice). Spoon the potatoes or rice onto a plate, press into a ring and pour the tuna sauce into the middle.

Do not leave the remainder of the tuna fish or soup in the cans. Put them into covered containers or cups in the fridge and use within 24 hours.

COD IN CIDER

Serves 1

White wine can be used instead of cider for a taste of real luxury!

Preparation and cooking time: 30–35 minutes.

1 small onion
Slice of lemon (optional)
Salt and pepper
6–8 oz (175–225g) piece of cod (or 1–2 frozen fish steaks)
½ cup cider
½ slice of bread
½ oz (12g) butter

Grease an oven-proof dish.

Peel and slice the onion finely, and arrange half in the dish. Add a squeeze of lemon, salt and pepper. Put the fish on top, cover with the rest of the onion and another squeeze of lemon. Carefully pour in the cider.

Crumble the bread into crumbs and sprinkle on top of the fish. Dot with the butter.

Bake in a moderate oven (375°F/190°C/Gas Mark 5) until golden brown.

9
BEEF

Generally the most expensive meat, especially if you buy the cuts for grilling or roasting. However, stewing steak and mince are much cheaper and can be made into delicious dishes, but they do take longer to prepare and cook, as the cheaper the meat the longer the cooking time.

BEEF CASSEROLE OR STEW   *Serves 1*

You can use any mixture of stewing beef and vegetables to make a casserole (cooked in the oven) or a stew (simmered in a covered pan on top of the stove), so just combine the vegetables you like. If you want the meal to go further add extra vegetables. Some supermarkets sell small packets of mixed root vegetables especially for casseroles. These are useful as you only need a small amount of each vegetable. As this dish is easier to cook in larger quantities (smaller quantities tend to dry up during cooking) why not double or triple the ingredients to make enough for 2 or 3 friends?

Preparation and cooking time: 1 hour 50 minutes – 2 hours 50 minutes.

(For one person cook 4 oz stewing steak for 1 hour 30 minutes; for 2 people cook 8 oz stewing steak for about 2 hours; for larger quantities cook for 2 hours 30 minutes.)

1 onion
Little oil or fat (for frying)
4–6 oz (100–175g) stewing steak
1 oz (25g) kidney (optional) – ox kidney is usually stewed
1 stock cube
½ glass of wine or beer (optional)

Vegetables – any mixture according to taste:
1 carrot – peeled and sliced
·Piece of swede (or small turnip) – peeled thickly, cut into 1 in (2.5cm) chunks
Stick of celery – washed and cut into ½ in (1.25cm) lengths
½ green pepper – washed, with the core and seeds removed, cut into short strips
1 courgette (or small aubergine) – washed, cut into ½ in (1.25cm) pieces
1 potato – peeled, cut into 1 in (2.5cm) chunks
1 oz (25g) mushrooms – washed, sliced
Clove of garlic – peeled, finely chopped
1 cup of water
Pinch of herbs
Garlic powder
Salt and pepper

For thicker gravy:
**½ tsp gravy flavouring powder and 1 tsp flour (or cornflour)
 or 2 tsp gravy granules
A little wine, beer or water to mix**

Peel and slice the onion and fry it gently in a casserole or a saucepan, until soft (about 2 to 3 minutes).

Cut the meat into 1 in (2.5cm) pieces, (kidney in ½ in (1cm) pieces), add to the onion in the pan, and fry until brown (3 to 5 minutes) stirring so that it cooks evenly. Stir in the stock cube and add the wine or beer if used.

Prepare the vegetables but do no cut them too small. Add them to the meat. Stir in the water so that it just covers the meat and vegetables. Add the herbs, salt, pepper and garlic powder. Bring to the boil and stir well.

Then either put the covered casserole dish in the middle of a moderate oven (325°F/170°C/Gas Mark 3–4), or lower the heat and leave to simmer with the lid on the pan for 1½ hours to 2½ hours according to the amount of meat used, stirring occasionally. If it seems to be drying up, add a little more wine, beer or water.

If you like the gravy thicker, mix the gravy flavouring powder and flour (or cornflour) or gravy granules into a thin paste with a little wine, beer or water, and add to the gravy in the dish for the last half hour of cooking time.

Serve very hot, on its own, or with jacket spuds (cooked in the oven with the casserole), boiled potatoes or hot French bread and butter.

SHEPHERD'S PIE *Serves 1*

Forget about school dinners, this can be made into a really delicious meal! For a change, add a little grated cheese to the potato topping, and sprinkle the top with grated cheese before grilling. The meat mixture can also be served on its own, or with boiled or mashed potatoes and vegetables.

Preparation and cooking time: 55 minutes.

1 small onion
2 tsp oil or fat (for frying)
4 oz (100g) minced beef
Little wine or beer (if you have any opened)
2 tsp tomato ketchup (optional)
Shake of Worcester sauce (optional)
½ stock cube
½ cup water
2–3 potatoes
½ oz (12g) butter or margarine
1 tomato (optional)

Peel and chop the onion. Put the oil or fat in a saucepan, and fry the onion gently for 2 to 3 minutes, until soft. Add the minced meat, and continue to fry gently, stirring all the time, until the meat is brown (about 2 to 3 minutes). Add the wine or beer, and sauces, stock cube and water. Stir well. Bring to the boil, then reduce the heat and leave to simmer for 20 to 30 minutes, until the meat is tender.

Meanwhile, peel the potatoes, cut them into evenly-sized pieces, and cook in boiling, salted water for 15 to 20 minutes, until soft. Drain and mash them with a potato masher or fork. Add the butter and beat until creamy. Pour the meat mixture into an oven-proof dish, cover with the mashed potato and fork down smoothly. Dot the top with a little butter, top with a sliced tomato if liked, and grill under a hot grill for a minute or two, until golden brown, or put on the top shelf of a hot oven (400°F/200°C/Gas Mark 6) for 5 to 10 minutes, until it is brown on top.

INSTANT SHEPHERD'S PIE   *Serves 1*

This really is an 'instant' meal, but is made quite tasty by adding a dash of your favourite sauces to the meat.

Preparation and cooking time: 10 minutes.

1 small tin (7 oz/198g) minced steak (or stewing steak)

Optional sauces:
Tomato ketchup
Brown sauce
Worcester sauce
Soy sauce
Few drops of tabasco sauce

Garlic powder (optional)
Pinch of dried herbs (optional)
1 small packet instant mashed potatoes – use the amount specified in the instructions on the packet
½ oz (12g) butter or margarine
Hot water
1 oz (25g) grated cheese (optional)
1 tomato (optional)

Empty the meat into a saucepan and bring it gently to the boil, stirring well. Add your chosen sauces and garlic powder and herbs. Simmer for 2 to 3 minutes until really hot.

Make up the instant mashed potato as directed on the packet using the butter and hot water and add most of the grated cheese (saving a little for the top).

Pour the meat mixture into an oven-proof dish, top with the mashed potato, and sprinkle with the remainder of the cheese and/or sliced tomato if used. Dot with a little butter or margarine. Cook under a hot grill, until golden brown (2 to 3 minutes).

POTATO BOLOGNESE   *Serves 1*

For those of you who don't like pasta, or want a change from spaghetti. Use either traditional or quick Bolognese sauce.

Preparation and cooking time: 45 minutes (traditional)
or 25 minutes (quick).

Traditional Bolognese sauce (see page 158) or
   Quick Bolognese sauce (see page 159)
3–4 potatoes
Knob of butter
1 oz (25g) grated cheese (or Parmesan cheese)

TRADITIONAL METHOD

Prepare the Bolognese sauce and leave to simmer.

Peel and slice the potatoes thickly and cook in boiling, salted water for 10 minutes, until soft (see page 71).

Drain and mash the potatoes with the butter, beating them well. Pile them onto a hot dish, forming them into a border or 'nest'. Pour the Bolognese sauce into the potato nest.

Serve with grated or Parmesan cheese.

QUICK METHOD

Peel and cook the potatoes first, preparing the quick sauce while the potatoes are cooking. Then prepare the dish as above in the traditional method.

BEEF CURRY

Serves 1

A change from the Indian take-away. This is a medium-hot curry, and is easier to prepare for two or more people, as very small amounts tend to dry up during cooking. Why not try double the quantity?

Serve with plain boiled rice (see page 81), poppadums and some side dishes (see overleaf).

Preparation and cooking time: 1 hour 50 minutes – 2 hours 50 minutes.

(For one person cook 4 oz stewing beef for 1 hour 30 minutes; for 2 people cook 8 oz stewing beef for about 2 hours; for larger quantities cook for 2 hours 30 minutes.)

1 onion
4–6 oz (100–175g) stewing beef
Little cooking oil (for frying)
2 level tsp curry powder (more or less according to taste)
1 small apple (preferably a cooker)
1 tomato
½ stock cube and 1 cup (¼ pt/150ml) boiling water (or ½ a 295g can mulligatawny soup)
2 tsp sultanas
1 tsp sugar
2 tsp pickle or chutney

Peel and slice the onion. Cut the beef into 1 in (2.5cm) cubes.

Heat the oil in a medium-sized saucepan and fry the onion gently, to soften it, for 3 to 5 minutes. Add the beef and fry for a further 5 minutes, until the meat is browned. Sprinkle the curry powder over the meat, and stir for a few minutes over a medium heat.

Peel and chop the apple, wash and chop the tomato, and add both to the meat and continue frying for 3 to 4 minutes, stirring gently.

Dissolve the stock cube in 1 cup of boiling water and add the stock to the meat, or add the mulligatawny soup. Wash and drain the sultanas. Add them to the curry with the sugar and pickle or chutney. Stir well and simmer gently, with the lid on, stirring occasionally, for 1½ to 2½ hours (the longer time is needed for larger quantities) until the meat is tender.

Side Dishes for Curries
Salted nuts
Chopped green peppers
Plain yoghurt
Sliced onions
Sliced banana (sprinkle with lemon juice to keep it white)
Chopped apple (sprinkle with lemon juice to keep it white)
Chopped cucumber
Chopped, hard-boiled egg
Washed, drained sultanas
Mango chutney
Desiccated coconut

POPPADUMS

Great fun to cook. Buy a packet of Indian poppadums, on sale at large supermarkets.

Heat 3–4 tbsp cooking oil in a frying pan over a medium heat (enough to cover the base of the pan). When the oil is hot float a poppadum on top, and it will puff up immediately, only taking a few moments to cook. Remove it carefully and leave it to drain on kitchen paper while cooking the next poppadum. Do not let the fat get too hot, or it will get smoky and burn.

HOME-MADE BEEFBURGERS *Serves 1*

These are quite a change from the commercially-produced beefburgers. You can make them bun-sized or 'half pounders'. Buy a good quality mince, as finely chopped as possible.

Serve in soft bread rolls (these are traditionally lightly toasted on one side) with tomato or barbecue sauce, or with potatoes, vegetables or a salad.

Preparation and cooking time: 20–25 minutes according to size.

½ small onion
4–8 oz (125–225g) minced beef, according to appetite
Salt and pepper
Pinch of dried herbs
Worcester (or tabasco) sauce
Little beaten egg (or egg yolk)
Little oil (for frying)

Peel and finely chop the onion, and mix well in a bowl with the minced beef, using a fork. Mix in the salt, pepper, herbs and sauce and bind together with a little egg. The mixture should be wet enough so the ingredients mould together, but not soggy. Divide this into 2 portions, shape each into a ball, and then flatten into a circle, about ¾ in (2cm) thick.

Heat the oil in a frying pan over a medium heat. Put the beefburgers carefully in the pan, and fry for 10 to 15 minutes, according to size, turning occasionally to cook both sides. Do not have the heat too high, as the beefburgers need to cook right through to the middle without burning the outside.

BOEUF STROGANOFF   *Serves 2*

Absolutely delicious, rather expensive and very impressive if you have a special friend to dinner. Serve with plain boiled rice, noodles or new potatoes, and a salad.

Preparation and cooking time: 25 minutes.

1 cup plain boiled rice (or 2 cups noodles or 3–6 new potatoes)
8 oz (225g) fillet (or rump) steak
1 medium onion
1 oz (25g) butter (or little cooking oil)
4 oz (100g) mushrooms
1 small green pepper
Salt and pepper
Garlic powder
3–4 tbsp soured cream (or double cream or plain yoghurt)
Chopped parsley

Cook the rice, noodles or scrubbed new potatoes in boiling salted water. Cut the steak into thin strips: 2 in (5cm) long by ½ in (1cm) wide by ¼ in (0.5cm) thick. Peel and chop the onion finely and fry in half the oil or butter in a frying pan or wok, until soft (2 to 3 minutes). Wash and slice the mushrooms. Wash the pepper, remove its core and seeds, and cut it into strips. Add the mushrooms and the pepper to the frying pan and fry gently for a further 4 to 5 minutes.

Remove all the vegetables from the pan and place onto a plate. Melt the remaining butter or oil in the pan, then add the steak strips and fry for 3 to 4 minutes, turning frequently so that they cook evenly. Return the onion, pepper and mushrooms to the pan. Add the salt, pepper and garlic powder. Gently stir in the cream or yoghurt and mix well. Heat carefully until piping hot, but try not to let the sauce boil. Sprinkle with chopped parsley if you want it to look impressive. Drain the rice, noodles or potatoes and serve at once.

CHILLI CON CARNE *Serves 1*

This is another dish which is easier to make in slightly larger quantities than are given below, so if possible double the ingredients and cook for 2 people. You can use mince or stewing steak. If using raw kidney beans be very careful: they must be fast boiled in water for half an hour before using in this recipe, otherwise they could be poisonous.

Preparation and cooking time: 2 hours 55 minutes (if using stewing steak) 1 hour 25 minutes (if using mince).

1 small onion
1 clove of garlic (or little garlic powder)
Little cooking oil
½ oz (12g) butter
1 rasher of bacon (or bacon trimmings)
4 oz (100g) stewing steak (or minced beef)
1 tbsp tomato purée (or ketchup)
1 cup water
Salt and pepper
½ level tsp chilli powder
½ small (7.5 oz/213g size) can cooked red kidney beans or 4 oz (100g) pre-cooked kidney beans (boiled for half an hour in fast boiling water, then drained)
Few drops of tabasco sauce (optional)

Peel and chop the onion and garlic. Put the oil and butter into a saucepan. Add the onion and fry gently until soft (2 to 3 minutes). Cut the bacon into small pieces. Add the bacon and stewing steak (or mince) to the pan and fry until browned, stirring so that it cooks evenly. Add the tomato purée (or ketchup), water, salt, pepper and chilli powder. Bring to the boil. Cover, lower the heat and leave to simmer for 1 hour (if using mince) or for 2½ hours (if using stewing steak), stirring occasionally (adding a little extra water if it gets too dry). Add the kidney beans. Simmer for a further 10 minutes. Taste (but be careful not to burn your tongue) and add tabasco sauce if liked. Serve hot.

GRILLED (OR FRIED) STEAK   *Serves 1*

A very special treat! Cheaper 'tenderised' steak can be bought in the supermarket. This is often good value, as it cooks very much like the more expensive cuts. You can buy a smaller amount of steak and add sausages, lamb's kidneys or beefburgers to your meal. Grilled tomatoes and mushrooms are also tasty with steak (see below). Serve with jacket spuds, sauté potatoes, boiled potatoes, baked stuffed potatoes or bread rolls, and a salad or peas. Prepare the vegetables before cooking the meat, as steak is best eaten immediately it is ready. To cook the vegetables see Chapter 5. Grilling is the best way to cook steak, but it can be fried too.

CUTS OF BEEF TO CHOOSE

Minute
Very thin slices, good for a steak sandwich.

Rump
Good flavour, quite lean. Cut it into portions at least ¾ in (2cm) thick.

Sirloin
Very tender, with some fat. Cut as rump.

Fillet
Very tender, very expensive! Cut into even thicker portions 1–1½ in (2.5–3.75cm) thick so that it stays juicy during cooking.

Tournedos
Fillet steak tied into rounds by the butcher; very, very expensive.

Preparation time: 2–3 minutes.
Cooking time: see method.

Allow 6–8 oz (175–225g) steak per serving
A little cooking oil (or butter)

GRILLED

Heat the grill. Put the steak on the greased grid of the grill pan and brush or wipe it with the oil or butter. Cook on one side, then turn it over carefully (do not stab the meat). Brush or wipe the second side with the oil or butter and cook to suit your taste:

Minute steak: 1 minute cooking on each side.

'Rare' steak: 2–4 minutes each side, depending on thickness.

Medium steak: Cook as 'rare', then lower the heat for a further 3–4 minutes each side.

Well done steak: Cook as 'rare', then lower the heat for a further 4–5 minutes each side.

FRIED

Heat the frying pan gently. Put a little oil or fat in the pan. Add the steak, and cook over a medium-high heat, as for grilled steak above. Serve immediately with chosen vegetables.

Sausages and beefburgers can be cooked with the steak. Thick sausages may need a bit longer to cook than the steak, so put them under the grill or in the frying pan first, then add the steak. (See page 88.) Cut lamb's kidney in half lengthways, remove the fatty 'core', and grill or fry for 3 to 5 minutes, with the steak. Cut tomatoes in half and grill under the steak in the grill pan, or fry in the frying pan with the meat, for 3 to 5 minutes. Mushrooms are best cooked in the bottom of the grill pan with a little butter, with the meat juices dripping onto them, or they can be fried in the frying pan with the steak. They will take from 3 to 5 minutes, according to size.

10
CHICKEN

Fresh and frozen chicken (whole, chicken joints, boneless or fillets) are extremely good value for money. There is very little waste, as all the scraps can be eaten cold or used up in sandwiches or risotto.

Chicken must be thoroughly defrosted before you start cooking, by leaving the chicken on a plate at room temperature for several hours, according to the instructions on the packet. You can hurry the defrosting process by putting the nearly-thawed chicken in a bowl of cold (not hot) water to get rid of all the ice crystals. Chicken defrosted too quickly in hot water will be tough when cooked. If chicken is not completely thawed before cooking it may not cook right through and any bacteria present will not be destroyed and could make you ill.

Chicken must be cooked thoroughly too. The juices should run clear, not tinged with pink, when pierced with a knife at the thickest part of the joint.

There are also lots of delicious, ready-prepared chicken dishes available at supermarkets, both chilled and frozen. These must be defrosted and cooked strictly according to the instructions on the packet.

FRIED CHICKEN   *Serves 1*

A quick and easy dinner, served with new or sauté potatoes, peas or a green salad. It is also tasty when eaten with new bread rolls and butter.

Preparation and cooking time: 20–22 minutes plus defrosting time.

1 chicken breast or leg joint – 6–8 oz (175–225g) according to your appetite
Little oil and a knob of butter (for frying)

Defrost the chicken for several hours at room temperature according to the instructions on the packet. (See page 134.) Wash the chicken pieces and dry them on kitchen paper.

Heat the oil and butter in a frying pan over a moderate heat, add the chicken and fry it gently for 15 to 20 minutes, according to size, turning it occasionally so that it browns on both sides. If the chicken seems to be getting too brown, lower the heat, but continue cooking, as the chicken needs to cook right through. Remove from the pan, and drain on kitchen paper. Serve hot or cold.

CHICKEN WITH SWEETCORN   *Serves 2*

The sweetcorn and potato sauce turns fried chicken into a complete meal. Serve with rice or potatoes.

Preparation and cooking time: 25–30 minutes plus defrosting time.

**2 chicken breasts or leg joints – each joint 6–8 oz (175–225g)
    according to your appetite**
Little oil and knob of butter (for frying)
1 onion
1 can (10 oz/284g) new potatoes
½ can (11½ oz/329g size) sweetcorn
½ oz (12g) butter
2 tsp flour
1 cup (5 fl oz/150ml) milk
Salt and pepper

Defrost the chicken for several hours at room temperature. (See page 134.)

Fry the chicken in the oil and butter, turning occasionally, for 15 to 20 minutes, until cooked and golden brown (see page 135).

Make the sauce while the chicken is frying. Peel and slice the onion. Drain the potatoes and sweetcorn. Melt the butter in a saucepan over a moderate heat, and fry the onion gently for 2 to 3 minutes. Add the potatoes and cook for a further 5 minutes, stirring gently.

Add the sweetcorn and mix well. Stir in the flour, and cook for 2 to 3 minutes. Remove from the heat, and gradually add the milk. Return to the heat and bring to the boil, stirring until the sauce thickens. Simmer for a few minutes, stirring gently, trying not to break up the potatoes. Season the sauce with the salt and pepper. Put the chicken onto a warm serving dish, cover with the sauce and serve at once.

CHICKEN IN TOMATO AND MUSHROOM
SAUCE   *Serves 1*

Fried chicken served in a tasty sauce. This dish is good with boiled rice or potatoes which can be cooked while the chicken is frying.

Preparation and cooking time: 40 minutes plus defrosting time.

1 chicken breast or leg joint – 6–8 oz (175–225g) according to your appetite
Little oil and knob of butter (for frying)
½ small onion
2–3 mushrooms
½ stock cube
½ cup hot water
2 tsp tomato purée (or tomato ketchup)
Pinch of dried mixed herbs
Salt and pepper
Pinch of garlic powder

Defrost the chicken for several hours at room temperature. (See page 134.)

Heat the oil and butter in a frying pan over a moderate heat, and fry the chicken for 15 to 20 minutes, turning occasionally, until cooked through and golden brown (see page 135). Remove the chicken to a warm dish and keep hot.

Peel and chop the onion, put it into the oil in the frying pan and fry gently for 2 to 3 minutes, until soft. Wash and slice the mushrooms, and add to the onion. Dissolve the stock cube in the hot water, add to the onion in the pan, bring to the boil, stirring all the time, then reduce the heat and cook for a further 5 minutes. Add the tomato purée, herbs, seasoning, and garlic powder, and continue cooking for another 4 to 5 minutes – the sauce should now be thick and will coat the chicken. Pour the sauce over the chicken.

ROAST CHICKEN PIECES   *Serves 1*

A quick and economical roast dinner. The chicken pieces are cooked in a roasting tin in the oven in the same way as a whole roast chicken, and can be served with thyme and parsley stuffing, sausages, bread sauce, apple sauce, roast potatoes and vegetables to make a traditional roast dinner.

Preparation and cooking time: 35–45 minutes according to size (plus defrosting time).

Quarter (6–8 oz/175–225g) of a chicken (breast or leg) or 2 chicken pieces
2 tsp oil and ½ oz (12g) butter (for cooking)
Dried herbs (optional)
Cooking foil

Defrost the chicken thoroughly for several hours at room temperature. (See page 134.)

Heat the oven at 400°F/200°C/Gas Mark 6–7. Rub the chicken with the oil and dot with the butter. Sprinkle with herbs, if liked. Place in a well-greased roasting tin and cover with cooking foil.

Roast for 30 to 40 minutes, according to the size of the chicken pieces, until the juices run clear (not pink) when tested with a fork. (If still pink, cook for a few more minutes.) Remove the foil for the last 10 minutes of cooking time to brown the chicken. Chipolata sausages, roast potatoes and parsnips can be cooked round the chicken pieces. Remove the chicken, and the sausages, potatoes and parsnips (if used) from the tin, and keep warm. Use the juices left in the roasting tin to make the gravy (see page 173).

EASY CHICKEN CASSEROLE   *Serves 2*

Make this for 2 people, otherwise the sauce will dry up
before the chicken is cooked. It can be prepared very quickly
and popped into the oven. Put a couple of jacket potatoes to
cook in the oven with it, and you have a complete meal.

*Preparation and cooking time: 1 hour 10 minutes plus
defrosting time.*

**2 chicken breast or leg joints – each joint 6–8 oz (175–225g)
   according to your appetite**
Little oil (for frying)
4 oz (100–125g) can or frozen mixed vegetables
1 small can (10.4 oz/295g) condensed chicken soup
Salt and pepper
Garlic powder or paste (optional)

Defrost the chicken for several hours at room temperature.
(See page 134.) Heat the oil in a frying pan over a moderate
heat, and fry the chicken for 5 minutes, turning so that it
browns on all sides. Remove the chicken. Put it into a
casserole with the frozen vegetables. Heat the soup in the
pan with the chicken juices, adding the seasoning and garlic.
Pour this sauce over the chicken. Cover with a lid, and cook
for about an hour, until the chicken is tender, either in a
moderate oven (350°F/180°C/Gas Mark 4) or over a very low
heat on top of the stove.

CHICKEN CURRY   *Serves 1*

Defrost the chicken joint at room temperature. (See page
134.) Make the curry using the recipe given for beef curry
(on page 127), substituting the chicken joint for the stewing
beef. Chicken cooks more quickly than stewing beef, so the
curry need only be simmered for about an hour. Serve with
boiled rice (see page 81) and curry side dishes as suggested
on page 128.

HAWAIIAN CHICKEN   *Serves 1*

Cook half the tin of pineapple with the chicken, then eat the
rest for pudding, with ice-cream, cream or yoghurt. Serve the
Hawaiian chicken with new or sauté potatoes, or potato
castles, and green beans or peas.

*Preparation and cooking time: 40 minutes plus defrosting
time.*

1 chicken joint (6–8 oz/175–225g)
1 tsp oil and knob of butter (for cooking)
½ small can (7¾ oz/220g size) pineapple pieces, chunks or
  slices in syrup
1 tsp flour or cornflour
1 tsp soy sauce
1 tsp Worcester sauce

Defrost the chicken for several hours at room temperature
(see page 134).

  Heat the oil and butter in a frying pan, and fry the chicken
over a moderate heat for 10 minutes, turning occasionally so
that it browns on all sides. Remove from the pan for a few
minutes.

· Drain the pineapple, saving the syrup. Mix the flour (or
cornflour) into a smooth paste with a little of the syrup. Add
the remainder of the syrup and stir this liquid into the juices
in the frying pan, stirring until the sauce thickens. Return the
chicken to the pan, add the pineapple pieces, and pour the
soy sauce and Worcester sauce over the chicken. Stir well,
then lower the heat and simmer for 15 minutes, stirring
occasionally.

CHICKEN IN WINE
Serves 1

This can be made with a chicken joint on the bone, but is super made with boneless chicken breast or filleted turkey, according to your taste and pocket. Serve with new potatoes and peas.

Preparation and cooking time: 45–60 minutes plus defrosting time (chicken on the bone takes the longest time).

1 chicken joint (6–8 oz/175–225g), boneless chicken breast or
    slice of turkey fillet
1 small onion
1 stock cube – preferably chicken flavour
½ cup hot water
1 tsp oil and knob of butter
1 wine glass of white wine (or cider)
½ tsp herbs
Salt and pepper
1 tsp flour (or cornflour)

Defrost the chicken thoroughly for several hours at room temperature (see page 134). Peel and finely chop the onion. Dissolve the stock cube in the ½ cup of hot water. Heat the oil and butter over a moderate heat, in a casserole or thick saucepan, and fry the chicken gently for a few minutes, turning it so that it browns on all sides. Remove from the pan. Add the onion to the pan, and stir over the moderate heat for a few minutes to soften.

Pour most of the wine (or cider) onto the onion, stir well and allow to bubble for a minute. Return the chicken to the sauce. Stir in the stock, herbs, salt and pepper (according to taste). Cover the pan, and simmer very gently for 30–45 minutes, until the chicken is tender. Mix the flour with the rest of the wine (or cider) to make a smooth paste, and gradually stir this into the chicken sauce, until it has thickened a little. Serve hot.

LAMB COUNTER

11

LAMB

Leg and shoulder are the dearest joints of lamb, with leg costing more than shoulder. These are strictly 'special occasion' meals, and are explained under 'Sunday Lunch Dishes' in Chapter 14. Lamb chops (loin, chump and leg chops are the big ones; cutlets are the small ones) make a quickly-cooked, tasty meal, but are also quite expensive. Stewing lamb (middle and best end of lamb, scrag end and breast of lamb) is much cheaper. These cuts of lamb are stewed with the meat left on the bone (so you buy more weight of meat than you do with beef) but need long, slow cooking. They make really delicious meals fairly cheaply. Breast of lamb can be boned, stuffed, rolled and roasted, and makes a very cheap and tasty Sunday dinner.

LAMB CHOPS – GRILLED OR FRIED *Serves 1*

Choose lean chops, but remember that lamb is basically a fatty kind of meat, and the fat gives the meat a good flavour. Chump and loin chops are larger than cutlets. Very small cutlets are sold in some supermarkets as 'breakfast chops', so decide how hungry you are feeling when you choose your chop.

Sausages, lamb's kidney or beefburgers can be cooked with the chops. Grill or fry the sausages first as they take longer to cook than the lamb. Tomatoes, mushrooms, new potatoes and peas go well with it too. Traditionally mint sauce (see page 177), mint jelly, redcurrant jelly or onion sauce (see page 175) are served with lamb.

Preparation and cooking time: 12–17 minutes.

1 chump or loin chop or 1–2 lamb cutlets
Little oil

GRILLED

Heat the grill. Brush or rub both sides of the chop with a smear of the oil. Place the chop on the greased grid of the grill pan and grill for 8 to 10 minutes, according to its size and your taste, turning the meat so that it browns evenly on both sides. Lamb is traditionally served pink and underdone in the middle, and brown and crispy on the outside, but cook the chops how you like them.

FRIED

Heat a little oil in a frying pan over a medium heat. Put the chops in the pan and fry, turning several times, for 8 to 10 minutes, until the chops are brown and crispy and cooked according to taste.

OVEN CHOP   *Serves 1*

A tasty dinner, served with a jacket potato which can cook in the oven with the casserole. This dish is equally good made with a pork chop.

Preparation and cooking time: 50–55 minutes.

1 small onion
3–4 mushrooms
½ tbsp oil (for frying)
1 chump or loin chop
½ small (8 oz/230g size) can tomatoes
Salt and pepper
Pinch of herbs

Peel and slice the onion. Wash and slice the mushrooms. Heat the oil in a frying pan over a medium heat. Fry the onion for 3 to 4 minutes to soften it. Add the chop to the pan, and cook on both sides for a few minutes, to brown. Add the mushrooms and cook for another minute. Put the chop into a casserole or oven-proof dish and pour the onion and mushrooms on the top.

Heat the tomatoes in the frying pan with the meat juices. Add these to the casserole, with the salt, pepper and herbs. Cover with a lid or cooking foil. Bake in a hot oven (400°F/200°C/Gas Mark 6) for 45 minutes, removing the lid for the last 15 minutes, to reduce the sauce to make it thicker.

If serving with a jacket potato, scrub and prick the potato, and cook it in boiling water for 10 minutes. Drain the potato. Lift it out carefully and put it into the oven to bake with the casserole for 30 to 45 minutes, according to size.

IRISH STEW WITH DUMPLINGS · *Serves 2*

This should satisfy even the hungriest Irishman. It makes a substantial meal on its own but can be served with extra potatoes or bread rolls, and a green vegetable.

Preparation and cooking time: 2 hours 20 minutes – 2 hours 50 minutes.

¾–1 lb (350–450g) middle neck or scrag end of lamb
2 onions
2 carrots
1–2 potatoes
1 tbsp oil (for frying)
1 stock cube
2–3 cups boiling water
½ tsp mixed herbs
Salt and pepper

For the dumplings:
4 oz (100g/4 heaped tbsp) self-raising flour
Salt and pepper
2 oz (50g/2 tbsp) shredded suet

For thicker gravy:
1 tbsp gravy granules
   or 2 tsp flour (or cornflour) and 1 tsp gravy flavouring powder
1 tbsp cold water, sherry, beer or wine

Cut the lamb into pieces suitable for serving. Trim off any large pieces of fat. Peel and slice the onions and carrots. Peel the potatoes and cut them into chunks.

Heat the oil in a large saucepan. Fry the onion and carrots over a medium heat for 3–4 minutes, stirring occasionally. Add the pieces of meat and fry for a further 2–3 minutes, trying to brown all the sides of the meat. Add the potato chunks. Dissolve the stock cube in 1 cup of boiling water, and pour it over the meat, adding enough extra water to cover the meat and vegetables. Add the herbs, salt and pepper. Stir gently and bring back to the boil, then reduce the heat and simmer over a very low heat for 1½ hours, with the lid on.

Make the dumplings by mixing together the self-raising flour, salt, pepper and suet. Add just enough cold water to make a dough – like very soft putty or plasticine. Divide this into 4 pieces and shape into dumplings. Carefully lower the dumplings into the stew and cook for a further 25–30 minutes, making sure the liquid is boiling gently all the time (keep the lid on the pan as much as possible, without letting it boil over).

If the gravy needs to be thicker, mix the gravy granules or the flour (or cornflour) and gravy flavouring powder into a smooth paste with a little cold water, sherry, wine or beer. Stir it into the stew, stirring well while the gravy thickens.

REAL LANCASHIRE HOT POT   *Serves 2*

This dish may also be eaten by Yorkshiremen, and those from other lesser counties!

Preparation and cooking time: 2 hours 15 minutes.

12–16 oz (350–450g) best end or middle neck of lamb
1 lamb's kidney
2 onions
1 carrot
1 very small turnip (optional)
3 or 4 potatoes, total weight 1 lb (450g)
1 tbsp oil (for frying)
1 stock cube
2 cups (½ pt/300ml) approx. boiling water
2 tsp flour or cornflour
Salt and pepper
Pinch of dried herbs
Knob of butter

Cut the lamb into pieces suitable for serving. Skin the kidney, cut in half lengthways, cut out the white fatty core and cut the kidney into pieces. Peel and slice the onions, carrot and turnip (if used). Peel and slice the potatoes and cut into thick slices (½ in/1.25cm).

Heat the oil in a frying pan, and brown the lamb pieces, over a medium heat, turning them so that they cook on all sides. Brown the kidney, and arrange all the meat in a casserole or oven-proof dish. Fry the onion in the pan for 3 to 4 minutes, to soften it. Add the sliced carrot and turnip (if used) and continue to fry gently, stirring all the time, for a further 3 minutes.

Add the vegetables to the meat in the casserole. Dissolve the stock cube in 2 cups of boiling water. Sprinkle the flour over the remaining juices in the frying pan, and stir. Gradually stir in the stock, stirring hard to make a smooth gravy and adding the salt, pepper and herbs. Pour the gravy over the meat in the casserole, to cover the meat and vegetables.

Then cover the meat with a thick layer of potato slices, placing them so that they overlap and form a thick crust. Dot with the butter. Cover with a lid or piece of tight-fitting foil, and cook in a moderate oven (325°F/170°C/Gas Mark 3–4) for 1½–2 hours, removing the lid for the last half hour of cooking time, to brown the top. If the top does not seem to be getting crispy enough, either increase the oven heat to 400°F/200°C/Gas Mark 6–7, or pop the casserole dish under a hot grill for a few minutes.

If you have to cook the casserole on top of the stove because an oven is not available, simmer the casserole very gently for 1½ to 2 hours, then brown the potato topping under the grill as described above.

12
PORK

Pork is quite a 'good buy', being generally cheaper than beef or the better cuts of lamb. It is a rich meat, so is filling too. It is important that pork is cooked thoroughly; it is better over-cooked than underdone, and must never, ever, be served pink, as rare pork can make you ill with food poisoning. The meat must look pale-coloured, right through. Cold roast pork should not be re-heated; eat it cold if you have any left over. If you are heating cooked pork dishes in a sauce, make sure this pork is really re-cooked right through to kill any bacteria, not just warmed up. Leg, shoulder and loin of pork are the more expensive cuts, and make far too much for one person. Details of how to cook them are given under 'Sunday Lunch Dishes', Chapter 14. Chops, spare ribs and belly are more suitable and economical for small quantities, so here are some ideas!

PORK CHOP – GRILLED OR FRIED   *Serves 1*

Quick and easy, and not too expensive. Tastes good with
sauté potatoes, a grilled or fried tomato, pineapple rings or a
spoonful of apple sauce. Pork is better grilled, as it can be a
bit fatty, but frying is quite acceptable if you don't have a
grill. Whichever way you choose to cook it, make sure it is
cooked thoroughly, the juices must run clear, not pink, and
the meat must be pale-coloured right through. Undercooked
pork can make you ill, so do cook it thoroughly.

Preparation and cooking time: 14–16 minutes.

1 pork chop
Little oil or butter
½ tsp dried mixed herbs (or dried sage)
1 tomato (or 1–2 pineapple rings or 1 tbsp apple sauce)
Cooked, cold, boiled potatoes to sauté

Heat the grill or heat a frying pan over a moderate heat with
a smear of oil. Rub both sides of the chop with the oil or
butter, sprinkle with the herbs. Either put the chop under the
hot grill, turning frequently, until brown and crispy, 12 to 15
minutes (lowering the heat if the chop starts getting too
brown); or, put the chop into the hot frying pan and fry over
a moderate heat for 12 to 15 minutes, turning frequently,
until brown and cooked thoroughly.

ACCOMPANIMENTS

Cut the tomato in half, dot with butter and put under the grill
or into the frying pan for the last 3 to 4 minutes of cooking
time; or, put the pineapple slices on top of the chop under
the grill or in the frying pan for 1 to 2 minutes to warm
slightly; or, prepare the apple sauce in advance from the
recipe on page 176 (or use apple sauce from a jar or can from
the supermarket). Fry the sauté potatoes while the chop is
cooking (see page 73). If you have only one frying pan you
can cook them in the pan with the chop.

MUSTARD-GLAZED PORK CHOP   *Serves 1*

A tangy hot grilled chop. Serve with new or sauté potatoes and a green vegetable.

Preparation and cooking time: 17–20 minutes.

1 tsp mustard
1 tsp brown sugar
Knob of butter
1 pork chop

Heat the grill.

Mix the mustard, sugar and small knob of butter together in a cup. Spread this mixture over both sides of the chop.

Cook the chop under the hot grill, turning frequently, until brown and crispy (12 to 15 minutes). Lower the heat if the chop gets too brown too quickly. The pork must be cooked right through. The juices must run clear not pink, and the meat must be pale-coloured right through. Under-cooked pork can make you ill, so do cook it thoroughly.

PORK CHOP IN CIDER   *Serves 1*

Absolutely delicious and the smell of the meal cooking gives you a real appetite.

Preparation and cooking time: 1 hour.

1 tsp cooking oil
½ oz (12g) butter
1 pork chop (preferably a loin chop) or 1 pork steak
1 small onion
1 small cooking apple (you can use an eating apple if necessary)
½–1 cup cider
Salt and pepper
Pinch of dried herbs
1 tbsp cream (you can use plain yoghurt or soured cream)

Heat the oil and butter in a frying pan. Fry both sides of the chop until brown (4 to 5 minutes). Place it in a casserole or an oven-proof dish.

Peel and slice the onion, peel and chop the apple, and fry them together in the frying pan, stirring frequently (4 to 5 minutes) until the onion is soft. Add to the meat in the casserole. Pour enough cider into the casserole so that it covers the meat. Add the salt, pepper and herbs.

Cover, with a lid or piece of foil, and bake in a moderate oven (350°F/180°C/Gas Mark 4–5) for approximately 45 minutes. (If you don't have an oven, this can be cooked very, very, gently in a saucepan on top of the stove for 45 minutes.) Stir in the cream and serve at once.

PORK IN A PACKET *Serves 1*

An easy way of cooking pork, without much washing up!

Preparation and cooking time: 1 hour.

1–2 tbsp uncooked long grain rice (or 3 tbsp cold cooked rice)
2 tbsp canned or frozen sweetcorn
2 tbsp frozen peas
1 spring onion (or ½ small onion)
Salt and pepper
Cooking oil
Butter (for greasing the foil)
1 pork chop
1 tsp soy (or Worcester) sauce
1 tbsp cider, white wine or beer

Cook the raw rice in boiling, salted water for 8 to 10 minutes, until just soft. Add the frozen sweetcorn and peas for the last 2 minutes and cook with the rice, or cook by themselves if you are using up cooked rice. (Canned sweetcorn does not need cooking and can be used straight from the can.)

Drain well. Wash and chop the spring onion or peel and chop the onion. Add the onion to the rice mixture, mix well and season with salt and pepper.

Cut a square of cooking foil, large enough to wrap the chop loosely. Grease the foil with the butter, and put the chop in the centre of the foil. Sprinkle with soy or Worcester sauce. Top with the rice mixture and moisten with the cider, wine or beer. Wrap the foil around the chop into a parcel, and put carefully onto a baking tin or dish. Bake in a moderate oven (350°F/180°C/Gas Mark 4–5) for 40 minutes.

CRUNCHY FRIED PORK
Serves 1

Shoulder and belly pork are cheap and tasty. Try to buy thin slices of meat for this dish and flatten them by banging them with a rolling pin. (If you don't have one, use an unopened can of beans etc., wrapped in a polythene bag, to stamp the slices flat.) A crisp green salad or a fresh tomato can accompany this dish.

Preparation and cooking time: 30 minutes.

1–2 potatoes (you can use up cooked potatoes if you have them)
4–6 oz (100–175g/1 or 2 slices) belly or shoulder pork
½ beaten egg (use the rest in scrambled egg)
1 tbsp packet sage and onion stuffing (or 1 tbsp porridge oats)
1 tbsp oil (for frying)
1 onion

Peel the potatoes, cut them in quarters and cook in boiling salted water for 15 minutes, until soft.

Flatten the pork as best you can and, if the pieces are large, cut them into portions. Beat the egg. Dip the pork pieces into the egg, and then toss them in the dry stuffing or porridge oats to coat the meat thoroughly.

Heat the oil in a frying pan. Put the pork pieces carefully into the hot fat and fry both sides of the pork over a medium heat, until brown and cooked right through (about 15 minutes). Put the pork onto a hot dish and keep warm.

Drain the potato when cooked. Cut into dice. Peel and chop the onion and cook in the fat in the frying pan. Add the diced potato and continue cooking until just turning brown and crispy, stirring occasionally. Sprinkle the onion and potatoes over the meat, and serve hot.

SPARE RIBS *Serves 1*

Cheap and cheerful. Messy but fun to eat, and filling if you serve with a large jacket potato and plenty of butter. You'll need finger bowls and lots of paper napkins!

Preparation and cooking time: 1 hour 30 minutes – 1 hour 45 minutes.

12–16 oz (350–450g) Chinese-style spare ribs
1 small clove of garlic (or ¼ tsp garlic powder)
1 tbsp soy sauce
1 tsp orange marmalade
1 small onion
Salt and pepper
½ stock cube
½ cup boiling water
1 tsp vinegar

Heat the grill. Put the ribs in the grill pan and brown them under the grill, turning frequently, to seal in the juices. If you don't have a grill, brown the ribs in a frying pan, with a little oil or butter, over a medium heat, for 2 to 3 minutes, turning often. Peel and crush the garlic clove.

Mix the soy sauce, marmalade and garlic, and spread over the ribs. Peel and slice the onion. Put the onion in a casserole or oven-proof dish. Place the ribs on top and season with salt and pepper.

Dissolve the stock cube in ½ cup of boiling water, add the vinegar and pour it all over the ribs. Cover and cook in a hot oven (400°F/200°C/Gas Mark 6–7) for 1¼ to 1½ hours (the longer time for the larger amount). Remove the lid for the last 20 minutes to allow the meat to become crisp. The sauce should be sticky when cooked. The jacket potato can be cooked in the oven with the casserole (see page 73).

13
PASTA

There are numerous shapes of pasta, but they are all cooked in the same way, and most of the different shapes are interchangeable in most recipes, with the exception of the lasagne and cannelloni types.

Spaghetti
Available in various lengths and thicknesses.

Tagliatelle and other Noodle varieties
Sold in strands and bunches.

Fancy shapes
Shells, bows, etc.

Macaroni types
Thicker tubular shapes.

Lasagne
Large flat sheets.

Cannelloni
Usually filled with a tasty stuffing.

Most makes of pasta have the cooking instructions on the packet, and the best advice is to follow these carefully.

Allow approximately 1 cup (3 oz/75g) pasta per serving.

Pasta must be cooked in a large pan of boiling, salted water, with a few drops of cooking oil added to the water to help stop the pasta sticking. Long spaghetti is stood in the pan and pushed down gradually as it softens. Let the water come to the boil, then lower the heat and leave to simmer (without the lid or it will boil over) for 8 to 10 minutes until the pasta is just cooked (*al dente*). Drain well, in a colander preferably, otherwise you risk losing the pasta down the sink. Serve at once.

MACARONI CHEESE　　　　　　　*Serves 1*

This is traditionally made with the thick, tubular macaroni pasta, but it is equally good made with spaghetti or pasta shapes, shells, bows, etc.

Preparation and cooking time: 30 minutes.

1 cup (3 oz/75g) macaroni or chosen pasta (uncooked)
Pinch of salt
½ tsp cooking oil

For the cheese sauce (or use packet sauce mix):
2 oz (50–75g) cheese
2 tsp flour or cornflour

1 cup (¼ pt/150ml) milk
½ oz (12g) butter
Salt, pepper, and mustard
Tomato (optional)

For the topping
1 oz (25g) grated cheese

Heat the oven (400°F/200°C/Gas Mark 6). Cook the macaroni or pasta in a large saucepan of boiling water, with a
pinch of salt and a few drops of cooking oil, for 10 to 15
minutes, until just cooked (*al dente*).

While the macaroni is cooking, make the cheese sauce
either according to the instructions on the packet or by using
the following method. Grate the cheese, put the cornflour or
flour in a small basin and mix it into paste with a little of the
milk. Bring the rest of the milk to the boil in a small pan,
then pour it into the flour mixture, stirring all the time. Pour
the mixture back into the pan, return to the heat and bring
back to the boil, stirring all the time until the sauce thickens.
Beat in the butter, salt, pepper, pinch of mustard and the
grated cheese.

Drain the macaroni well, and put it into a greased, oven-
proof dish. Pour the cheese over the macaroni, and mix
slightly. Sprinkle the rest of the cheese on top. Put into the
hot oven for 10 minutes, until the cheese is crisp and
bubbling, and the macaroni is hot.

This dish can be topped with sliced, fresh tomato and
served with a salad. The top can be browned under the grill
instead of in the oven, provided the sauce and macaroni are
hot when mixed.

TRADITIONAL BOLOGNESE SAUCE   *Serves 1*

This thick meaty sauce can be used with spaghetti, pasta shapes, lasagne or even mashed potato, for a cheap and cheerful dinner.

Preparation and cooking time: 45 minutes.

1 small onion
½ carrot (optional)
½ rasher of bacon (optional)
Clove of garlic or pinch of garlic powder (optional)
2 tsp oil or a little fat (for frying)
3–4 oz (75–100g) minced beef
½ small can (8 oz/230g size) tomatoes or 2 fresh tomatoes
2 tsp tomato purée or tomato ketchup
½ beef stock cube and ½ cup water or ½ small tin
**   (10.4 oz/295g size) of tomato soup**
Pinch of salt and pepper
Pinch of sugar
Pinch of dried herbs

Peel and chop the onion. Peel and chop or grate the carrot. Chop the bacon. Peel, chop and crush the garlic clove.

· Fry the onion and bacon gently in the oil or fat in a saucepan, stirring until the onion is soft (2 to 3 minutes). Add the minced beef and continue cooking, stirring until it is lightly browned. Add the carrot, tinned tomatoes (or chopped fresh ones), tomato purée (or ketchup), stock cube and water (or the soup) stirring well. Add the salt, pepper, sugar and herbs.

Bring to the boil, then lower the heat and simmer, stirring occasionally, for 20 to 30 minutes, until the meat is tender.

QUICK BOLOGNESE SAUCE *Serves 1*

Very fast and easy to prepare. Use instead of Bolognese sauce made with fresh minced beef.

Preparation and cooking time: 10 minutes.

1 small tin (7 oz/198g) minced steak
1 or 2 tomatoes (tinned or fresh)
2 tsp tomato purée (or tomato ketchup)
Pinch of garlic powder (optional)
Pinch of salt and pepper
Pinch of sugar
½ tsp dried herbs

Empty the minced steak into a saucepan. Chop the tinned or fresh tomatoes, add to the beef, with the tomato purée (or ketchup), garlic powder, salt, pepper, sugar and herbs. Bring gently to the boil, stirring well, then lower the heat and simmer for 5 minutes, stirring occasionally. Use as traditional Bolognese sauce.

SPAGHETTI BOLOGNESE   *Serves 1*

Grated Cheddar cheese can be used instead of Parmesan, but a drum of Parmesan keeps for ages in the fridge and goes a long way.

Preparation and cooking time: 25–55 minutes.

Traditional Bolognese Sauce (see page 158) or Quick Bolognese Sauce (see page 159)
3 oz (75g) spaghetti (or 1 cup pasta shells, bows, etc)
½ tsp cooking oil
2 tsp Parmesan cheese (or 1 oz/25g grated Cheddar cheese)

Prepare the Bolognese sauce.

Cook the spaghetti or chosen pasta in a pan of boiling, salted water with ½ tsp cooking oil for 10 to 12 minutes. (If you want to have long spaghetti, stand the bundle of spaghetti in the boiling water and, as it softens, coil it round into the water without breaking.)

Drain the spaghetti and put it onto a hot plate. Pour the sauce into the centre of the spaghetti and sprinkle the cheese on the top. Serve at once.

SPAGHETTI PORK SAVOURY *Serves 1*

Belly pork is one of the cheapest cuts of meat you can buy.

Preparation and cooking time: 30 minutes.

1 generous cup (3 oz/75g) pasta – spaghetti, shells, noodles,
   etc.
Little cooking oil
2 oz (50g/1–2 slices) belly pork
1 onion
2 fresh tomatoes (or 1 small tin (8 oz/230g) tomatoes)
1 oz (25g) Cheddar cheese (or a little Parmesan)

Cook the chosen pasta in a large saucepan of boiling, salted water, with a few drops of cooking oil, for 10 to 12 minutes. Drain and keep hot. Meanwhile, cut the pork into tiny strips, discarding any rind and gristly bits. Peel and chop the onion and chop the fresh tomatoes (if used).

Heat some oil in a frying pan. Add the onion and fry for a few minutes to soften it. Add the pork strips and fry, stirring well, until browned. Add the tomato pieces or tinned tomatoes (not the juice) and stir well.

Cook over a low heat for another 10 minutes, stirring to break up the tomatoes, making a thick, saucy mixture. Grate the cheese. Pour the hot sauce over the spaghetti, and serve at once, sprinkled with the grated cheese.

QUICK LASAGNE
Serves 1

For this recipe you can use the traditional Bolognese sauce
(page 158), or else make it up using the first four ingredients
listed here. Serve with a green salad.

Preparation and cooking time: 25–30 minutes.

Small tin minced steak (7 oz/198g)
2 tsp tomato purée or tomato ketchup
Pinch of garlic powder
Salt and pepper
3–4 sheets (2 oz/50g) instant lasagne – plain or verdi
½ can (10.4 oz/295g size) condensed chicken (or mushroom)
soup mixed with milk or water (enough to fill ¼ of the soup
can)
1 oz (25g) cheese – grated or thinly sliced

Put the canned meat into a small saucepan with the tomato
purée, garlic, salt and pepper, or put the Bolognese sauce in
a pan, and heat gently for 3 to 5 minutes, stirring well, to
make a runny sauce (add a little water if needed).

Grease an oven-proof dish – the square foil dishes are
excellent for one portion. Put layers of the meat sauce,
lasagne sheets and the soup in the dish, ending with a layer of
soup. Make sure the lasagne is completely covered with the
sauce. Top with the grated or thinly-sliced cheese. Bake for
15 to 20 minutes in an oven (375°F/190°C/Gas Mark 5–6)
until the cheese is golden and bubbling.

CHEESY NOODLES
Serves 1

A cheap dish for using up the contents of the cupboard or fridge. Serve with a piece of cheese, tomato or a salad.

Preparation and cooking time: 15 minutes.

1 cup (3 oz/75g) uncooked noodles
1 tsp oil
2 oz (50g) cheese
1 oz (25g) butter
Salt and pepper

Cook the noodles in a large saucepan of boiling, salted water with 1 tsp cooking oil, until just soft (about 7 to 10 minutes).

Grate the cheese, or chop it finely into very small cubes.

Drain the noodles, return to the hot, dry pan and shake for a moment in the pan over the heat, to dry them and keep them hot. Remove from the heat and stir in the cheese and the butter. Season with the salt and pepper and pile onto a hot dish. Serve at once.

14
'SUNDAY LUNCH'
DISHES

This chapter shows simply and clearly how to cook the traditional Sunday lunch: how to roast beef, chicken, lamb and pork. For those who don't eat meat, I've included a recipe for a Nut Roast. At the end of the chapter, there are also recipes on how to make gravy and all the other different sauces that accompany the various meats. All the traditional 'Sunday Lunch' recipes are for several people – according to the size of joint you buy – which is useful when you have weekend visitors.

ROAST BEEF
It is best if several people can share a joint, as a very small joint is not an economical buy, for it tends to shrink up

during cooking. Therefore you get better value with a larger joint which should turn out moist and delicious.

JOINTS TO CHOOSE FOR ROASTING:
Topside
Lean.

Sirloin
Delicious, but it does have a fair amount of fat around the lean meat.

Rolled Rib
May be a little cheaper than sirloin.

Choose a joint of beef that looks appetising with clear bright red lean meat and firm pale-cream fat. A good joint must have a little fat with it, or it will be too dry when roasted.

Make sure you know the weight of the joint you buy, as cooking time depends on the weight. *You should allow approximately 6 oz (175g) uncooked weight of beef per person*, so a joint weighing 2½–3 lb (1–1.5kg) should provide 6 to 8 helpings (remember you can save some cold meat for dinner next day). For underdone 'rare' beef allow 15 minutes per lb (450g) plus an extra 15 minutes. For medium-done beef allow 20 minutes per lb (450g) plus an extra 20 minutes. Remember that a small joint will cook through quicker, as it is not so thick as a big joint, so allow slightly less time.

Serve beef with Yorkshire pudding, horseradish sauce, gravy, roast potatoes and assorted vegetables or a green salad.

Place the joint in a greased roasting tin, with a little lard, dripping, margarine or oil on top. The joint, or the whole tin, may be covered with foil, to help keep the meat moist. Roast in a hot oven (400°F/200°C/Gas Mark 6–7) for the appropriate time (as explained above). Test that the meat is cooked by stabbing it with a fork or vegetable knife, and note the colour of the juices that run out: the redder the juice the more rare the meat. When the meat is cooked, lift it out carefully onto a hot plate and make the gravy (see page 173).

For the roast potatoes: calculate when the joint will be ready and allow the potatoes 45 to 60 minutes roasting time, according to size. They can be roasted around the joint, or in a separate tin in the oven. (See page 72.)

YORKSHIRE PUDDING

Individual Yorkshire puddings are baked in patty (bun) tins, but a larger pudding can be cooked in any baking tin (not one with a loose base!), but they do not cook very well in a pyrex-type dish.

Preparation and cooking time: 25 minutes (small)
40–45 minutes (large).

4 heaped tbsp PLAIN flour
Pinch of salt
1 egg
2 cups (½ pt/300ml) milk
Little oil or fat

Put the flour and salt in a basin (use a clean saucepan if you do not have a large basin). Add the egg and beat into the flour, gradually adding the milk, and beating to make a smooth batter. (The easiest way of doing this is with a hand or electric mixer, but with a bit more effort you get just as good a result using a whisk, a wooden spoon or even a fork.) Beat well.

Put the tins, with the fat in, on the top shelf of the oven (400°F/200°C/Gas Mark 6–7) for a few minutes to get hot. Give the batter a final whisk, and pour it into the tins. Bake until firm and golden brown. Try not to open the oven door for the first 10 minutes so that the puds rise well. If you want meat and puds ready together, start cooking the puds 25 minutes before the meat is ready for small puds, 40–45 minutes before for large puds.

ROAST CHICKEN

It may sound odd, but larger chickens are far more economical: you get more meat and less bone for your money, so it's worth sharing a chicken between several people, and keeping some cold for the next day (keep it in the fridge and don't keep it too long). The scrappy bits left on the carcass can be chopped up and used to make a risotto.

Before cooking a frozen chicken, make sure the chicken is completely defrosted by leaving it out at room temperature for several hours according to the instructions on the wrapper. It can be soaked in cold (not hot) water to get rid of the last bits of ice and hurry the thawing process but do not try to thaw it in hot water as the chicken will be tough when cooked. (See page 134.)

A 2–2½ lb (900–1100g) chicken will serve 2 to 3 people, while a 3–4 lb (1350–1800g) chicken will serve 4 to 6 people, according to appetite. Make sure you know the weight of the bird as cooking time depends on the weight. Allow 20 minutes per lb (450g) plus 20 minutes extra. Very small chickens (2–2½ lb/900–1100g) may only need 15 minutes per lb (450g) plus 15 minutes extra.

Chicken is traditionally served with chipolata sausages, thyme and parsley stuffing and bread sauce. We like apple sauce or cranberry sauce with it as well. Roast potatoes, parsnips, carrots and sprouts are tasty with chicken in the winter, while new potatoes and peas make a good summer dinner.

1 chicken (completely defrosted)
Small potato (optional)
Oil and butter (for roasting)
Cooking foil

Heat the oven (400°F/200°C/Gas Mark 6–7). Rinse the chicken in cold water and dry with kitchen paper. It is now thought best to roast chicken without putting stuffing inside. The stuffing sometimes causes the meat not to be thoroughly cooked. If you are making stuffing, cook it separately in a greased dish, according to the instructions on the packet (see page 177), or only put a little inside the chicken. I sometimes put a small, peeled raw potato inside the chicken as the steam from the potato keeps the chicken moist.

Spread the butter and oil liberally over the chicken (you can cover the breast and legs with butter papers if you have any) and either wrap the chicken loosely in foil and put it into a tin, or put it into a greased roasting tin and cover the tin with foil. Put the chicken in the tin into the hot oven. Calculate the cooking time so that the rest of the dinner is ready at the same time.

Sausages, roast potatoes and parsnips can be cooked round the chicken or in a separate roasting tin. Sausages will take 20 to 30 minutes; potatoes and parsnips about 45 minutes to 1 hour.

Remove or open the foil for the last 15 minutes of cooking time, to brown the chicken. Test that the chicken is cooked by prodding it with a pointed knife or fork in the thickest part, inside the thigh. The juices should run clear; if they are still pink, cook for a little longer. Remove the chicken carefully onto a hot plate, and use the juices in the tin to make the gravy. (See page 173.)

ROAST LAMB

Leg and shoulder are both expensive joints. Shoulder is cheaper than leg, but tends to be more fatty. These joints are usually sold on the bone, so you have to allow more weight of meat for each person than you do with beef. However, trying to carve a shoulder of lamb can provide quite an entertaining cabaret act! *Allow at least 8 oz (225g) per serving*; so a joint weighing 2¼–2½ lb (about 1kg) should serve 4 people adequately.

Stuffed breast of lamb is a far more economical joint and makes a cheap Sunday dinner. A large breast of lamb will serve at least 2 generous helpings. The traditional accompaniments for lamb are mint sauce, mint jelly, redcurrant jelly or onion sauce. Serve with roast potatoes, parsnips or other vegetables.

ROAST LEG OR SHOULDER OF LAMB

You don't have to buy a whole leg or shoulder; half legs and shoulders, or a piece of a very large joint can be bought. Make sure you know the weight of the meat you buy as cooking time depends on the weight. *Allow 20 minutes per lb (450g) plus an extra 20 minutes.*

Joint of leg or shoulder of lamb
Oil or dripping (for roasting)
2–3 cloves of garlic (optional)
2–3 sprigs of rosemary (optional)

Heat the oven (400°F/200°C/Gas Mark 6–7). Place the joint in a roasting tin, with a little oil or dripping. If you like the flavour of garlic, you can insert 1 or 2 peeled cloves under the skin of the meat, near the bone, to impart a garlic flavour to the meat, but lamb has a lovely flavour so this is not really necessary. Rosemary sprigs can be used in the same way.

Cover the joint, or the whole tin, with cooking foil. (This helps to stop the meat shrivelling up.) Roast it in the hot oven for the calculated time, removing the foil for the last 20 to 30 minutes of the cooking time, to brown the meat, if it is a bit pale under the foil. Roast potatoes and parsnips can be cooked with the joint for the last hour of cooking time.

Test that the lamb is cooked at the end of the cooking time by stabbing it with a fork or vegetable knife. Lamb is traditionally served pink in the middle, but many people prefer it cooked more; it is entirely a matter of personal preference. The meat juices should run slightly tinged with pink for underdone lamb, and clear when the lamb is better cooked. When the meat is cooked satisfactorily, lift it carefully onto a hot plate and make the gravy. Serve with mint sauce.

ROAST STUFFED BREAST OF LAMB

An extremely economical roast. A large breast of lamb will serve 2 people and makes a very cheap roast dinner. Try to buy boned meat or ask the butcher to bone it for you. If you purchase one with the bones in, it is fairly easy to remove them yourself with a sharp knife, but be careful not to bone your fingers at the same time!

Serve with gravy, mint sauce, roast potatoes and parsnips, or other vegetables.

Preparation and cooking time: 1 hour 40 minutes – 2 hours 10 minutes.

1 packet (3 oz/75g size) thyme and parsley stuffing
Juice of ½ lemon (optional)
1 large breast (2 lb/900g approx.) of lamb (boned if possible)
½ yard (0.5 metre) clean string or 6 wooden cocktail sticks or toothpicks
1 tbsp oil (for cooking)
Piece of cooking foil

Heat the oven (350°F/180°C/Gas Mark 4–5). Make the stuffing as directed on the packet, adding lemon juice to the hot water before mixing the stuffing to give a tangy flavour.

Spread the stuffing over the lamb, and roll it up carefully, not too tightly. Tie it up in 2 or 3 places with the string, or secure in a roll with cocktail sticks. Lightly rub the outside of the meat with the oil, and either wrap the meat in the foil and place it in a roasting tin, or put the meat in a greased roasting tin and cover the tin with the foil.

Cook in the oven for 1½ to 2 hours, according to the size of the joint (a bigger joint will take longer) unwrapping or removing the foil for the last half hour of the cooking time to brown the meat.

ROAST PORK

Most pork joints are sold with the bone in, so you have to allow more weight of meat per serving to make up for this. (It also makes it more difficult to carve.)

Joints to choose for roasting:
Leg: the leanest and most expensive.
Shoulder: cheaper and just as tasty.
Loin: chops, left in one piece, not cut up.

Allow about 8 oz (250g) per serving; a 2½–3 lb (1125–1350g) joint should serve 4 to 6 people. Make sure you know the weight of your joint, as cooking time depends on the weight. *Allow 25 minutes per lb (450g) plus 25 minutes extra.*

Pork is traditionally served with sage and onion stuffing, and apple sauce. Also serve it with roast potatoes and parsnips or other vegetables.

Heat the oven (400°F/200°C/Gas Mark 6–7) so that the joint goes into a hot oven, to make the crackling crisp. Rub the pork skin with oil, and sprinkle with salt to give the cracking a good flavour. Place the joint in the roasting tin with a little oil or fat to stop it sticking to the tin. Put the tin into the hot oven and calculate the cooking time so that the rest of the dinner can be ready at the right time.

After 20 minutes or so, when the crackling is looking crisp, the joint or the whole tin can be covered with foil to stop the meat getting too brown (smaller joints will brown more easily). Roast potatoes or parsnips can be cooked around the meat for the last hour of the cooking time, or in a separate roasting tin. Cook the stuffing in a greased dish, according to the instructions on the packet (see page 177).

Test that the meat is cooked at the end of the cooking time: the juices should run clear when prodded with a knife or fork. If they are still pink, cook for a bit longer. Pork must be cooked right through (it is better overcooked than underdone) as rare pork can cause food poisoning. The meat should be pale-coloured, not pink. When it is completely cooked, lift it onto a hot plate and make the gravy.

NUT ROAST   *Serves 2*

The traditional vegetarian 'Sunday Lunch' meal that everyone has heard of. This recipe makes enough for two portions
since cold nut roast is tasty too. If you have a freezer, the
second portion can be frozen, uncooked, for use later. Serve
with tomato sauce.

Preparation and cooking time: 45 minutes (individual dishes)
60 minutes (larger dishes).

1 onion
1 stick of celery
4 oz (100g/1 very full cup) mixed nuts, roughly chopped (a
    processor or liquidiser is useful for this)
2 large fresh tomatoes or use the tomatoes from a small (7 oz/
    230g) can of tomatoes (you can use the juice as an aperitif)
1 tbsp oil and a knob of butter (for frying)
3 oz (75g/3 full cups) fresh wholemeal breadcrumbs
Salt and pepper
½ tsp mixed herbs
Pinch of chilli powder
1 egg
Piece of foil (for covering the dishes)

Grease two individual dishes or one larger tin (foil dishes are
useful for this). Heat the oven to 400°F/200°C/Gas Mark 6–7.

Peel and chop the onion. Wash and chop the celery. Chop
the nuts. Chop the tomatoes.

Heat the oil and butter in a large frying pan or saucepan
over a moderate heat and fry the onion and celery gently for
4 to 5 minutes until softened but not browned. Remove from
the heat. Add the nuts, breadcrumbs, chopped tomatoes,
salt, pepper, herbs and chilli powder.

Beat the egg in a small basin or cup and stir into the
mixture. Taste, and adjust the seasoning and herbs if
necessary.

Spoon into the well-greased tins and cover lightly with
greased cooking foil. Bake in the hot oven as follows: small

tins – 20 to 30 minutes, removing the foil after 15 minutes; large tins – 45 to 60 minutes, removing the foil after 30 minutes.

GRAVY

Often the meat juices alone from grilled or fried meat make a tasty sauce poured over the meat. But if you want to make 'real' gravy remember the more flour you use the thicker the gravy. The liquid can be any mixture of water, vegetable water, wine, sherry, beer or cider.

Preparation and cooking time: 4 minutes.

1–2 tsp cornflour or flour and 1 tsp gravy flavouring powder or 2 tsp gravy granules
1 cup (¼ pt/150ml) water or vegetable water and/or wine, beer, sherry, cider
Any juices from the meat

Mix the cornflour or flour and the gravy flavouring powder (if used) into a smooth paste with a little of the cold water, wine, cider, sherry or even beer (depending on what you're drinking). Add the rest of the water and the meat juices from the roasting tin.

Pour the mixture into a small saucepan, and bring to the boil, stirring all the time. Stir gravy granules, if used, straight into the hot liquid. Add more liquid if the gravy is too thick, or more flour mixture if it is too thin.

To thicken the gravy used in stews and casseroles, make the gravy mixture as above. Stir the mixture into the stew or casserole and bring to the boil so that the gravy can thicken as it cooks.

WHITE SAUCE

This is a quick way to make a basic sauce, to which you can add other ingredients or flavourings.

Preparation and cooking time: 5 minutes.

2 tsp cornflour (or flour)
1 cup (¼ pt/150ml) milk
½ oz (12g) butter (or margarine)
Salt and pepper

Put the cornflour or flour in a large cup or small basin. Mix it into a runny paste with 1 tbsp of the milk. Boil the rest of the milk in a saucepan. Pour it onto the well-stirred flour mixture, stirring all the time. Pour the mixture back into the saucepan, return to the heat and bring to the boil, stirring all the time, until the sauce thickens. Beat in the butter or margarine. Season with the salt and pepper.

CHEESE SAUCE
Grate 1–2 oz (25–50g) cheese. Add to the white sauce with the butter, and add a dash of mustard if you have any.

PARSLEY SAUCE
Wash and drain a handful of sprigs of parsley. Chop them finely with a knife or scissors, and add to the sauce with the salt and pepper.

ONION SAUCE

A quick and easy method. Onion sauce is traditionally served with lamb, and is also tasty poured over cauliflower.

Preparation and cooking time: 25 minutes.

1 onion
1 cup (¼ pt/150ml) water
2 tsp flour or cornflour
1 cup (¼ pt/150ml) milk
Knob of butter
Salt and pepper

Peel and finely chop the onion. Put it into a small saucepan, with the cup of water. Bring to the boil, then lower the heat and cook gently for 10 to 15 minutes, until the onion is soft.

In a bowl mix the flour or cornflour into a paste with a little of the milk. Gradually add this to the onion mixture, stirring all the time as the mixture thickens. Add more milk, until the sauce is just thick enough – not runny, but not like blancmange. Beat in the knob of butter, and season with the salt and pepper. Serve hot.

'INSTANT' SAUCE MIX

Several makes of sauce mix are now widely available at supermarkets. Follow the instructions on the packet, and only make up as much sauce as is needed for the recipe. Keep the rest of the packet for later, tightly closed, in a dry cupboard or fridge.

BREAD SAUCE

Serve it with chicken. I generally use a packet of bread sauce mix, which is very easy to make, cooks quickly and tastes good, especially with the addition of a little extra butter and a spoonful of cream. Allow 1 cup (¼ pt) milk for 1 to 2 servings; 2 cups (½ pt) milk will make enough sauce for 2 to 4 people, according to your appetites.

1 packet bread sauce mix (you may only need to use part of the packet, but the rest will keep in the store cupboard)
1 cup (¼ pt/150ml) milk
Knob of butter (¼ oz/8g) – optional
2 tsp cream – optional

Make the sauce according to the instructions on the packet. Stir in the butter and cream just before serving. Left-over sauce will keep overnight in the fridge and can be used on cold chicken sandwiches.

APPLE SAUCE

You can buy jars or tins of apple purée, but it is cheaper and very easy to make your own. Apple sauce is served with roast pork or poultry.

Preparation and cooking time: 10–15 minutes.

1–2 cooking apples
2–3 tbsp water
1–2 tbsp sugar

Peel, core and slice the apples. Put them in a saucepan with the water and bring to the boil gently. Simmer for 5 to 10 minutes, until the apples are soft (do not let them boil dry). Add the sugar to taste (be careful, the apples will be *very* hot) and mash with a fork until smooth.

MINT SAUCE

You can buy jars of mint sauce at the supermarket, but I think they taste better if you re-mix the sauce with a little sugar and 1 to 2 teaspoons of fresh vinegar. Mint sauce is traditionally served with lamb.

'BOUGHT' MINT SAUCE

3–4 tsp 'bought' mint sauce
1 tsp granulated sugar
1–2 tsp vinegar

Mix all the above ingredients together in a small glass or dish.

'FRESH' MINT SAUCE

Handful of fresh mint sprigs
2–3 tbsp vinegar (wine vinegar if you have it)
1–2 tsp granulated sugar

Strip the leaves from the stems. Wash well, drain and chop the mint as finely as possible. Mix the mint, vinegar and sugar in a small glass or dish, and serve with the lamb. This sauce will keep in a small, covered jar in the fridge.

STUFFING

Traditionally, sage and onion stuffing goes with pork, while thyme and parsley goes with chicken, but any mixture of herbs is tasty.

Preparation and cooking time: 35–45 minutes.

1 packet (3 oz/75g size) stuffing
A little butter or margarine
Hot water – you can use water from the kettle or vegetable water

Make up the stuffing according to the packet. Grease an oven-proof dish, put the stuffing into the dish, dot with the butter. Bake in the oven (400°F/200°C/Gas Mark 6–7) with the joint, for 30 to 40 minutes, until crispy on top.

15

PUDDINGS AND CAKES

A few easy recipes for those with a sweet tooth.

Lots of delicious chilled and frozen desserts, gooey gateaux and sticky buns are widely available ready-made in the shops and can provide an instant treat.

Scan the packets of cake, pudding and biscuit mixes on the supermarket shelves. With the addition of butter and eggs, you can easily produce a home-made cake.

QUICK CHOCOLATE SAUCE – FOR ICE-CREAM

Serves 1

Fast, easy and most effective. It has a lovely, chocolatey flavour but is not too rich.

Preparation and cooking time: 5 minutes.

1 chocolate bar (1–2 oz/25–50g size)
1 tsp cold water

Break the chocolate into a pottery or pyrex basin or jug, with 1 tsp of water. Stand the basin in 1 in (2.5cm) hot water in a saucepan over a low heat, and simmer gently until the chocolate melts. Stir well, and pour the chocolate sauce over scoops of ice-cream.

HOT CHOCOLATE SAUCE – SERVE WITH
ICE-CREAM
Serves 1

A rich fudgy sauce, delicious with vanilla, chocolate or coffee-flavoured ice-cream.

Preparation and cooking time: 10 minutes.

2 oz (50g) chocolate chips, chocolate cake covering or a
chocolate bar
1 tbsp brown sugar
1 tbsp cold water
1 oz (25g) butter (unsalted is best)
2 tsp rum (optional)

Put the chocolate, sugar and water into a small saucepan, over a low heat, and stir until the chocolate melts and the mixture is smooth and creamy. Remove from the heat. Add the butter in small flakes. Beat well. Beat in the rum, if used. Serve, poured over scoops of ice-cream. If necessary, re-heat the sauce later by putting it into a pyrex or pottery basin or jug, and stand this in 1 in (2.5cm) hot water in a saucepan. Put the saucepan over a low heat and simmer gently until the sauce melts again, stirring well.

BANANA SPLIT   *Serves 1*
Full of calories, but absolutely delicious!

Preparation time: 5 minutes (plus the time for making the chocolate sauce).

1 large banana
2–3 tbsp ice-cream
1 tbsp chocolate sauce (bought or home-made – see page 179)
1 tbsp thick cream – spooning cream is ideal
Chopped nuts (for decoration – optional)
Chocolate sprinkles (for decoration – optional)

Split the banana in half, lengthways, then place it on a plate. Sandwich the banana halves together with spoonfuls of ice-cream. Spoon the chocolate sauce over the top. Decorate with the cream and sprinkle nuts or chocolate sprinkles on the top. Eat immediately.

FRUIT PAVLOVA   *Serves 1*
A super summer sweet. Make it with cream, ice-cream – or both!

Preparation time: 5 minutes.

1–2 tbsp fresh or canned fruit – raspberries, strawberries, canned peaches, mandarins, pineapples, pears
1–2 tbsp thick cream (spooning cream is good) and/or 1–2 tbsp ice-cream
1–2 meringue nests (available in packets from supermarkets)

Prepare this dish just before you are ready to eat it. Wash and drain the fresh fruit, or drain the canned fruit. Spread the ice-cream over the meringue nests. Arrange the fresh or canned fruit carefully on top of the cream or ice-cream. Decorate with a spoonful of thick cream. Serve at once.

SPONGE FRUIT FLAN
Serves 2

So easy, yet looks most impressive. Choose fruit and jelly whose flavours complement each other.

Preparation and cooking time: 10 minutes (plus setting time).

½ tin (15½ oz/439g size) fruit in natural juice or syrup (oranges, peaches, pineapples, pears, etc.)
Water if necessary
1 packet (1 pt size) jelly – any flavour
A 6 in/15cm sponge flan case or 2 individual flan cases (available from large supermarkets)

Open the tin of fruit and strain the juice or syrup into a cup. Make up ½ pint (2 cupfuls) of the fruit juice by adding water if necessary. Heat the juice and water in a saucepan, until it is just boiling. Remove from the heat and add the jelly. Stir until the jelly melts. Leave a few minutes to cool, then put into the fridge, freezer or other cold place, until the jelly is half-set. (This will take about ½ to 1 hour according to the temperature; the colder it is, the quicker the jelly will set.)

When the jelly is half-set, arrange the fruit in the sponge flan in pretty patterns. Spoon the half-set jelly on the top and leave in a cool place to set completely (15–30 minutes, depending on the temperature). Leave any spare jelly to set, then mash with a fork and serve separately with any spare fruit. (If the jelly gets too set before you remember to finish the flan, it can be thinned down by carefully adding 1 to 2 tbsp boiling water to the set jelly and stirring hard, to make it soft again.)

CRUNCHY CREAM PIE   *Serves 2–3*

Easy to make, and delicious served with cream or ice-cream.
You can use any flavour of instant flavoured milk dessert for
the filling – chocolate or butterscotch are lovely.

Preparation time: 15 minutes.

3–4 oz (75–100g) plain digestive biscuits
2 oz (50g) butter or block margarine
2 heaped tbsp brown sugar (use white if you haven't any
   brown)
1 packet instant flavoured milk dessert
2 cups (½ pt/300ml) milk

Put the biscuits into a deep bowl or a clean polythene bag
and crush them into crumbs with a rolling pin or wooden
spoon. Melt the butter in a saucepan over a very low heat (do
not let it brown or burn), then stir in the sugar and biscuit
crumbs and mix well. Press this mixture into a greased deep
pie plate, pie dish or baking tin (6–7 in/15–18cm in
diameter), spreading it round to make a flan case (there is no
cooking, so it does not have to be an oven-proof dish).

Put the flan in a cold place to cool. Make up the instant
flavoured milk dessert with the milk as instructed on the
packet. Whisk with a whisk, mixer or fork. Leave for a
minute so that it partly sets. Pour into the biscuit crust and
smooth the top. Leave it in a cool place or fridge for a few
minutes to set.

PANCAKES   *Makes 6–8 pancakes*

These can be sweet or savoury, and are delicious any day, not just on Shrove Tuesday (Pancake Day). Sweet pancakes are traditionally served sprinkled with 1 tsp sugar and a squeeze of lemon. For sweet and savoury fillings see page 30.

Preparation time: 10 minutes (plus 1 minute per pancake cooking time).

4 heaped tbsp (4 oz/100g) plain flour
1 egg
2 cups (½ pt/300ml) milk
Oil or lard for frying – not butter

Prepare the filling if used. Put the flour into a bowl (use a medium-sized saucepan if you don't have one). Add the egg, and beat it into the flour. Gradually add the milk and beat to make a smooth batter (the easiest way of doing this is with a hand or electric mixer, but with a bit of effort you get just as good a result using a wooden spoon or even a fork).

Heat a clean frying pan over a moderate heat, and when hot, but not burning, grease the pan with a smear of oil or lard (approximately ½ tsp). Pour in a little batter, enough to cover the pan thinly. Tilt the pan to spread the batter over it. Fry briskly, until just set on top, and lightly browned underneath, shaking the pan occasionally to stop the pancake sticking – this will only take a few moments.

Toss the pancake, or flip it over with a knife, and fry for a few more moments to cook the other side. Turn it out onto a warm plate. Sprinkle with lemon and sugar, or add the filling, and roll up or fold into four.

Pancakes taste best eaten at once, straight from the pan, but they can be filled, rolled up and kept warm while you cook the rest. Wipe the pan with a pad of kitchen paper, re-heat and re-grease the pan, and cook the next pancake as before.

SYRUPY PEACHES   *Serves 1*

Make this lovely pudding when fresh peaches are cheap in the greengrocer's. Serve hot with cream or ice-cream. (This dish can be prepared, but not cooked, in advance, the cold fruit being left to soak in the syrup, and then put in the oven to cook while you are eating your first course.)

Preparation and cooking time: 15 minutes.

2 tbsp brown sugar
½ cup water
1–2 peaches

Make the syrup: put the brown sugar and water into a small saucepan, bring to the boil, stirring occasionally, and simmer gently for 3 to 4 minutes to dissolve the sugar. Wash the peaches (do not peel) and cut them in half, from top to bottom. Remove the stones. Put the peaches into an oven-proof dish with the cut sides face upwards, and pour the hot syrup over the fruit, spooning it into the holes left by the stones. Put into a warm oven (350°F/180°C/Gas Mark 4), for 10 to 15 minutes, until the fruit is hot and the syrup bubbling.

GRILLED PEACHES   *Serves 1*

Absolutely delicious with fresh peaches, but very good with tinned fruit too. Buy cheap peaches in the summer for a treat. Serve with cream or ice-cream.

Preparation and cooking time: 5 minutes.

1–2 fresh peaches or ½ a tin (15 oz/425g size) of peaches
1 oz (25g) butter
2 tbsp demerara sugar

Peel and slice the fresh peaches or drain and slice the tinned peaches. Butter an oven-proof dish, and place the peach slices in the dish. Sprinkle thickly with the brown sugar, dot with some butter. Place the dish under a hot grill for a minute or two, so that the sugar melts and the peach slices warm through. Serve at once.

LIQUEUR ORANGES   *Serves 2*

Delicious, simple and rather unusual, so save it for when you
are entertaining a special friend.

Preparation time: 5 minutes.
Chilling time: 1–2 hours, but longer if possible; all day is best.

2 large, sweet oranges
2 tbsp sugar
1 tbsp orange liqueur – Cointreau, Grand Marnier or
    Curaçao (you can buy a miniature bottle of liqueur)
Thick cream (optional)

Peel the oranges and scrape away any white pith. Cut the
oranges into thin rings, and arrange the slices in a shallow
serving dish. Sprinkle with the sugar and liqueur. Cover the
dish with a plate or cling film and leave it in the fridge or in a
cold place for at least an hour, but all day if possible, to chill
and let the liqueur soak in. Serve alone or with thick cream.

PEANUT CRUNCH

A crunchy cake to eat with coffee.

Preparation time: 10 minutes (plus setting time).

1 packet (7–8 oz/200–225g) plain digestive, rich tea or other
    plain biscuits
2 oz (50g) butter or block margarine
2 tbsp brown sugar (white will do)
4 tbsp golden syrup or honey
4 tbsp crunchy peanut butter

Grease a square or round shallow tin (approximately 7 in
(17.5cm) in diameter). Put the biscuits in a deep bowl or a
polythene bag and crush them not too finely with a rolling
pin or wooden spoon. Melt the butter, sugar and syrup in a
saucepan over a low heat, stirring well, until the butter is
melted and the sugar has dissolved. Remove from the heat,
and stir in the peanut butter. Mix in the biscuits, stir well.
Press into the greased tin, and leave in the fridge or a cool
place until set (½–1 hour according to temperature). Cut
into squares or fingers.

CHOCOLATE CRUNCHIES

This has to be the easiest cake recipe there is, anywhere.

Preparation and cooking time: 5 minutes.

4 oz (100g) chocolate cake covering, cooking chocolate or chocolate bar
2 cups (2 oz/50g) cornflakes or rice crispies
12–15 paper cases

Break the chocolate into a pyrex or pottery basin. Stand this in 1 in (2.5cm) of hot water in a saucepan. Simmer this over a gentle heat until the chocolate melts. Remove the basin from the pan (use a cloth, the basin will be hot) and stir in the cornflakes or crispies, and mix until they are well-coated with the chocolate. Spoon into heaps in the paper cases, and leave to set. Store in a tin or plastic box.

CHOCOLATE KRISPIES

Almost everyone likes these, and they're cheap too. Instead of the sugar and cocoa you can use 4 tbsp drinking chocolate.

Preparation and cooking time: 15 minutes.

2 oz (50g) butter or block margarine
2 tbsp sugar
2 tbsp golden syrup
2 tbsp (level) cocoa
3 cups (3 oz/75g) cornflakes or rice crispies
12–15 paper cases

Put the butter (or margarine), sugar and syrup in a medium-sized saucepan, and heat over a gentle heat until melted. Stir in the cocoa (or drinking chocolate) and stir well to make a chocolate syrup. Stir in the cornflakes or crispies, and mix well to coat them thoroughly. Heap them into the paper cases and leave to set. Store in a tin or plastic box.

CHOCOLATE BISCUIT CAKE

This can be made in any shape of shallow baking tin or dish. It does not need baking, just leave it to cool, then cover with melted chocolate and cut into squares.

Preparation and cooking time: 20 minutes (plus setting time).

1 packet (7–8 oz/200–225g) plain digestive or rich tea biscuits
4 oz (100g) butter or block margarine
2 tsp sugar
2 tsp cocoa or 4 tsp drinking chocolate
1 tbsp golden syrup or honey
½ packet (4 oz/100g) chocolate cake covering (you can use cooking chocolate or chocolate bars)

Grease a square or round shallow sandwich cake baking tin (approximately 7–8 in/17.5–20cm in diameter). Crush the biscuits (not too finely) by putting them into a deep bowl or a clean polythene bag, and crushing them with a rolling pin or wooden spoon.

Put the butter, sugar, cocoa and syrup into a medium-sized saucepan, and melt slowly over a low heat, stirring occasionally. Remove from the heat. Add the crushed biscuits and mix well. Press into the prepared tin, spread flat and leave to cool (10 to 15 minutes).

Melt the chocolate by breaking it into a pyrex or pottery basin or jug and standing this in 1 in (2.5cm) hot water in a saucepan over a low heat. Simmer gently until the chocolate melts. Pour the chocolate over the biscuit cake, spread evenly and leave to set for 15–30 minutes in a cool place. Cut into squares or fingers and store in a tin or plastic box.

DROP SCONES OR SCOTCH PANCAKES

Fun to make for tea on a cold weekend afternoon.

Preparation and cooking time: 20 minutes.

4 heaped tbsp self-raising flour
or 4 heaped tbsp plain flour and 1 tsp cream of tartar and
½ tsp bicarbonate of soda
1 egg
1 cup (¼ pt/150ml) milk
Little oil or lard (not butter) for greasing
Clean tea-towel or napkin

Put the flour (and cream of tartar and bicarbonate of soda if using plain flour) into a bowl. (Use a medium-sized saucepan if you don't have a bowl.) Add the egg, and beat it into the flour, gradually adding the milk and beating to make a smooth batter. (Use a hand or electric mixer if you have one, but you get just as good a result using a wooden spoon or a fork.) The batter will be much thicker than pancake or Yorkshire Pudding batter.

Heat a clean frying pan, or a griddle (a flat iron pan for baking cakes), over a moderate heat. When it is quite hot, but not burning, grease it lightly with the oil or lard, and drop one tablespoon of the batter at a time onto the pan. Drop the tablespoonfuls so that they fall far enough apart from each other to allow room for each of them to spread slightly. You can probably cook 3 or 4 pancakes at a time. Cook for 1½ to 2 minutes, until there are little bubbles on the top of the pancakes and the underneath is light brown. Turn them over gently with a knife and cook the other side for a few minutes. Remove them from the pan and place them on a clean cloth, folding it over to keep the scones moist as they cool. Serve with lots of butter, jam, or clotted cream for a treat.

INDEX

189

HOW TO BOIL
AN EGG

... and 184 other
recipes fo

KT-432-919

In the same series

Man Alone Cook Book
*The Big Occasion Cook Book
*The Bride's Guide

*By the same author

HOW TO
BOIL
AN EGG

...and 184 other simple
recipes for one

Jan Arkless

RIGHT WAY

CONTENTS

For Jon Jon,
whose architectural aspirations
inspired this book.

1

INTRODUCTION

I originally wrote this book to help my son with his cooking when he first went to university. I have since realised that the recipes contained here are not only useful for students but for anyone, of any age, who find themselves alone, and for the first time have to cook for themselves, whether in their own home or in new accommodation.

Other cookery books assume some basic knowledge of cooking techniques but in this book I have assumed none as I wrote it specifically for the person who knows *absolutely nothing* or *very little* about cooking, or meal planning.

The book explains the simple things that one is supposed to know by instinct, such as how to boil an egg or fry sausages, how to prepare and cook vegetables *and* have them ready to eat at the same time as the main course! It includes recipes and suggestions for a variety of snacks and main meals (not all cooked in the frying pan or made from mince), using fish, chicken, beef, lamb and pork. The majority of the meals are quick, easy and economical to make, but there is a 'Sunday Lunch' chapter near the end of the book.

There are just a few recipes for desserts and cakes as you can easily buy biscuits and ready-made or frozen cakes. Remember that yoghurt makes a good, cheap sweet, and that fresh fruit is the best pud you can eat. Also, fresh fruit juice or milk is far better for you than fizzy drinks or alcohol.

Most recipes in other cookery books are geared towards feeding four or six people, but the recipes contained here are designed for the single person living on his or her own. However, this book does include a few recipes which cater for two people. This is because it is easier to cook larger portions of stews and casseroles as very small helpings tend to dry up during cooking.

AMOUNTS TO USE WHEN COOKING FOR ONE

Pasta, Noodles, Shapes, etc.
1 very generous cup (3 oz/75g) of uncooked pasta.

Potatoes
3–4 (8 oz/225g) according to size.

Rice
½ cup (2–3 oz/50–75g) dry uncooked rice.

Vegetables
See the individual vegetables in Chapter 5.

Oily Fish
1 whole fish (trout, mackerel, herring).

White Fish
6–8 oz (175–225g) fillet of cod, haddock, etc.

Roast Beef
Approximately 6 oz (175g) per person. A joint weighing 2½–3 lb (1–1.5kg) should serve 6–8 helpings; remember you can use cold meat for dinner the next day.

Minced Beef
4–6 oz (100–175g).

Beef Steak
6–8 oz (175–225g) is a fair-sized steak.

Stewing Steak
4–6 oz (100–175g).

Chicken
Allow a 6–8 oz (175–225g) chicken joint (leg or breast) per person. A 2½–3 lb (1–1.5kg) chicken serves 3–4 people.

Lamb or Pork Chops
1 per person.

Lamb Cutlets
1–3 according to size and appetite.

Roast Lamb
Because you are buying meat with a bone in, you need to buy a larger joint to account for the bone. A joint weighing about 2½ lb (1kg) will serve 4 people well.

Roast Pork
Approximately 8 oz (225g) per serving. A boneless joint weighing 2½–3 lb (1–1.5kg) will give 5–6 generous helpings.

Pork or Gammon Steaks
1 per person or 6 oz (175g).

USING THE OVEN
Temperatures are given for both gas and electric ovens.

Remember always to heat the oven for a few minutes before cooking food in it, so that the whole of the oven reaches the appropriate temperature.

REHEATING FOOD

One note of warning: be very careful about reheating cooked dishes. If you must do this, always be sure that the food is re-cooked right through, not merely warmed. *Food just reheated can make you extremely ill if not cooked thoroughly, especially pork and chicken – you have been warned!*

FOLLOWING THE RECIPES

I have given 'preparation and cooking' times for the recipes in this book so that, before you start cooking, you will know approximately how much time to set aside for preparing and cooking the meal. Read the recipe right the way through so that you know what it involves.

The ingredients used in each recipe are all readily available and listed in the order they are used in the method. Collect all the specified ingredients *before* you start cooking, otherwise you may find yourself lacking a vital ingredient when you have already prepared half the meal. When the meal is ready, there should be no ingredients left – if there are, you have missed something out!

Measurements

The ingredients are given in both imperial and metric measurements. Follow one type of measurement or the other, but do not combine the two, as the quantities are not exact conversions.

I have used size 2 or 3 eggs in the recipes so you can use whichever you happen to have in stock. Meat, fish and vegetables can be weighed in the shop when you buy them, or will have the weight on the packet. Don't buy more than you need for the recipe; extra bits tend to get left at the back of the cupboard or fridge and wasted. But it is worthwhile buying some goods in the larger size packets – rice, pasta, tomato ketchup, etc. – as they will keep fresh for ages and be on hand when you need them.

In case you don't own kitchen scales many of the measurements are also given in spoonfuls or tea cups (normal drinking size, which approximates to ¼ pint/5 fl oz/ 150ml; it isn't the American measure of a cup). The following measurements may also be helpful:

Butter, margarine or lard, etc.
1 inch cube (2.5cm cube) = 1 oz (25g); it is easy to divide up a new packet and mark it out in squares.

Cheese
1 inch cube (2.5cm cube) = 1 oz (25g) approximately.

Flour, cornflour
1 very heaped tbsp = 1 oz (25g) approximately.

Pasta (shells, bows, etc.)
1 very full cup = 3 oz (75g) approximately.

Rice
½ cup dry uncooked rice = 2 oz (50g) approximately.

Sugar
1 heaped tbsp = 1 oz (25g) approximately.

Sausages
Chipolatas: 8 sausages in an 8 oz (225g) packet.
Thick sausages: 4 sausages in an 8 oz (225g) packet.

Abbreviations
tsp   = teaspoon
dsp   = dessertspoon
tbsp   = tablespoon (serving spoon)
1 spoonful   = 1 slightly rounded spoonful
1 level spoonful   = 1 flat spoonful

| 1 cupful | = 1 tea cup (drinking size cup) approximately ¼ pint/5 fl oz/150ml (*not* the American measure) |
| pt | = pint |

USEFUL STORES & KITCHEN EQUIPMENT

This section may be particularly useful if you're a student living away from home and cooking for yourself for the first time in your life. Beg or borrow these items from home or try to collect them at the beginning of term, then just replace them during the year as necessary.

Beef, chicken and vegetable stock cubes
Coffee (instant)
Coffee (real)
Cooking oil
Cornflour
Curry powder
Dried mixed herbs
Drinking chocolate
Flour
Garlic powder (or paste)
Gravy granules
Horseradish sauce
Mustard
Milk powder (for coffee)

Orange/lemon squash
Pasta
Pepper
Pickle
Rice (long grain)
Salt
Soy sauce
Sugar
Tabasco sauce
Tea bags
Tomato purée (in a jar or tube)
Tomato sauce
Vinegar
Worcester sauce

Also
Dish cloth, washing-up liquid, tea towels, pan scrubber, oven cleaning powder, oven cloth.

Store sugar, rice, flour, pasta, biscuits and cakes in airtight containers rather than leaving them in open packets on the shelf. This keeps them fresh and clean for much longer and protects them from ants and other insects. Try to collect

some storage jars and plastic containers for this purpose.
(Large, empty coffee jars with screw lids, and plastic ice-
cream cartons are ideal.)

Perishable Foods
These don't keep so long but are useful to have as a start.

Bacon	Frozen vegetables
Biscuits	Honey
Bread	Jam
Butter	Margarine
Cereals (such as cornflakes)	Marmalade
Cheese	Milk
Chocolate spread	Peanut butter
Eggs	Potatoes
Fruit juice	

Handy Cans for a Quick Meal

Baked beans	Spaghetti hoops
Beans with sausages	Stewed steak
Chicken in white sauce	Sweetcorn
Corned beef	Tinned fruit
Evaporated milk	Tuna fish
Frankfurter sausages	Vegetables (peas, carrots,
Italian tomatoes	etc.)
Luncheon meat	
Minced beef	*Also*
Rice pudding	Blancmange powders
Sardines	Instant whip
Soups (also packet soups)	Jellies
Spaghetti	Pot noodles

Useful Kitchen Equipment
Basin (small)
Bottle opener

Casserole pan (thick heavy ones are the best)
Chopping/bread board
Cling film
Cooking foil
Cooking tongs
Dessertspoons
Fish slice
Frying pan
Grater
Kettle
Kitchen paper
Kitchen scissors
Knives: bread knife with serrated edge;
      sharp chopping knife for meat;
      vegetable knife
Measuring jug
Oven-proof dish (pyrex-type): 1 pint/0.5 litre size is big
    enough for one
Plastic storage containers (large ice-cream tubs are useful, to
    store biscuits, cakes, pasta, etc.)
Saucepans: 1 small; 1 or 2 large ones
Storage jars (large empty coffee jars are ideal)
Tablespoons
·Teaspoons
Tin opener
Wooden spoon

Handy but not Essential Kitchen Equipment
Baking tin (for meat)
Baking tins (various)
Basin (large) or bowl
Bread bin
Colander
Egg whisk or egg beater
Electric frying pan/multi cooker (very useful if your cooker is
    very small, old or unreliable)
Electric kettle

Foil dishes (these are cheap and last for several bakings; useful if you need a tin of a particular shape or size)
Kitchen scales
Liquidiser
Measuring jug (can also be used as a basin)
Mixer or food processor
Potato masher
Saucepans (extra) and/or casserole dishes
Sieve
Toaster

GLOSSARY

Various cooking terms used in the book (some of which may be unfamiliar to you) are explained in this glossary.

Al dente
Refers to pasta that is cooked and feels firm when bitten.

Basting
Spooning fat or butter or meat juices over food that is being roasted (particularly meat and poultry) to keep it moist.

Beating
Mixing food with a wooden spoon or whisk so that the lumps disappear and it becomes smooth.

Binding
Adding eggs, cream or butter to a dry mixture to hold it together.

Blending
Mixing dry ingredients (such as flour) with a little liquid to make a smooth, runny lumpfree mixture.

Boiling
Cooking food in boiling water (i.e. at a temperature of 212°F/100°C) with the water bubbling gently.

Boning
Removing the bones from meat, poultry or fish.

Braising
Frying food in a hot fat so that it is browned, and then cooking it slowly in a covered dish with a little liquid and some vegetables.

Casserole
An oven-proof dish with lid; also a slow-cooked stew.

Chilling
Cooling food in a fridge without freezing.

Colander
A perforated metal or plastic basket used for straining food.

Deep-frying
Immersing food in hot fat or oil and frying it.

Dicing
Cutting food into small cubes.

Dot with butter
Cover food with small pieces of butter.

Flaking
Separating fish into flaky pieces.

Frying
Cooking food in oil or fat in a pan (usually a flat frying pan).

Grilling
Cooking food by direct heat under a grill.

Mixing
Combining ingredients by stirring.

Nest (making a)
Arranging food (such as rice or potatoes) around the outside of a plate to make a circular border and putting other food into the middle of this 'nest'.

Poaching
Cooking food in water which is just below boiling point.

Purée
Food that has been passed through a sieve and reduced to pulp (or pulped in a liquidiser or electric mixer).

Roasting
Cooking food in a hot oven.

Sautéing
Frying food quickly in hot, shallow fat, and turning it frequently in the pan so that it browns evenly.

Seasoning
Adding salt, pepper, herbs and/or spices to food.

Simmering
Cooking food in water which is just below boiling point so that only an occasional bubble appears.

Straining
Separating solid food from liquid by draining it through a sieve or colander, e.g. potatoes, peas, etc., that have been cooked in boiling water.

2
EGGS

Eggs are super value, quick to cook and can make a nourishing snack or main meal in minutes.

In view of the publicity over salmonella in eggs, take care about the eggs you buy and store them sensibly and hygienically – eggs have porous shells and should never be stored where they are in contact with uncooked meat or fish, dust or dirt of any kind. They also absorb smells through the shells, so beware if you are buying fresh fruit, washing powder, household cleaners, firelighters, etc., and keep them in separate shopping bags. Heed the advice on fresh eggs given out by the health authorities: only buy eggs from a reputable supplier and *do not serve raw or lightly cooked egg dishes to babies, pregnant women or the elderly unless you're sure that the eggs are free from bacteria*. There are egg substitutes available in the shops (although you may have to search for them) which you may prefer for safety reasons instead of fresh eggs. Don't panic, but do take reasonable care with egg cookery.

BOILED EGG

Use an egg already at room temperature if possible, not one straight from the fridge as otherwise it may crack. If you prick the top of the shell once with a special gadget or a clean pin, the egg will not crack while cooking (my daughter-in-law Barbara taught me this, and it really does work). Slip the egg carefully into a small saucepan, cover with warm (not boiling) water and add ½ tsp salt (to seal up any cracks). Bring to the boil, note the time and turn down the heat before the egg starts rattling about in the pan. Simmer gently, timing from when the water begins to boil, using the table below:

Size	Time	Description
Large (sizes 1 or 2)	3 mins.	soft-boiled
Standard (sizes 3 or 4)	2½ mins.	soft-boiled
Large	4 mins.	soft yolk, hard white
Standard	3½ mins.	soft yolk, hard white
Large	10 mins.	hard-boiled
Standard	9 mins.	hard-boiled

SOFT-BOILED
Remove carefully from the pan with a spoon, put into an egg cup and tap the top to crack the shell and stop the egg continuing to cook inside.

HARD-BOILED
Remove the pan from the heat and place under cold, running water to prevent a black ring forming round the yolk. Peel off shell and rinse in cold water to remove any shell still clinging to the egg.

POACHED EGG

Put about 1 in (2.5cm) water into a clean frying pan and bring to the boil. Reduce the heat so that the water is just simmering. Crack the egg carefully into a cup, and slide it into the simmering water. Cook very gently, just simmering in the hot water, for about 3 minutes, until the egg is set to your liking. Lift it out with a slotted spoon or fish slice, being careful not to break the yolk underneath.

FRIED EGG

Heat a small amount of cooking oil, butter or dripping in a frying pan over a moderate heat (not too hot, or the egg white will frazzle). Carefully break the egg into a cup to check that it is not bad, then pour it into the frying pan and fry gently for 2 to 3 minutes. To cook the top of the egg, either baste the egg occasionally by spooning a little of the hot fat over it, or put the lid on the pan and let the heat cook it. You may prefer the egg carefully flipped over when half done to cook on both sides, but be prepared for a broken yolk. Remove the egg from the pan with a fish slice or wide-bladed knife.

SCRAMBLED EGGS

Usually you will want to scramble 2 or more eggs at a time.

Chopped chives are tasty with scrambled eggs. Simply wash them, cut off their roots and chop them.

Beat the egg well with a fork in a basin or large cup. Add salt, pepper and chopped chives. Melt a large knob of butter in a small, preferably thick, saucepan. Turn heat to low, and pour in the beaten egg, stirring all the time, until the egg looks thick and creamy. Do not overcook, as the egg will continue to cook even when removed from the heat. Stir in (if required) 1 to 2 tsp cream or top of the milk, or a small knob of butter (this helps to stop the egg cooking any more).

CHEESY SCRAMBLED EGGS

Add 1 oz (25g) grated or chopped cheese to the beaten eggs, before cooking.

PAN SCRAMBLE

If you are cooking sausages or bacon as well as scrambled eggs, fry the meat first and then cook the eggs in the same hot fat.

PIPERADE   *Serves 1*

Scrambled eggs plus a bit extra.

Preparation and cooking time: 30 minutes.

1 small onion
Small green pepper
2 tomatoes (fresh or tinned)
1 tbsp oil, or knob of butter (for frying)
Pinch of garlic powder
Salt and pepper
2–3 eggs

Peel and slice the onion. Wash, core and chop the green pepper. Wash and chop the fresh tomatoes or drain the tinned tomatoes and chop roughly. Heat the butter or oil in a saucepan and cook the onion and pepper over a medium heat, stirring well, until soft (about 5 minutes).

Add the chopped tomatoes, garlic, salt, pepper and stir. Put a lid on the pan and continue to cook gently over a low heat, stirring occasionally, for about 15 to 20 minutes, to make a thick saucy mixture.

Break the eggs into a small basin or large cup. Lightly beat them with a fork, then pour them into the vegetable mixture, stirring hard with a wooden spoon, until the eggs are just setting. Pour onto a warm plate, and eat with hot buttered toast or crusty fresh bread rolls.

SAVOURY EGGS
Serves 1

A cheap and tasty variation on the bacon 'n egg theme; makes a good, quick supper.

For a change, cooked sliced sausages or slices of salami can be used instead of bacon.

Preparation and cooking time: 25 minutes.

1 small onion
1 small eating apple
1 rasher of bacon
2 tsp cooking oil or large knob of butter (for frying)
Salt and pepper
¼ tsp sugar
2 eggs

Peel and slice the onion. Wash, core and slice the apple. De-rind the bacon and cut into ½ in (1.25cm) pieces. Heat the oil or butter in a frying pan over a moderate heat. Add the bacon, onion and apple, and fry, stirring occasionally, until soft (about 5 minutes). Stir in the salt, pepper and sugar.

Remove from the heat. Break the eggs into a cup, one at a time, and pour on top of the onion mixture. Cover the pan with a lid, and cook for a further 3 to 5 minutes over a very low heat, until the eggs are as firm as you like them.

CHEESY BAKED EGG   *Serves 1*
Quite delicious, and so easy to make.

Preparation and cooking time: 20 minutes.

3–4 oz (75–100g) cheese
2 eggs
Salt and pepper
Large knob of butter

Heat the oven (350°F/180°C/Gas Mark 4). Grease an oven-proof dish well with some butter.

Grate the cheese and cover the base of the dish with half of the cheese. Break the eggs, one at a time, into a cup, then slide them carefully on top of the cheese. Season well with the salt and pepper, and cover the eggs completely with the rest of the cheese.

Dot with the butter and bake in the hot oven for about 15 minutes, until the cheese is bubbling and the eggs are just set. Serve at once, with crusty French bread, rolls or crisp toast, or a salad.

EGG NESTS   *Serves 1*

These can be served plain, or with the addition of grated
cheese, to make a very cheap lunch or supper.

Preparation and cooking time: 30 minutes.

2–4 potatoes
Large knob of butter
2 oz (50g) cheese (optional)
Salt and pepper
2 eggs

Peel the potatoes, cut into thick slices and cook in boiling,
salted water in a saucepan for 10 to 15 minutes, until soft.
Drain and mash with a fork, then beat in the large knob of
butter, using a wooden spoon. Grate the cheese, if used, and
beat half of it into the potato. Season with the salt and
pepper.

1.   Egg nest

   Grease an oven-proof dish. Spread the potato into this,
and make a nest for the eggs. Keep it warm. Boil 1 in (2.5cm)
water in a clean frying pan and poach the eggs. If making
cheesy eggs, heat the grill. Carefully lift the eggs out of the
water when cooked and put them into the potato nest. If
making plain eggs serve at once, otherwise cover the eggs
with the remainder of the grated cheese and brown for a few
moments under the hot grill. Can be served with a fresh
tomato or a salad.

SICILIAN EGGS
Serves 1

Saucy tomatoes with eggs and bacon. Serve with hot toast.

Preparation and cooking time: 25 minutes.

2 eggs
1 small onion
Knob of butter
1 small tin (8 oz/230g) tomatoes
Salt and pepper
Pinch of sugar
Pinch of dried herbs
2 rashers of bacon (de-rinded)

Hard boil the eggs for 10 minutes. Cool them in cold, running water. Shell them, rinse clean, slice thickly and arrange in a greased, heat-proof dish.

Peel and slice the onion, and fry it in the butter in a small saucepan over a moderate heat, until soft (about 5 minutes). Add the tomatoes, salt, pepper, sugar and herbs, and cook gently for a further 5 minutes. Heat the grill.

Pour the tomato mixture over the eggs, top with the de-rinded bacon rashers and place under the hot grill until the bacon is cooked.

If you do not have a grill, fry the bacon in the pan with the onions, remove it and keep it hot while the tomatoes are cooking, then top the tomato mixture with the hot, cooked bacon.

EGG, CHEESE AND ONION SAVOURY   *Serves 1*
Cheap and cheerful, eaten with chunks of hot, crusty bread.

Preparation and cooking time: 30 minutes.

2 eggs
1 onion
Knob of butter (for frying)
1 oz (25g) cheese

For the cheese sauce (you can omit this and just use grated cheese or alternatively use packet sauce mix):
1 oz (25g) cheese
2 tsp flour (or cornflour)
1 cup (¼ pt/150ml) milk
½ oz (12g) butter
Salt and pepper
Pinch of mustard

Hard boil the eggs for 10 minutes. Peel and slice the onion and fry gently in the knob of butter in a small saucepan over a moderate heat, for 4 to 5 minutes, until soft and cooked. Grate the cheese.

For the cheese sauce: EITHER mix the flour or cornflour into a smooth paste with a little of the milk in a small basin. Boil the rest of the milk and pour onto the flour mixture, stirring all the time. Then pour the whole mixture back into the saucepan and stir over the heat until the mixture thickens. Stir in the butter and beat well. Add the 1 oz (25g) grated cheese, salt, pepper and mustard. OR make up the packet sauce mix.

Put the onion into a greased oven-proof dish. Slice the cold, peeled hard-boiled eggs, and arrange on top of the onion. Cover with the cheese sauce and sprinkle with the rest of the grated cheese. Brown under a hot grill for a few minutes, until the cheese is melted, crisp and bubbly.

MURPHY'S EGGS   *Serves 1*

A cheap and filling supper dish if you have time to wait for it to cook in the oven.

Preparation and cooking time: 1 hour 15 minutes.

½ lb (225g) potatoes (about 3 or 4 according to appetite)
1 onion
1 rasher of bacon
Salt and pepper
½–1 cup (¼ pt/150ml approx.) hot milk
Knob of butter
2 eggs

Peel the potatoes, cut into small ½ in (1.25cm) dice. Peel and slice the onion. De-rind and chop the bacon. Grease an oven-proof dish. Mix the potatoes, onion and bacon in a bowl, and put into the dish, seasoning well with the salt and pepper. Add the hot milk (enough to come halfway up the dish) and dot with the butter.

Bake in a hot oven (400°F/200°C/Gas Mark 6), covered with a lid or foil, for 45 minutes to 1 hour, until the potatoes are cooked and all the milk is absorbed.

Break each egg into a cup. Remove the dish of potatoes from the oven, make two hollows in the top of the potatoes with a spoon, and slip the raw eggs into the hollows. Return the dish to the oven for 6 to 8 minutes until the eggs are set. Serve at once.

EGGY BREAD OR FRENCH TOAST *Serves 1*

A boarding school favourite.

Serve with golden syrup, honey or jam, or sprinkled with white or brown sugar.

Or to make it savoury, sprinkle with salt, pepper, and a blob of tomato sauce. Savoury eggy bread goes well with bacon, sausages and baked beans.

Preparation and cooking time: 15 minutes.

1 egg
1–2 tsp sugar (according to taste)
½ cup milk
3–4 thick slices of white bread
2 oz (50g) butter (for frying)

Break the egg into a basin or a large cup, add the sugar and beat well with a whisk, mixer or fork, gradually adding the milk. Pour this egg mixture into a shallow dish or soup plate, and soak each slice of bread in the egg, until it is all soaked up.

Heat a frying pan over a moderate heat. Melt the butter in the pan and fry the soaked bread slices in the hot butter, turning to cook both sides, until golden brown and crispy. Serve at once as above.

FRENCH OMELETTE

Serves 1

The best-known type of omelette: light golden egg, folded over into an envelope shape. Served plain or with a wide variety of sweet or savoury fillings, folded inside. There is no need for a special omelette pan (unless you happen to own one, of course). Use any clean, ordinary frying pan.

Preparation and cooking time: 10 minutes.

2–3 eggs
1 tsp cold water per egg
Pinch of salt and pepper (omit for sweet omelettes)
Knob of butter
Filling as required (see opposite)

Prepare the filling (see list opposite). Warm a plate. Break the eggs into a basin or large cup, add the water, salt and pepper and beat with a fork.

Put the butter in a frying pan and heat over a moderate heat until it is just sizzling (but not brown). Place the egg mixture in the pan at once. Carefully, with a wide-bladed knife or wooden spoon, draw the mixture from the middle to the sides of the pan, so that the uncooked egg in the middle can run onto the hot pan and set. Continue until all the egg is very lightly cooked underneath and the top is still running and soft (about one minute). The top will cook in its own heat, when it is folded over.

With the wide-bladed knife or a fish slice loosen the omelette so that you can remove it easily from the pan. Put the filling across the middle of the omelette and fold both sides over it to make an envelope. If using a cold filling, cook for a further minute. Remove from the pan and place on the warm plate. Serve at once, with French bread, bread rolls, sauté or new potatoes, a side salad or just a fresh tomato. Delicious!

OMELETTE AND PANCAKE FILLINGS
For pancakes, see page 183.

Savoury
Asparagus
Use ½ small can (10 oz/298g size) asparagus tips. Heat them through in a small saucepan. Drain and keep hot.

Bacon
Fry 1–2 rashers of bacon in a little oil or fat. Keep hot.

Cheese
1–2 oz (25–50g) grated or finely cubed.

Chicken
2–3 tbsp chopped, cooked chicken. (You can use the pickings from a roast chicken.)

Fresh or Dried Herbs
Add 1 tsp chopped herbs to the beaten eggs, water and seasoning.

Cooked Meat
Chop 1–2 slices cooked ham, salami or garlic sausage, etc.

Mushrooms
Wash and chop 2 oz (50g or 4–5 mushrooms). Cook gently in a small pan, with a knob of butter, for 2–3 minutes, stirring occasionally. Keep hot.

Tomato
Wash 1–2 tomatoes, slice and fry them in a little oil or fat and keep hot.

Sweet
Choose one of the following fillings, then sprinkle the omelettes with 1 tsp icing or granulated sugar, just before serving.

Fruit
Add 2–3 tbsp sliced, tinned fruit (peaches, pineapple or apricot) or 2–3 tbsp sliced fresh fruit (bananas, peaches, strawberries or raspberries).

Honey
Add 2–3 tbsp honey.

Honey and Walnut
Use 2–3 tbsp honey, 1 tbsp chopped walnuts.

Jam
Add 1–2 tbsp jam or bramble jelly. Warm the jam by standing it in a saucepan with 2 in (5cm) hot water, and warming gently over a low heat.

Marmalade
Add 2–3 tbsp orange or ginger marmalade.

SPANISH OMELETTE   *Serves 1*

A delicious, filling, savoury omelette. Served flat like a thick pancake, mixed with onion, potato, cooked meat and other vegetables – a good way of using up cold, cooked, leftovers. (A large omelette, made with 4 eggs and some extra vegetables, can be cut in half, serving 2 people.)

Preparation and cooking time: 15 minutes.

EXTRAS (optional):
Bacon: 1–2 rashers of bacon, chopped and fried with the onion
Cooked meat: 1–2 slices of chopped, cooked ham, salami, or garlic sausage, etc.
Green peppers: 1–2 tbsp green peppers, chopped and mixed with the onion
Sausages: 1–2 cold, cooked sausages, sliced

Vegetables: 1–2 tbsp cold cooked vegetables (peas, sweetcorn, green beans, mixed vegetables)

1 small onion
2–3 boiled potatoes
2–3 eggs
1 tsp cold water per egg
Salt and pepper
Pinch of dried herbs (optional)
1 tbsp oil (for frying)

Prepare the 'extras' if used. Peel and chop the onion. Dice the cooked potatoes. Beat the eggs, water, seasoning and herbs lightly with a fork in a small basin.

Heat the oil in an omelette or frying pan over a medium heat, and fry the onion for 3 to 5 minutes, until soft. Add the diced potato and continue frying until the potato is thoroughly heated. Add the extra meat or vegetables (if used) and heat through again. Heat the grill and warm a plate. Pour the beaten egg mixture into the pan, over the vegetables, and cook without stirring until the bottom is firm, but with the top remaining creamy and moist (about 1 to 2 minutes). Shake the pan occasionally to prevent sticking.

Place under the hot grill for ½ minute, until the top is set – beware in case the pan handle gets hot. Slide the omelette flat onto the warm plate and serve at once.

QUICK EGG AND VEGETABLE CURRY   *Serves 1*
A fast and easy curry recipe.

Preparation and cooking time: 35 minutes.

1 onion
Knob of butter
1 tsp cooking oil
1 tsp curry powder (or more or less according to taste)
1 tsp flour or cornflour
Small can (10 oz/295g) mulligatawny soup
2 eggs
½ cup (2–3 oz/50-75g) long grain rice
1 cup or 2 oz (50g) frozen mixed vegetables

Peel and chop the onion, and fry in the oil and butter in a saucepan over a medium heat, until soft (about 3 to 4 minutes). Stir in the curry powder and flour, and cook very gently for a further 2 minutes, stirring all the time. Gradually stir in the soup, bring to the boil, reduce the heat to a simmer, put on the lid, and cook gently for about 20 minutes, stirring occasionally, to make a thick sauce.

Hard boil the eggs for 10 minutes. Rinse them under cold, running water, peel them, wash off the shell and cut in half, lengthways. Cook the rice for 10 to 12 minutes in a large pan of boiling salted water (see page 81). Drain and keep hot, fluffing with a fork to stop it going lumpy. Add the mixed vegetables to the curry sauce, bring back to the boil and simmer for a few minutes to cook the vegetables.

Put the rice onto a warm plate, spreading round with a spoon to form a ring. Arrange the eggs in the centre and cover with the vegetable curry sauce. Serve with any side dishes you like (see page 128).

DRINKING EGG OR EGG NOG   *Serves 1*

A nourishing breakfast for those in a hurry, or an easily-digested meal for those feeling fragile!

Preparation time: 5 minutes.

1 egg
2 tsp sugar
2 cups (½ pt/300ml) milk (cold or warm)
2 tsp brandy, rum or whisky (optional, but not for breakfast!)
   or 1 tbsp sherry (optional, but not for breakfast!)
Pinch of nutmeg or cinnamon

Break the egg into a basin, beat it lightly with a mixer, egg whisk or fork, adding the sugar and gradually beating in the milk. Add the spirits (if used). Pour into a tall glass, sprinkle nutmeg or cinnamon on top and serve at once.

HOW TO SEPARATE AN EGG

METHOD 1

Have 2 cups or basins ready. Crack the egg carefully, and pull the 2 halves apart, letting the white drain into one basin, and keeping the yolk in the shell, until all the white has drained out. Tip the yolk into the other basin. If the yolk breaks, tip the whole lot into another basin and start again with another egg.

METHOD 2

Carefully break the egg and tip it onto a saucer, making sure the yolk is not broken. Place a glass over the yolk, and gently tip the white into a basin, keeping the yolk on the saucer with the glass.

3

CHEESE

Here are some delicious snacks using cheese – they're simple and quick to make.

EASY WELSH RAREBIT (CHEESE ON TOAST)

Serves 1

This is the quickest method of making cheese on toast. It can be served plain, or topped with pickle, sliced tomato or crispy, cooked bacon.

Preparation and cooking time: 5–10 minutes.

1–3 rashers of bacon (optional)
1–2 tomatoes (optional)
2–3 oz (50–75g/2–3 slices) cheese   *(continued overleaf)*

(Easy Welsh Rarebit continued)
2–3 slices of bread (white or brown)
Butter (for spreading)
1 tbsp pickle (optional)

Heat the grill. Lightly grill the bacon, if used. Slice the tomatoes, if used. Slice the cheese, making enough slices to cover the pieces of bread. Toast the bread lightly on both sides and spread one side with the butter. Arrange the slices of cheese on the buttered side of the toast and put under the grill for 1 to 2 minutes, until the cheese begins to bubble. Top with the tomato slices, bacon or pickle and return to the grill for another minute, to heat the topping and brown the cheese. Eat at once.

TRADITIONAL WELSH RAREBIT   *Serves 1*

More soft and creamy than cheese on toast, and only takes a few more minutes to prepare.

Preparation and cooking time: 10 minutes.

1–3 rashers of bacon (optional)
1–2 tomatoes (optional)
2–3 oz (50–75g) cheese
1 tsp milk
Pinch of mustard
Shake of pepper
1 tbsp pickle (optional)
2–3 slices of bread, and butter

Heat the grill. Lightly grill the bacon, if used. Slice the tomatoes, if used. Grate the cheese and mix into a stiff paste with the milk in a bowl, stirring in the mustard and pepper. Lightly toast the bread, and spread one side with butter, then generously cover it with the cheese mixture. Put under the hot grill for 1 to 2 minutes, until the cheese starts to bubble. Top with the bacon, tomato slices or pickle, and return to the grill for another minute, to heat the topping and brown the cheese. Serve at once.

BUCK RAREBIT
Serves 1

Welsh Rarebit with poached eggs. When the toast is covered with the cheese, and ready to pop back under the grill to brown, prepare 1 or 2 poached eggs, by cooking them gently in simmering water for 2 to 3 minutes. While the eggs are cooking, put the toast and cheese slices under the grill to brown. When they are golden and bubbling, and the eggs are cooked, carefully remove the eggs from the water, and slide them onto the hot cheesy toast. Serve immediately.

BOOZY WELSH RAREBIT
Serves 1

Open a can of beer, use a little in the cooking, and drink the rest with your meal.

Preparation and cooking time: 10–15 minutes.

2–3 oz (50–75g) cheese
Knob of butter
1–2 tbsp beer
Shake of pepper
Pinch of mustard
1–2 slices of bread (white or brown)

Grate the cheese and heat the grill. Melt the butter in a small saucepan over a moderate heat. Add the cheese, beer, pepper and mustard, and stir well over the heat, until the cheese begins to melt, and the mixture begins to boil. Remove the saucepan from the heat. Toast the bread lightly on both sides. Carefully pour the cheese mixture onto the toast, and put back under the grill for a few moments, until the cheese is hot, bubbling and golden brown. Serve at once, delicious!

CHEESY FRANKFURTER TOASTS   *Serves 1*

A quick snack, made with food from the store cupboard.

Preparation and cooking time: 15 minutes.

2–3 slices of bread
½ oz (12g) butter
**2–3 slices of cooked ham, garlic sausage or luncheon meat
   (optional)**
**Small can (8 oz/227g; actual weight of sausages 4 oz/163g)
   Frankfurter sausages**
2–3 slices of cheese (pre-packed slices are ideal)

Heat the grill. Lightly toast the bread on one side. Butter the
untoasted side of the bread. Lay the ham or garlic sausage on
the untoasted side and top with the Frankfurters. Cover with
the cheese slices, and cook under the hot grill until the
cheese has melted. Eat at once.

   If you don't have a grill the bread can be heated in a hot
oven (400°F/200°C/Gas Mark 6) for a few minutes, and then
buttered. Place the 'toast' with the topping back into the
oven, on an oven-proof dish, and cook for 5 to 10 minutes,
until the cheese has melted.

CAULIFLOWER CHEESE *Serves 1*

Filling enough for a supper dish with crusty French bread and butter, or serve as a vegetable dish with meat or fish.

Preparation and cooking time: 30 minutes.

1 portion (3–4 florets) cauliflower
1 slice of bread (crumbled or grated into crumbs)
Knob of butter
1 sliced tomato (optional)

For the cheese sauce (alternatively use packet sauce mix or 2 oz/50g grated cheese):
2 oz (50g) cheese
2 tsp cornflour or flour
1 cup (¼ pt/150ml) milk
½ oz (12g) butter or margarine
Salt and pepper
Pinch of mustard

Trim the cauliflower's stalk, divide it into florets and wash thoroughly. Cook it in boiling, salted water for 5 minutes, until just tender. Drain well.

Make the cheese sauce (see page 174).

Put the cauliflower into a greased oven-proof dish. Cover with the cheese sauce, sprinkle the breadcrumbs on top and add a knob of butter and the tomato slices. Place under a hot grill for a few minutes, until golden-brown and crispy. (If you do not have time to make the cheese sauce, cover the cauliflower with 2 oz (50g) grated cheese and grill as above.)

4

SNACKS, SAVOURIES
AND SALADS

Just a few ideas and suggestions for quick snacks and packed lunches. Other recipes can be found in Chapters 2 and 3.

SANDWICHES FOR PACKED LUNCHES
Try and ring the changes with different kinds of bread – white, brown, granary, sliced, crusty rolls, soft baps, French bread and Arab bread are a few suggestions. Crisp breads make a change too.

Butter the bread lightly, this stops it going soggy if the

filling is moist, and holds the filling in place (have you ever tried eating unbuttered egg sandwiches?). Wrap the sandwiches in cling film to keep them fresh – it's worth buying a roll if you take sandwiches often – or put them into a polythene bag. A plastic container will stop them getting squashed.

Lettuce, tomato, cucumber, celery and green peppers are a good addition, either sliced in the sandwiches or eaten separately, with them. Treat yourself to some fresh fruit as well, according to what is in season.

Cheese
Slice or grate the cheese.

Cheese and Pickle
As above, and mix with a little pickle or chutney.

Cheese Slices
Quick and easy. Use straight from the packet. Spread pickle on top of the cheese if liked.

Cheese and Tomato
Slice a tomato layer on top of the cheese.

Cheese and Onion
Peel and thinly slice an onion, lay it thinly on top of the sliced cheese.

Cold Meat
Sliced, cooked meat, from the supermarket or delicatessen: ham, tongue, turkey roll, chicken roll, salami, garlic sausage, etc. Buy according to your taste and pocket. Buy fresh as you need it; do not store too long in the fridge.

Cold Meat from the Joint
Beef and mustard or horseradish sauce
Slice the beef thinly, and spread with the mustard or horseradish.

Cold Lamb and Mint Sauce
Slice the meat, cut off any excess fat. Add the mint sauce.

Cold Pork and Apple Sauce and Stuffing
Slice the pork, spread with any leftover apple sauce and stuffing.

Cold Chicken
Use up the fiddly bits from a roast chicken or buy chicken roll slices. Spread with cranberry jelly and stuffing. Do not store for too long in the fridge; buy just a little at a time.

Egg
Cook for 10 minutes in boiling water. Shell, wash and mash with a fork. Mix it either with a little mayonnaise or tomato chutney. One egg will fill two rounds of cut bread sandwiches.

Marmite
Very good for you, especially with a chunk of cheese, or topped with sliced cheese.

Peanut Butter
No need to butter the bread first. Top with seedless jam (jelly) if liked.

Salad
Washed lettuce, sliced tomato, sliced cucumber, layered together.

Salmon
Open a can, drain off any excess juice, and tip the salmon into a bowl. Discard the bones and skin, and mash with a little vinegar and pepper. Spread on the buttered bread, top with cucumber slices or lettuce if liked.

Tuna Fish
Open a can, drain off the oil. Tip the tuna fish into a bowl

and mash with vinegar and pepper, or mayonnaise. Spread on the buttered bread, top with lettuce or cucumber slices.

Liver Pâté
Choose from the numerous smooth or rough pâtés in the supermarket. Brown or granary bread is particularly good with pâté.

Eat with your Packed Lunch:
Cottage Cheese (plain or flavoured)
Eat from the carton with a fresh buttered roll, or an apple if you're slimming. Don't forget to take a spoon.

Yoghurt
Eat from the carton – remember to take a spoon.

Hard-boiled Egg
Hard boil an egg. Shell and wash it. Pop it into a polythene bag and eat with a fresh buttered roll.

Scotch Egg
Buy fresh from the supermarket.

FRIED BREAD
Serves 1

Best cooked in the frying pan in the fat left from frying bacon or sausages.

Preparation and cooking time: 4–5 minutes.

1–2 slices of bread
Fat left in the pan from cooking sausages or bacon (or 2 tsp cooking oil and large knob of butter)

Remove the sausage or bacon from the pan and keep hot. Cut the bread slices in half, and fry in the hot fat over a moderate heat for 1 to 2 minutes on each side, until golden brown and crispy, adding a little extra butter to the pan if necessary.

FRIED CHEESE SANDWICHES

Serves 1

A very quick and tasty snack.

Preparation and cooking time: 10 minutes.

2–4 slices of bread
½ oz (12g) butter
2–4 thin cheese slices (you can use pre-packed cheese slices if you wish)
1 tbsp cooking oil and a large knob of butter (for frying)

Extra fillings (optional):
1 thinly-sliced tomato
1 tsp pickle
1–2 rashers of crisply fried bacon – fry this ready before you start the sandwiches

Lightly butter the slices of bread. Make them into sandwiches with 1 to 2 slices of cheese in each sandwich, adding any of the optional extras you like.

Heat the oil and knob of butter in a frying pan, over a moderate heat. Put the sandwiches into the hot fat, and fry for a few minutes on each side, until the bread is golden and crispy, and the cheese is beginning to melt.

Remove from the pan, drain on a piece of kitchen paper if they seem a bit greasy. Eat at once while hot.

GARLIC BREAD   *Serves 1*
A sophisticated alternative to hot bread rolls.

Preparation and cooking time: 18–20 minutes.

1 clove of garlic (or ½ tsp garlic powder or paste)
2 oz (50g) butter
½ French loaf or 1–2 bread rolls (according to appetite)
Large piece of cooking foil (for wrapping)

Peel, chop and crush the garlic clove, if used, until smooth.
(You can crush it with a pestle and mortar or garlic press, if
you have one, or use the flat side of a knife but this is more
fiddly.) Cream together the butter and crushed garlic (or
garlic powder or paste), until soft and well-mixed.

Cut the loaf nearly through into 1 in (2.5cm) slices (be
careful not to cut the slices completely or the loaf will drop
into bits) or cut the rolls in half. Butter the slices of the loaf,
or the rolls, generously on both sides with the garlic butter
and press the loaf or rolls together again. Wrap the loaf or
rolls loosely in the foil. Heat the bread in a hot oven (400°F/
200°C/Gas Mark 6–7) until hot and crisp (approximately 5
minutes). Serve at once, with the foil unfolded.

HERB BREAD   *Serves 1*
If you don't like garlic, omit garlic from the above recipe and
make a herb loaf, adding a really generous handful of freshly
chopped or snipped mixed herbs and a tsp lemon juice to the
butter.

BEANS (OR SPAGHETTI) ON TOAST   *Serves 1*

If you've never cooked these before, here is the method.

Preparation and cooking time: 5 minutes.

1 oz (25g) cheese (optional)
1 small (8 oz/225g) tin beans, spaghetti, spaghetti hoops, etc.
2–3 slices of bread
Butter

Grate the cheese, or chop it finely (if used).

Put the beans or spaghetti into a small saucepan, and heat slowly over a moderate heat, stirring occasionally. Toast the bread and spread one side of it with butter. When the beans are beginning to bubble, stir gently until they are thoroughly heated.

Put the toast onto a warm plate, and pour the beans on top of the buttered side (some people prefer the toast left at the side of the plate). Sprinkle the cheese on top. Eat at once.

GARLIC MUSHROOMS   *Serves 1*

Delicious, but don't breathe over other people after eating these! Serve with fried bacon to make it more substantial.

Preparation and cooking time: 10 minutes.

3–4 oz (75–100g) mushrooms
1 clove of fresh garlic (or garlic powder or garlic paste)
1–2 rashers of bacon (optional)
1 oz (25g) butter with 1 tsp cooking oil
2 thick slices of bread

Wash the mushrooms. Peel, chop and crush the fresh garlic, if used. Fry the bacon and keep hot. Melt the butter and oil in a saucepan over a moderate heat. Add the garlic (fresh, powder or paste) and mushrooms.

Stir well, and fry gently for 3 to 5 minutes, stirring and spooning the garlic-flavoured butter over the mushrooms. While the mushrooms are cooking, toast the bread lightly, cut in half and put onto a hot plate. Spoon the mushrooms onto the toast and pour the remaining garlic butter over the top. Top with bacon, if used. Eat at once.

PIZZA

There are so many makes, shapes and sizes of pizza available now, both fresh and frozen, that it hardly seems worth the effort of making your own. However, these commercial ones are usually improved by adding your own extras during the cooking, either when under the grill or in the oven according to the instructions on the packet.

Add these extras for the last 5 to 10 minutes of cooking time by spreading them on top of the pizza:

Cheese
Use grated or thinly sliced.

Ham
Chop and sprinkle over the pizza.

Salami, Garlic Sausage
Chop or fold slices and arrange on top of the pizza.

Mushrooms
Wash and slice thinly, spread over the pizza.

Tomatoes
Slice thinly, spread over the pizza.

Olives
A few spread on top add colour and flavour.

Anchovies or Sardines
Arrange criss-cross over the pizza.

BASIC GREEN SALAD   *Serves 1*

Preparation time: 5 minutes.

3–4 washed lettuce leaves
½ small onion
1 tbsp vinaigrette

Leave the lettuce leaves whole if small, or shred as finely as you like. Peel and slice the onion. Put the lettuce and onion into a salad bowl, add the vinaigrette and lightly turn the lettuce over in the dressing, until well mixed.

Other salad vegetables can be added:

Beetroot (cooked, if necessary, and sliced)
Celery (washed, scraped, if necessary, cut into 1 in (2.5cm) lengths)
Cucumber (washed, cut into rings or chunks)
Pepper (washed, cored, cut into rings)
Radishes (with tops cut off, roots removed and washed)
Spring onion (washed, cut off roots and yellow leaves, cut into rings or leave whole)
Tomatoes (washed, sliced or cut into quarters)
Watercress, mustard and cress (washed, sprinkled on top of the other vegetables).

WINTER SALAD   *Serves 1*

Trim, shred and wash a quarter of a white or green cabbage. Drain well and dry in a salad shaker (if you have one) or put into a clean tea-towel and shake or pat dry. Put the cabbage in a dish, with any other salad vegetables, such as raw, grated carrot, tomato quarters, cucumber, celery, peppers, peeled sliced onion.

It can either be served on its own, or with a dressing made from the following ingredients mixed together thoroughly: 4 tsp salad oil, 2 tsp vinegar, pinch of salt, pepper and sugar.

COLESLAW

Serves 1

A quick and tasty way of using up extra raw cabbage. Serve with cold meat, or with hot dishes.

Preparation time: 15 minutes.

¼ crisp white cabbage
1 small carrot
1 eating apple (red-skinned if possible)
Lemon juice (if possible)
1 small onion
1–2 tbsp mayonnaise
Salt and pepper

Trim off the outer leaves and stalk of the cabbage. Shred it finely, wash it well in cold water. Scrape the carrot. Chop it finely or grate it. Peel and core the apple. Chop it finely or grate it. Sprinkle with a little lemon juice. Peel the onion. Chop or grate it finely. Drain the cabbage well.

Mix all the vegetables together in a bowl. Toss lightly in the mayonnaise until all the ingredients are well-coated. Season to taste.

Many different fruit or vegetables can be used in this recipe. A few chopped salted nuts, a tbsp of washed, dried sultanas, a little chopped green pepper are some ideas you might like to try.

5

VEGETABLES, VEGETABLE
DISHES AND RICE

This chapter gives basic instructions on preparing and
cooking fresh vegetables (listed in alphabetical order) to be
eaten as part of a meal, together with recipes using
vegetables which are substantial enough to be used as a lunch
or supper dish by themselves.

When cooking vegetables in water, remember that a lot of
the goodness and flavour soaks from the vegetables into the
cooking water. So do not use too much water or overcook
them. When possible, use the vegetable water for making
gravy. Frozen vegetables are convenient but are generally
dearer than fresh vegetables. Vegetable prices vary tremendously according to the season, so look out for the best buys
at the vegetable counter.

GLOBE ARTICHOKES

2. Globe Artichokes

These are the green, leafy type of artichoke. They look large, but as you only eat the bottom tip of each leaf, you do need *a whole artichoke for each person*. As they are expensive, cook them mainly for special occasions.

Cut off the stem of the artichoke to make the base level, snip off the points of the leaves, and wash the artichoke well in cold water. Put in a large saucepan, cover with boiling salted water, and boil for 30 to 40 minutes, until a leaf will pull off easily.

Drain the water from the pan and then turn the artichoke upside down in the pan for a few moments to drain any remaining water. Serve with plenty of butter.

JERUSALEM ARTICHOKES

3. Jerusalem Artichokes

These artichokes look like knobbly potatoes. Cook them immediately they are peeled, as they go brown very quickly even in cold water. A little lemon juice in the cooking water helps to keep them white.

8 oz (225g) serves 1–2 portions.

BOILED
Peel the artichokes and cut them into evenly-sized lumps about the size of small potatoes. Boil them in a pan of salted water for 20 to 30 minutes, until tender. Drain and serve with a dab of butter.

BOILED WITH CHICKEN SAUCE
Cook in salted water (as above) until tender. Drain, and put back in the saucepan with ½ can (10 oz/300g size) of condensed chicken soup. Bring back to the boil, stirring occasionally. Tip the artichokes onto a warm plate, pouring the chicken sauce over them.

FRIED
Peel the artichokes and cut them into thick slices or chunks. Put 1 tsp cooking oil and ½ oz (12g) butter into a frying pan, add the artichoke pieces and cook gently, turning frequently, for 15 to 20 minutes, until soft. Tip the artichokes onto a warm plate, pouring the buttery sauce over them.

ASPARAGUS
A very expensive treat! *Usually sold in bundles, enough for 2–4 servings.*

Cut off the woody ends of the stems and then scrape off the white tough parts of the stems. Rinse. Tie the stems into a bundle, with clean string or white cotton, and stand them tips uppermost in a pan with 1 in (2.5cm) boiling water. Cover the pan with a lid or a dome of foil, and boil for 8 to 10 minutes, until tender. Remove them carefully from the pan. Asparagus is traditionally eaten with the fingers. To eat, just dip the tips in butter and leave any woody parts that still remain on the stems.

AUBERGINES

The English name for the aubergine is the 'egg plant'. These lovely, shiny purple-skinned vegetables are best left unpeeled.

Fry 1 medium-sized aubergine per person.

To get rid of any bitter taste before cooking, slice the aubergine into ½ in (1.25cm) pieces. Put into a colander or strainer (if you do not have one, lay the slices on a piece of kitchen paper), sprinkle with salt, press a heavy plate down on top and leave for 30 minutes so that the bitter juices are pressed out. Wash and dry the slices. Heat a little oil in a frying pan, and fry gently until soft (about 5 minutes).

AVOCADO PEARS

Buy avocados when the price is down – the price varies considerably during the year, as they are imported from several countries. They make a nourishing change.

Choose pears that yield slightly when pressed gently. Unripe pears feel very hard.

Slice the avocado in half lengthways, cutting through to the stone. Then separate the two halves by twisting gently. Remove the stone with the tip of the knife, trying not to damage the flesh, which should be soft and buttery in texture.

Cut avocados discolour very quickly, so prepare them just before serving, or rub the cut halves with lemon juice to stop them going brown. Serve avocados plain with a squeeze of lemon juice, with a vinaigrette dressing or with any one of the numerous fillings spooned into the cavity from where the stone was removed. Brown bread and butter is the traditional accompaniment, with a garnish of lettuce, tomato and cucumber.

Some Filling Ideas

Vinaigrette: Mix well 2 tsp oil, 1 tsp vinegar, salt, pepper and a pinch of sugar.

Mayonnaise: 1 tbsp mayonnaise.

Cottage Cheese: Mix well together 2 tbsp cottage cheese (plain or with chives, pineapple, etc.) and 1 tsp mayonnaise.

Prawn or Shrimp: Mix gently together 1–2 tbsp shelled prawns or shrimps (fresh, frozen or canned), 1 tbsp mayonnaise and/or cottage cheese. A sauce can also be made with a mixture of 1 tbsp salad cream and a dash of tomato ketchup.

Egg: Shell and chop 1 hard-boiled egg. Mix gently with 1 tbsp mayonnaise and/or cottage cheese.

Yoghurt: 2 tbsp yoghurt on its own, or mixed with a chopped tomato and a few slices chopped cucumber.

CREAMY AVOCADO TOAST   *Serves 1*

Use a soft avocado pear for this. They are often sold off cheaply when they become very ripe and the shop wants to sell them quickly.

Preparation time: 5 minutes.

1 ripe avocado
Salt and pepper
2 thick slices of bread (brown or granary)
Knob of butter

Cut the avocado in half, lengthways and remove the stone. Scoop out the soft flesh with a teaspoon, put it into a small basin, and mash to a soft cream. Season with the salt and pepper.

Toast the bread on both sides, spread one side with butter, then spread the avocado cream thickly on the top. Eat while the toast is hot.

SAVOURY AVOCADO SNACK *Serves 1*

If you're a vegetarian and don't want to eat bacon, you may prefer to sprinkle ½ tbsp chopped walnuts on top of the cheese instead.

Preparation and cooking time: 15 minutes.

1–2 rashers of bacon
Oil (for frying)
1 small avocado pear
1 oz (25g) cheese
Chunk of French bread
Knob of butter

De-rind the bacon. Fry it in a little oil in a frying pan over a moderate heat until crisp.

Peel the avocado pear and slice it, removing the stone. Grate or slice the cheese.

Cut the French bread in half lengthways, and spread with the butter. Arrange layers of the avocado and bacon on the bread. Top with the cheese slices or grated cheese.

Grill under a hot grill for a few minutes, until the cheese is golden, bubbling and melted. Eat at once.

BROAD BEANS

Buy 4–8 oz (100–225g) unshelled beans per person, according to the size of the beans. The smaller, younger beans go further, as you can cook them whole, like French beans, whereas older, larger beans need to be shelled.

TINY NEW BROAD BEANS

Top and tail the beans with a vegetable knife or a pair of scissors. Either leave them whole or cut them into shorter lengths (4 in/10cm) depending on their size. Boil them in water for 5 to 10 minutes, according to size, until tender. Drain and serve with a knob of butter.

LARGER BROAD BEANS

Remove the beans from the pods. Cook in boiling water for 5 to 10 minutes, until tender. Drain and serve with a knob of butter, or parsley sauce, if you feel very ambitious.

FROZEN BROAD BEANS

Allow approximately 4 oz (100g) per serving. Cook as instructed on the packet, and serve as above.

FRENCH BEANS

Can be rather expensive, but as there is very little waste you need only buy a small amount. *Allow approximately 4 oz (100g) per serving.*

Top and tail the beans with a vegetable knife or a pair of scissors. Wash the beans and cut the longer beans in half (about 4 in/10cm). Put them into a pan of boiling, salted water and cook for 2 to 5 minutes, until just tender. Drain well and serve them with a knob of butter.

FROZEN WHOLE FRENCH BEANS

Allow approximately 3–4 oz (75–100g) per serving. Cook in boiling, salted water as directed on the packet and serve as above with a knob of butter. Very tasty, but be careful not to overcook them.

RUNNER BEANS

These are sold frozen and ready to cook all year round, but lovely fresh beans are available in August and September. Choose crisp, green beans; limp, pallid ones are not as fresh as they should be. *Allow 4 oz (100g) beans per person.*

Top and tail the beans. Cut down the sides of the large beans to remove any tough stringy bits, and slice the beans evenly into whatever size you prefer, up to 1 in (2.5cm) long. Wash them in cold water. Cook in boiling, salted water for 5 to 10 minutes, according to size, until just tender. Drain well and serve hot.

FROZEN BEANS

Allow 3–4 oz (75–100g) per serving. Cook according to the instructions on the packet, in boiling, salted water.

BEAN SPROUTS

These can be cooked on their own, but are better when cooked with a mixture of stir-fried vegetables. *Allow 4 oz (100g) per portion.* Soak for 10 minutes in cold water, then drain the bean sprouts well. Heat 1 tbsp oil in a frying pan or a wok, add the bean sprouts and fry for 1 to 2 minutes, stirring all the time. Serve at once.

BROCCOLI

Green broccoli and purple sprouting broccoli are both cooked in the same way. *Allow 2–3 pieces or 8 oz (225g) per serving.*

Remove any coarse outer leaves and cut off the ends of the stalks. Wash well in cold water. Boil for 5 to 10 minutes in salted water, until tender. Drain well; press out the water gently with a fork if necessary. Serve with a knob of butter.

FROZEN BROCCOLI

Allow 4–6 oz (100–150g) per serving, according to appetite. Cook as directed on the packet, in boiling, salted water.

BRUSSELS SPROUTS

Try to buy firm, green sprouts of approximately the same size. Yellow outside leaves are a sign of old age.

Allow 4–6 oz (100-150g) per serving.

Cut off the stalk ends, and trim off the outer leaves if necessary. Wash well. Cook in boiling, salted water for 5 to 10 minutes, until tender. Drain well.

FROZEN SPROUTS

Allow 3–4 oz (75–100g) per serving. Cook in boiling, salted water as directed on the packet.

WHITE OR GREEN CABBAGE

A much maligned vegetable, evoking memories of school days. If cooked properly, cabbage is really delicious and much cheaper than a lot of other vegetables. Cabbage goes a very long way, so either buy a *small cabbage* and use it for several meals (cooked, or raw in a winter salad) or *just buy half or a quarter of a cabbage*.

Trim off the outer leaves and the stalk. Cut into quarters and shred, not too finely, removing the central core and cutting that into small pieces. Wash the cabbage. Boil it in salted water for 2 to 5 minutes. Do not overcook. Drain well, serve with a knob of butter, or with a cheese sauce.

To make cabbage cheese, instead of cauliflower cheese, substitute the cabbage for the cauliflower on page 39.

CRISPY CABBAGE CASSEROLE   *Serves 1*

This is filling enough to serve as a cheap supper dish, with hot bread rolls, butter and a chunk of cheese. It is delicious as a vegetable accompaniment with meat.

Preparation and cooking time: 35 minutes.

1 portion of cabbage (¼ of a cabbage)
1 small onion
1–2 sticks of celery
1 tsp oil and ½ oz (12g) butter (for frying)
1 slice of bread

For the white sauce (or use 1 packet of sauce mix):
2 tsp cornflour (or flour)
1 cup (¼ pt/150ml) milk
½ oz (12g) butter (or margarine)
Salt and pepper

Grease an oven-proof dish or casserole. Trim the outer leaves and stalk from the cabbage. Shred it, not too finely, wash it well and drain. Peel and chop the onion. Scrape and wash the celery and cut into 1 in (2.5cm) lengths. Heat the oil and butter in a frying pan, and fry the onion gently for 2 to 3 minutes until soft. Add the celery and drained cabbage, fry gently for a further 5 minutes, stirring occasionally.

Heat the oven at (400°F/200°C/Gas Mark 6–7). Make the white sauce (see page 174). Put the vegetable mixture into the greased dish. Pour the white sauce over the top. Crumble or grate the bread into crumbs, and sprinkle these on top of the sauce. Dot with a knob of butter. Bake for 15 minutes in the hot oven until the top is crunchy and golden brown.

RED CABBAGE   *Serves 1*

Usually cooked in a casserole, to make a lovely warming winter vegetable dish. Why not put some jacket potatoes in the oven to eat with it?

Preparation and cooking time: 1 hour (cooked on top of the stove); 1 hour 15 minutes (cooked in the oven).

1 rasher of bacon (optional)
1 small onion
½ small red cabbage
1 eating apple
1 tsp oil
½ oz (12g) butter
Salt and pepper
1 tsp sugar (brown if possible, but white will do)
1 tsp vinegar
½ cup boiling water

Chop the bacon with a sharp knife or a pair of scissors. Peel and chop the onion. Cut off the stalk from the cabbage. Remove any battered outside leaves. Shred the cabbage finely, wash and drain. Peel, core and slice the apple. Melt the oil and butter in a frying pan and fry the bacon until crisp. Remove the bacon, put it on a plate. Add the onion to the pan and fry gently for 2 to 3 minutes, until soft.

PAN METHOD

In a saucepan, put layers of the cabbage, apple, onion and bacon, seasoning each layer with salt, pepper, sugar and vinegar. Pour ½ cup of boiling water over it and lightly sprinkle with sugar. Put on the saucepan lid and simmer gently for 45 minutes, stirring occasionally.

OVEN METHOD

Use a casserole dish (with a lid) that can be put in the oven. Put the vegetables in layers as in the pan method, adding ½ cup of boiling water and the sugar and cook in the oven

(350°F/180°C/Gas Mark 4), stirring occasionally, for about an hour. Jacket potatoes can be cooked with the casserole. Serve hot. Red cabbage cooked in this way is tasty with pork and lamb.

CARROTS

New carrots can simply be scrubbed and cooked whole, like new potatoes. Older, larger carrots should be scraped or peeled, then cut in halves, quarters, slices, rings or dice, as preferred. The smaller the pieces the quicker the carrots will cook.

Allow 4 oz (100g) per serving.

Scrub, peel and slice the carrots as necessary. Boil them in salted water for 5 to 20 minutes, according to their size, until just tender. Serve with a knob of butter.

BUTTERED CARROTS

Prepare the carrots as above: leaving tender, young carrots whole, or slicing old carrots into rings. Put the carrots in a saucepan, with ½ a cup of water, ½ oz (12g) butter, 1 tsp sugar and a pinch of salt. Bring to the boil, then reduce the heat and simmer for 20 minutes, until the carrots are tender. Take the lid off the saucepan, turn up the heat for a few minutes, and let the liquid bubble away until only a little sauce is left. Put the carrots onto a plate, and pour the sauce over them.

FROZEN CARROTS OR MIXED VEGETABLES

Allow 3–4 oz (75–100g) per serving. Cook in boiling, salted water as directed on the packet, and serve as above.

CAULIFLOWER

Most cauliflowers are too large for one person, but they can be cut in half and the remainder kept in the fridge for use in the next few days. Try not to bruise the florets when cutting them, as they will discolour easily. Very small caulis and packets of cauliflower florets are sold in some supermarkets.

Allow 3–4 florets per serving.

Trim off tough stem and outer leaves. The cauli can either be left whole or divided into florets. Wash thoroughly. Cook in boiling, salted water for 5 to 15 minutes, according to size, until just tender. Drain well. Serve hot, with a knob of butter, a spoonful of soured cream, or white sauce (see page 174). For cauliflower cheese, see page 39.

FROZEN CAULIFLOWER
Allow 4–6 oz (100–150g) per serving. Cook as directed on the packet and serve as above.

CELERIAC

4. Celeriac

The root of a variety of celery, celeriac is one of the more unusual vegetables now available in good greengrocers and larger supermarkets.

Allow 4–8 oz (100–225g) per person.

Peel fairly thickly, and cut into evenly-sized chunks. Put into a saucepan with boiling water, and cook for 30 to 40 minutes. Drain well. Serve with butter, or mash with a potato masher, fork or whisk, with a little butter and top of the milk. Season with salt and pepper.

CELERY

Most popular eaten raw, with cheese, or chopped up in a salad. It can be cooked and served as a hot vegetable; the tougher outer stems can be used for cooking, leaving the tender inner stems to be eaten raw.

Allow 3–4 stalks of celery per serving.

Trim the celery stalk. Divide it into separate stems. Wash each stem well and scrape off any stringy bits with a knife. The celery is now ready to eat raw. To cook, chop the celery into 1 in (2.5cm) lengths. Put it into a saucepan, with boiling, salted water, and cook for 10 minutes, until just tender. Drain well, serve with a knob of butter, or put into a greased, oven-proof dish, top with 1–2 oz (25–50g) grated cheese, and brown under a hot grill.

CHICORY

This can be used raw in salads, or cooked carefully in water and butter, and served hot.

Allow 6–8 oz (175–225g/one head) per serving.

5. Chicory

Remove any damaged outer leaves and trim the stalk. With a pointed vegetable knife, cut a cone-shaped core out of the base, to ensure even cooking and reduce bitterness. Wash in cold water. Put the chicory into a saucepan with a knob of butter, 2–3 tbsp water and a pinch of salt. Cook gently for about 20 minutes, until just tender, making sure that all the liquid does not disappear. Serve with melted butter.

CHINESE LEAVES

These can be used raw in salads. Keep the Chinese leaves in a polythene bag in the fridge to keep them crisp until you want to use them.

Allow ¼–½ small cabbage per serving.

Trim off any spoiled leaves and stalks. Shred finely. Wash and drain well (in a salad shaker or a clean tea-towel). Use in salad with any other salad vegetables (cucumber, tomato, cress, spring onions, raddish etc.) and a vinaigrette dressing (2 tbsp oil, 1 tsp vinegar, pinch of salt, pepper and sugar, all mixed well together).

COURGETTES

These are baby marrows. They are very quick and easy to prepare, and are quite economical as there is almost no waste with them. *Allow 1 or 2 courgettes (4–6 oz/100–175g) per serving, according to size.*

Top and tail very tiny courgettes, and leave them whole. Slice larger ones into rings (½–1 in/1.25–2.5cm) or large dice. Wash well.

BOILED

Prepare the courgettes as above. Boil them gently in salted water for 2 to 5 minutes, until just tender. Drain them very well, as they tend to be a bit watery. (You can get them really dry by shaking them in the pan over a very low heat for a moment.) Serve topped with a knob of butter, or tip them into a greased, oven-proof dish and top with 1 oz (25g) grated cheese, and brown under a hot grill. Courgettes can also be served with white, cheese or parsley sauce.

FRIED

Prepare the courgettes as above. Wash and drain them well and dry on kitchen paper. Melt a little cooking oil and butter in a frying pan, add the courgettes and fry gently for a few minutes, until tender. Drain on kitchen paper. Serve hot.

CUCUMBER

Most widely used as a salad vegetable and eaten raw, although it can be cut in chunks and added to casseroles, or cooked in the same way as courgettes or celery. Cucumbers are usually bought *whole, or cut in half*. They keep best in the fridge, wrapped in a polythene bag.

Wash the cucumber. Peel thinly (if you wish) or leave unpeeled. Cut into thin slices and use with salad, or munch a chunk like an apple, with a ploughman's lunch.

LEEKS

These must be thoroughly washed or they will taste gritty.

Allow 1 or 2 leeks per serving, according to size and appetite.

Cut off the roots and the tough green part, just leaving any green that looks appetising. Slit down one side and rinse well in cold, running water to get rid of all the soil and grit – this is a bit fiddly and it will take a few minutes to get them thoroughly clean. Leave them whole, or cut them into shorter lengths if they are very large, or into rings.

Cook in a very little boiling, salted water for 5 to 10 minutes, according to size, or sauté in a little oil or butter for a few minutes. Drain well. Serve at once, or put into a greased oven-proof dish, cover with 1 oz (25g) grated cheese and brown under a hot grill or serve with white sauce which can be prepared while the leeks are cooking.

LETTUCE

Cheapest and best in spring and summer, when various kinds are available. Choose a lettuce that looks crisp and firm, with a solid heart; if it looks limp and flabby it is old and stale. Lettuce will keep for a few days in a polythene bag or a box in the fridge, but goes slimy if left too long, so buy *a small lettuce* unless you're going to eat a lot of salad.

Cut off the stalk and discard any brown or battered leaves. Pull the leaves off the stem and wash separately in cold, running water. Dry thoroughly in a salad shaker or clean tea-towel. Put into a polythene bag or box in the fridge if not using immediately, to keep it crisp. Serve as a basic green salad or as a garnish with bread rolls, cheese or cold meat, or as a side salad with hot dishes (alone or with a French dressing).

MARROW

Very cheap when in season, during the autumn. *A small marrow* will serve three or four people as a vegetable with meat or fish, or can be stuffed with meat or rice to make a dinner or supper dish.

Wash the marrow in cold water. Peel thinly. Cut into 1 in (2.5cm) rings or cubes, according to size. Boil gently in salted water for 3 to 6 minutes, until just tender. Drain very well, as marrow can be a bit watery. (You can get the pieces really dry by shaking them in the pan over a very low heat for a few moments.) Serve topped with a knob of butter, or tip the pieces into a greased oven-proof dish and top with 1 oz (25g) grated cheese, and brown under a hot grill. Marrow can also be served with white, cheese or parsley sauce.

MUSHROOMS

Buy in small amounts, *2 oz (50g)*, so that they can be eaten fresh. Fresh mushrooms are pale-coloured and look plump and firm; older ones look dried-up and brownish. Keep mushrooms in the fridge. Mushrooms can be fried or grilled with bacon, sausages, chops or steaks. Add them to casseroles or stews or make a tasty snack by cooking them in butter and garlic and serving on toast (see page 46).

Allow 2–3 mushrooms each, according to size, or 1–2 oz (25–50g).

FRIED
Wash the mushrooms in cold water. Leave them whole or slice large ones if you wish. Fry them gently in a little butter

and oil for a few minutes, until soft. They can be put in the frying pan with bacon or sausages, or cooked alone in a smaller saucepan.

GRILLED

Put a small knob of butter in each mushroom and grill them for a few minutes in the base of the grill pan. If you are grilling them with bacon, sausages or chops put them under the grill rack; the juice from the meat and mushrooms makes a tasty sauce.

OKRA

6. Okra

Known as Ladies' Fingers, okra consists of curved seed pods. It can be served as a vegetable with meat or curry, or fried with tomatoes, onions and spices with rice as a supper dish.

Allow 2 oz (50g) per serving.

Top and tail the okra. Wash it in cold water. Put 1–2 tbsp cooking oil in a pan, add the okra and cook gently, stirring occasionally for 15 to 20 minutes, until the okra feels tender when tested with a pointed knife. It should have a slightly glutinous texture.

ONIONS

The best way to peel onions without crying is to cut off their tops and tails and then peel off their skins with a vegetable knife under cold running water.

To chop onions evenly, peel them under cold water, then slice them downwards vertically into evenly-sized rings. If you want finely-chopped onion pieces, slice the rings through again horizontally.

ROAST ONION

Allow 1 medium or large onion per person. Spanish onions are good for roasting. Top, tail and peel the onion. Heat a little oil or fat in a roasting tin (400°F/200°C/Gas Mark 6). When hot (3 to 5 minutes) place the onion carefully in the hot fat – it will spit, beware! Roast for 45 minutes to 1 hour. Onions are delicious roasted with a joint of meat and roast potatoes.

BAKED ONION

Allow 1 large onion per person. Spanish onions are the best. Rinse the onion, top and tail it, but do not peel it. Put it in a tin or baking dish, and bake for 45 minutes to 1 hour (400°F/ 200°C/Gas Mark 6). Slit and serve with butter.

BOILED ONION

Allow 1 medium onion per person. Top, tail and peel the onion. Put it in a pan of boiling water and simmer for 20 to 30 minutes, according to its size, until tender.

FRIED ONION

Allow 1 onion per person. Top, tail and peel the onion and slice into rings. Fry them gently in a saucepan with a little oil and butter, for 5 to 10 minutes, until soft and golden, stirring occasionally. Delicious with liver and bacon.